W9-AUJ-127

What happened in

LIFE ON EARTH · BOOK 1
LOSING THE GIRL

Claudia Jones, one of Blithedale High's brightest students, has gone missing, and rumors are swirling.

Emily Hiroko Baker has terminated an unplanned pregnancy and started to realize that her hookup, Brett Hathaway, isn't letting her into his life.

Brett is struggling with his own unrequited crush, on his lifelong friend Johanna, and with family problems he'd rather keep to himself.

Nigel Jones is growing up—slowly—after getting dumped and figuring out how to be a friend to a girl without pressuring her for something more.

Paula Navarro has told Emily their friendship is over. Maybe Emily was too self-absorbed. Maybe Paula was just jealous. Even Paula's not sure.

But things are only going to get weirder. Paula and Nigel have seen signs of Claudia around town—at least it *might* have been Claudia—and felt some strange effects . . .

Content warning: Sexual assault

Graphic Universe™
A division of Lerner Publishing Group, Inc.
241 First Avenue North
Minneapolis, MN 55401 USA

For reading levels and more information, look up this title at
www.lernerbooks.com.

Library of Congress Cataloging-in-Publication Data

Names: MariNaomi, author, illustrator.
Title: Gravity's pull / MariNaomi.
Description: Minneapolis : Graphic Universe, [2018] | Series: Life on Earth ; [2] |
    Summary: Claudia Jones has returned to Blithedale High School, but rumors
    about her possible alien abduction persist as everyone begins to feel the
    strange effects of her presence.
Identifiers: LCCN 2018014446 (print) | LCCN 2018020403 (ebook) |
    ISBN 9781541542693 (eb pdf) | ISBN 9781512449112 (lb : alk. paper) |
    ISBN 9781541545267 (pb : alk. paper)
Subjects: LCSH: Graphic novels. | CYAC: Graphic novels. | Alien abduction—
    Fiction. | Missing children—Fiction. | High schools—Fiction. | Schools—Fiction.
Classification: LCC PZ7.7.M339 (ebook) | LCC PZ7.7.M339 Gr 2018 (print) | DDC
    741.5/973—dc23

LC record available at https://lccn.loc.gov/2018014446

Manufactured in the United States of America
1-42843-26507-8/24/2018

LIFE ON EARTH · BOOK 2

GRAVITY'S PULL

MARINAOMI

Graphic Universe™ · Minneapolis

FOR MYRIAM GURBA, WHOSE GRAVITATIONAL
PULL I CAN NEVER RESIST

PART ONE

Nigel Q. Jones

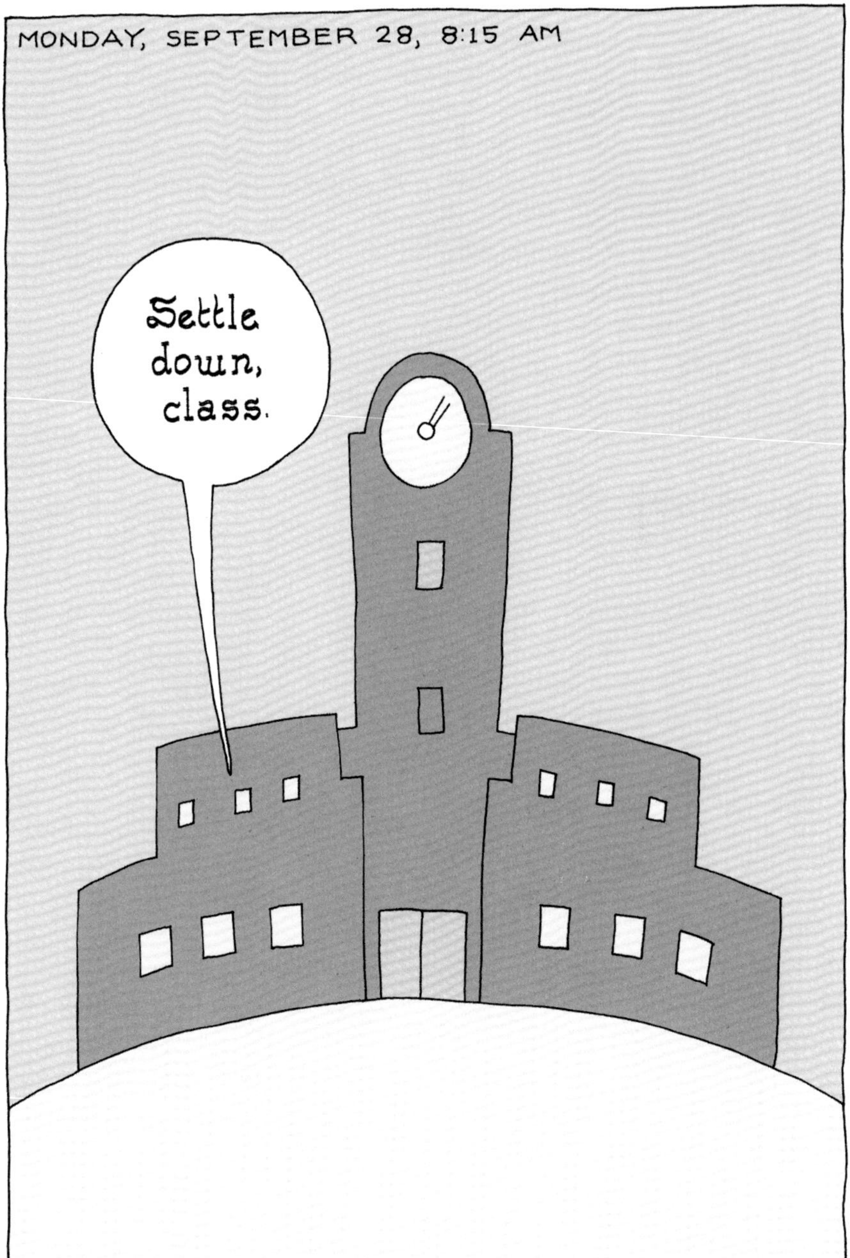
MONDAY, SEPTEMBER 28, 8:15 AM
Settle down, class.
BLITHEDALE HIGH SCHOOL - JUNIOR HOMEROOM

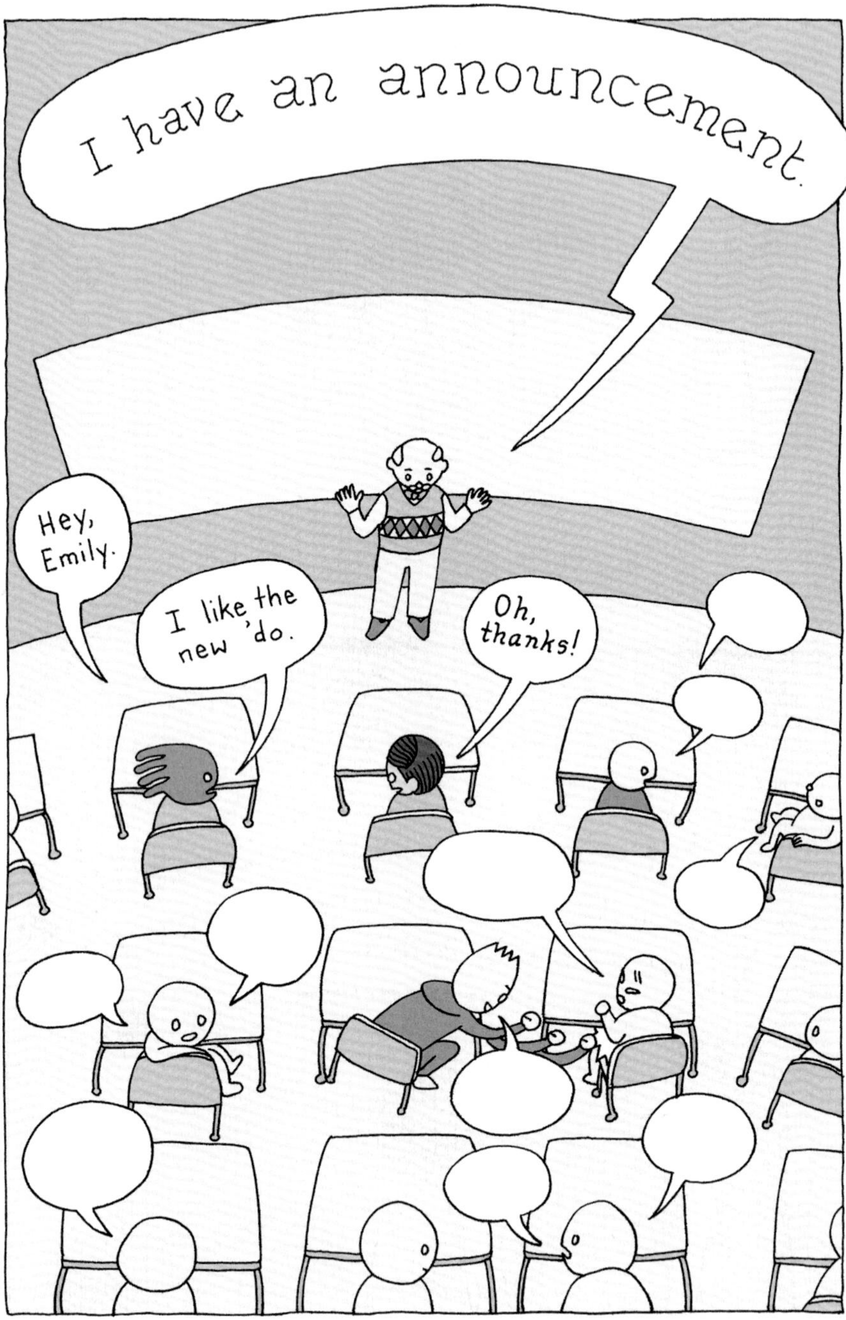
I have an announcement.
Hey, Emily.
I like the new 'do.
Oh, thanks!

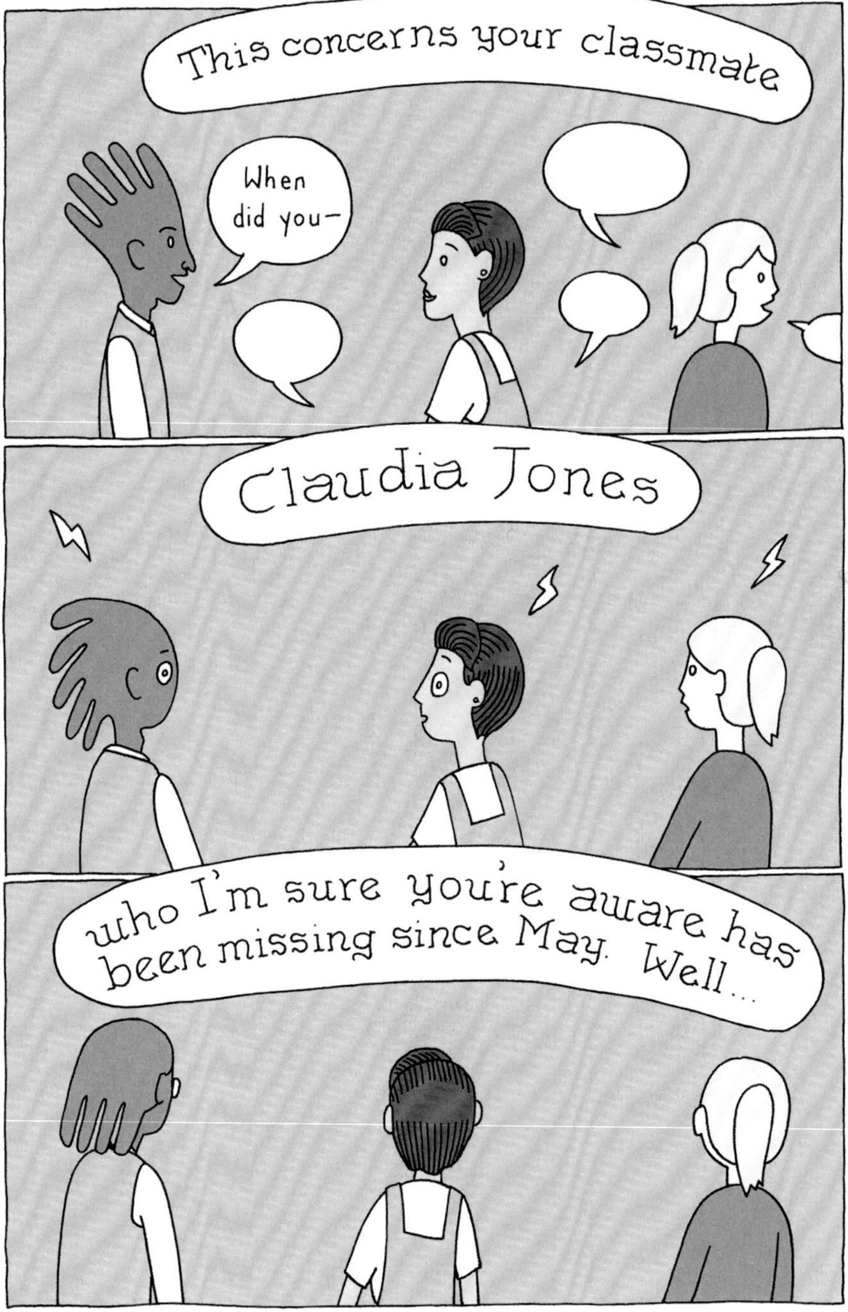
This concerns your classmate
When did you-
Claudia Jones
who I'm sure you're aware has been missing since May. Well...

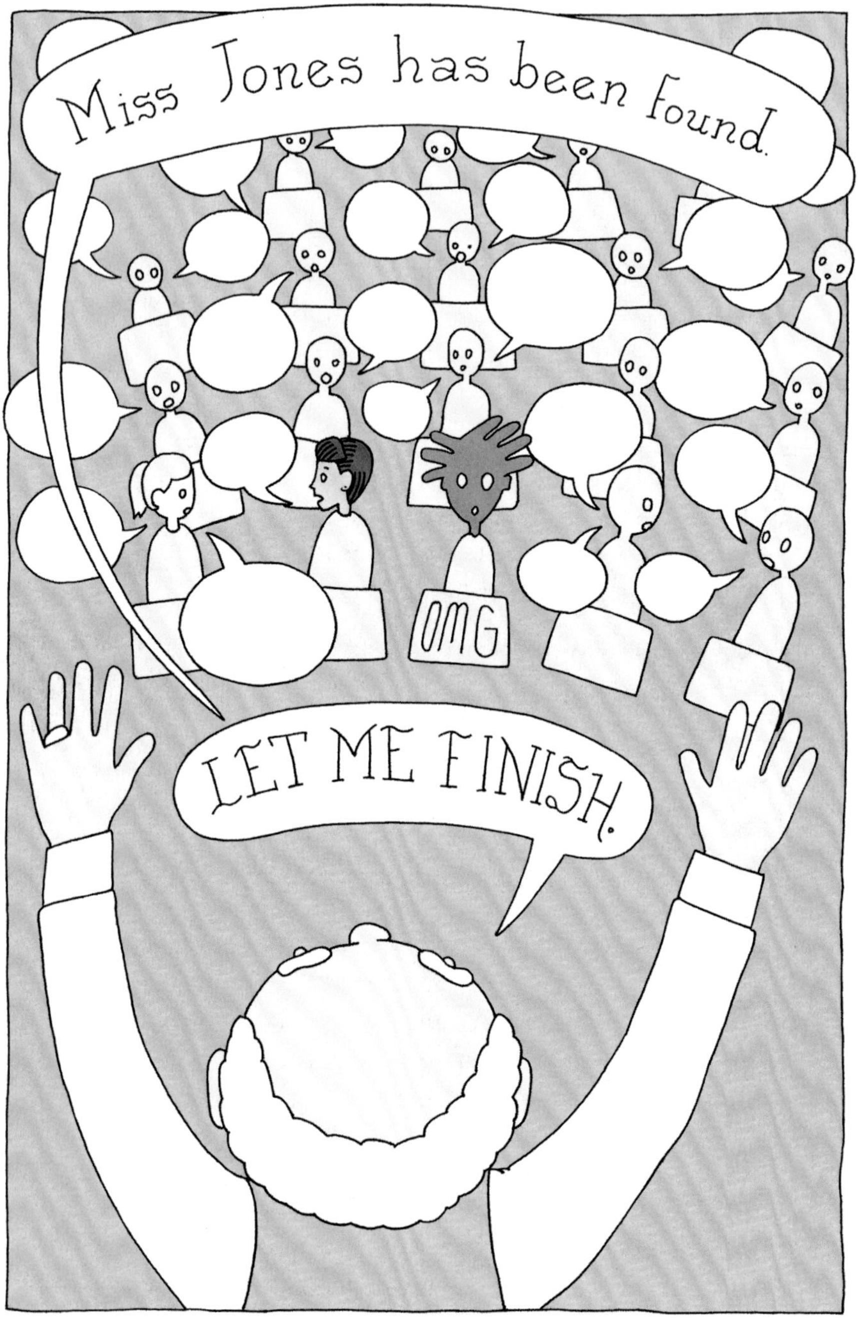
Miss Jones has been found.
OMG
LET ME FINISH.

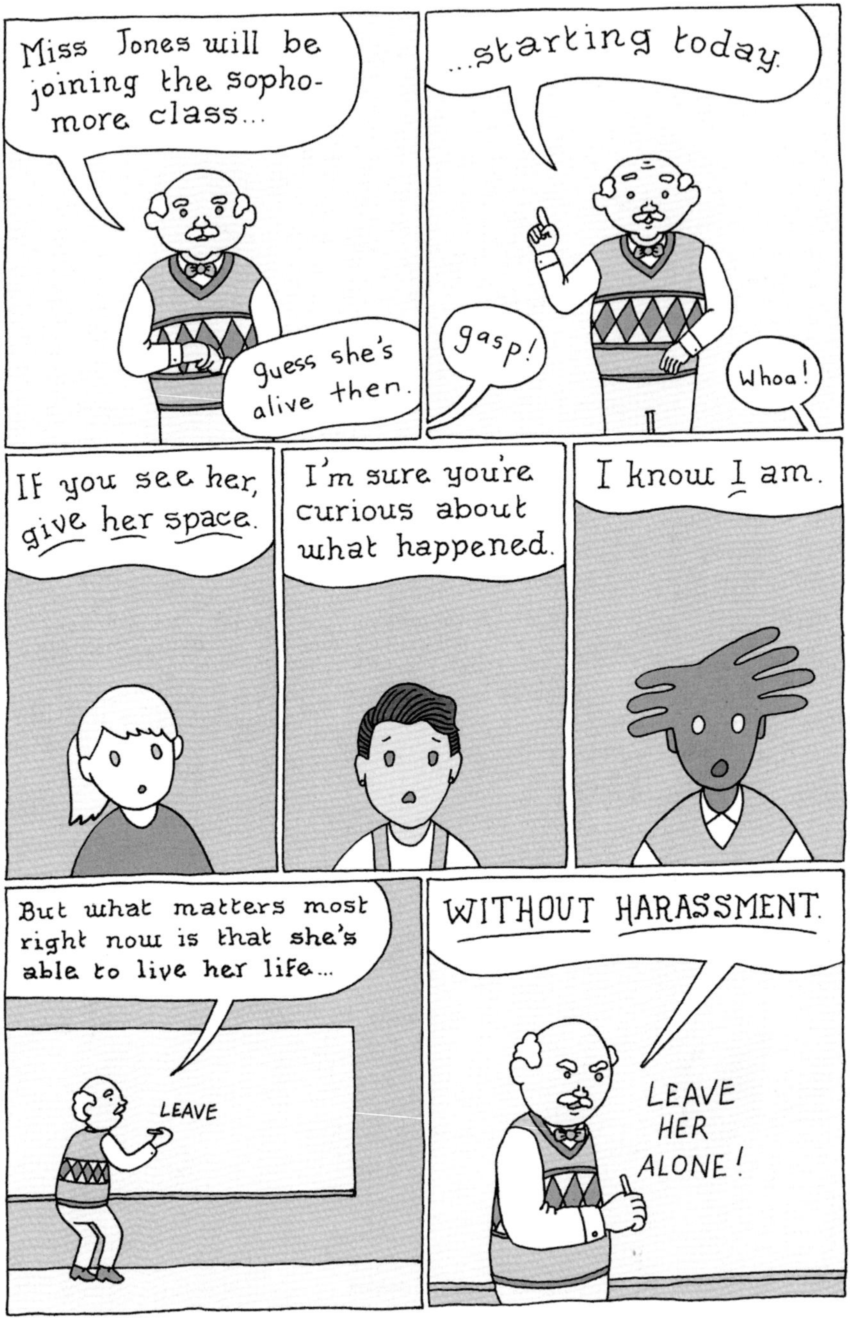
Miss Jones will be joining the sophomore class...
Guess she's alive then.
...starting today.
gasp!
Whoa!
If you see her, give her space.
I'm sure you're curious about what happened.
I know I am.
But what matters most right now is that she's able to live her life...
LEAVE
WITHOUT HARASSMENT.
LEAVE HER ALONE!

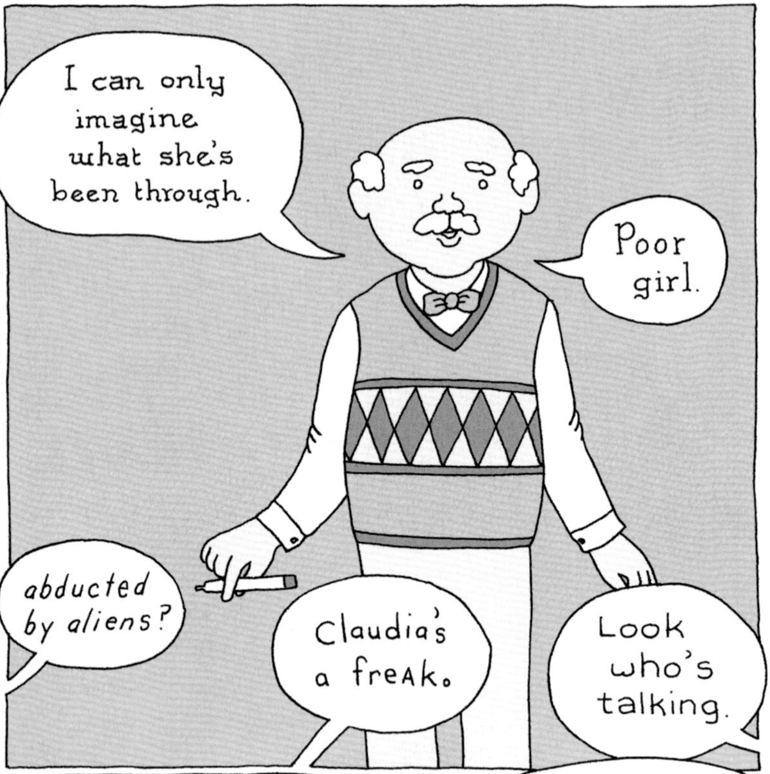
I can only imagine what she's been through.
Poor girl.
abducted by aliens?
Claudia's a freak.
Look who's talking.

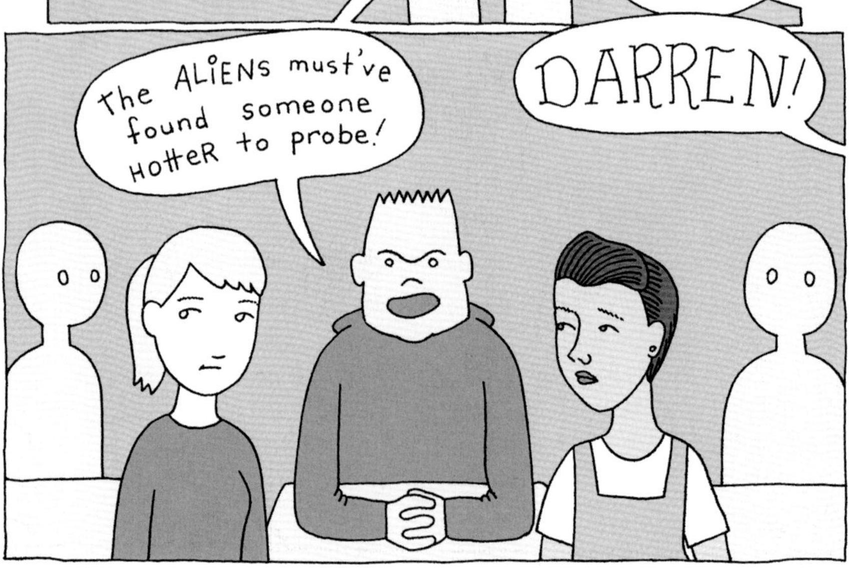
The ALIENS must've found someone HOTTER to probe!
DARREN!

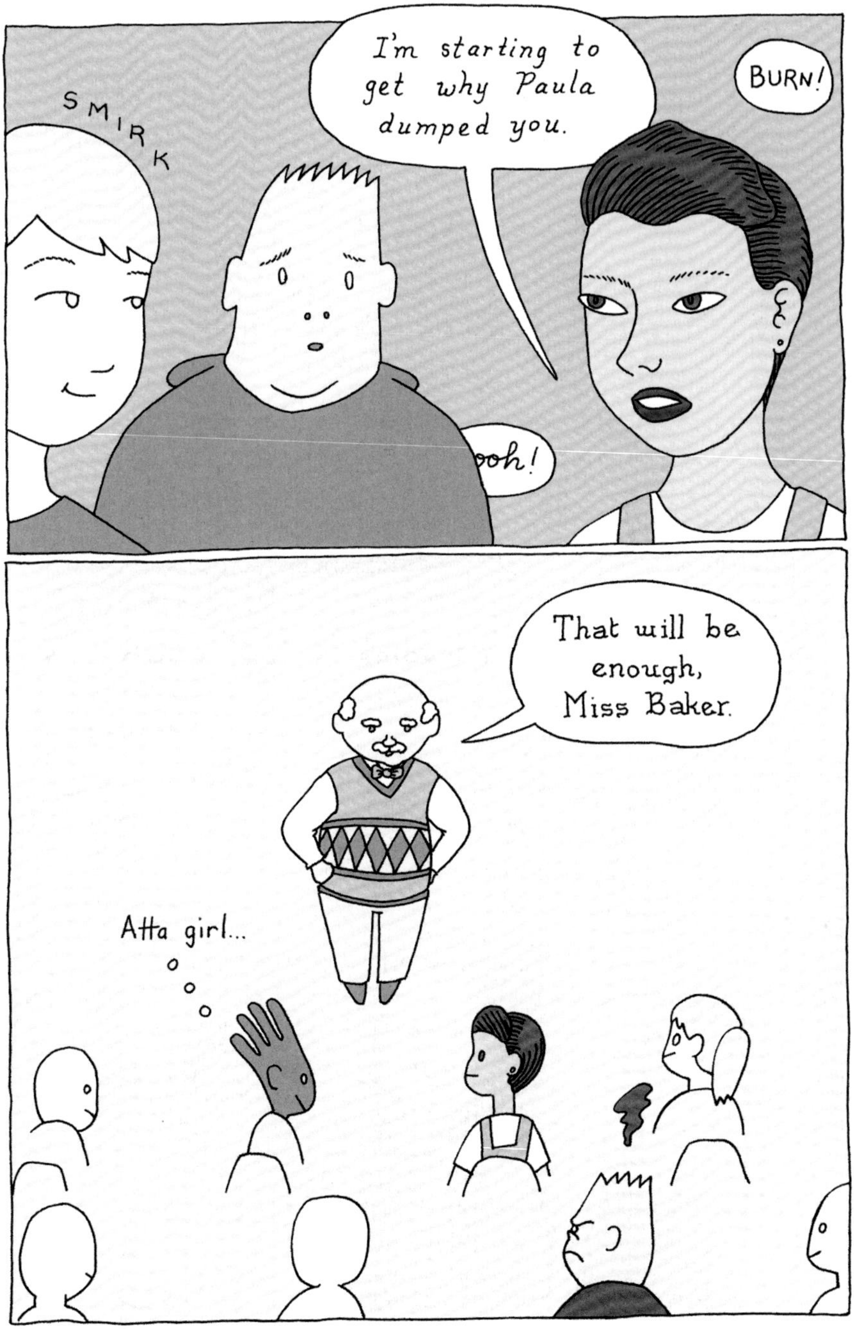
SMIRK
I'm starting to get why Paula dumped you.
BURN!
ooh!
That will be enough, Miss Baker.
Atta girl...

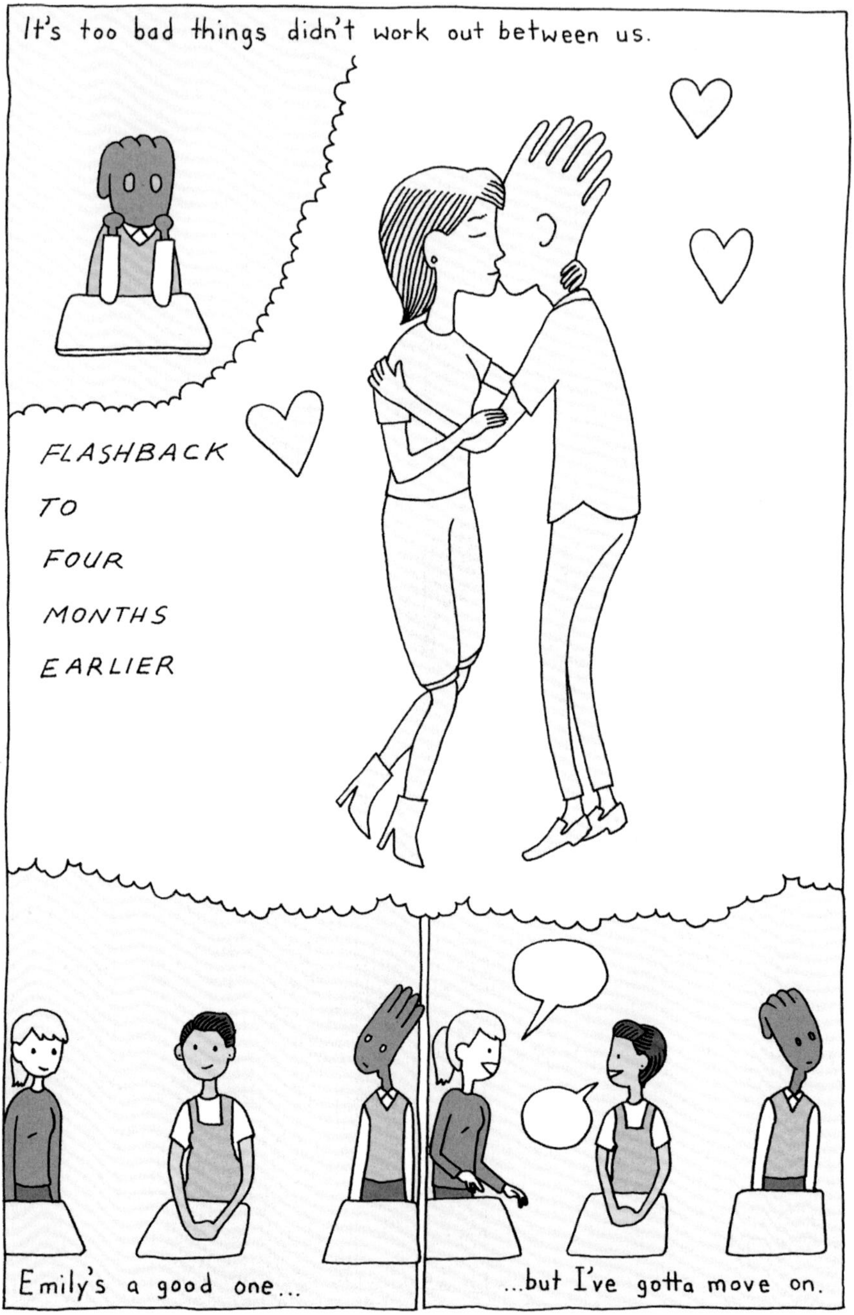
It's too bad things didn't work out between us.
FLASHBACK TO FOUR MONTHS EARLIER
Emily's a good one...
...but I've gotta move on.

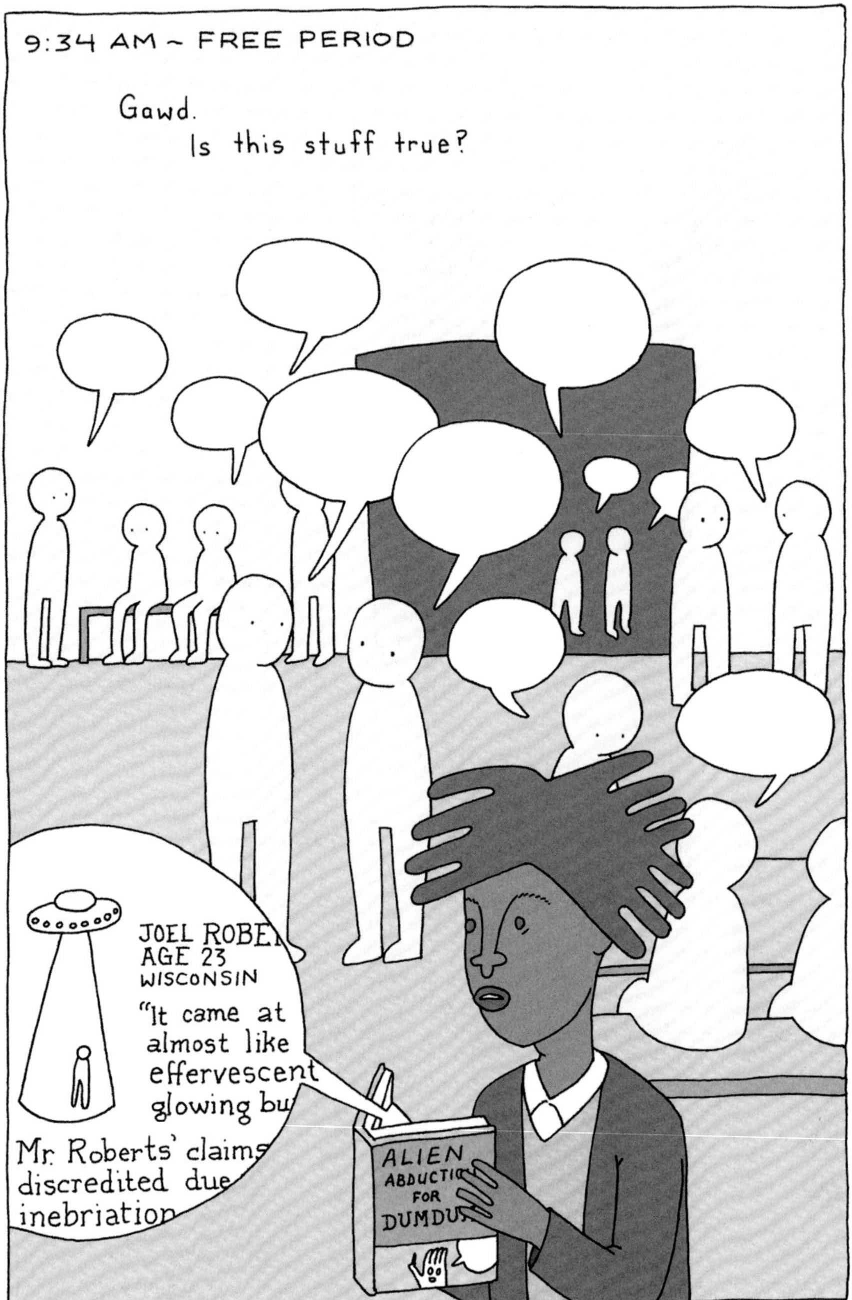
9:34 AM ~ FREE PERIOD
Gawd.
Is this stuff true?
JOEL ROBE
AGE 23
WISCONSIN
"It came at
almost like
effervescent
glowing bu
Mr. Roberts' claims
discredited due
inebriation
ALIEN
ABDUCTIO
FOR
DUMDU

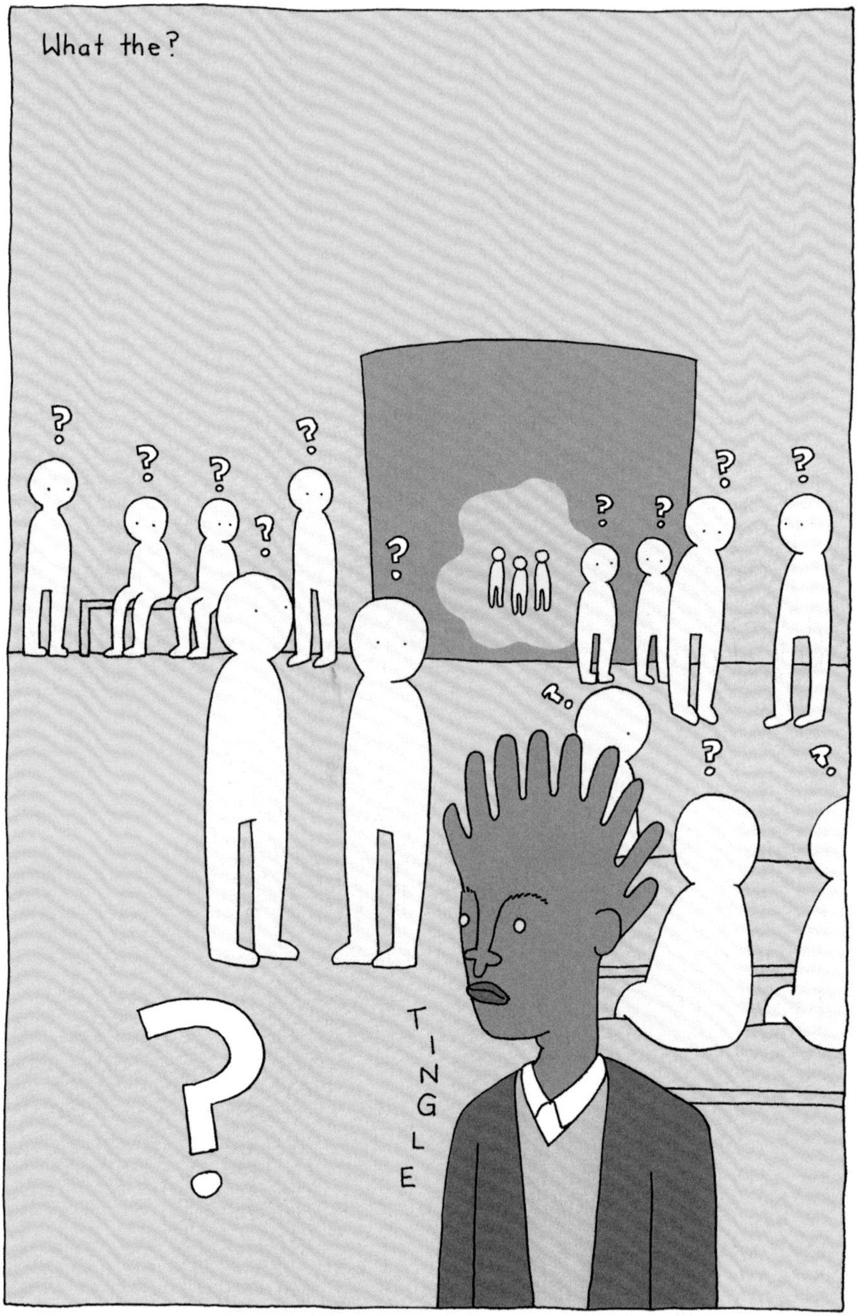
What the?
?
TINGLE

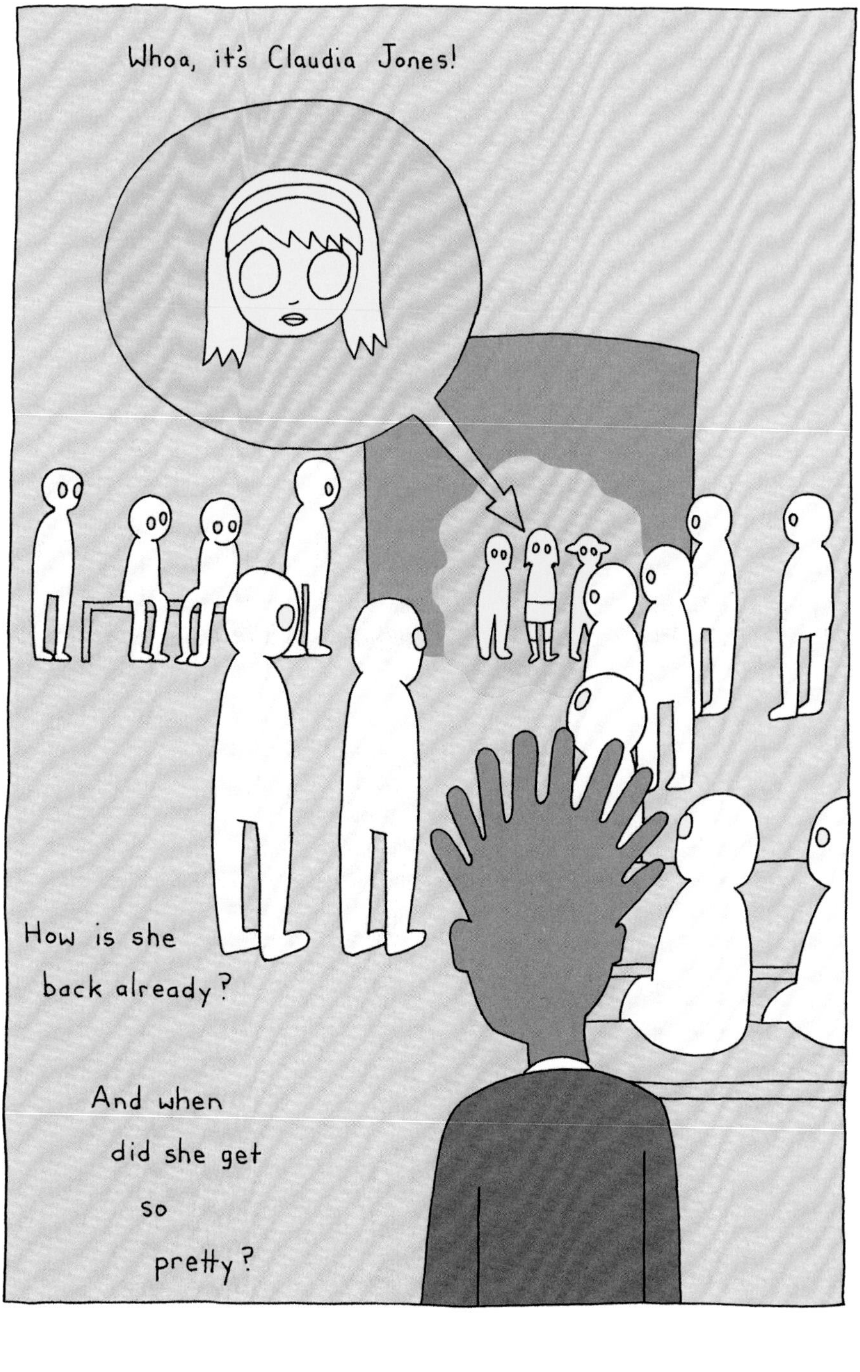
Whoa, it's Claudia Jones!
How is she back already?
And when did she get so pretty?

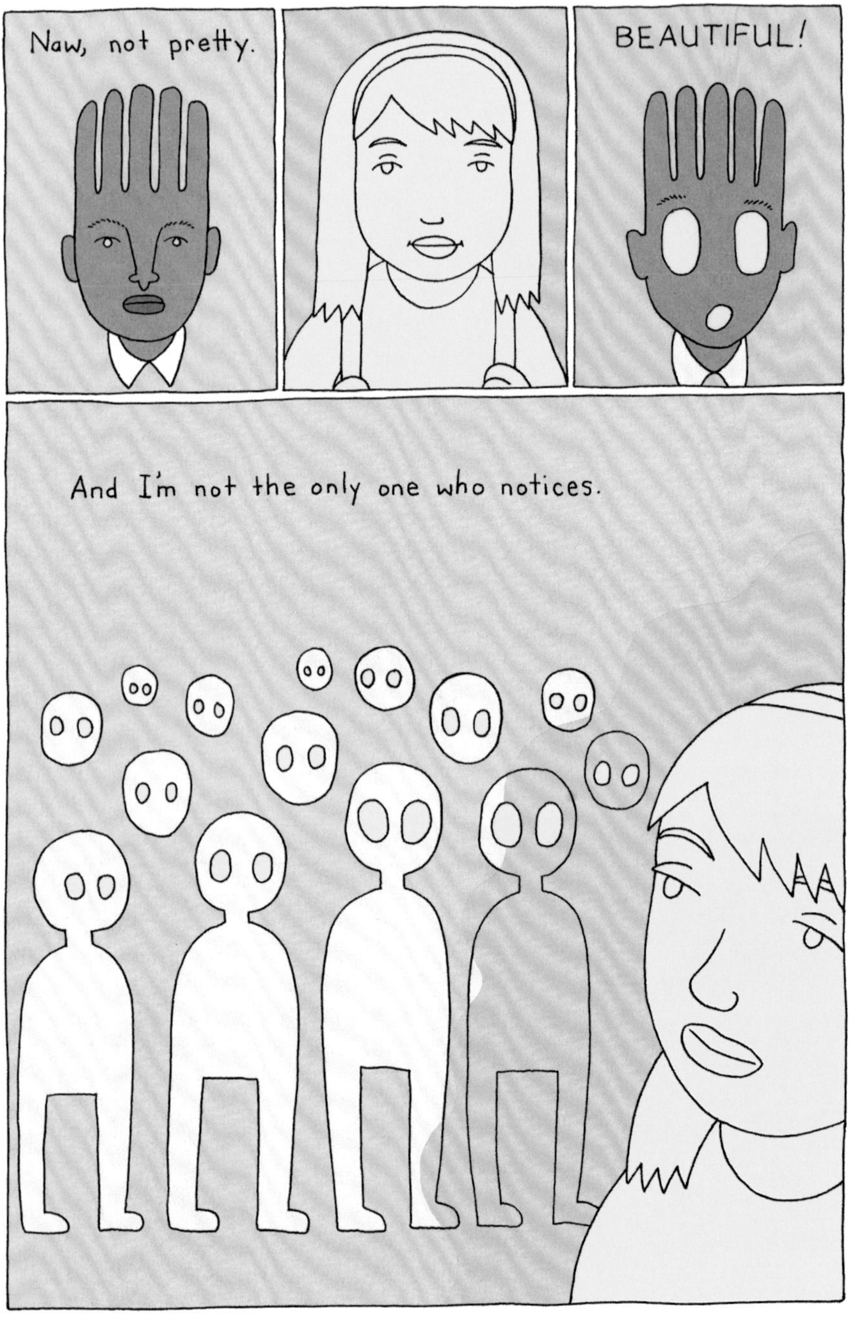
Naw, not pretty.
BEAUTIFUL!
And I'm not the only one who notices.

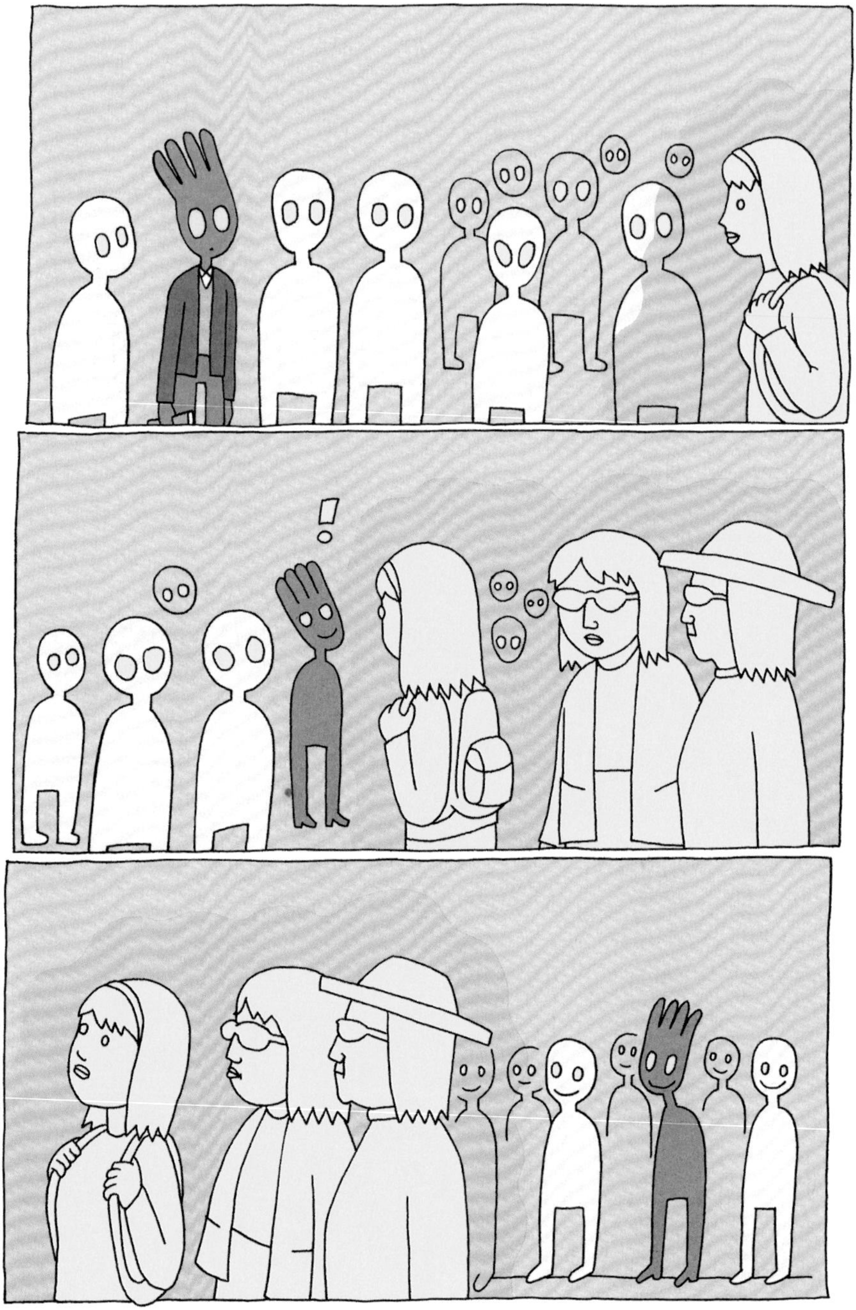
!

It's like she's got some kind of hold over us.

She used to be a nobody.

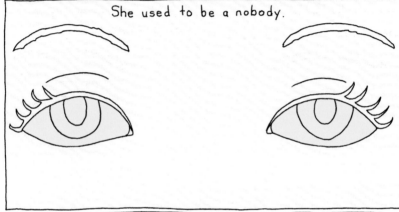

Right now, nobody can take their eyes off her.

14

Maybe it's 'cause she's famous now.

Or maybe they feel sorry for her. Or maybe the aliens gave her some kind of mind-control abilities!

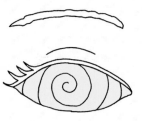 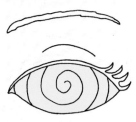

HA HA!
Good one, Nigel!

Hm...but maybe it's too soon for that kind of joke.

Gotta save that one for later.

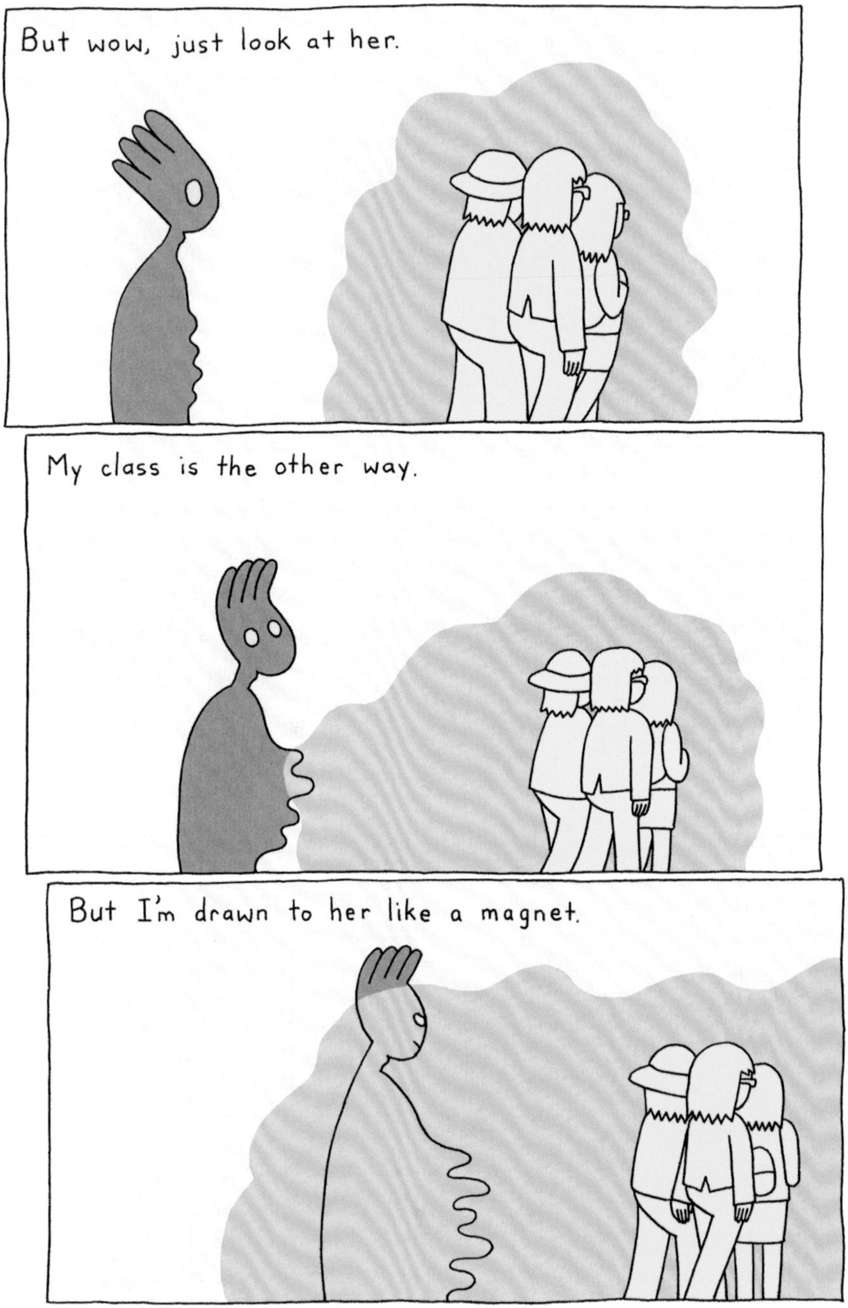
But wow, just look at her.
My class is the other way.
But I'm drawn to her like a magnet.

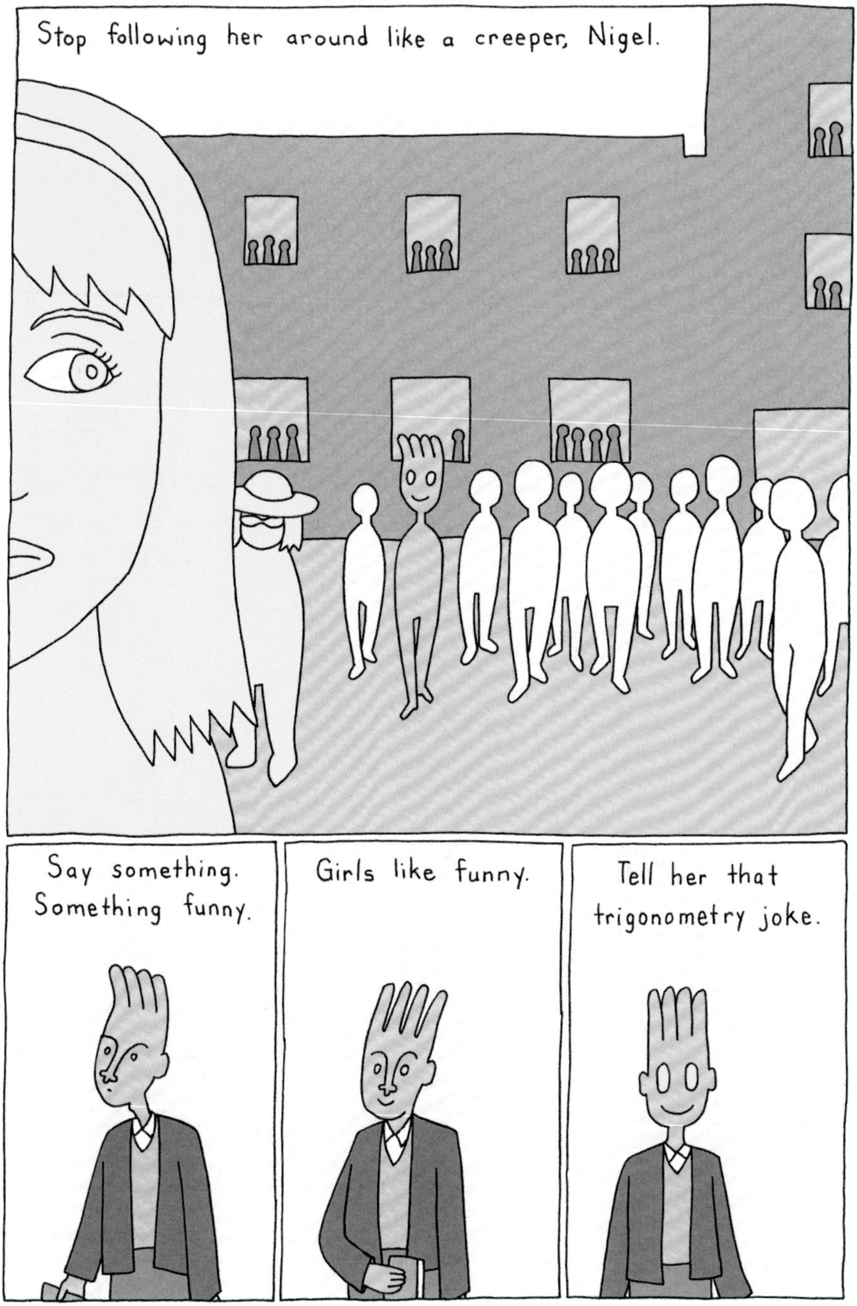
Stop following her around like a creeper, Nigel.
Say something. Something funny.
Girls like funny.
Tell her that trigonometry joke.

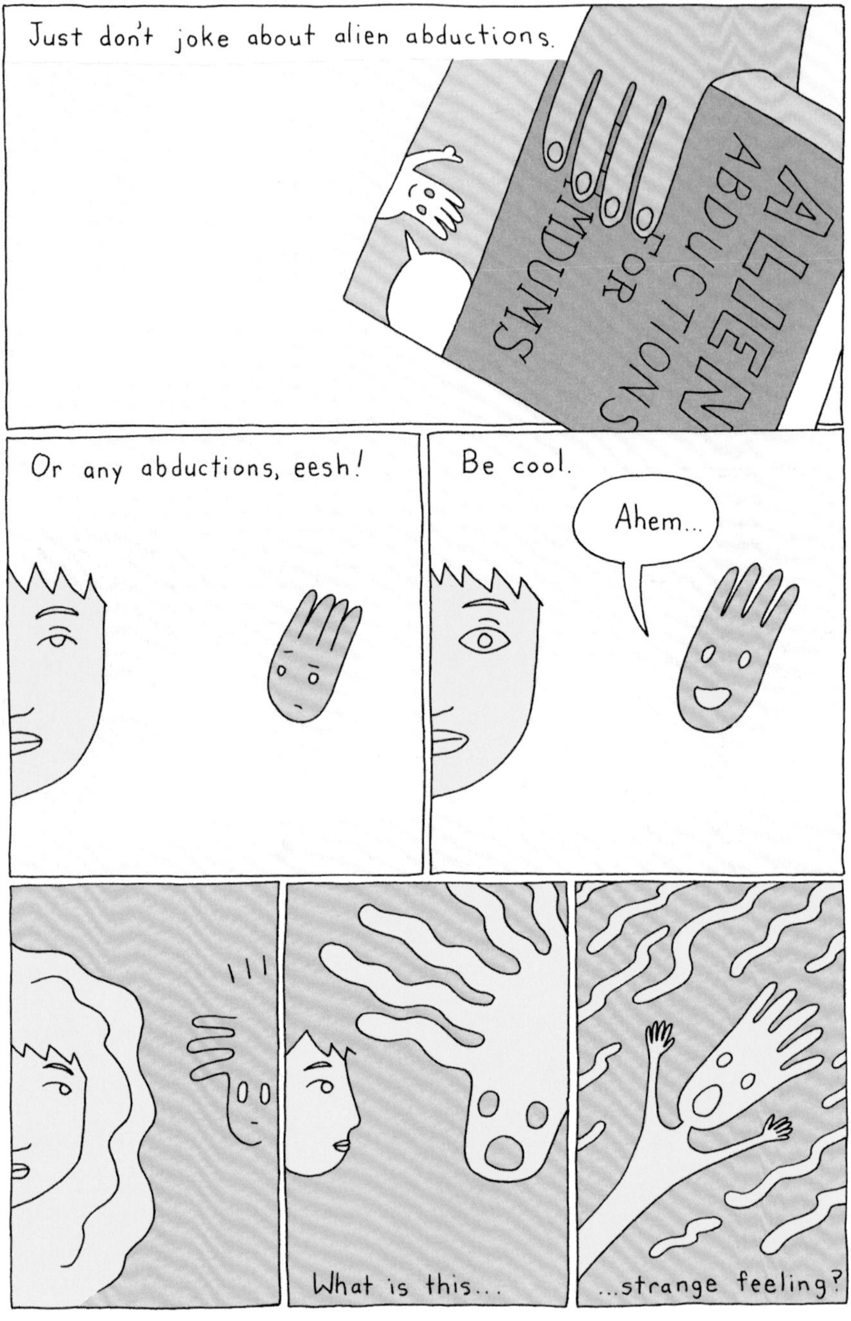
Just don't joke about alien abductions.
ALIEN ABDUCTIONS FOR DUMS
Or any abductions, eesh!
Be cool.
Ahem...
What is this...
...strange feeling?

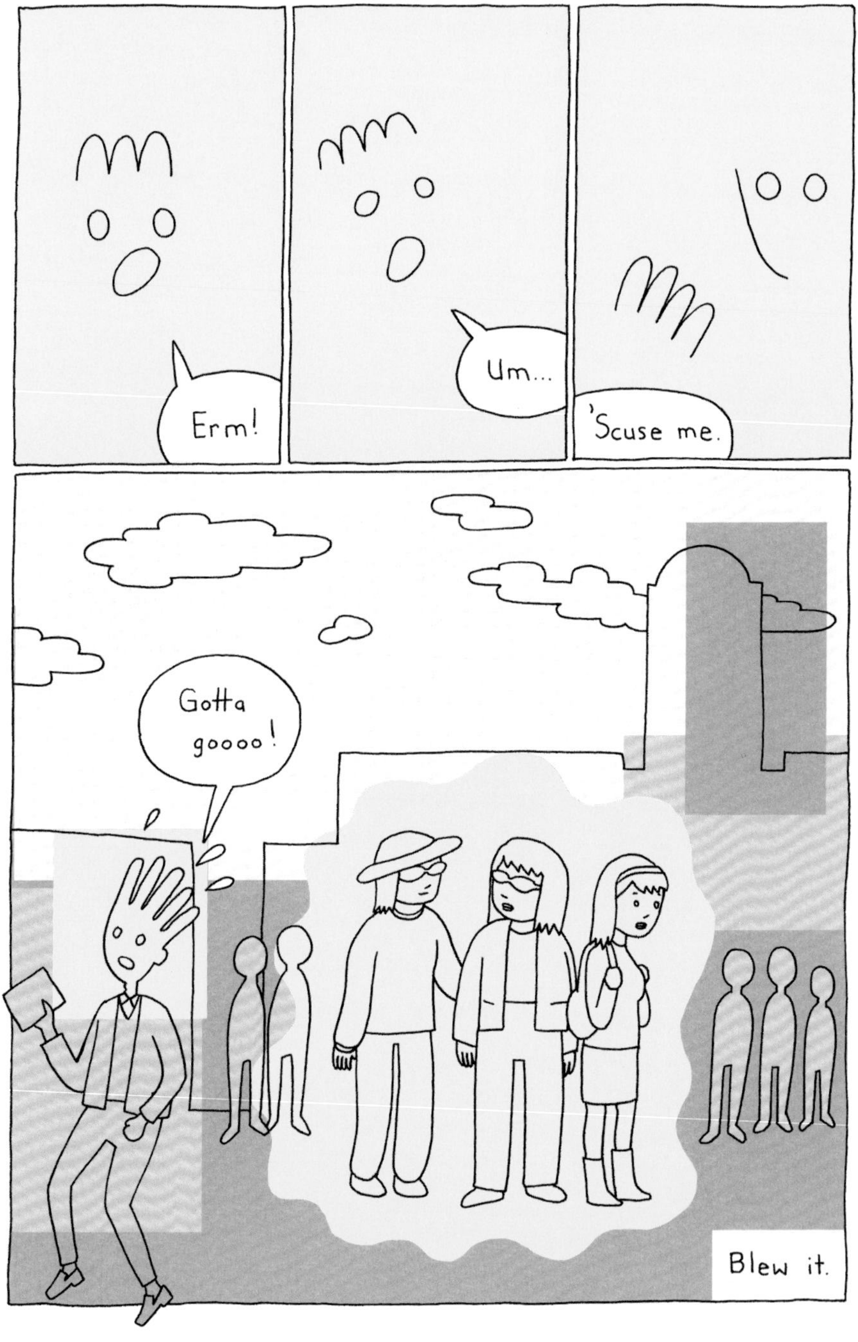
Erm!
Um...
'Scuse me.
Gotta goooo!
Blew it.

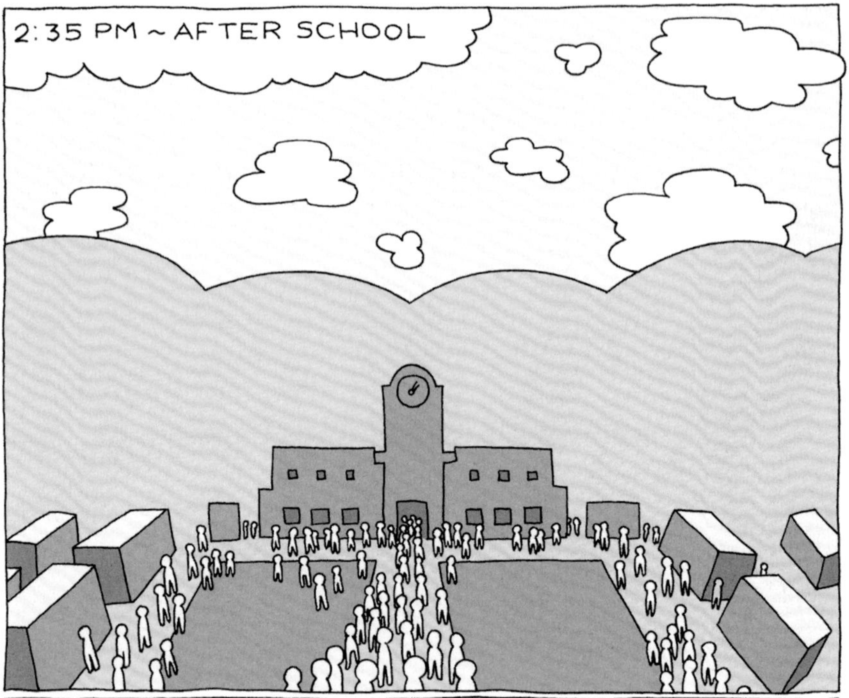
2:35 PM ~ AFTER SCHOOL

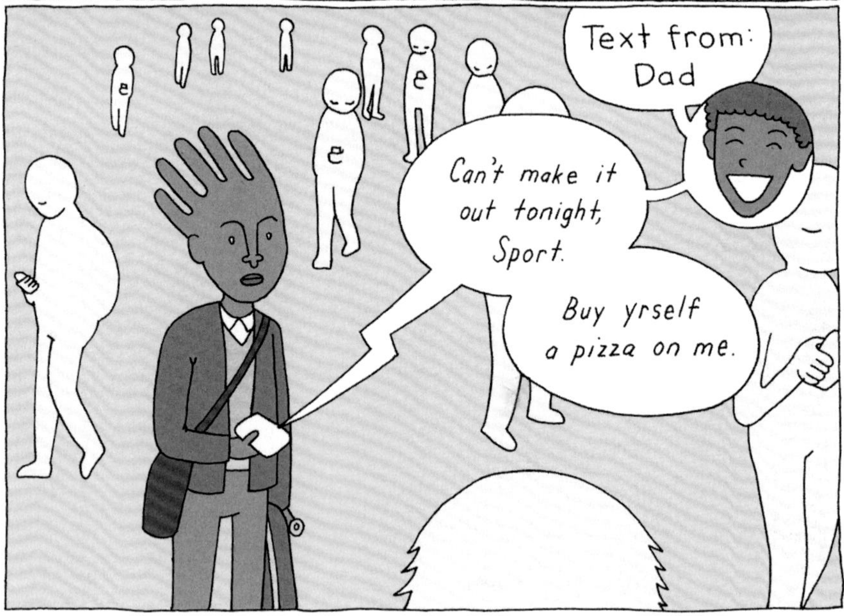
Text from: Dad
Can't make it out tonight, Sport.
Buy yrself a pizza on me.

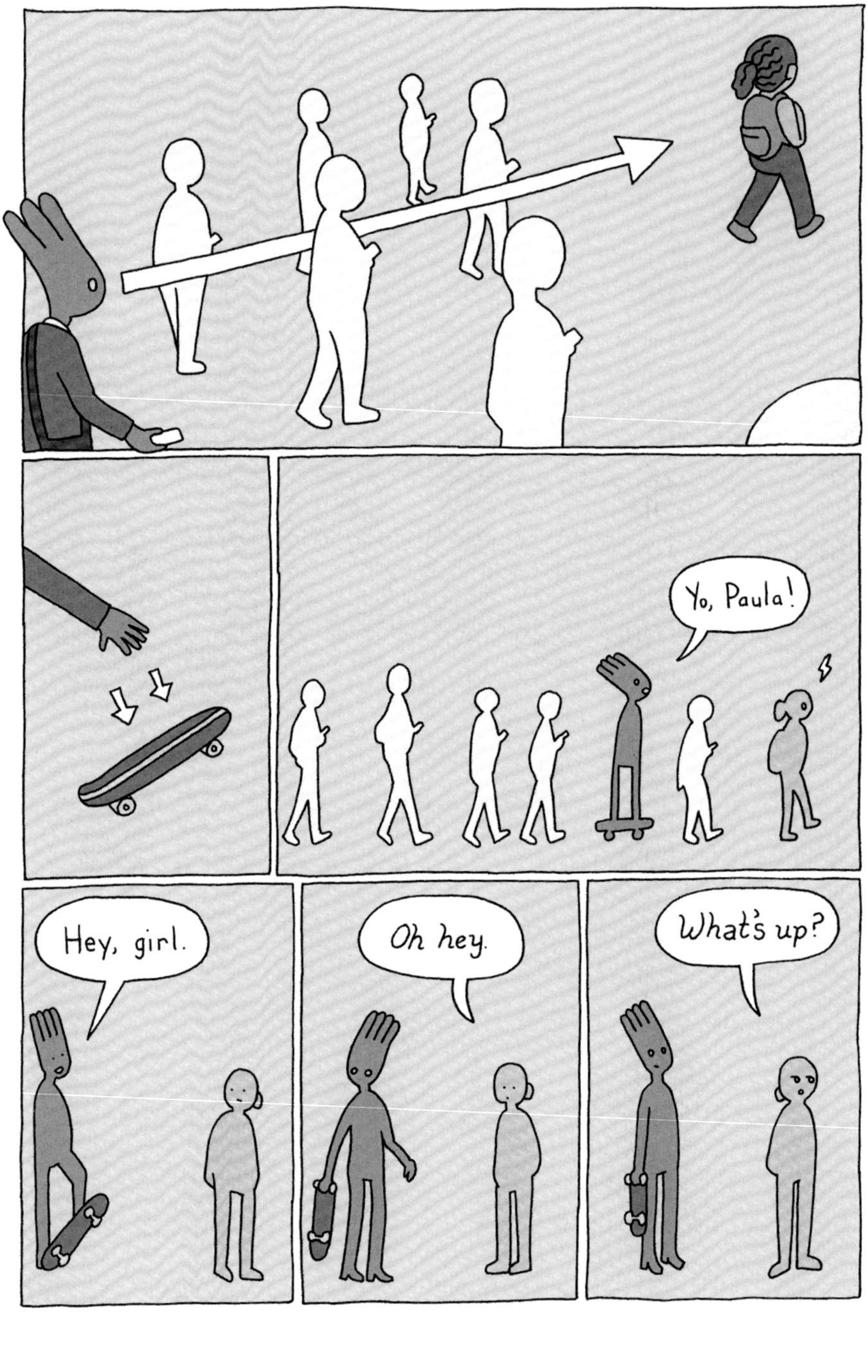
Yo, Paula!
Hey, girl.
Oh hey.
What's up?

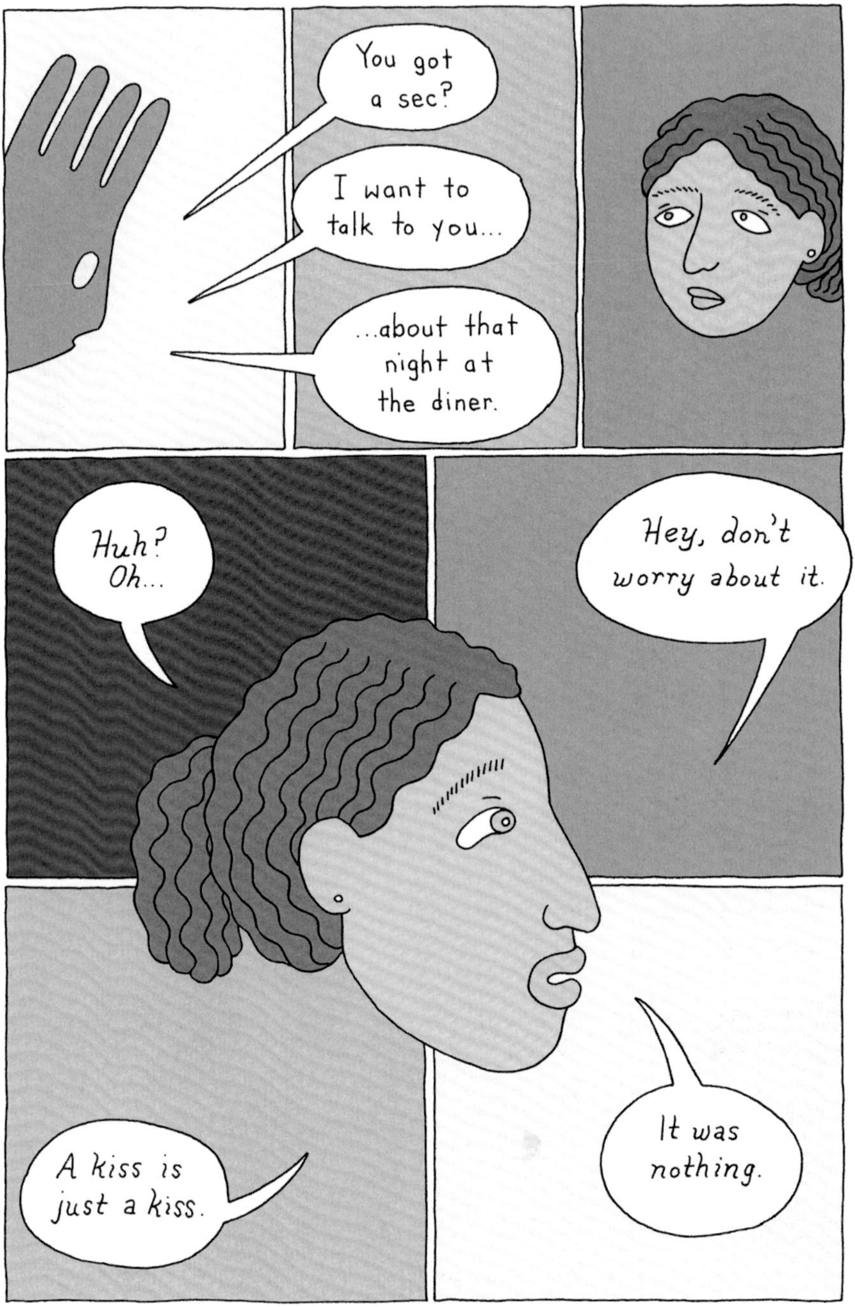
You got a sec?
I want to talk to you...
...about that night at the diner.
Huh? Oh...
Hey, don't worry about it.
A kiss is just a kiss.
It was nothing.

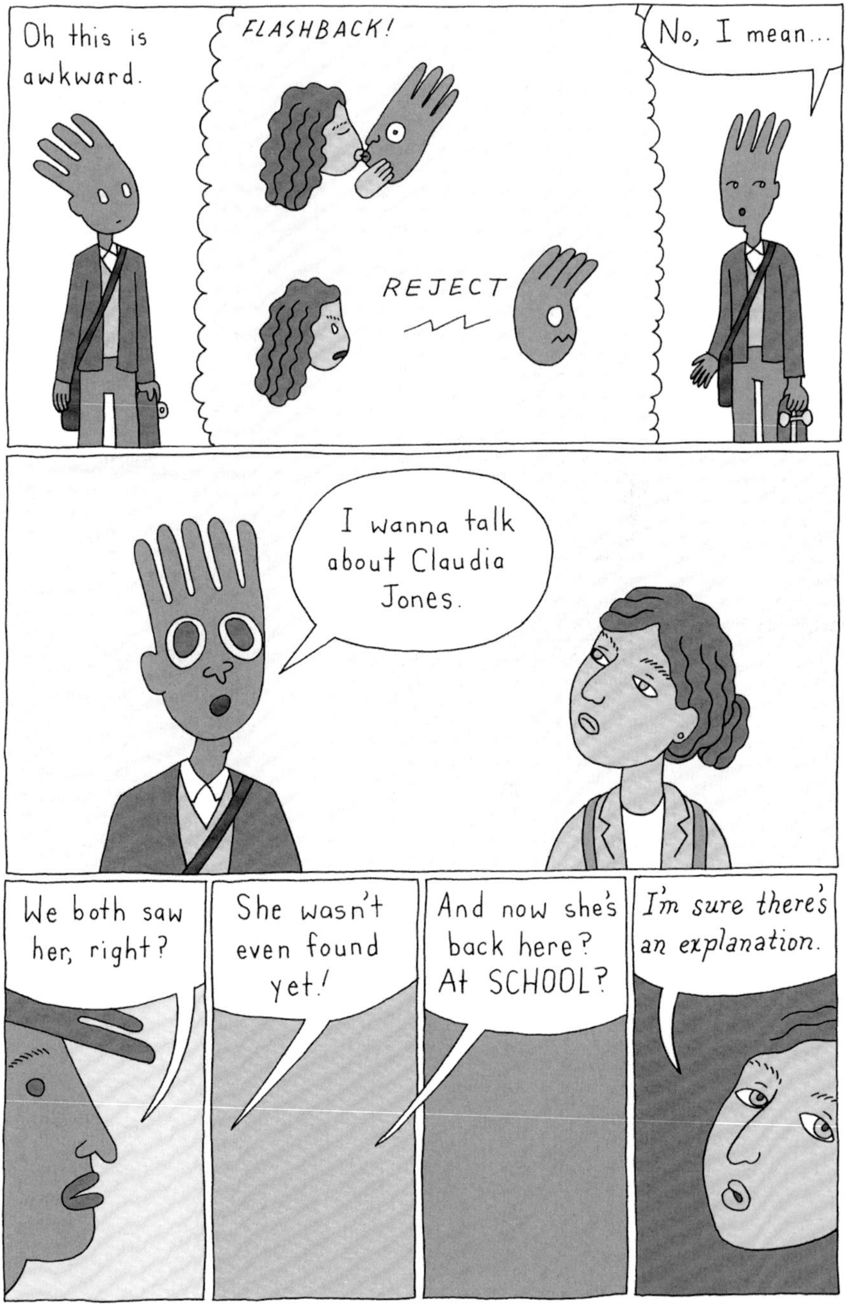
Oh this is awkward.
FLASHBACK!
REJECT
No, I mean...
I wanna talk about Claudia Jones.
We both saw her, right?
She wasn't even found yet!
And now she's back here? At SCHOOL?
I'm sure there's an explanation.

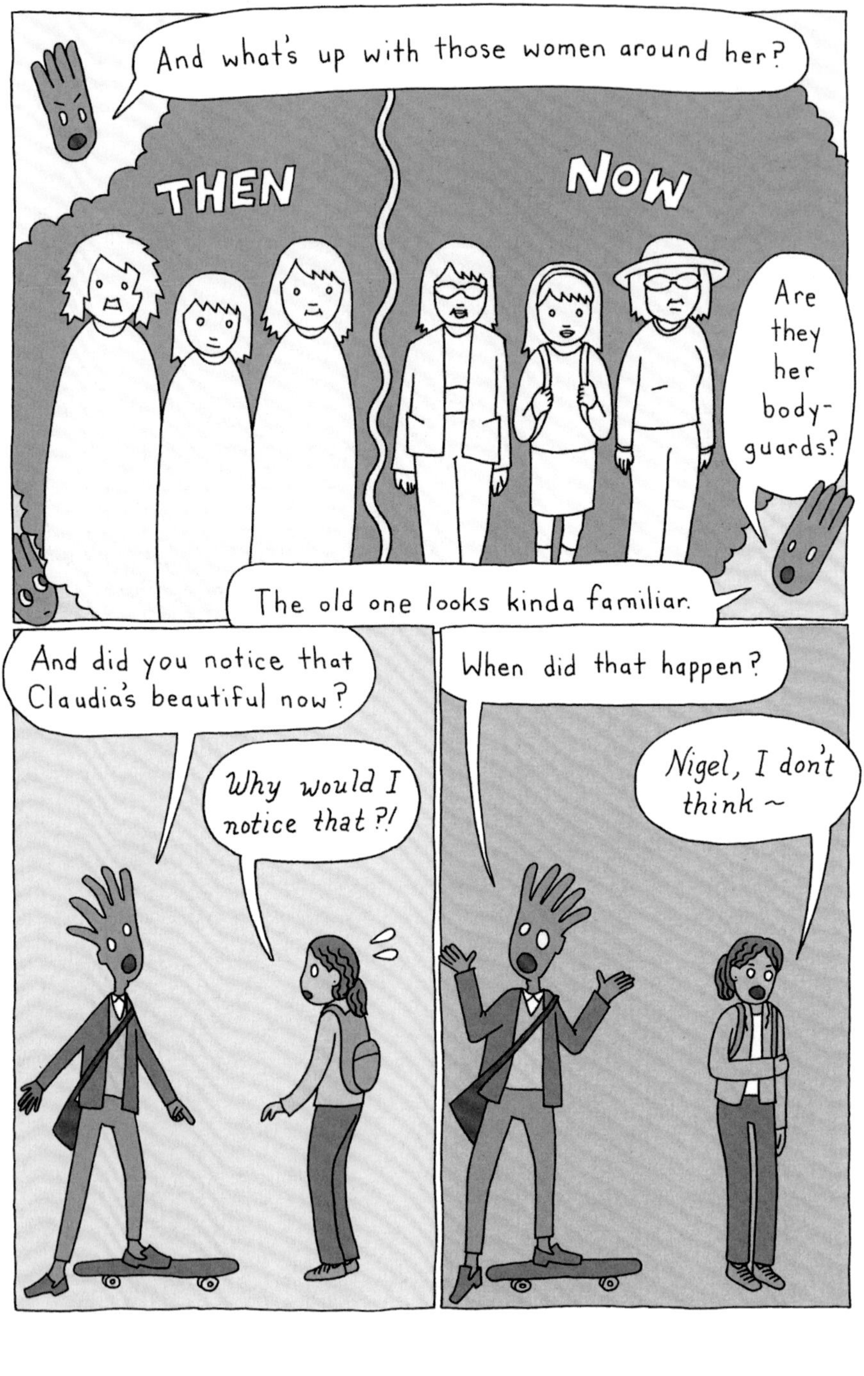
And what's up with those women around her?
THEN
NOW
Are they her body-guards?
The old one looks kinda familiar.
And did you notice that Claudia's beautiful now?
Why would I notice that?!
When did that happen?
Nigel, I don't think ~

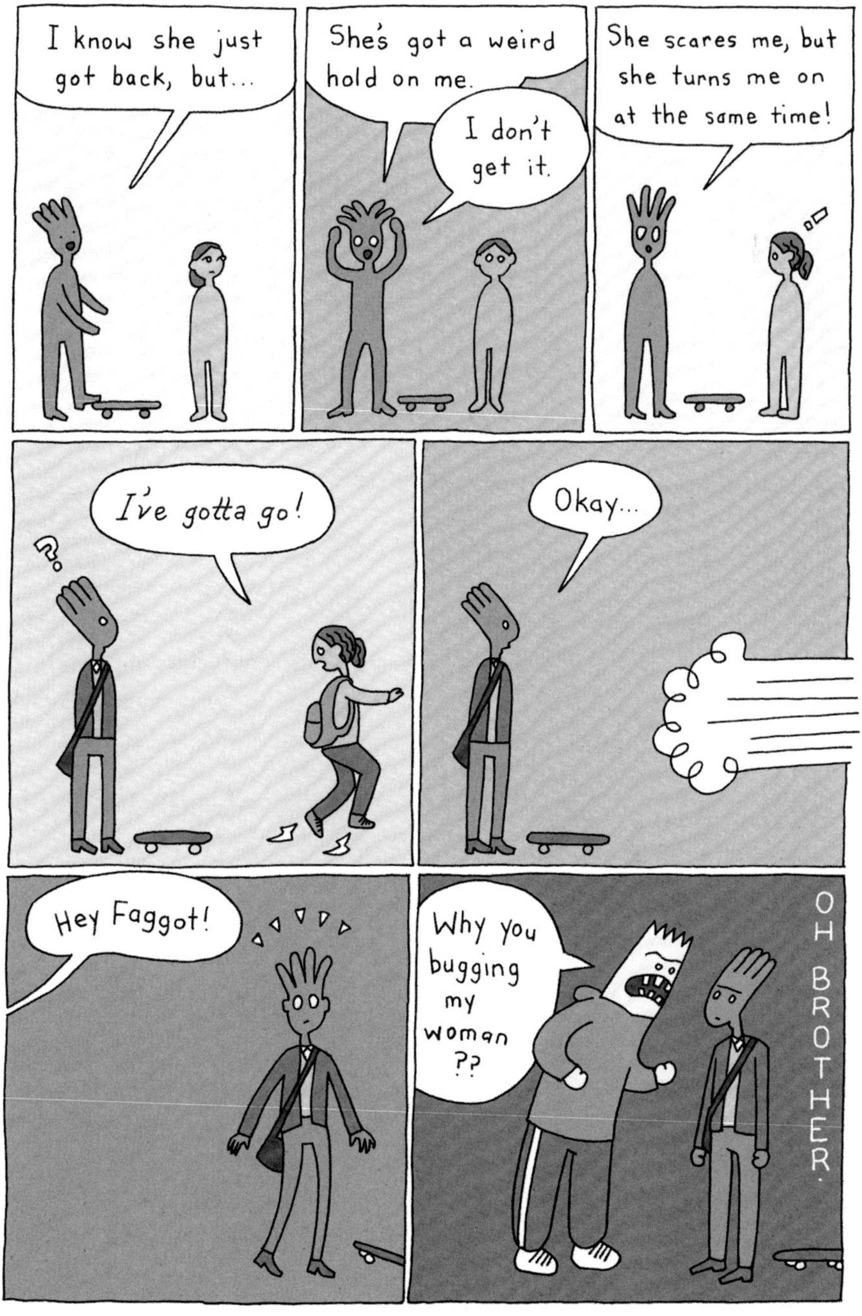
I know she just got back, but...
She's got a weird hold on me.
I don't get it.
She scares me, but she turns me on at the same time!
I've gotta go!
Okay...
Hey Faggot!
Why you bugging my woman ??
OH BROTHER.

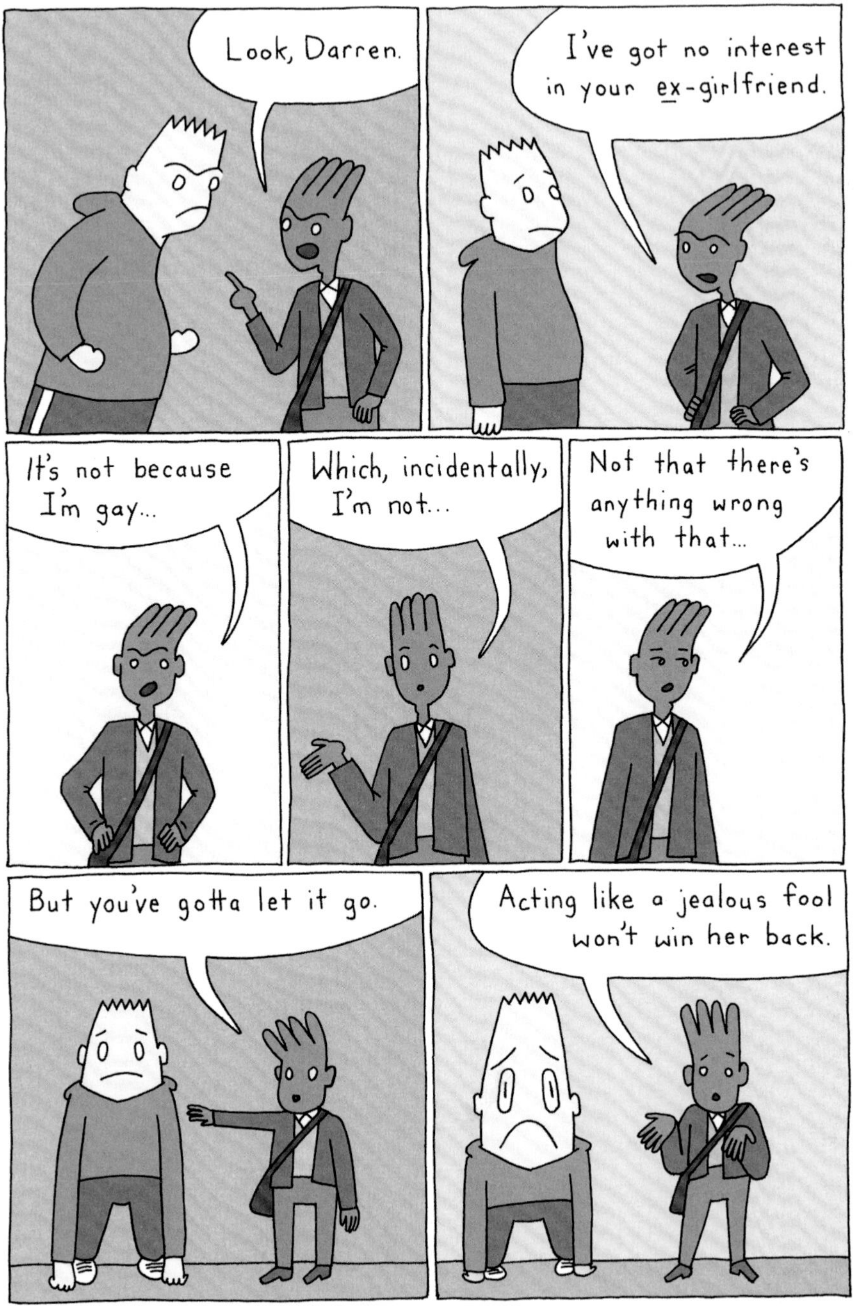
Look, Darren.
I've got no interest in your ex-girlfriend.
It's not because I'm gay...
Which, incidentally, I'm not...
Not that there's anything wrong with that...
But you've gotta let it go.
Acting like a jealous fool won't win her back.

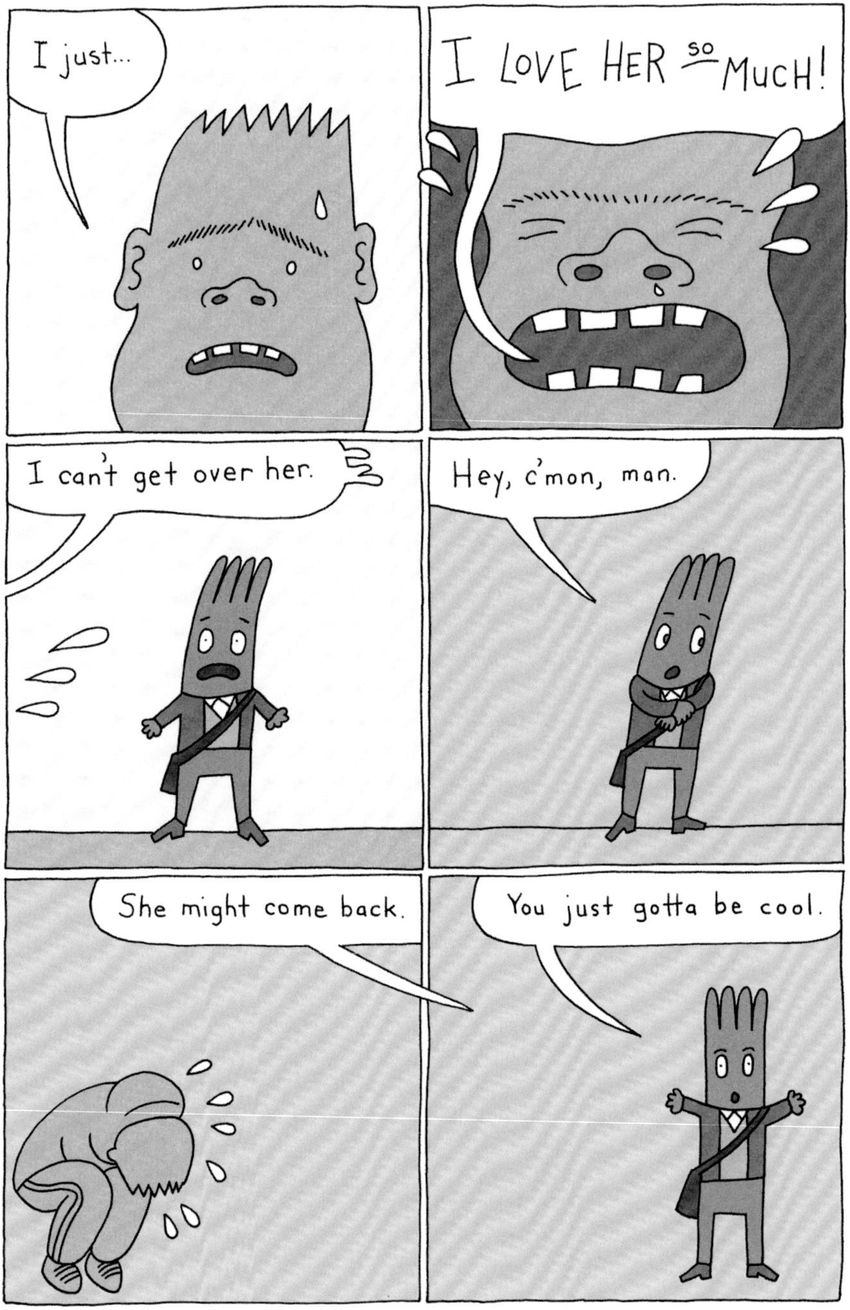
I just...
I LOVE HER SO MUCH!
I can't get over her.
Hey, c'mon, man.
She might come back.
You just gotta be cool.

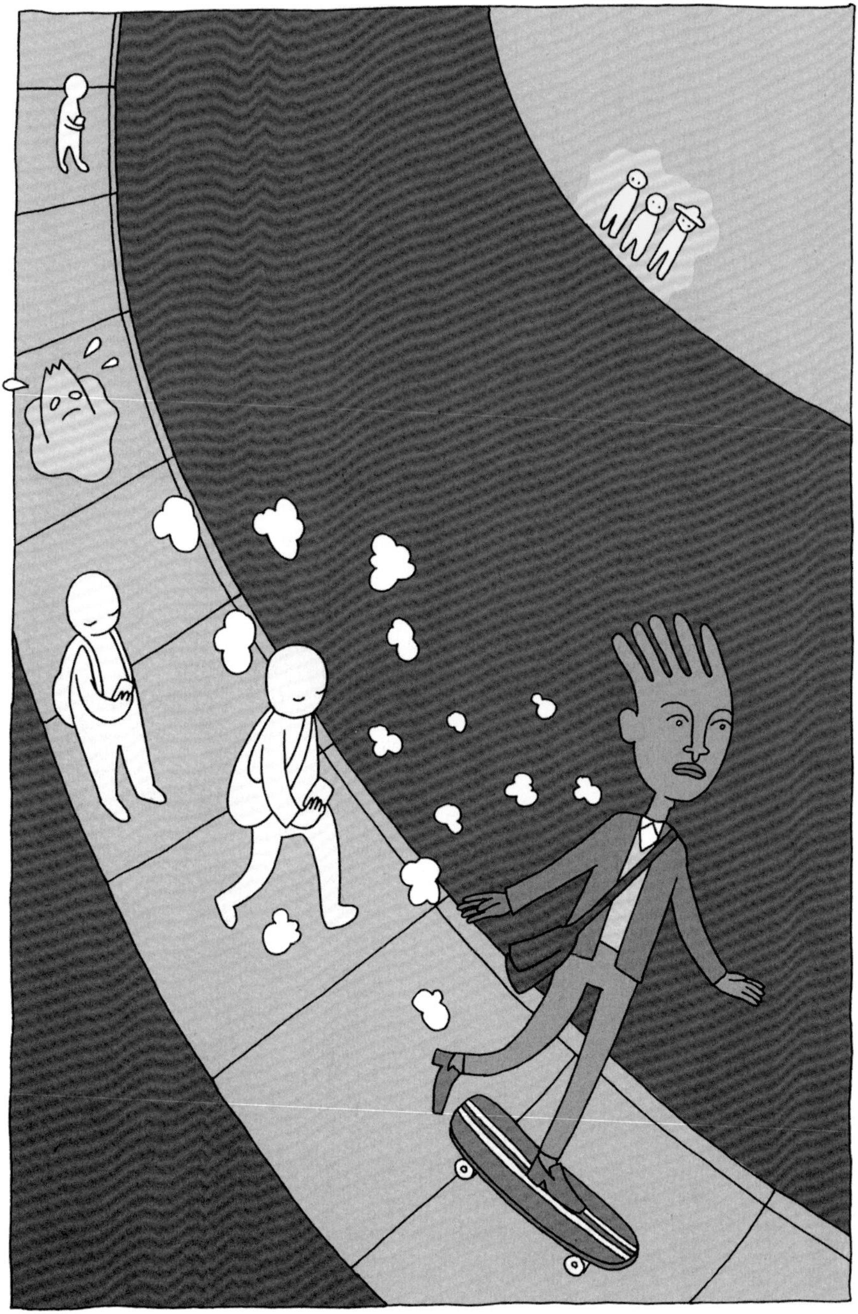

PART TWO

Paula Navarro

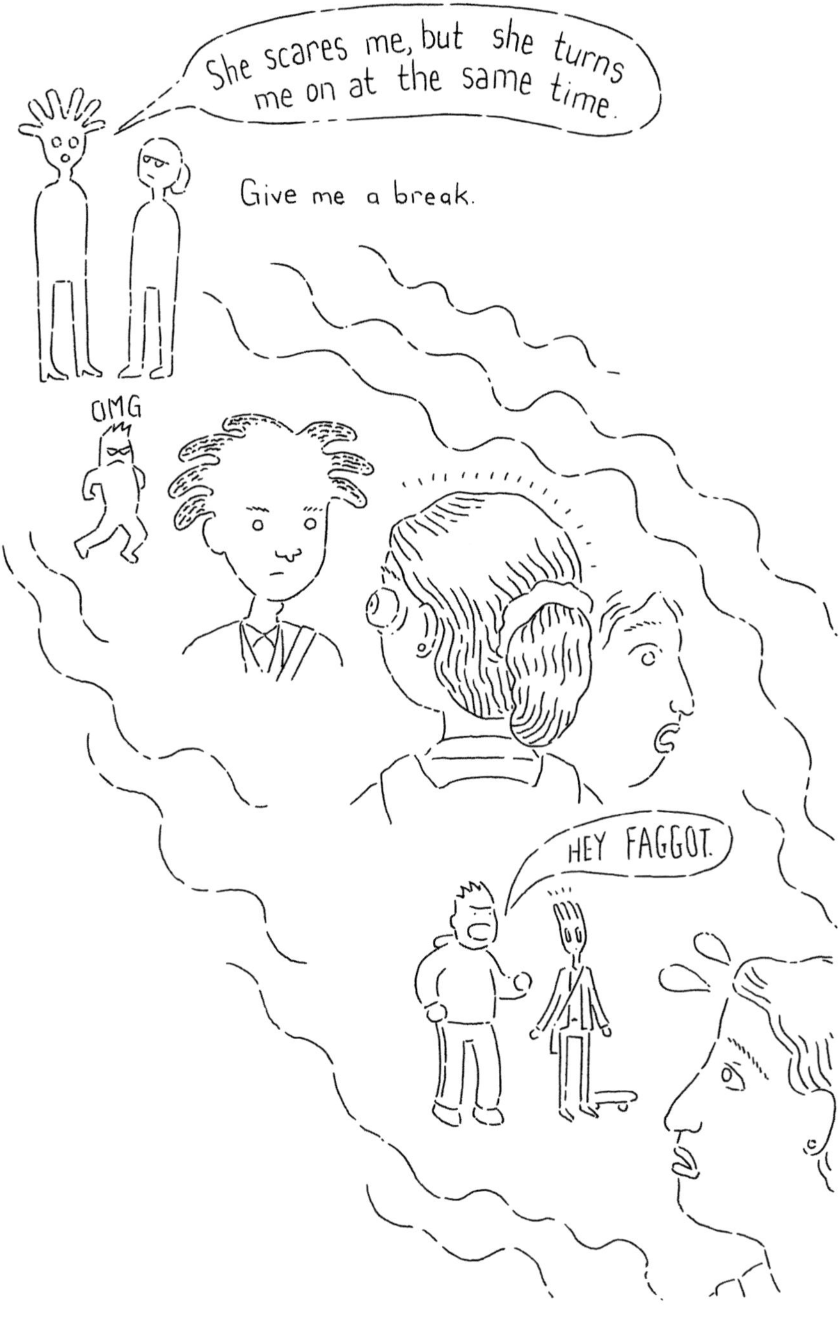
She scares me, but she turns me on at the same time.
Give me a break.
OMG
HEY FAGGOT.

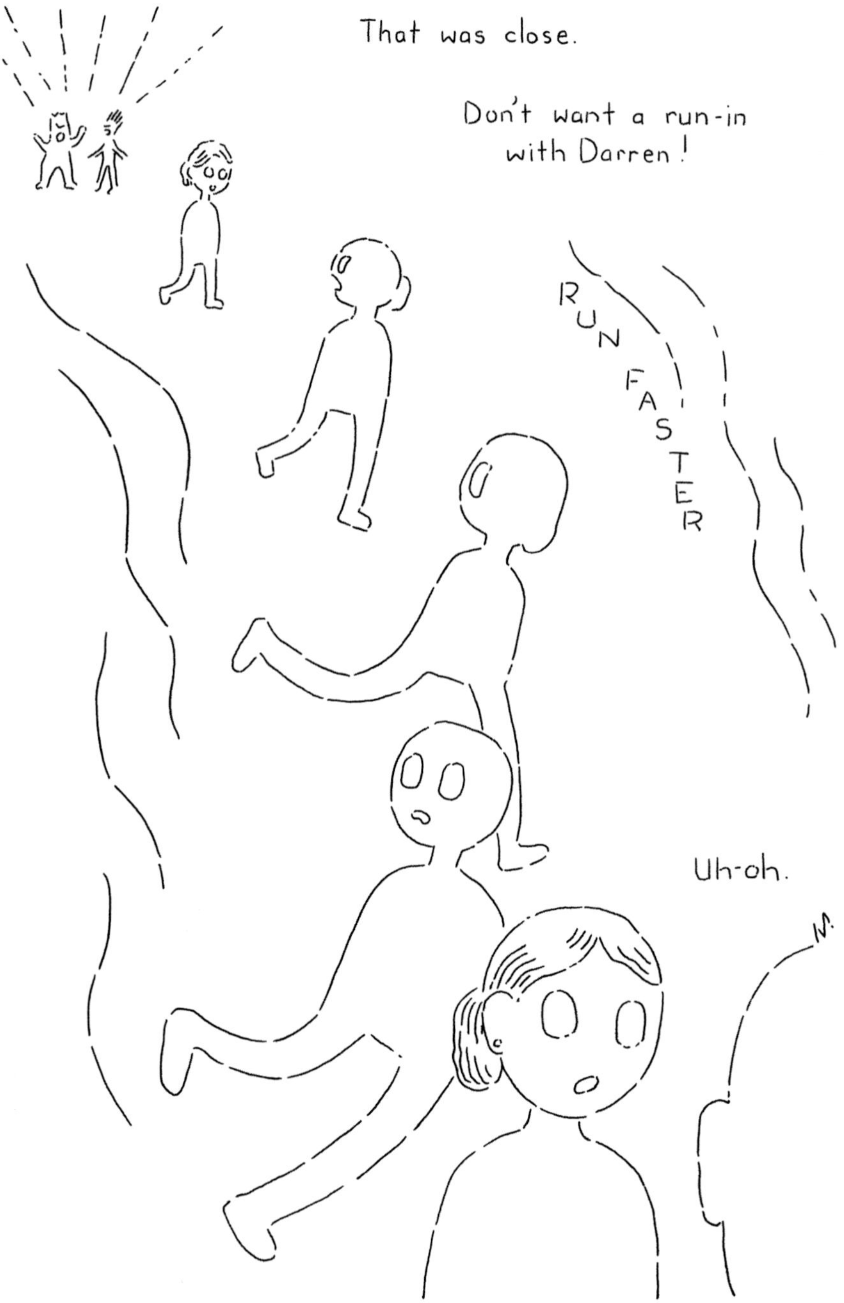
That was close.
Don't want a run-in with Darren!
RUN FASTER
Uh-oh.

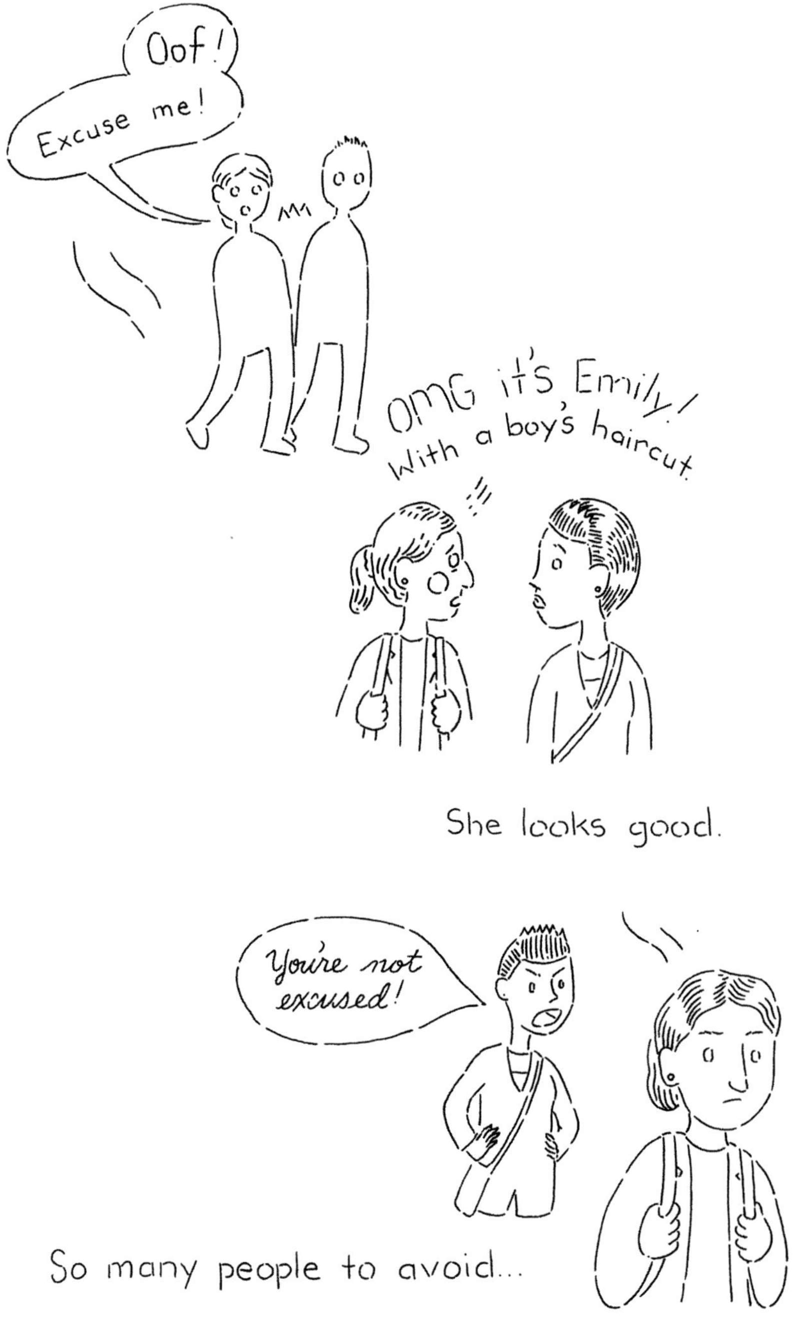
Oof!
Excuse me!
OMG it's Emily!
With a boy's haircut.
She looks good.
You're not excused!
So many people to avoid...

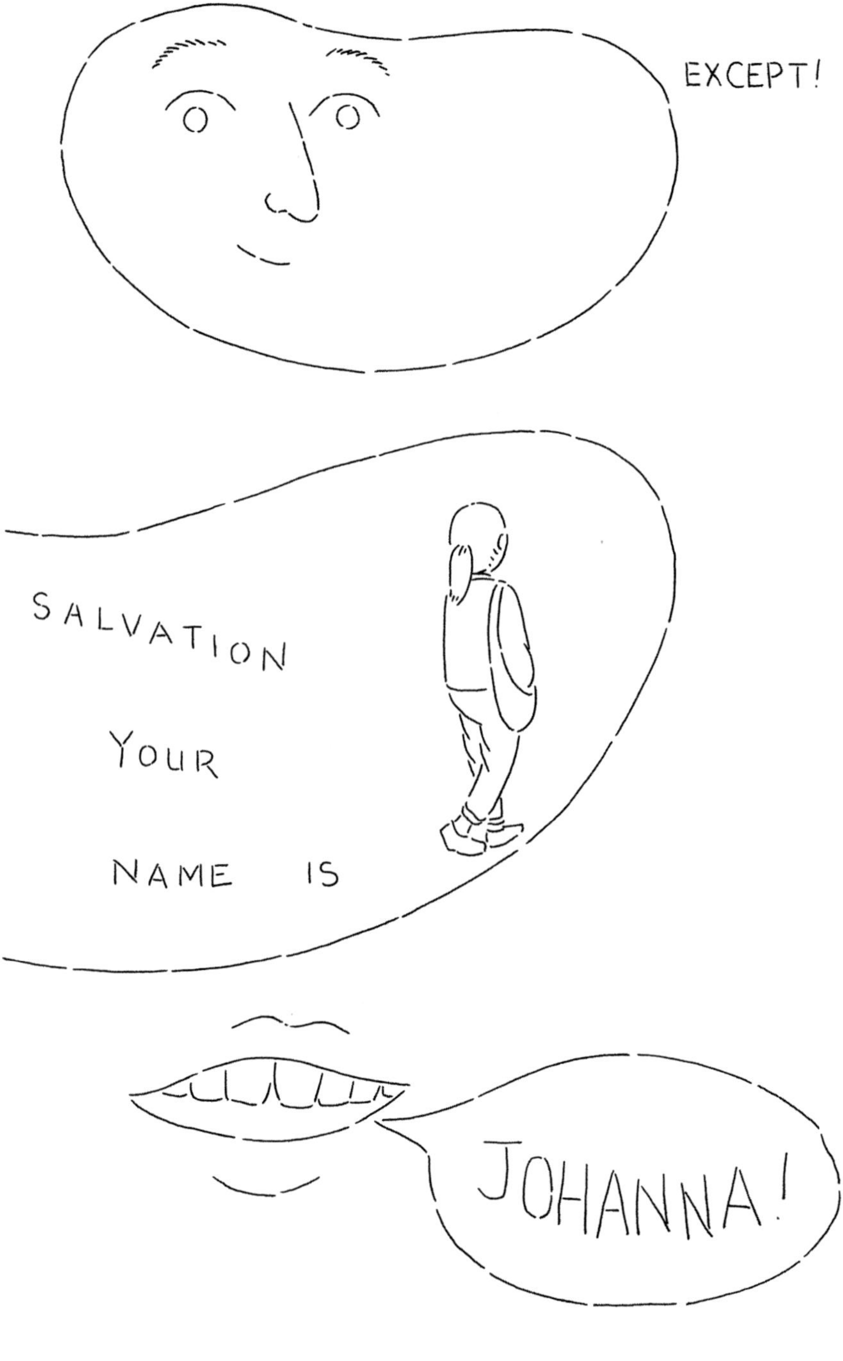
EXCEPT!
SALVATION
YOUR
NAME IS
JOHANNA!

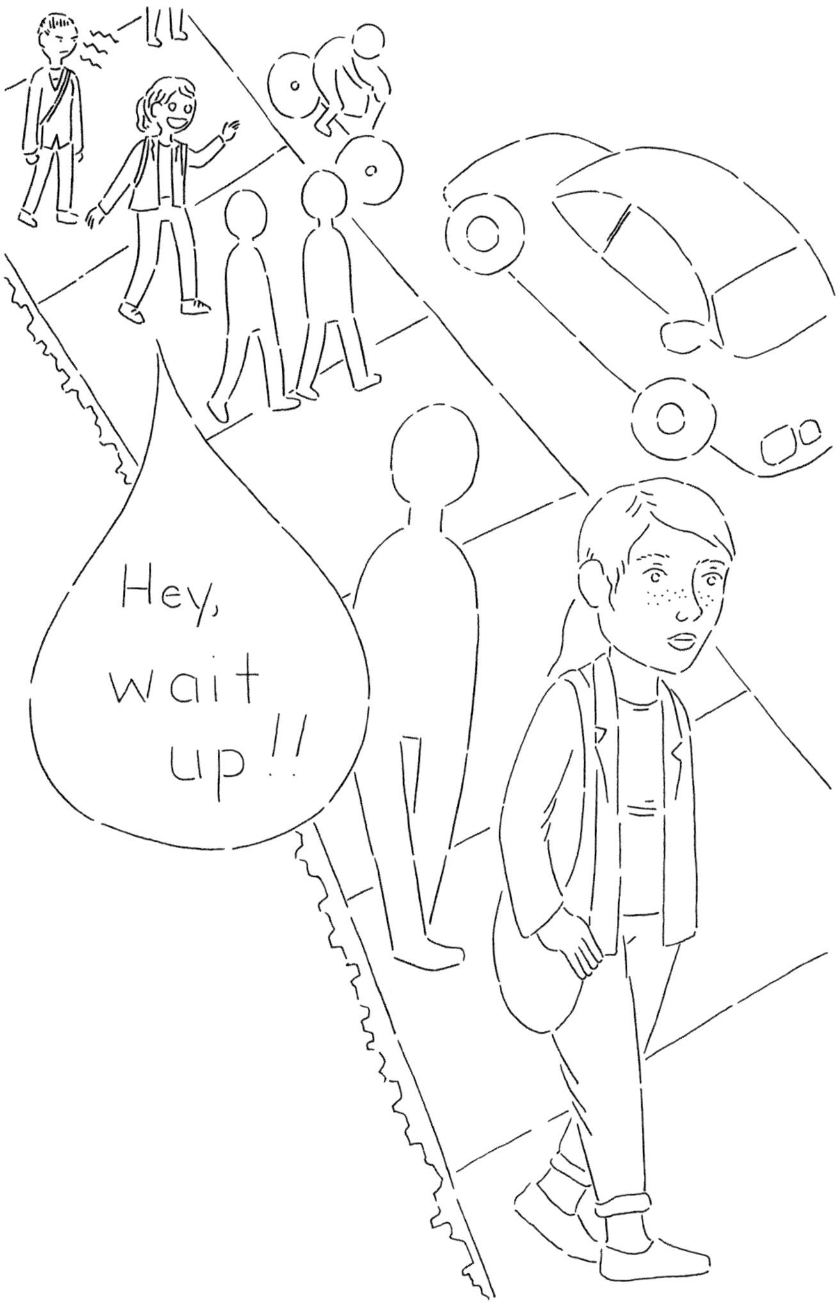
Hey, wait up!!

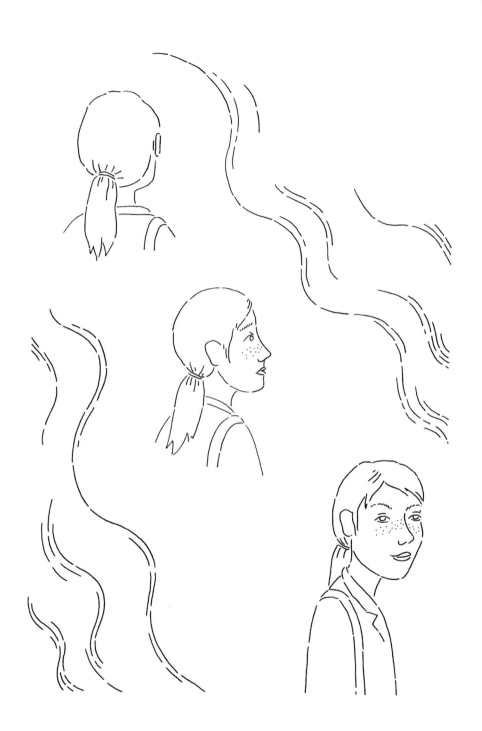

She actually looks happy to see me.
When has that ever happened?

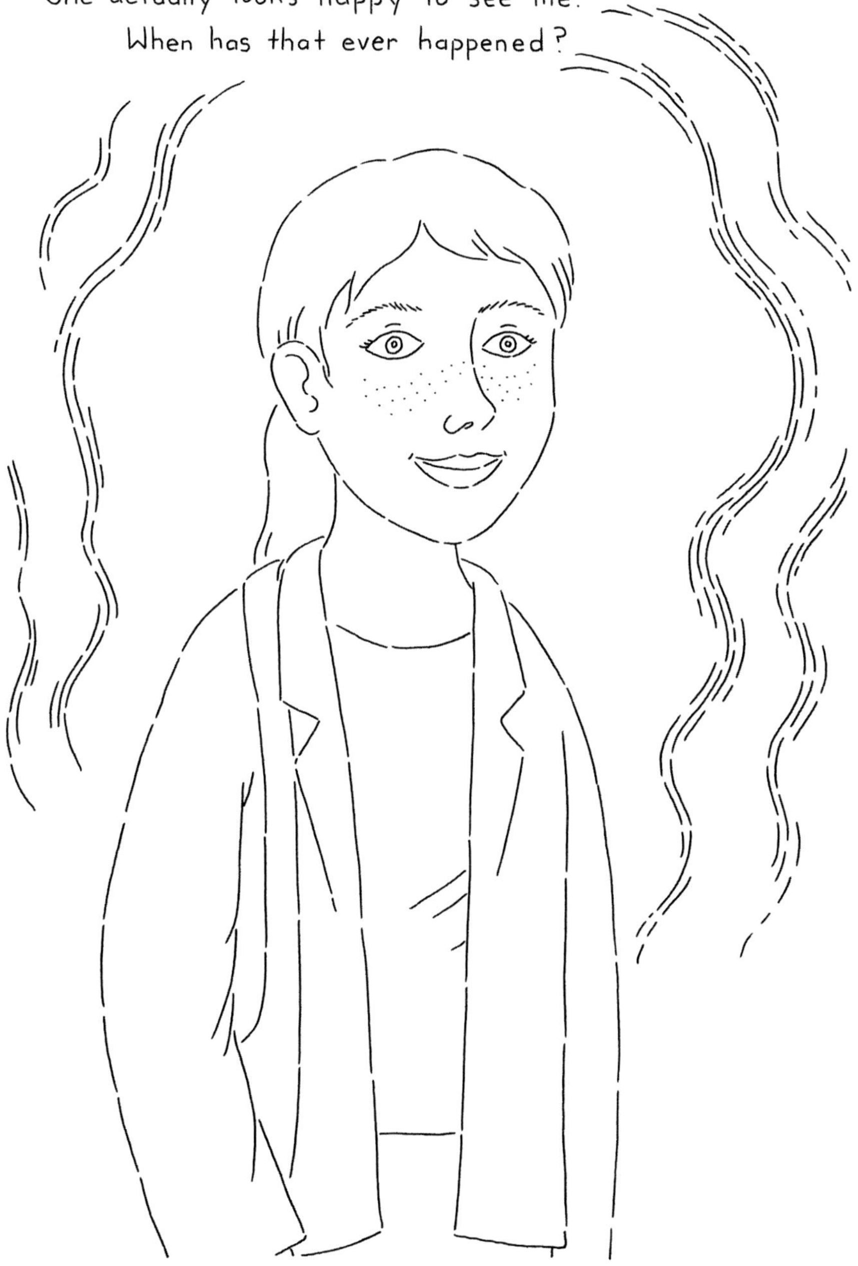

Here goes...

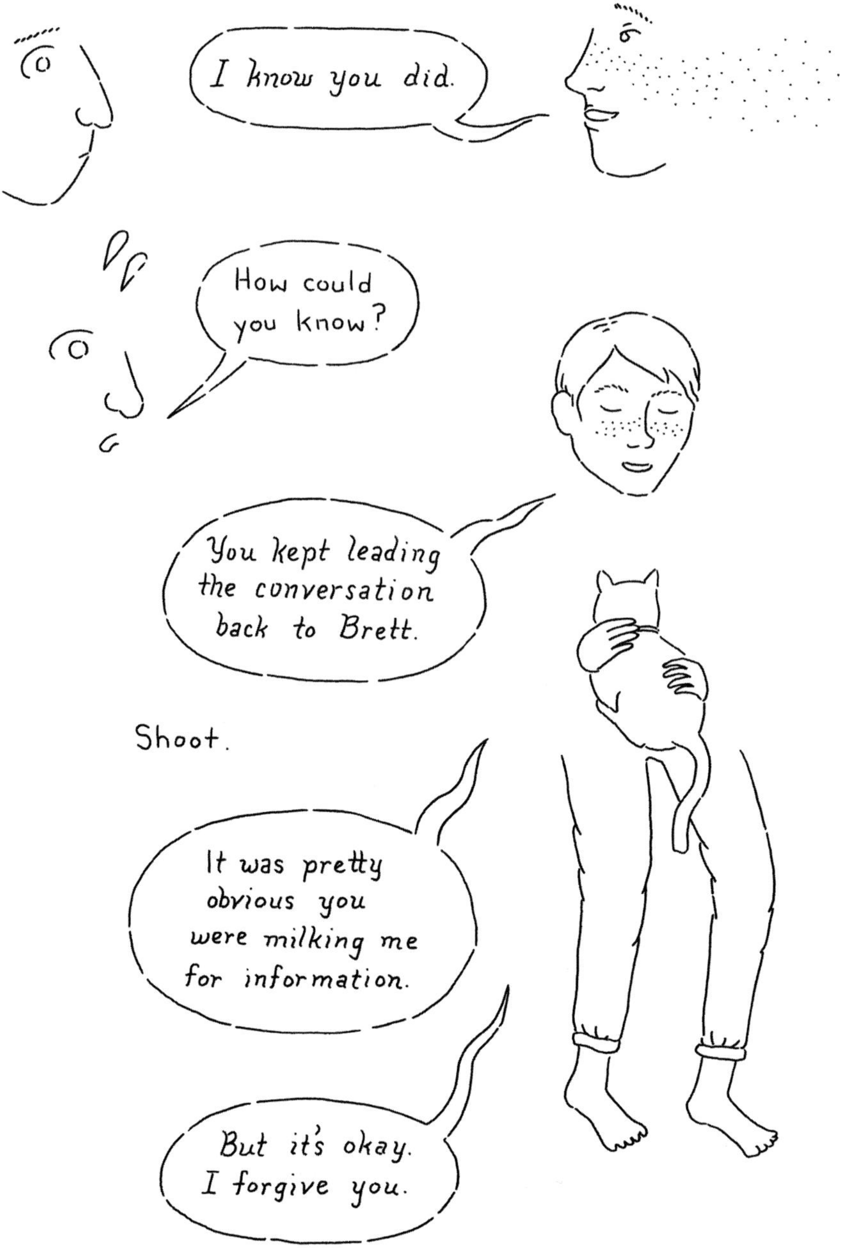
I know you did.
How could you know?
You kept leading the conversation back to Brett.
Shoot.
It was pretty obvious you were milking me for information.
But it's okay. I forgive you.

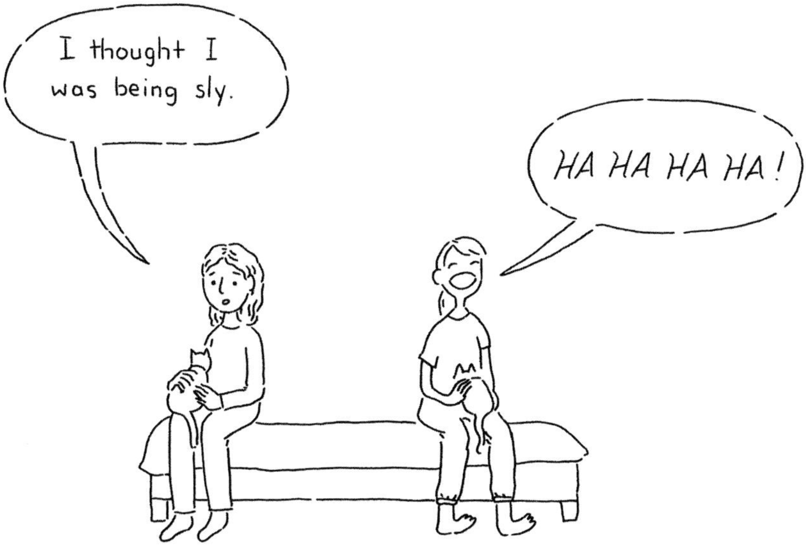
I thought I was being sly.
HA HA HA HA!

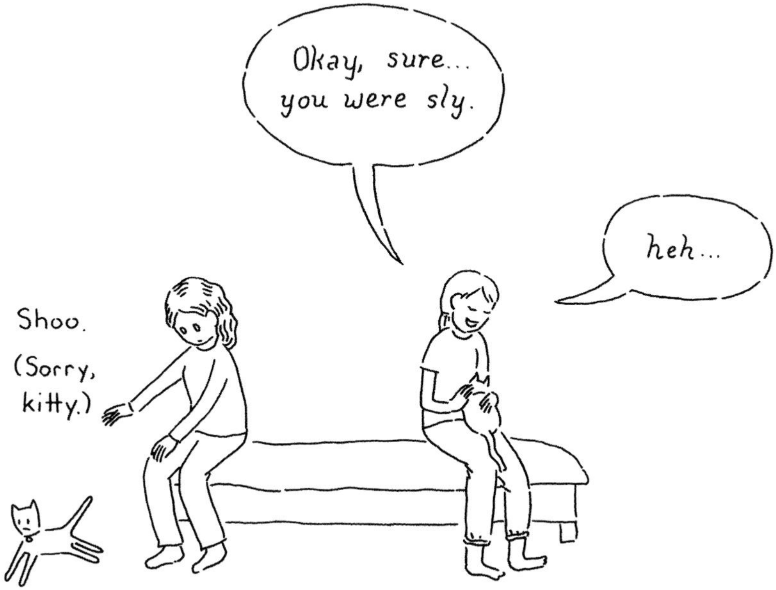
Okay, sure... you were sly.
heh...
Shoo.
(Sorry, kitty.)

You get that that's not why I hang out with you, right?
If you say so.

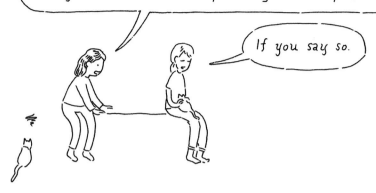

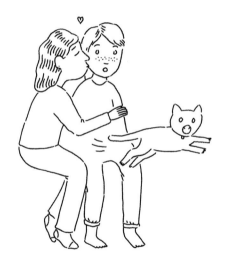

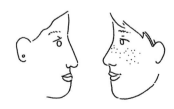

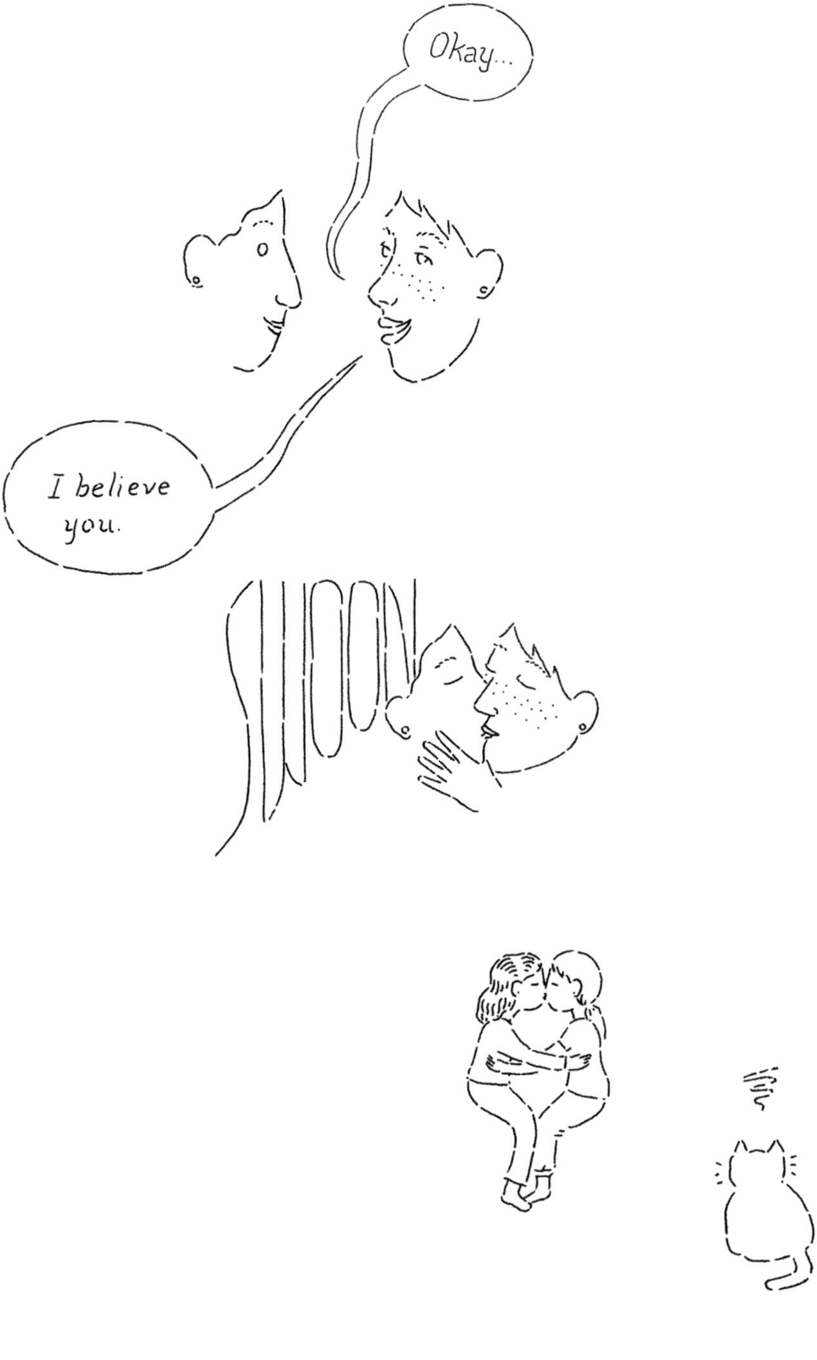
Okay...
I believe you.

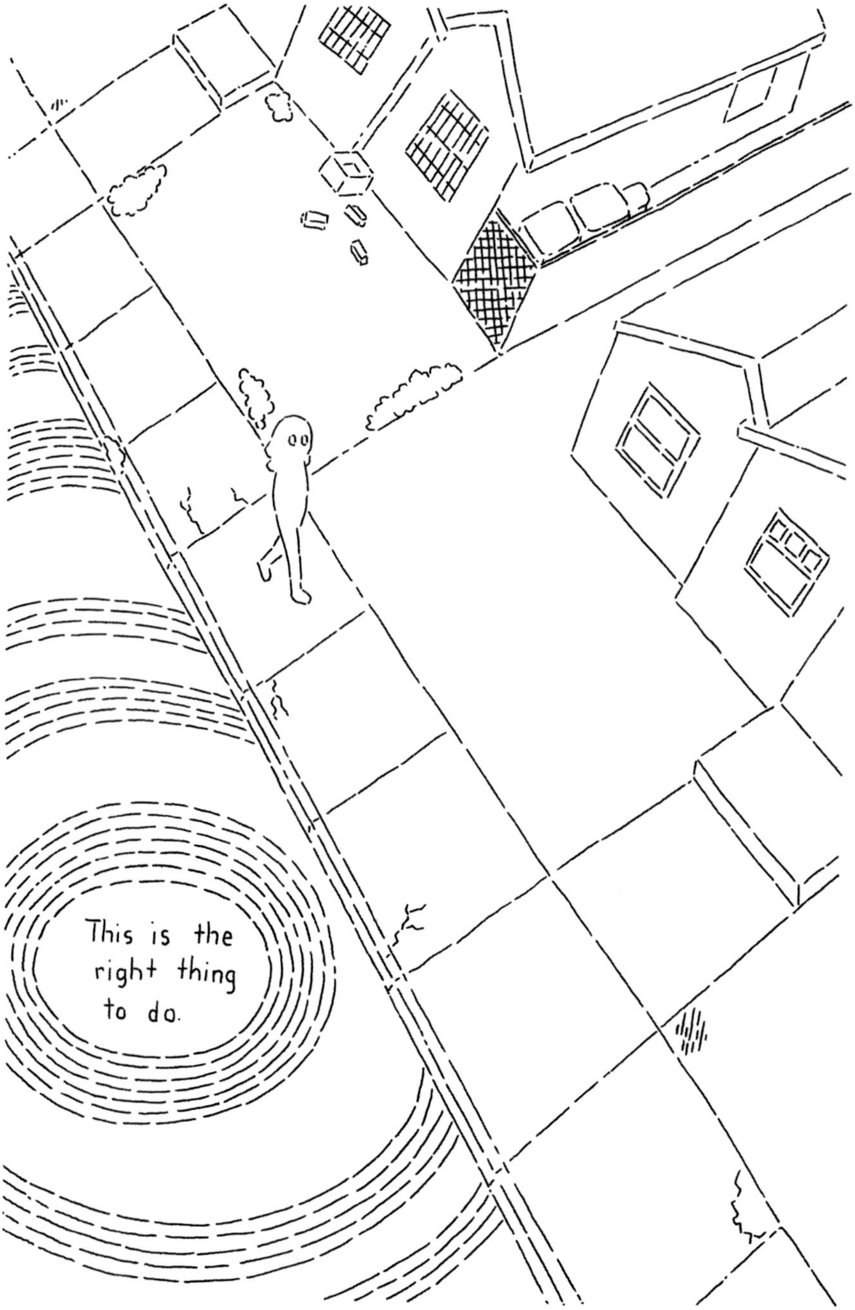
This is the right thing to do.

47

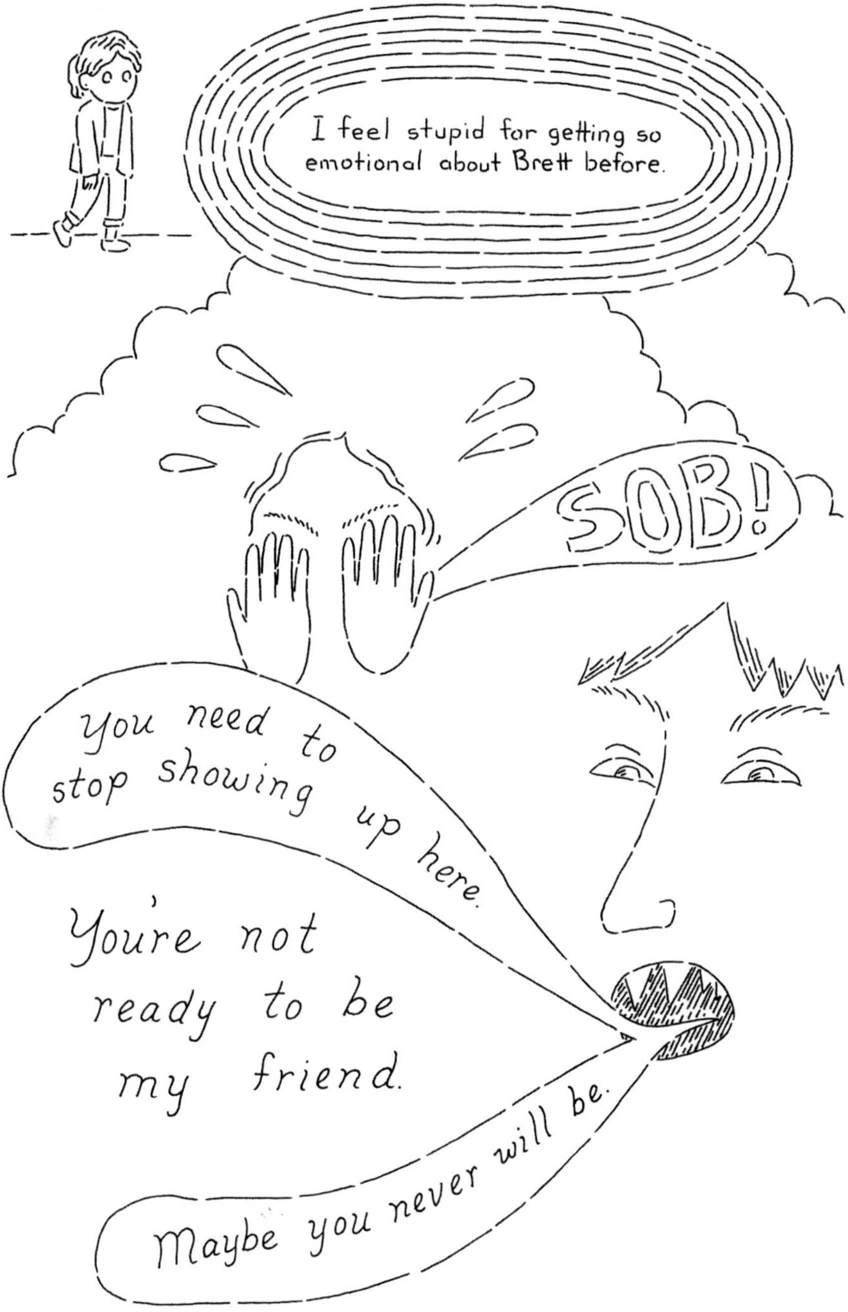
I feel stupid for getting so emotional about Brett before.
SOB!
you need to stop showing up here.
You're not ready to be my friend.
Maybe you never will be.

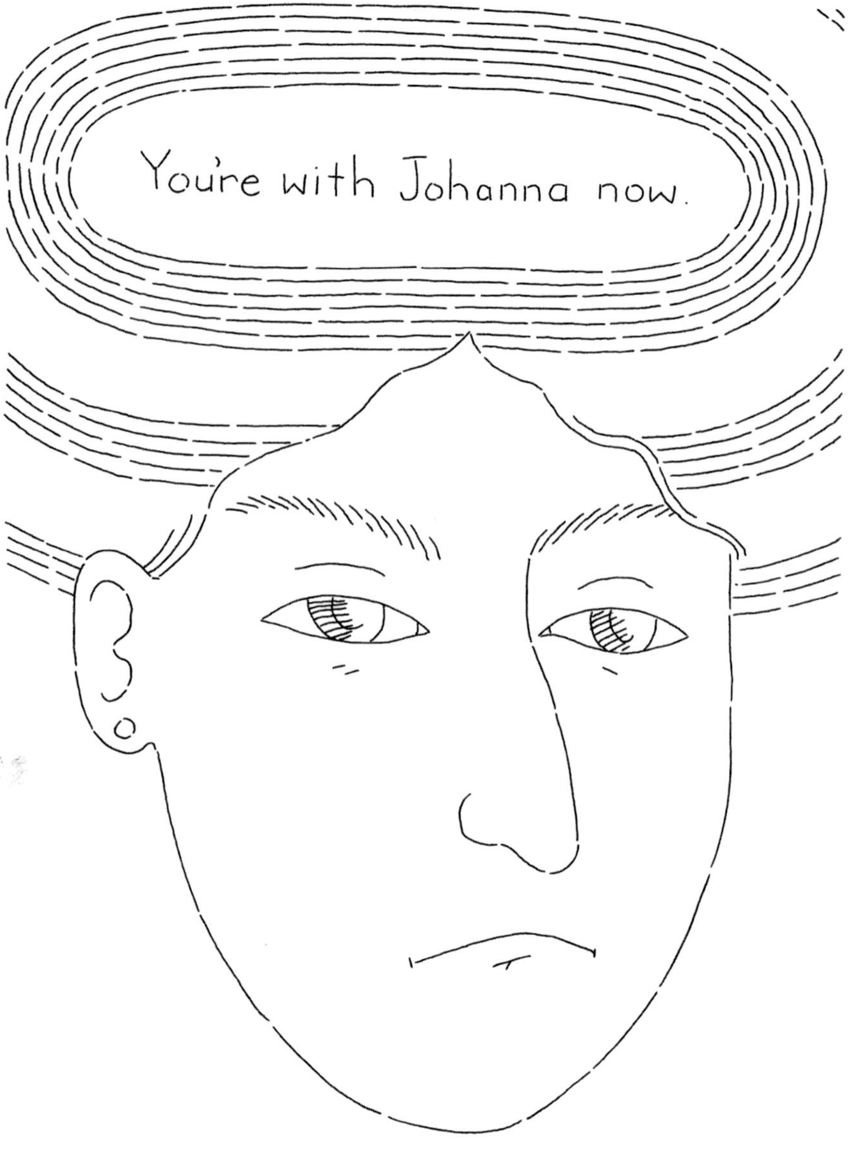
You're with Johanna now.

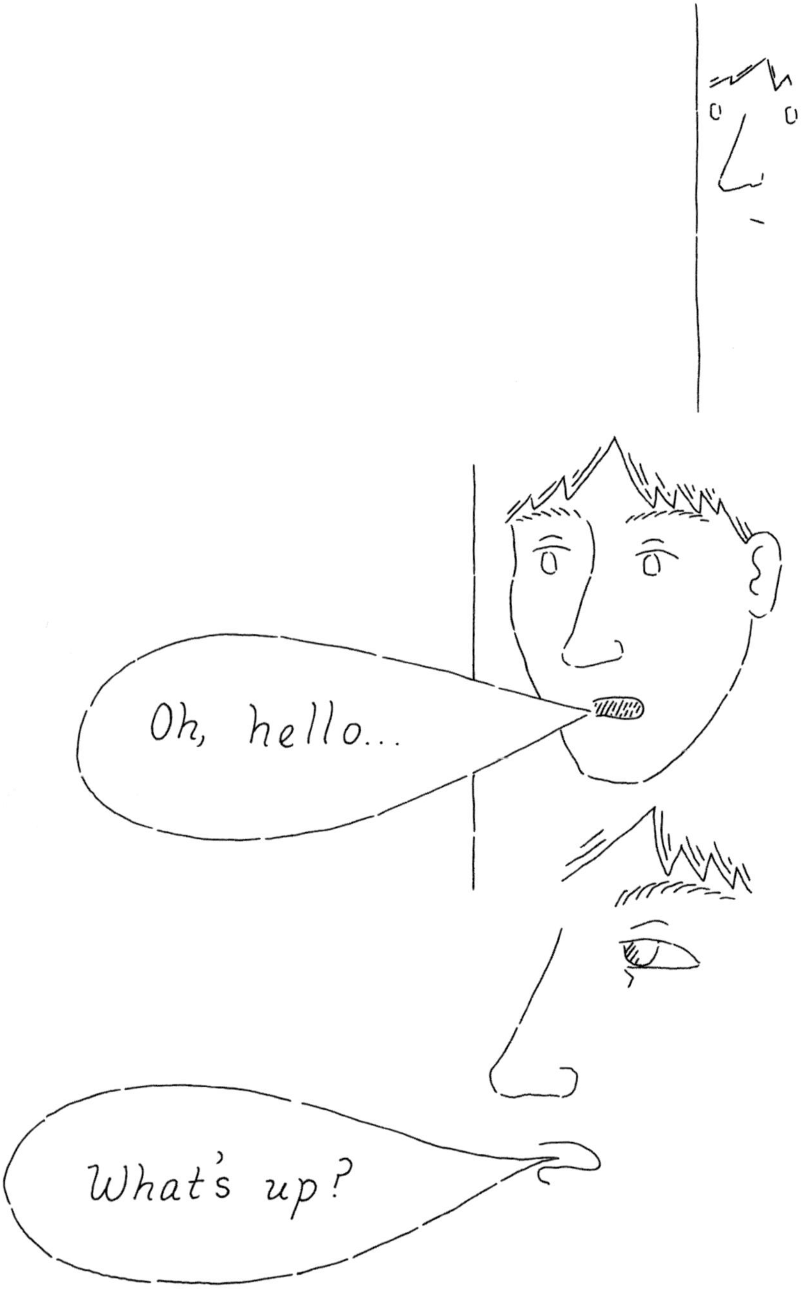
Oh, hello...
What's up?

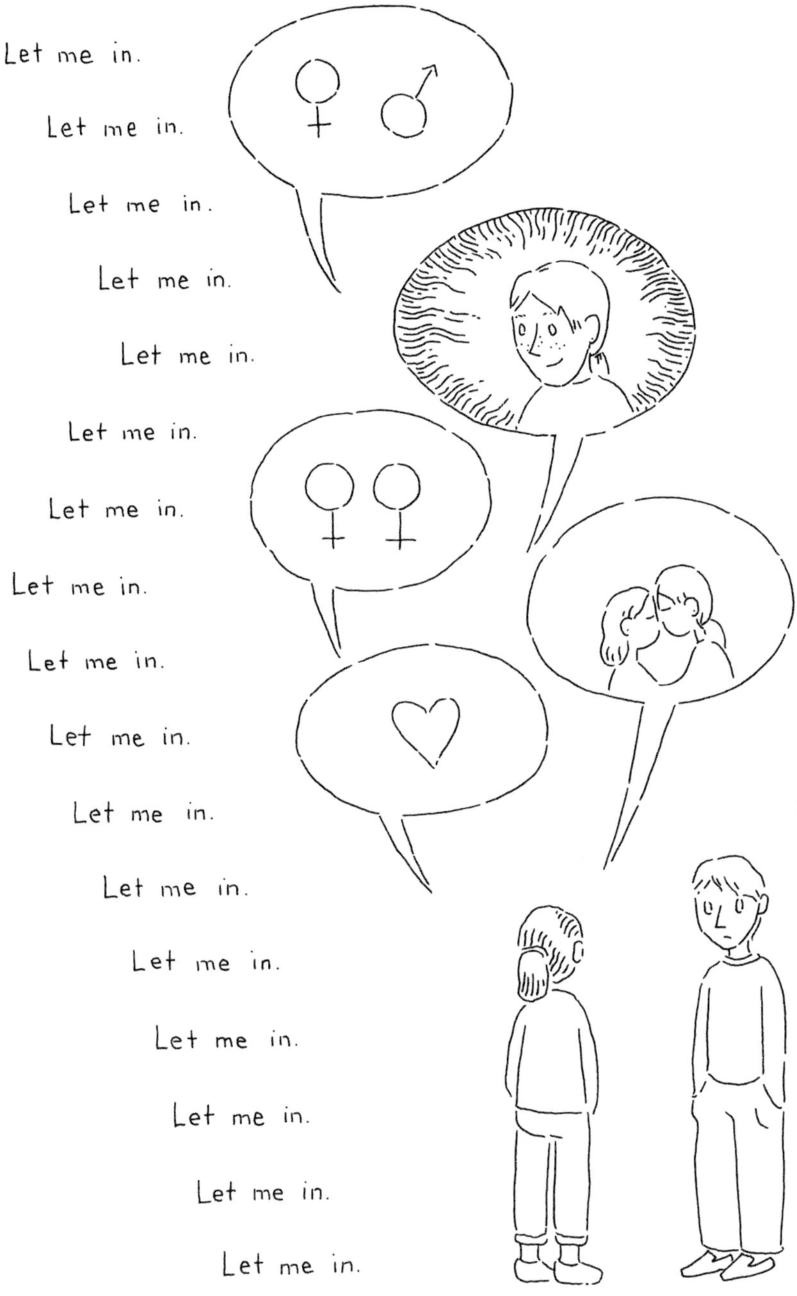
Let me in.
Let me in.
Let me in.
Let me in.
Let me in.
Let me in.
Let me in.
Let me in.
Let me in.
Let me in.
Let me in.
Let me in.
Let me in.
Let me in.
Let me in.
Let me in.
Let me in.

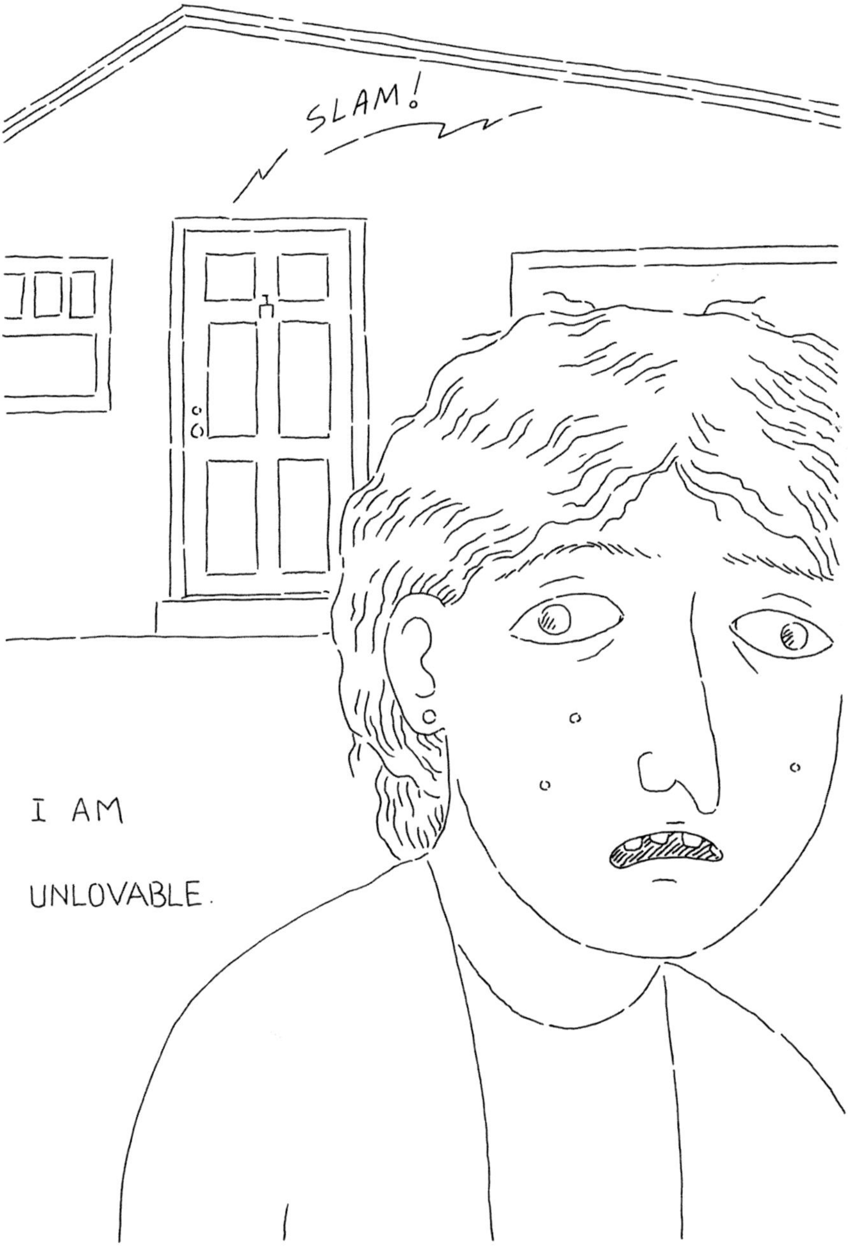
SLAM!
I AM
UNLOVABLE.

PART THREE

NOT
PICTURED

Brett Hathaway

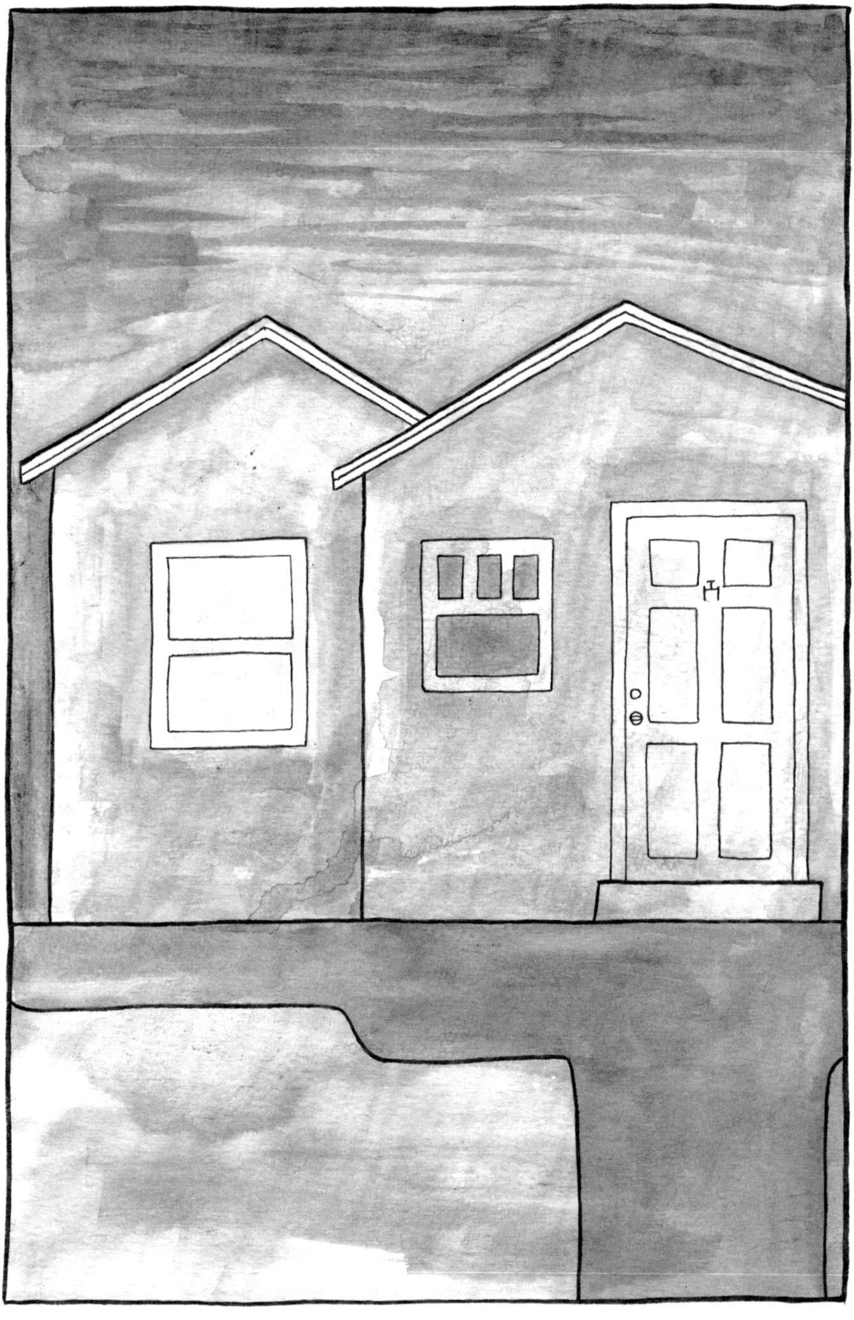

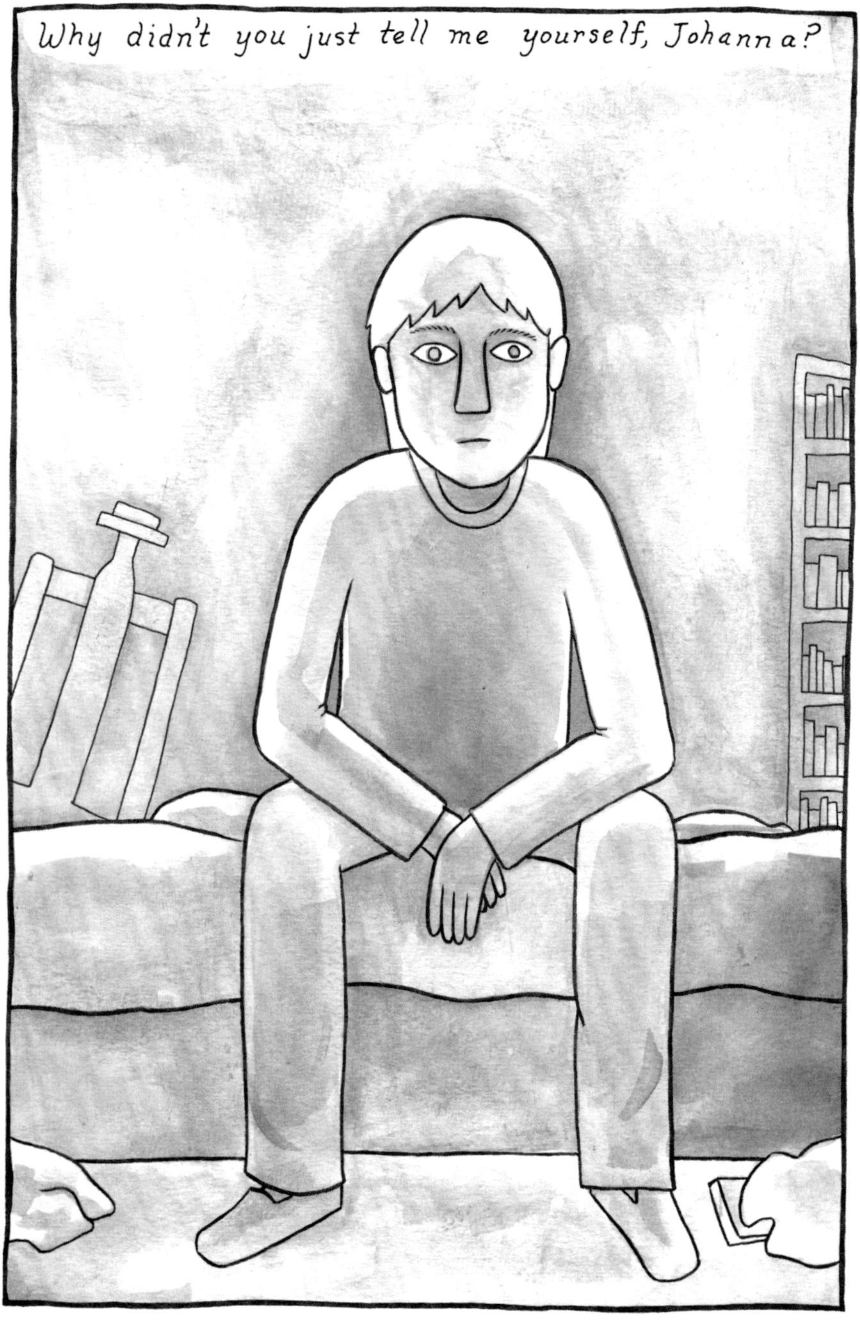
Why didn't you just tell me yourself, Johanna?

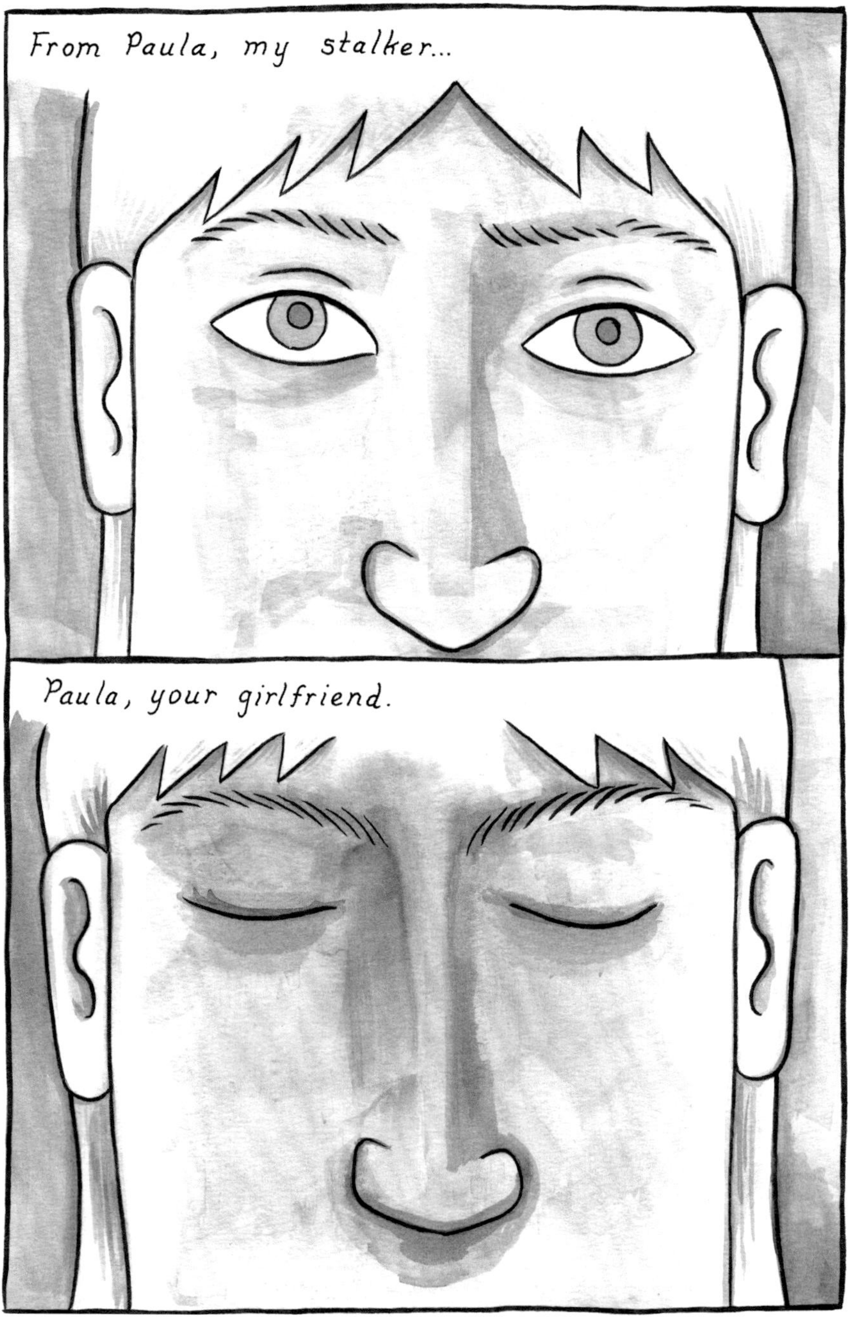
From Paula, my stalker...
Paula, your girlfriend.

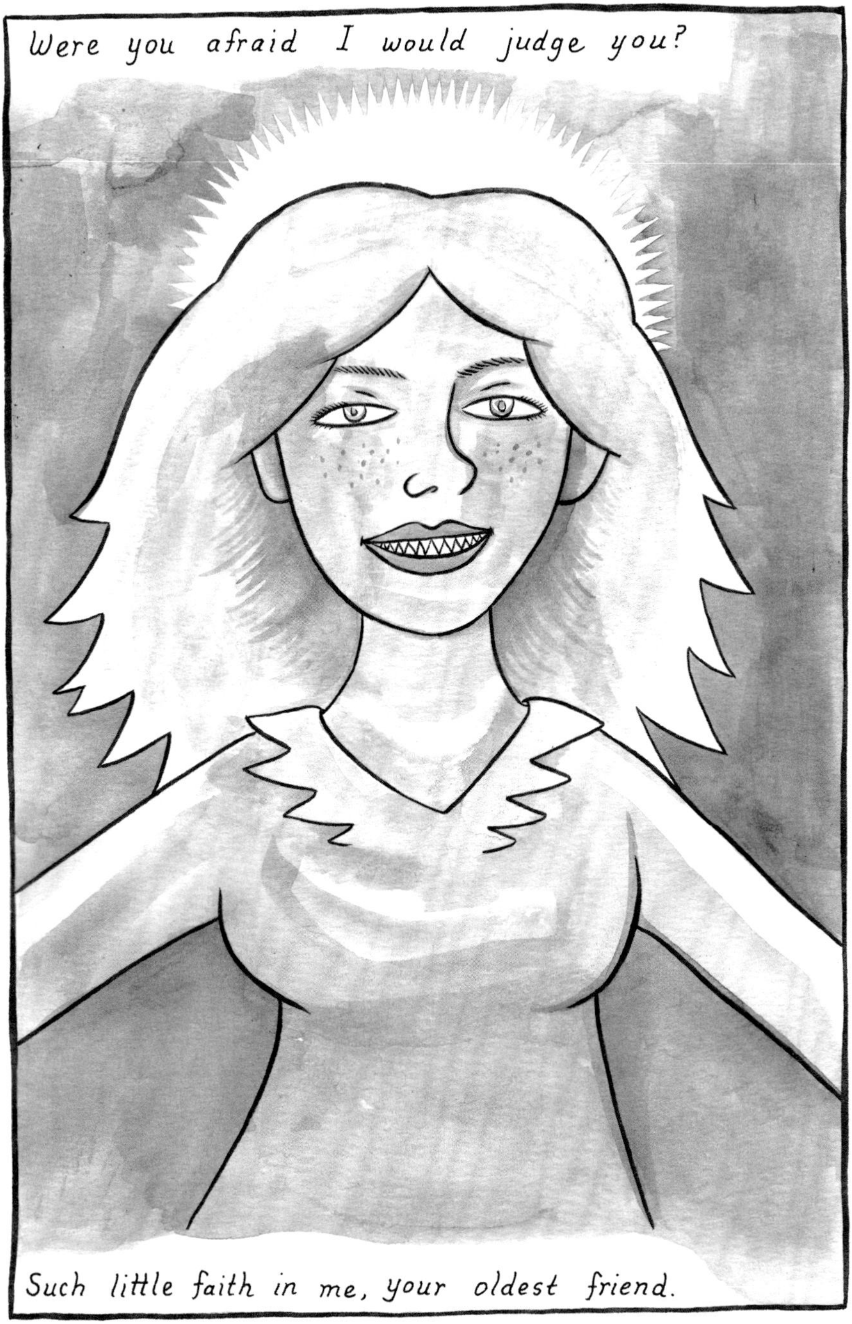
Were you afraid I would judge you?
Such little faith in me, your oldest friend.

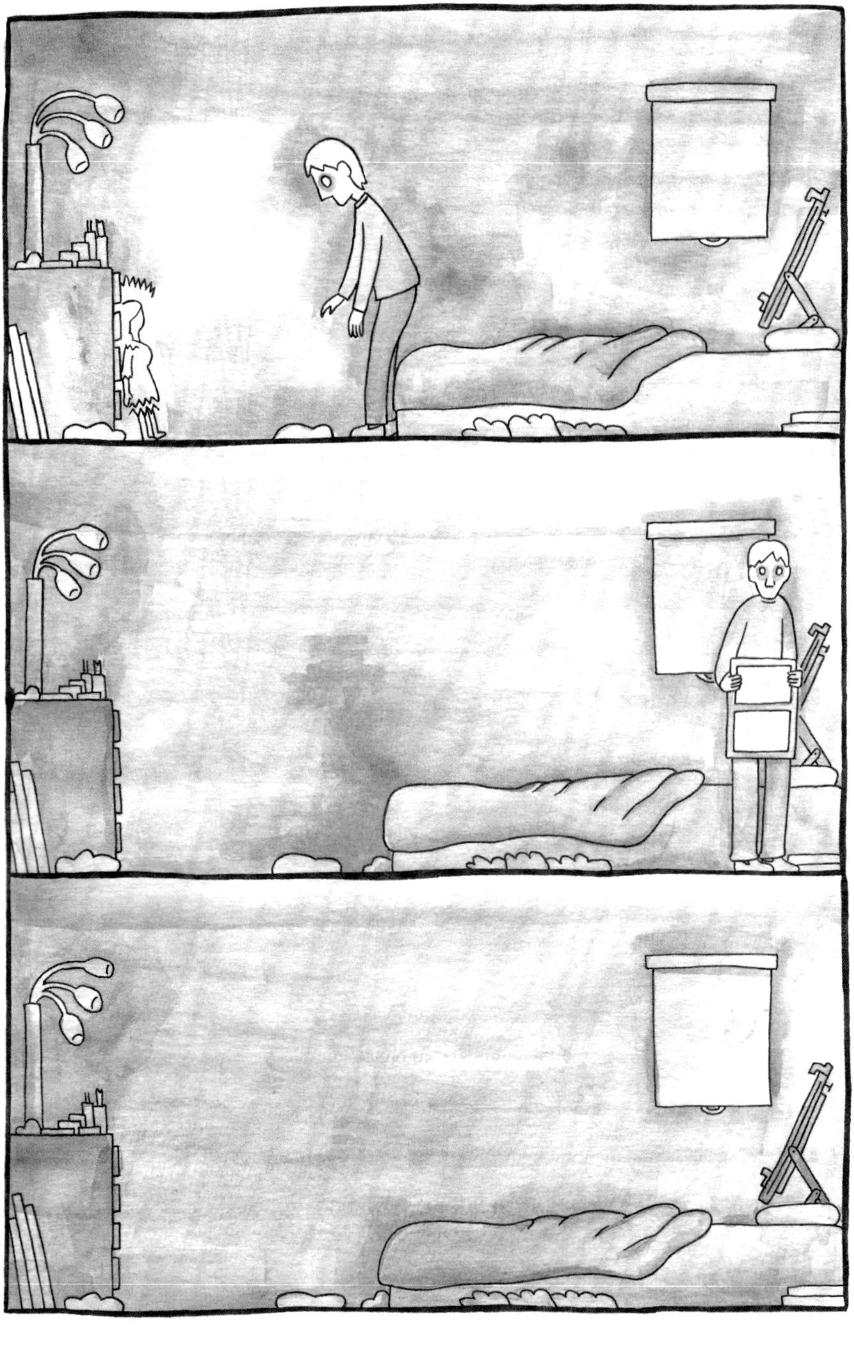

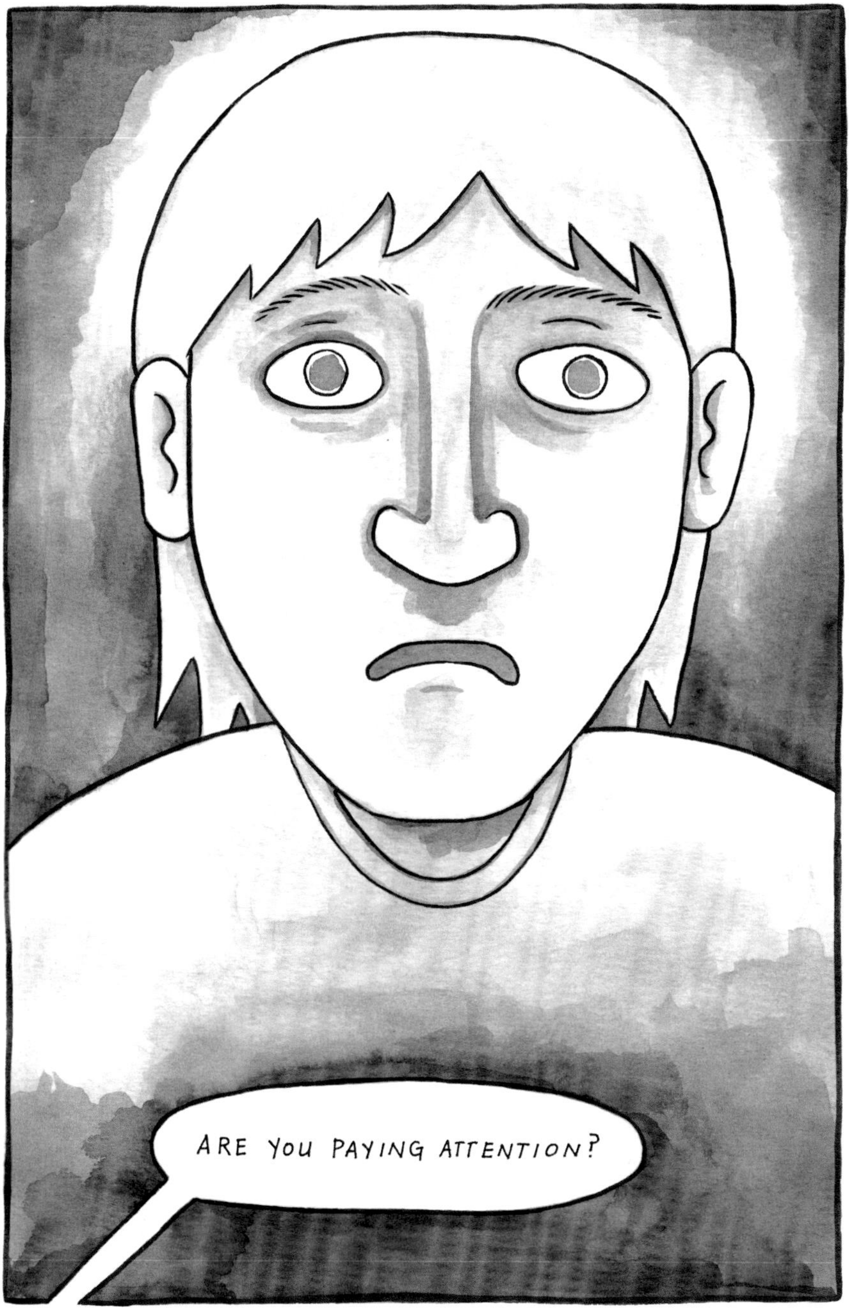
ARE YOU PAYING ATTENTION?

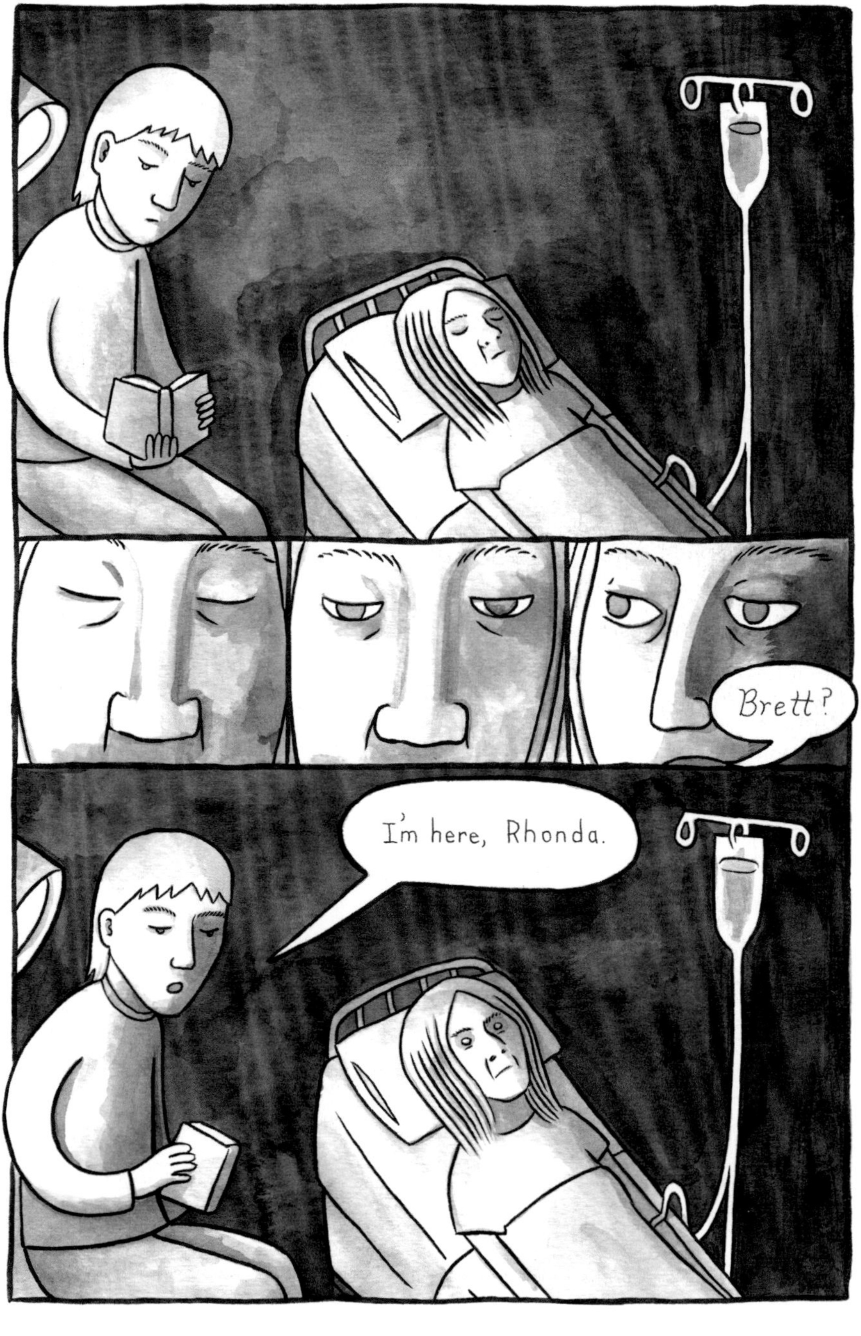
Brett?
I'm here, Rhonda.

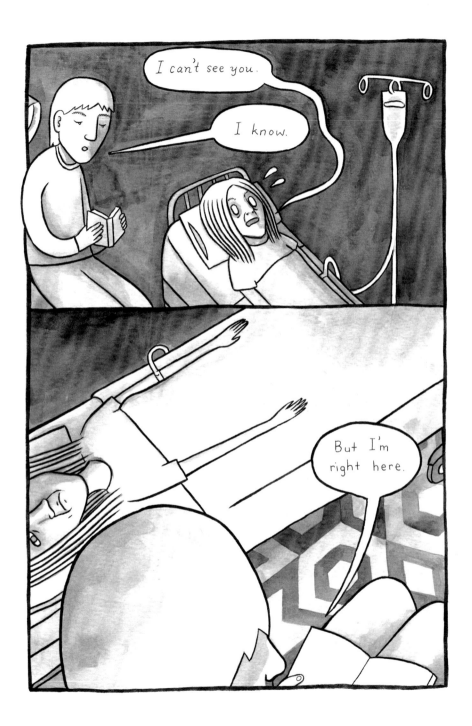

71

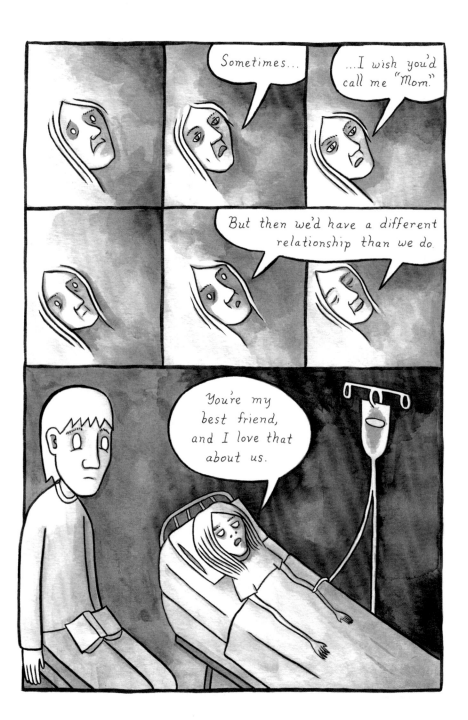

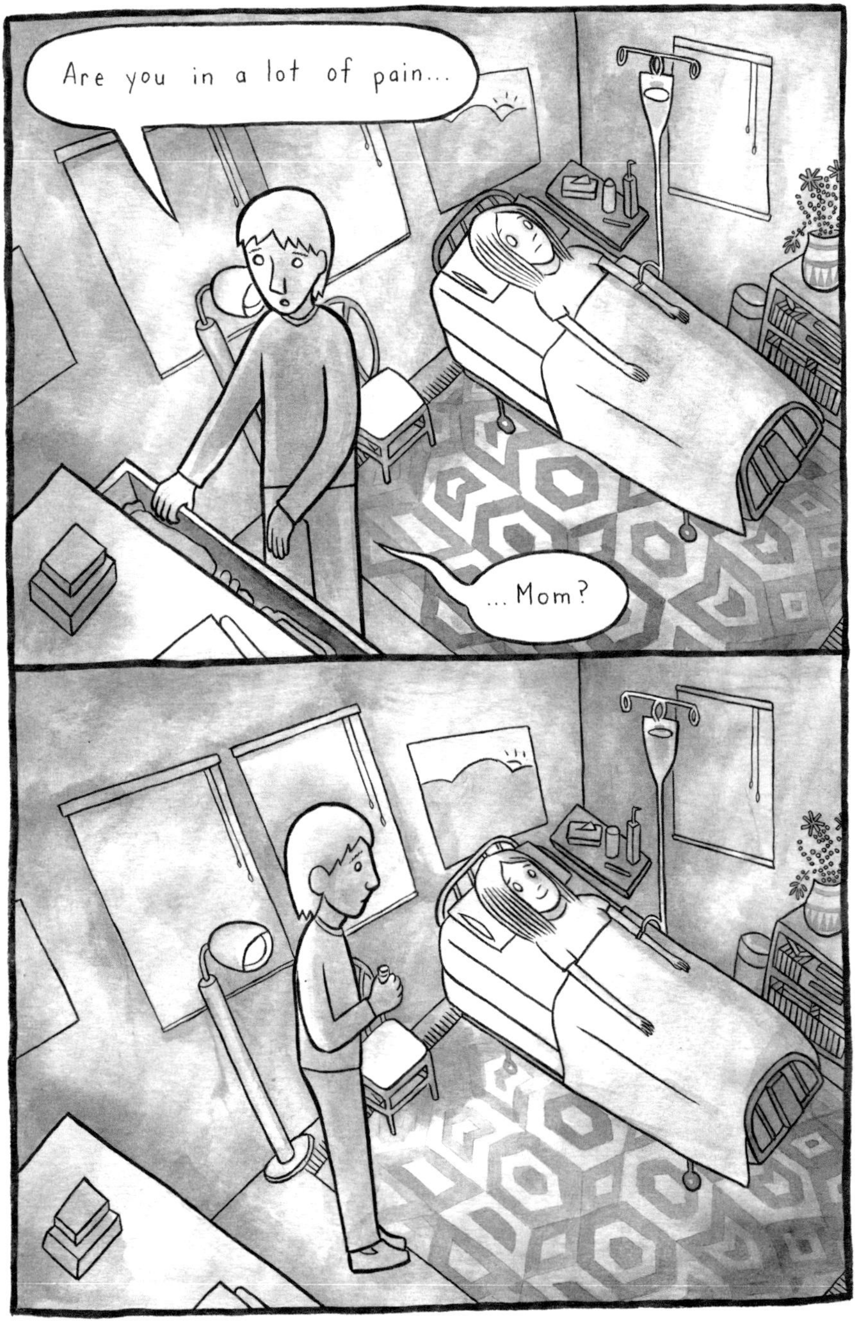
Are you in a lot of pain...
...Mom?

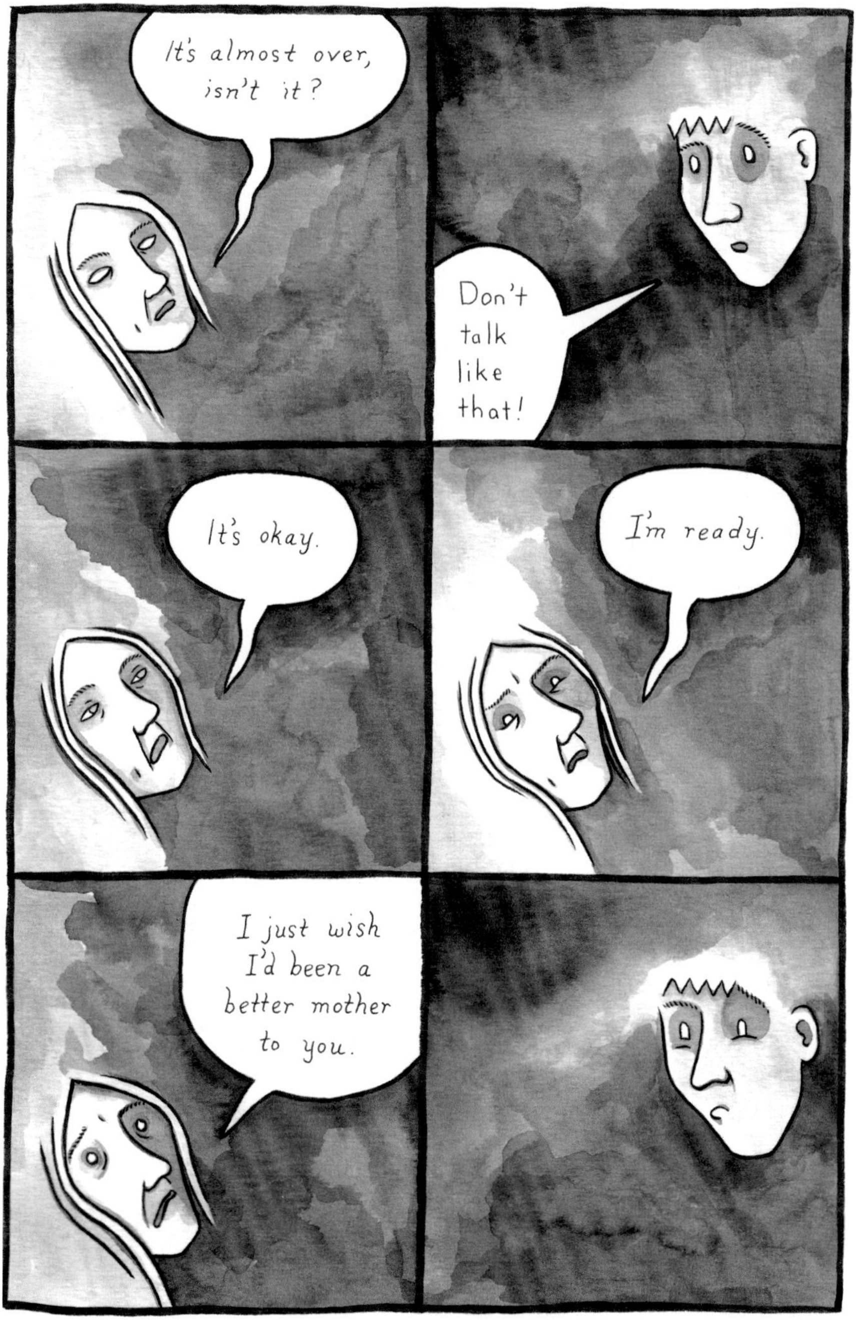
It's almost over, isn't it?
Don't talk like that!
It's okay.
I'm ready.
I just wish I'd been a better mother to you.

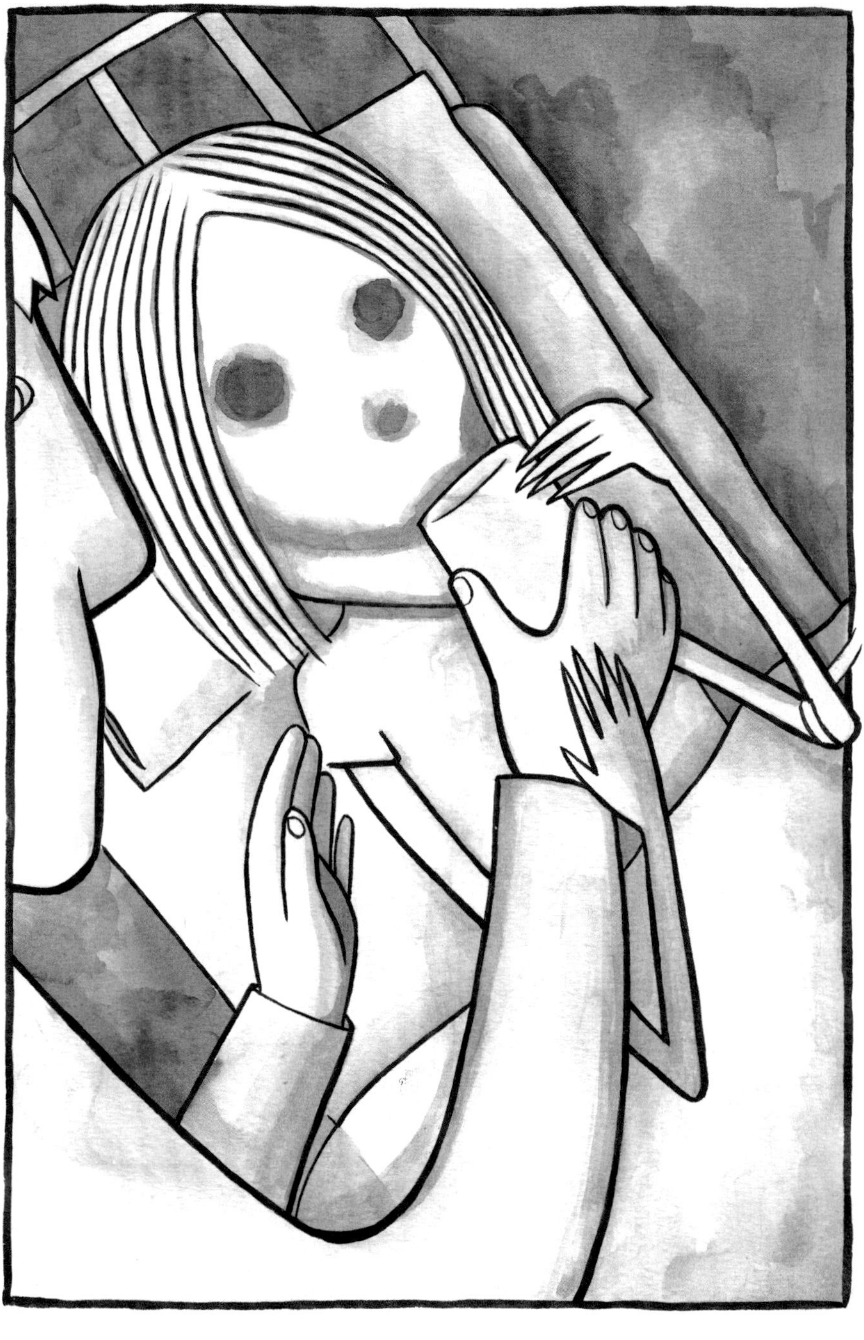

Soon I will have nobody.

PART FOUR

Emily H. Baker

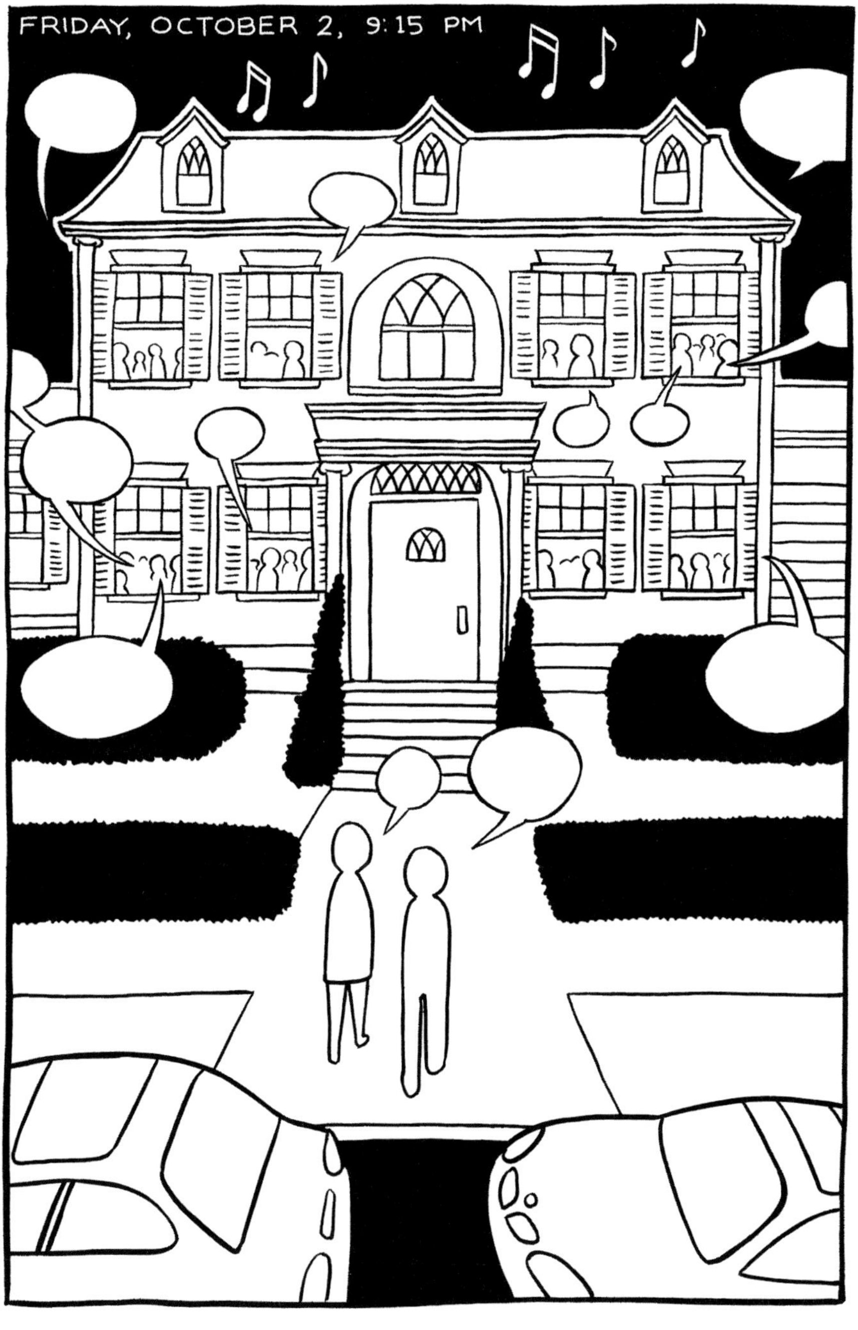
FRIDAY, OCTOBER 2, 9:15 PM

84

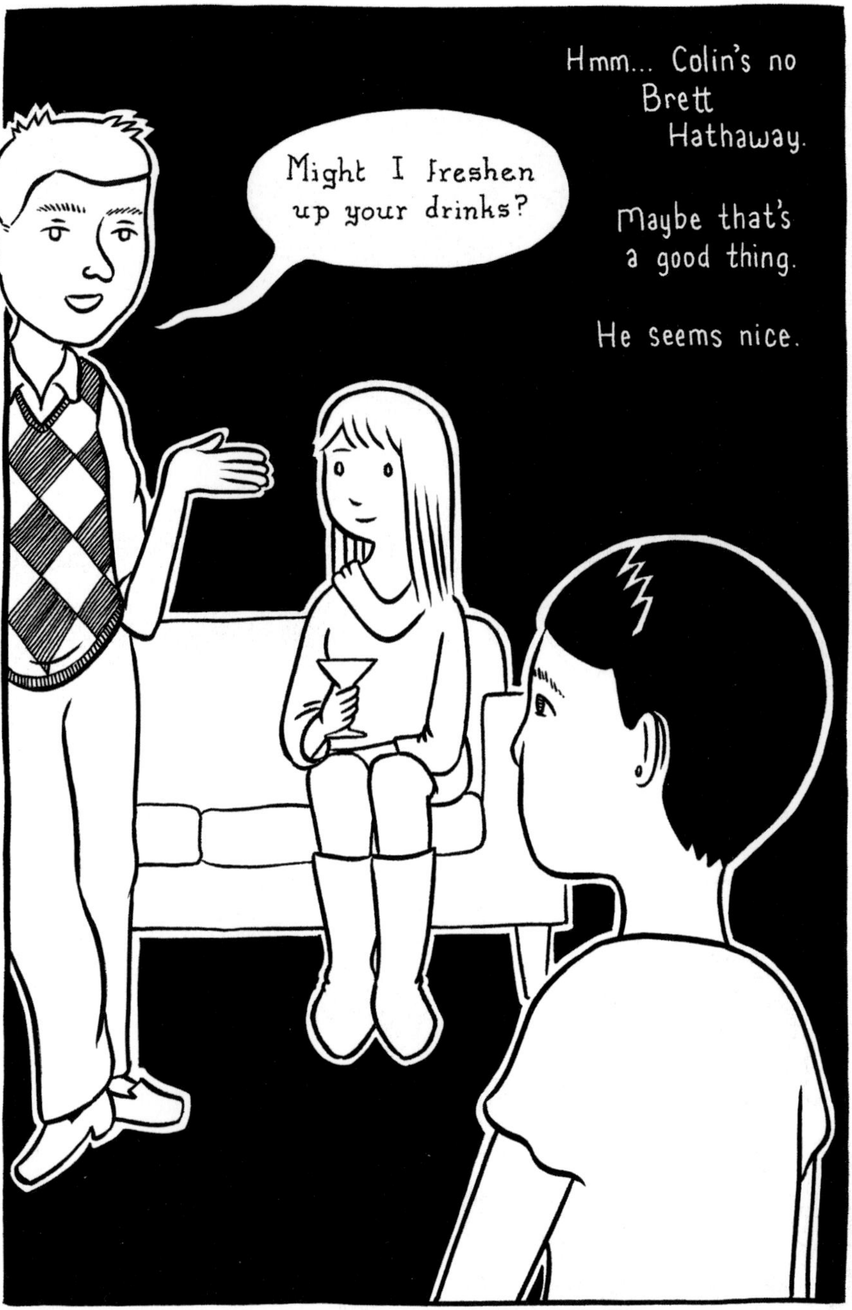
Might I freshen up your drinks?
Hmm... Colin's no Brett Hathaway.
Maybe that's a good thing.
He seems nice.

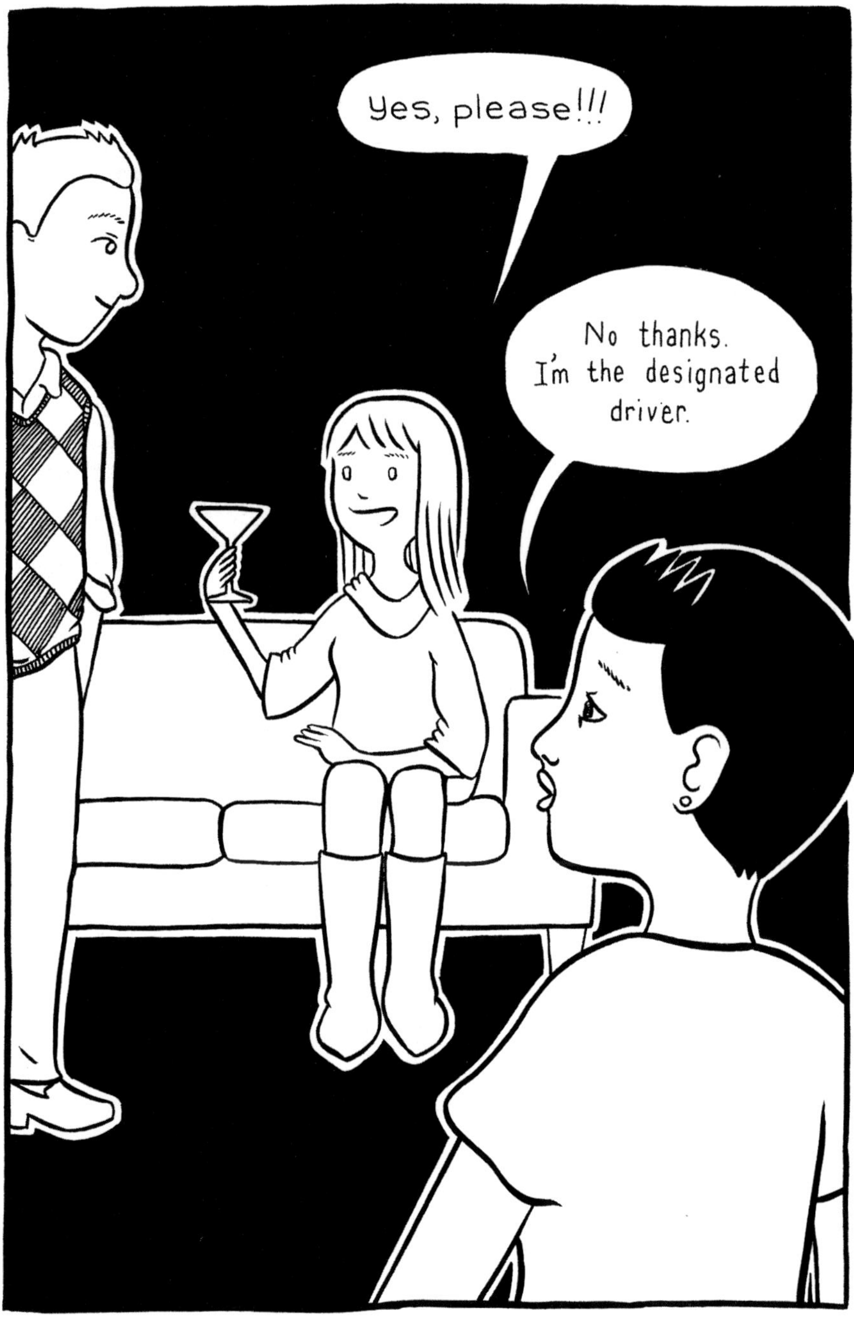
Yes, please!!!
No thanks. I'm the designated driver.

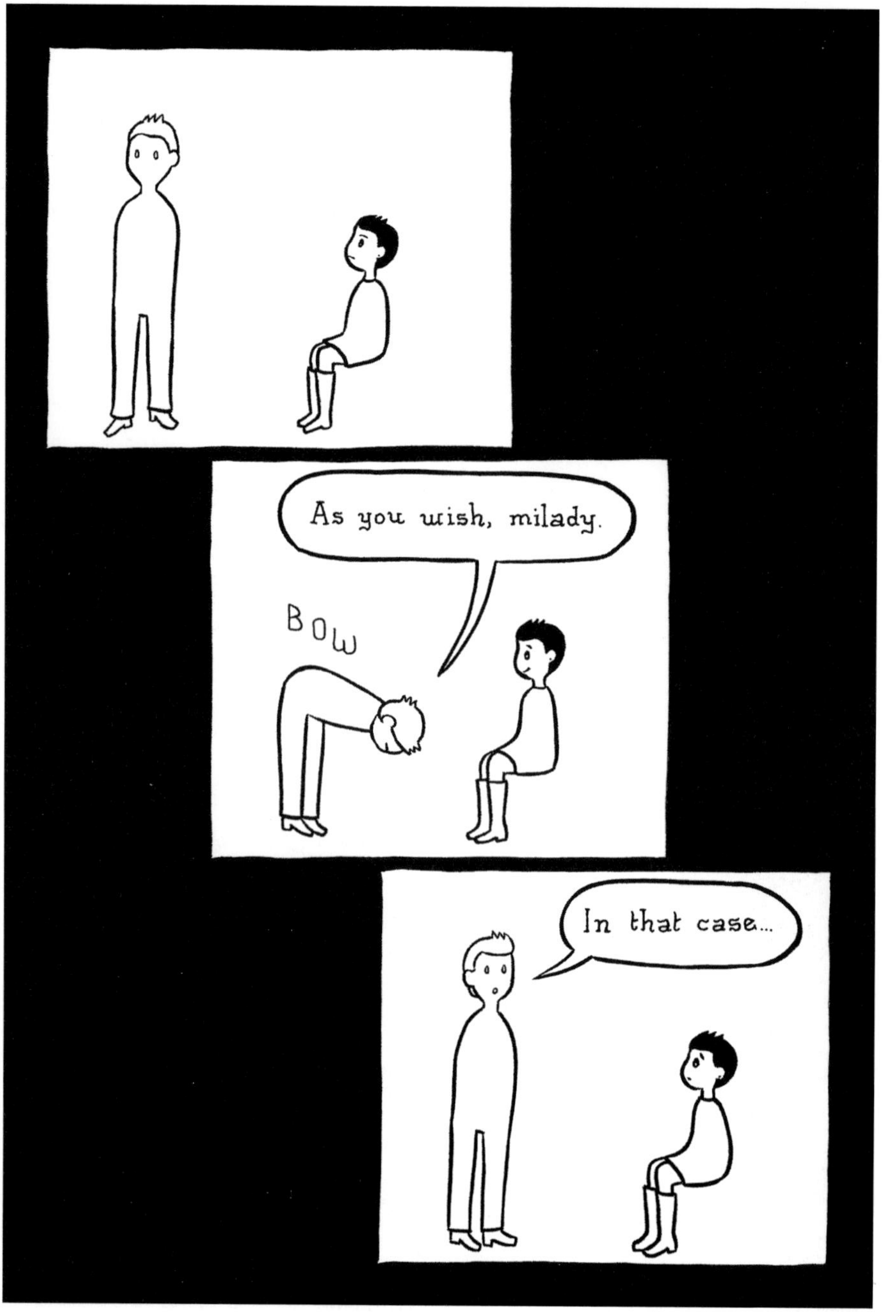
As you wish, milady.
BOW
In that case...

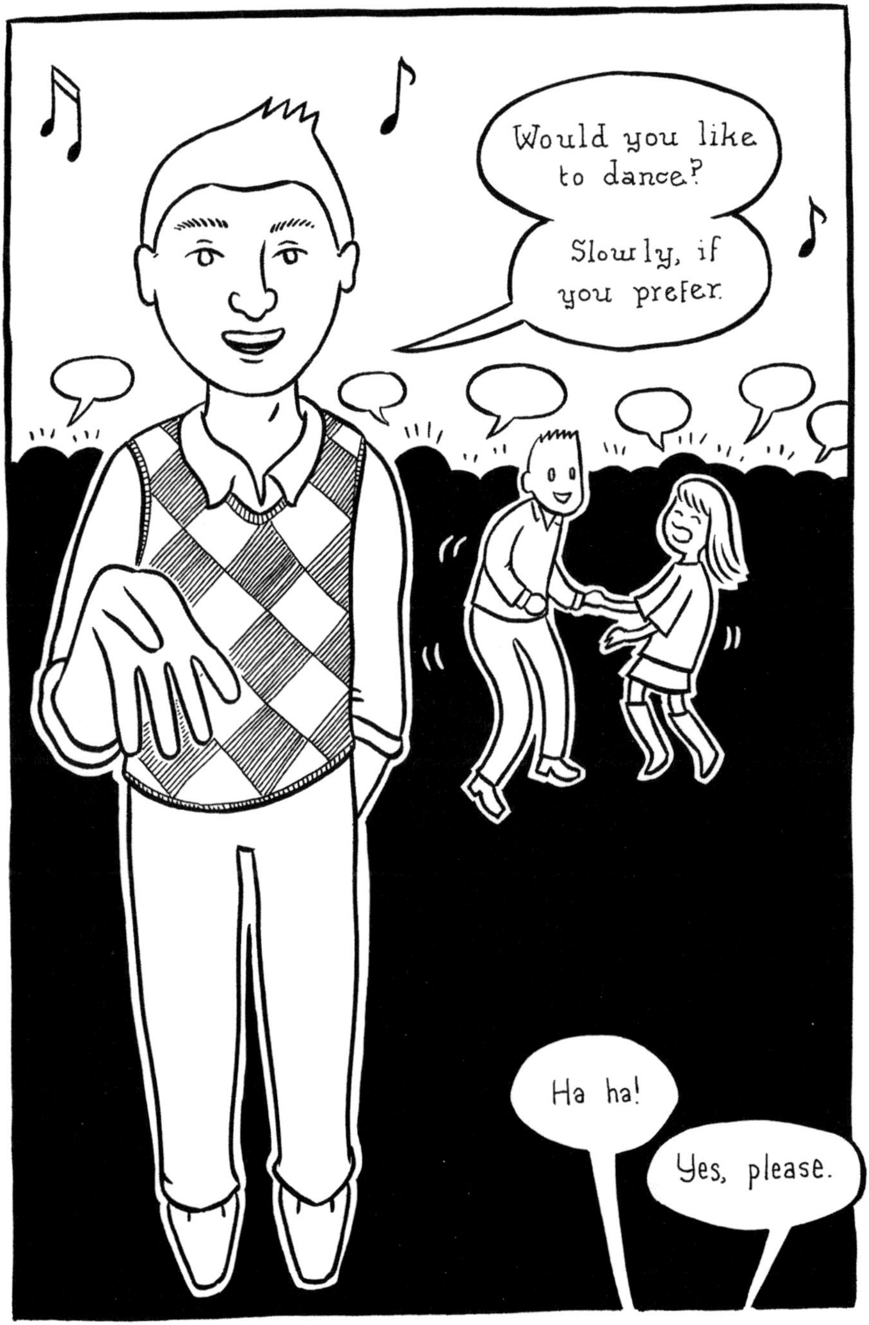
Would you like to dance?
Slowly, if you prefer.
Ha ha!
Yes, please.

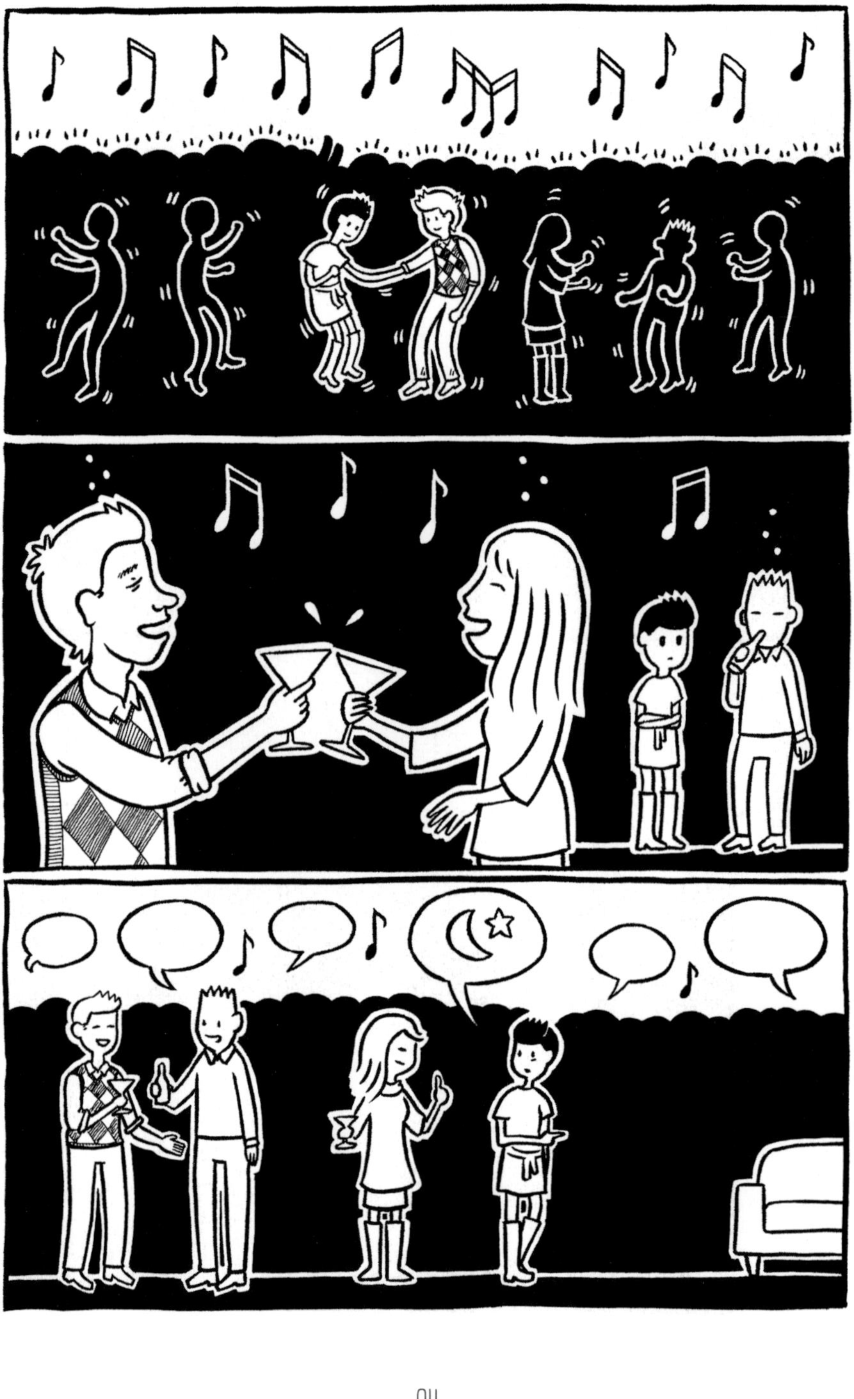

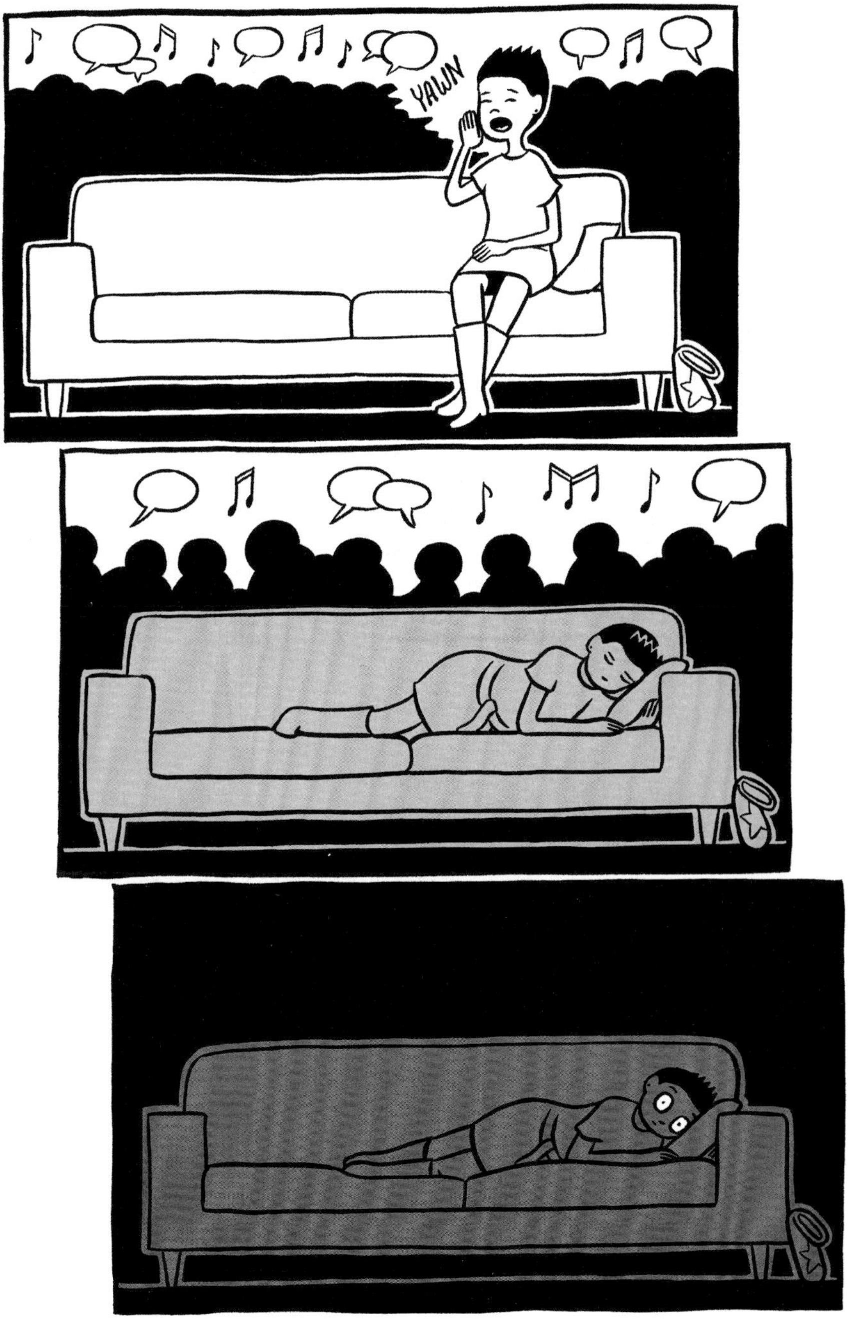
YAWN

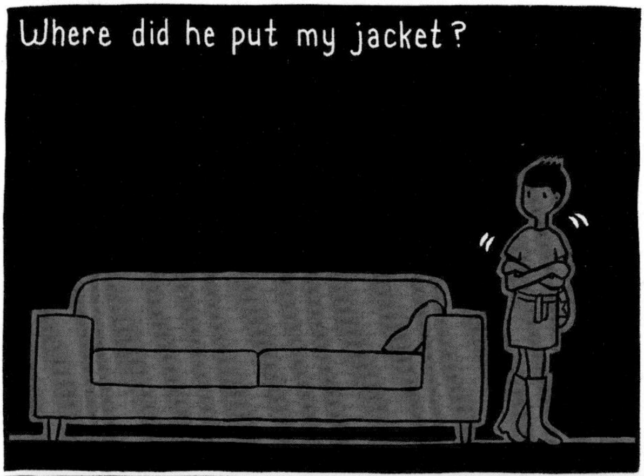
Where did he put my jacket?

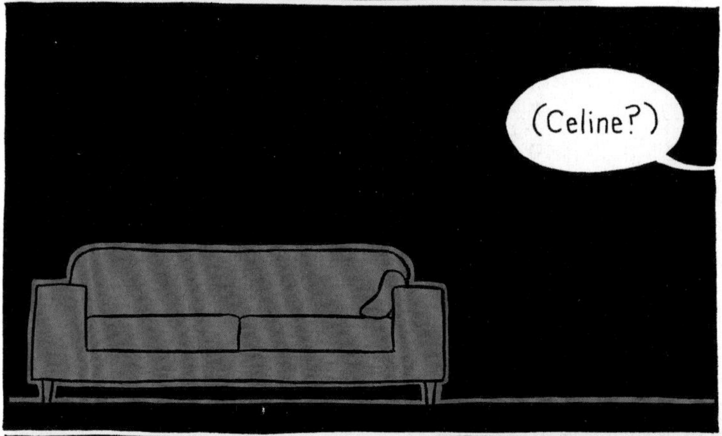
(Celine?)

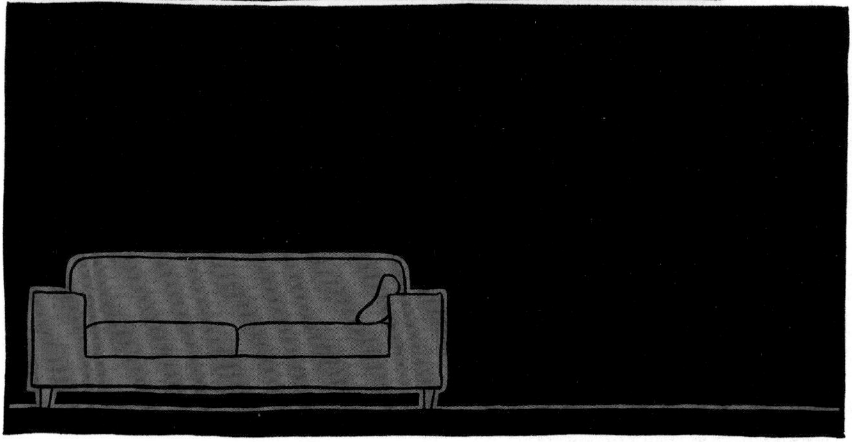

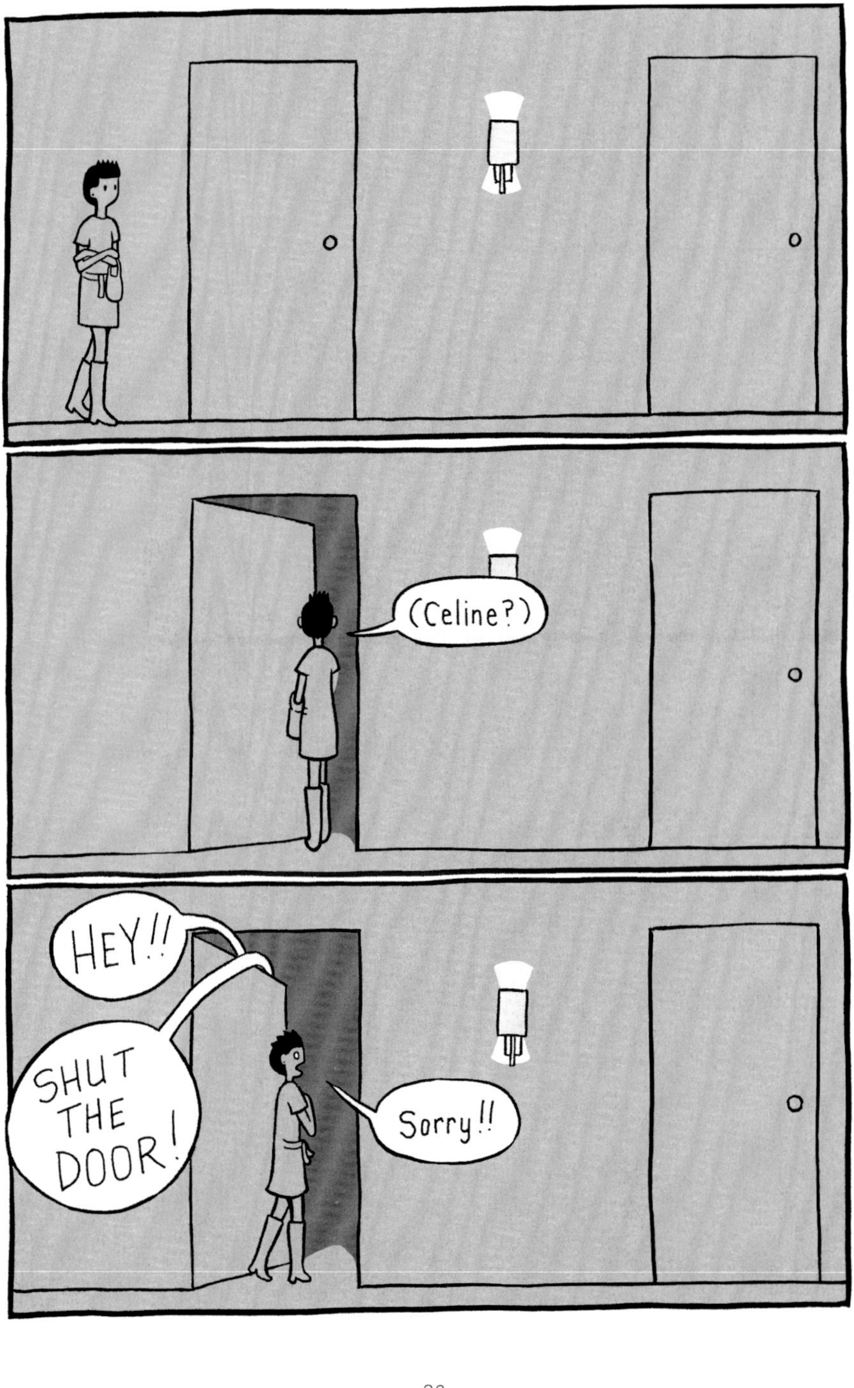
(Celine?)
HEY!!
SHUT THE DOOR!
Sorry!!

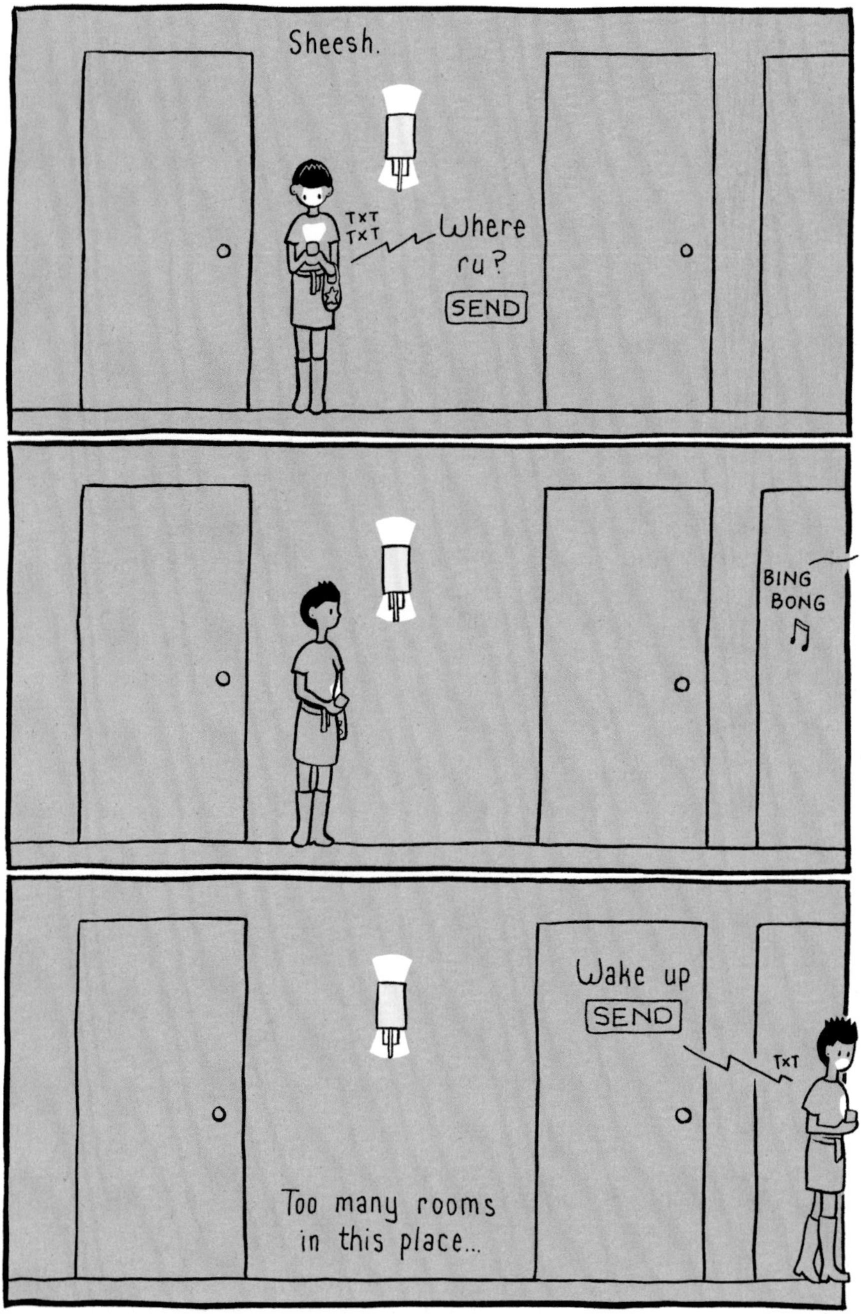
Sheesh.
TXT TXT
Where ru?
SEND
BING BONG
Wake up
SEND
TXT
Too many rooms in this place...

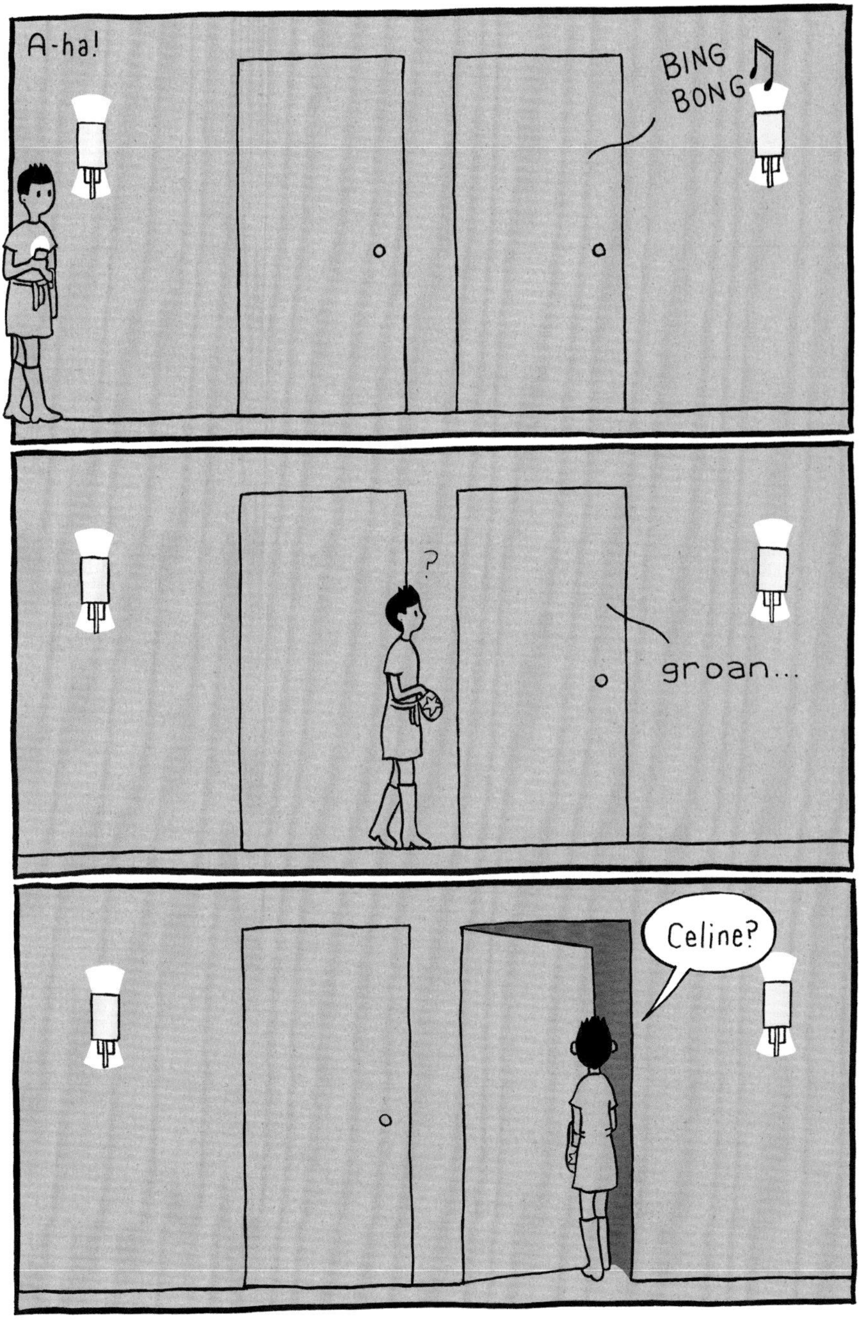

A-ha!
BING BONG
?
groan...
Celine?

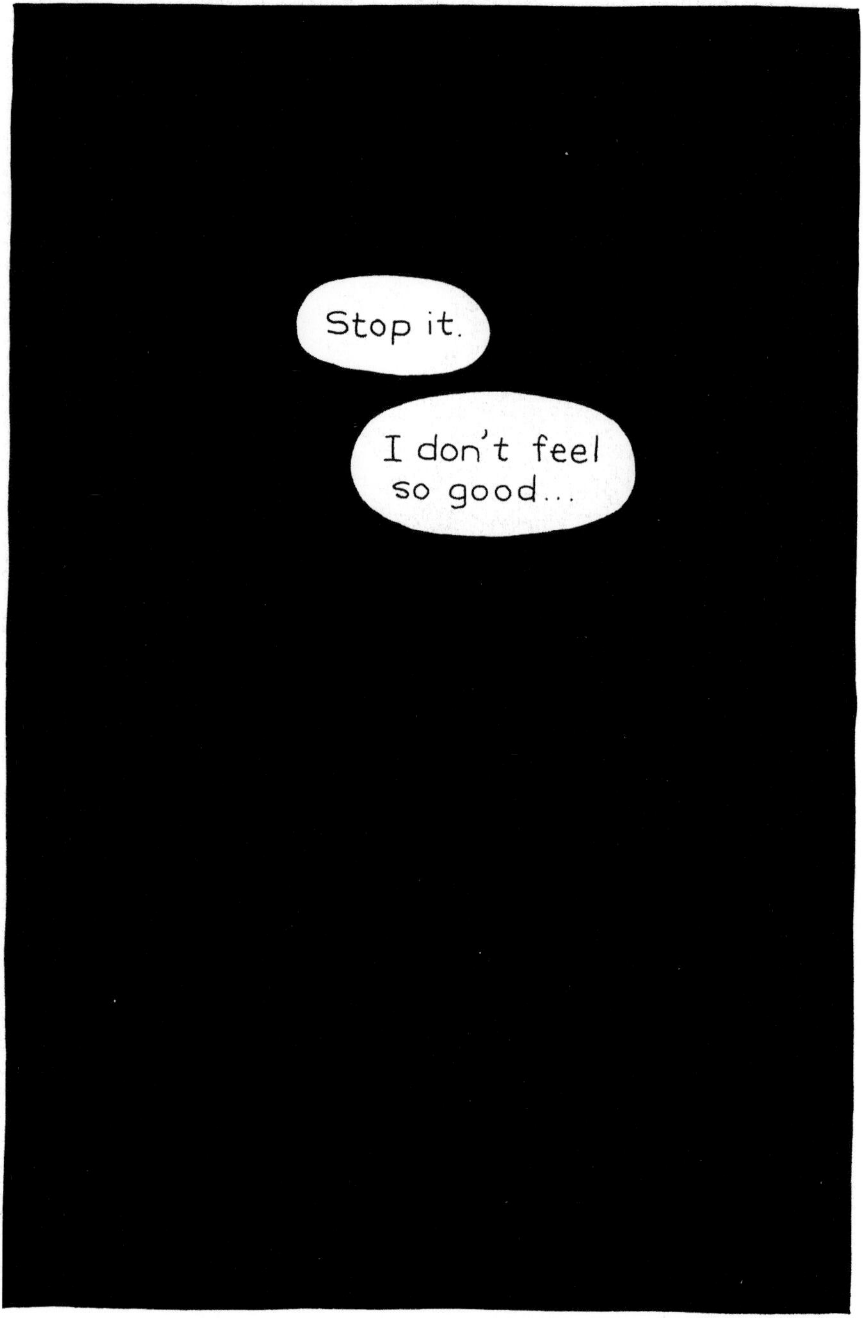
Stop it.
I don't feel so good...

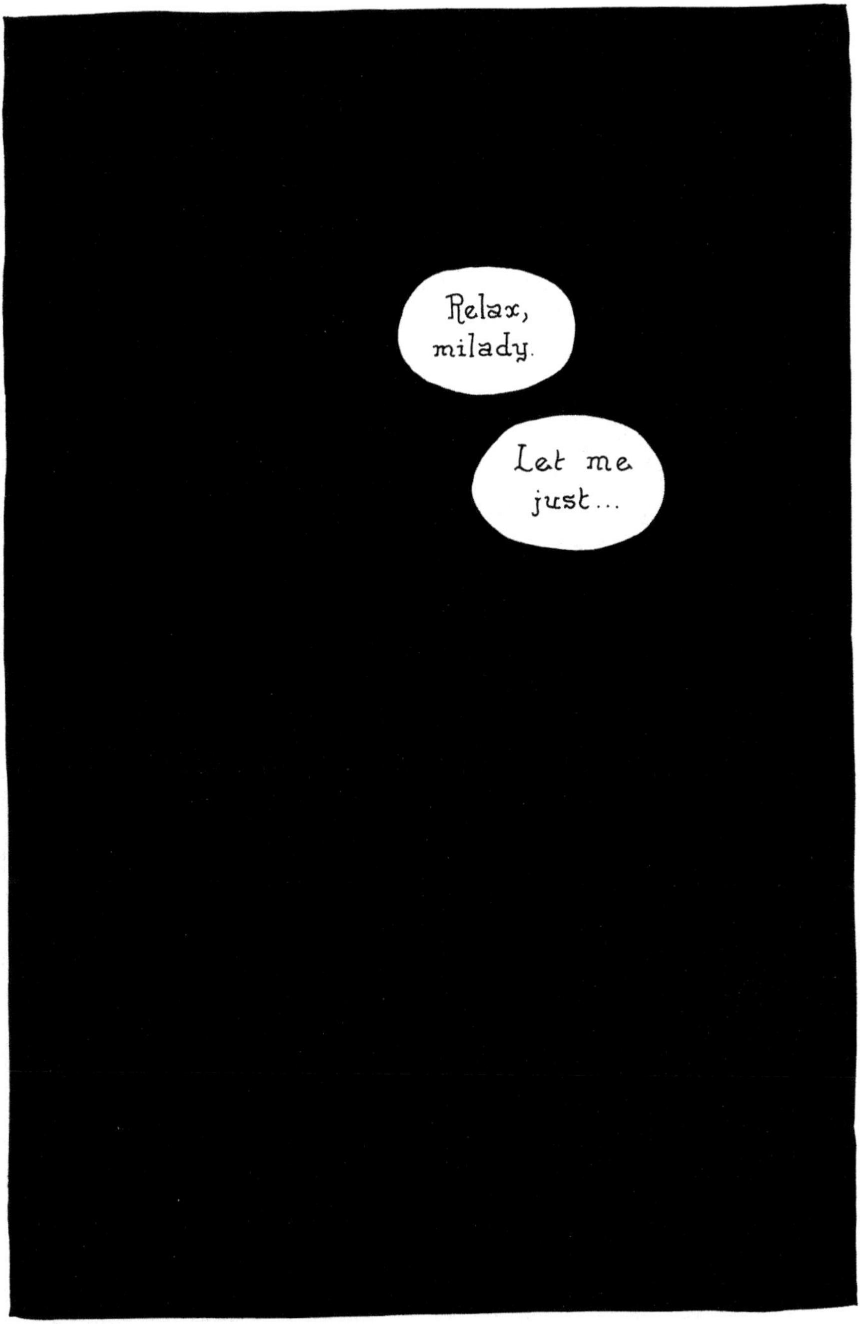
Relax, milady.
Let me just...

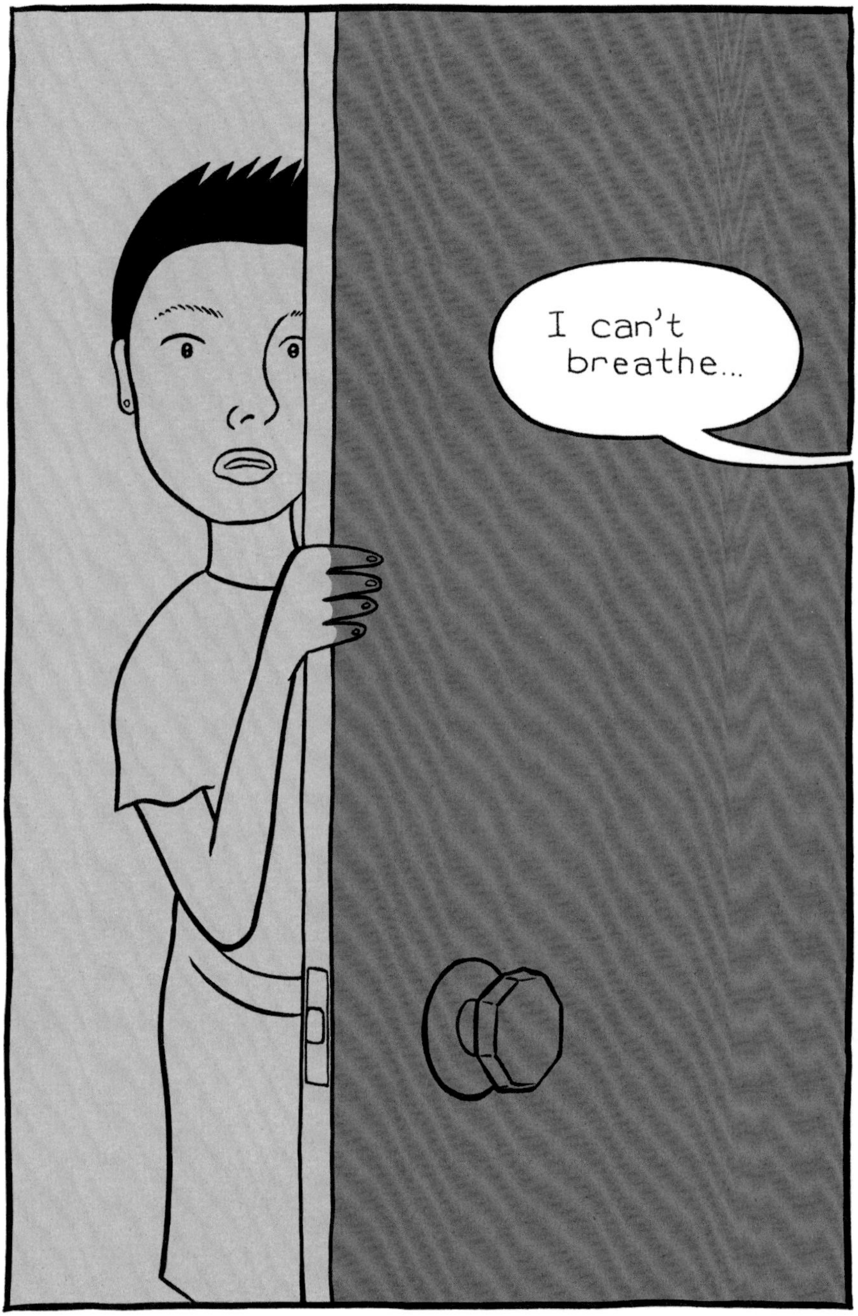
I can't breathe...

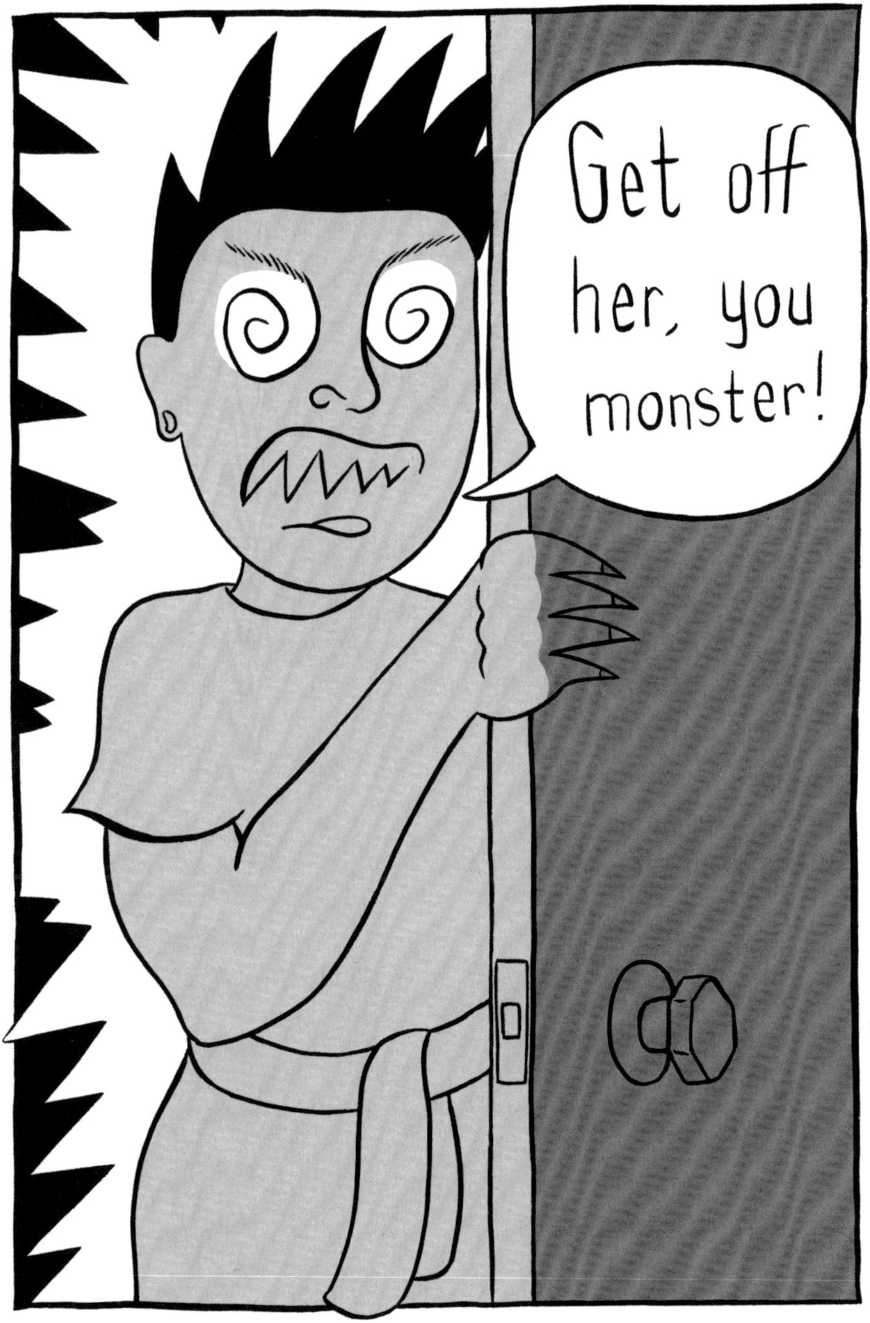
Get off her, you monster!

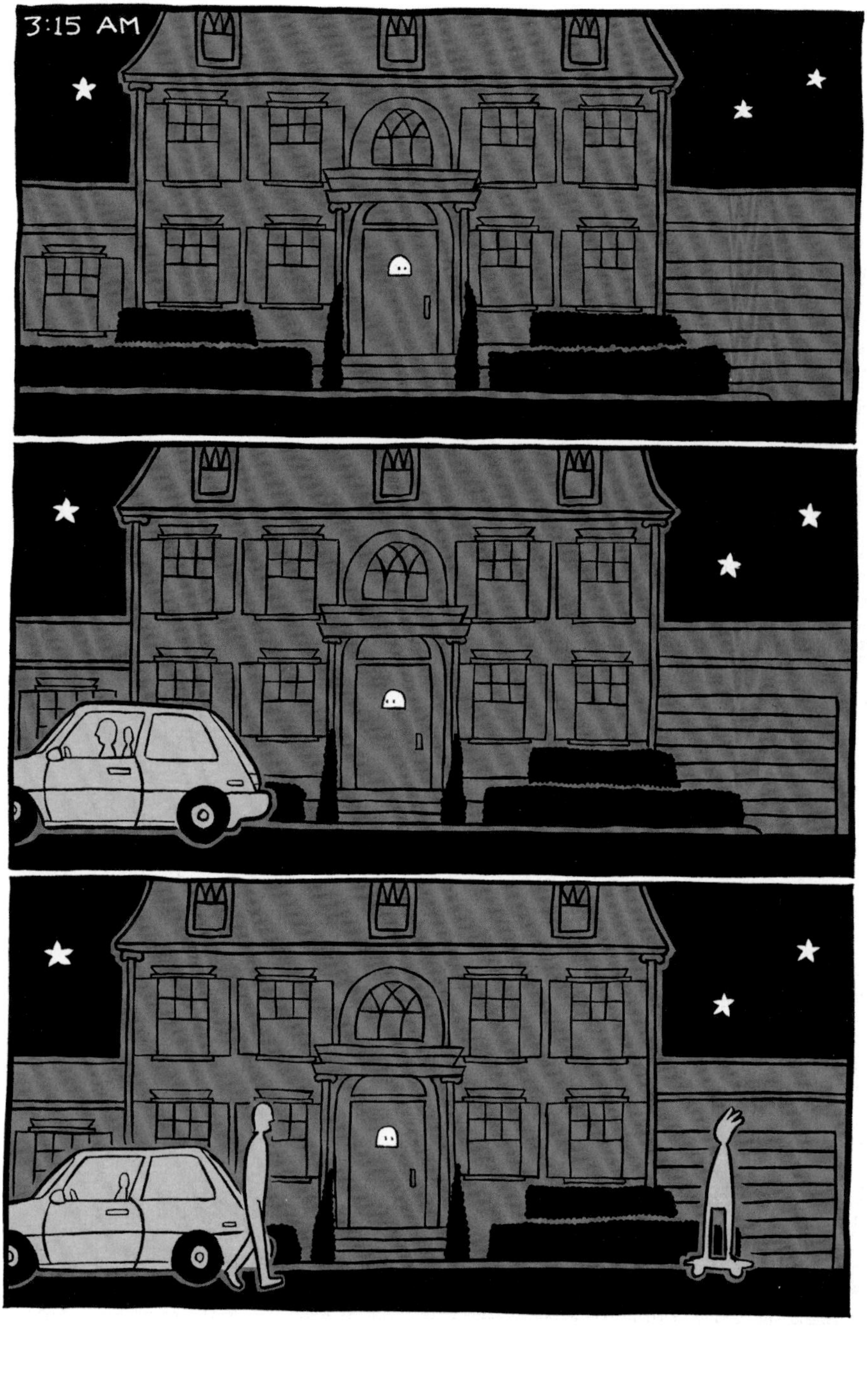
3:15 AM

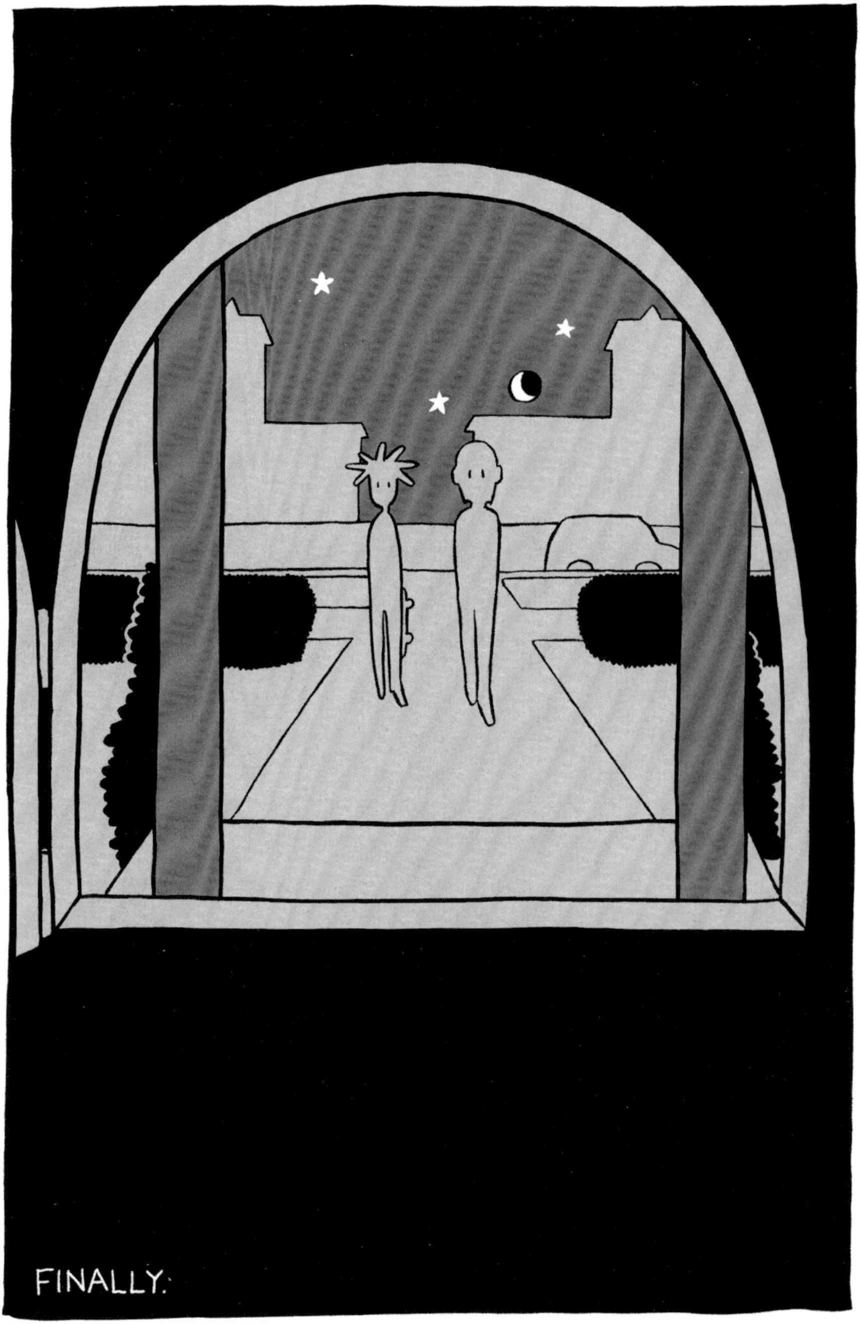
FINALLY.

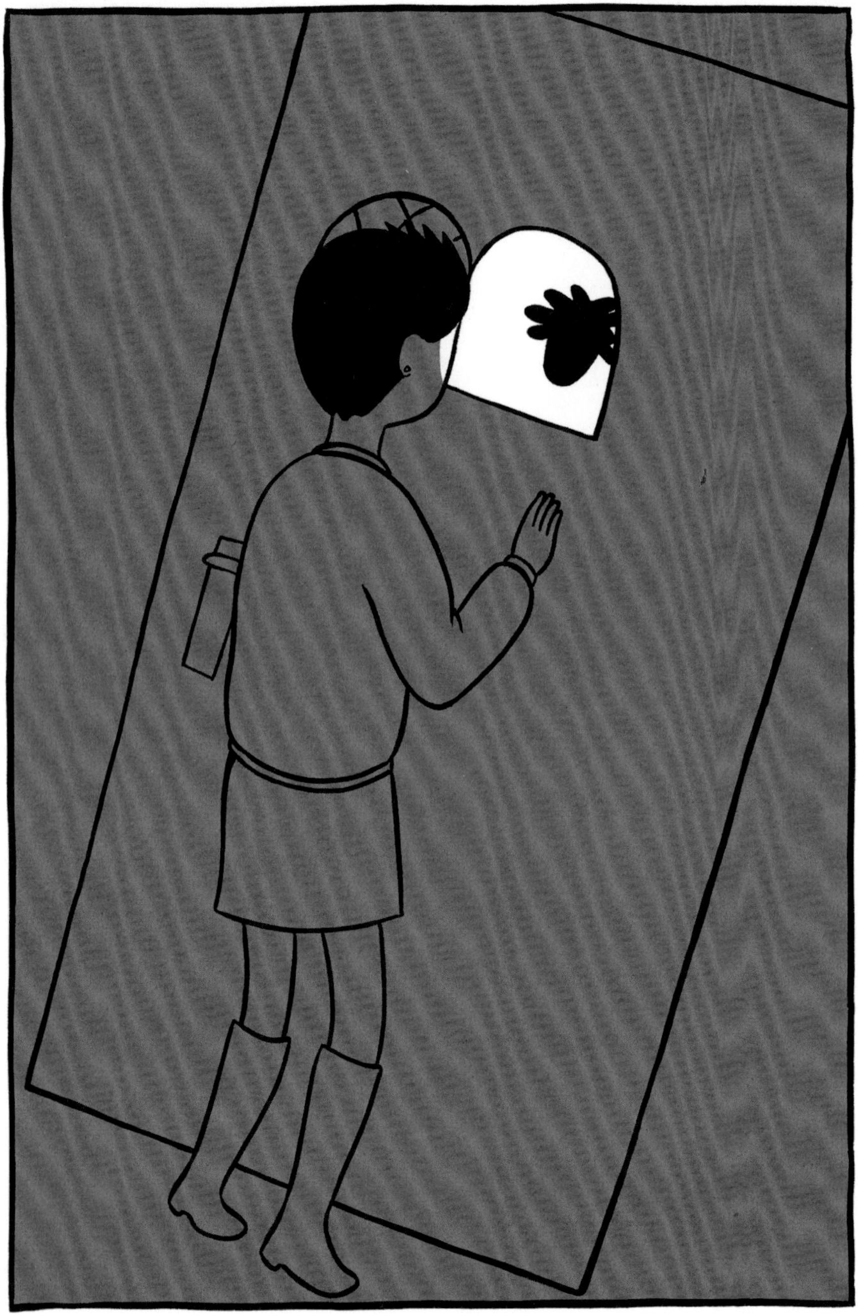

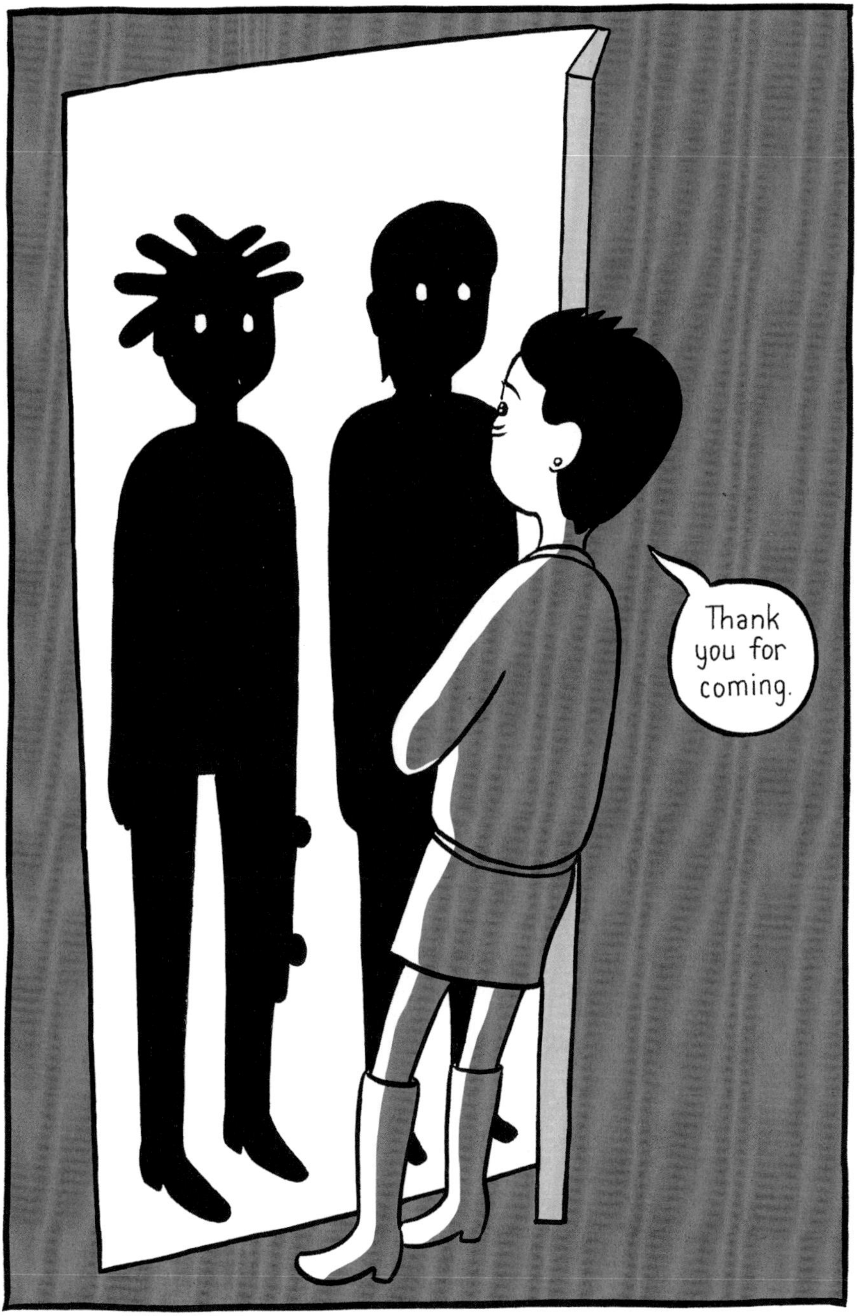
Thank you for coming.

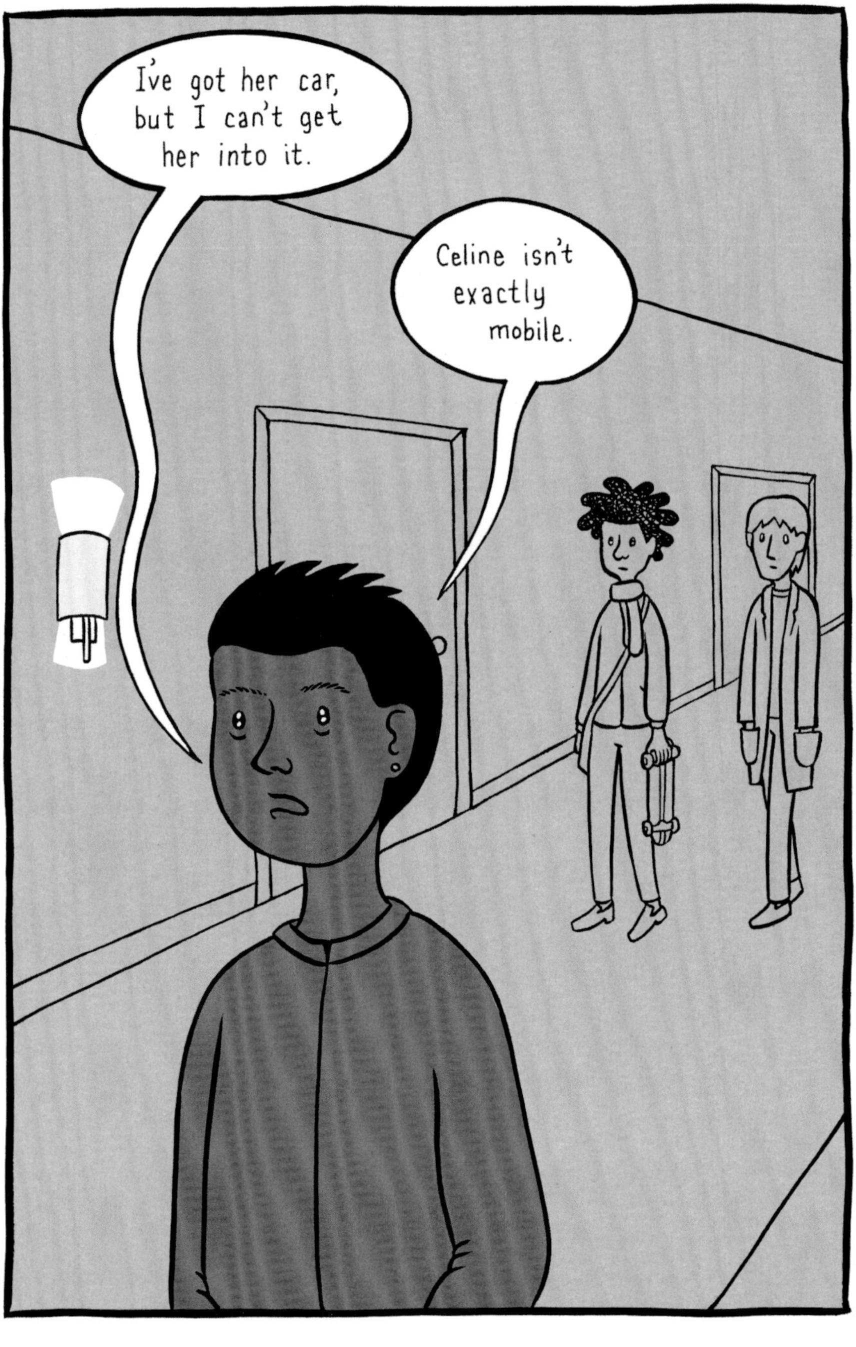
I've got her car, but I can't get her into it.
Celine isn't exactly mobile.

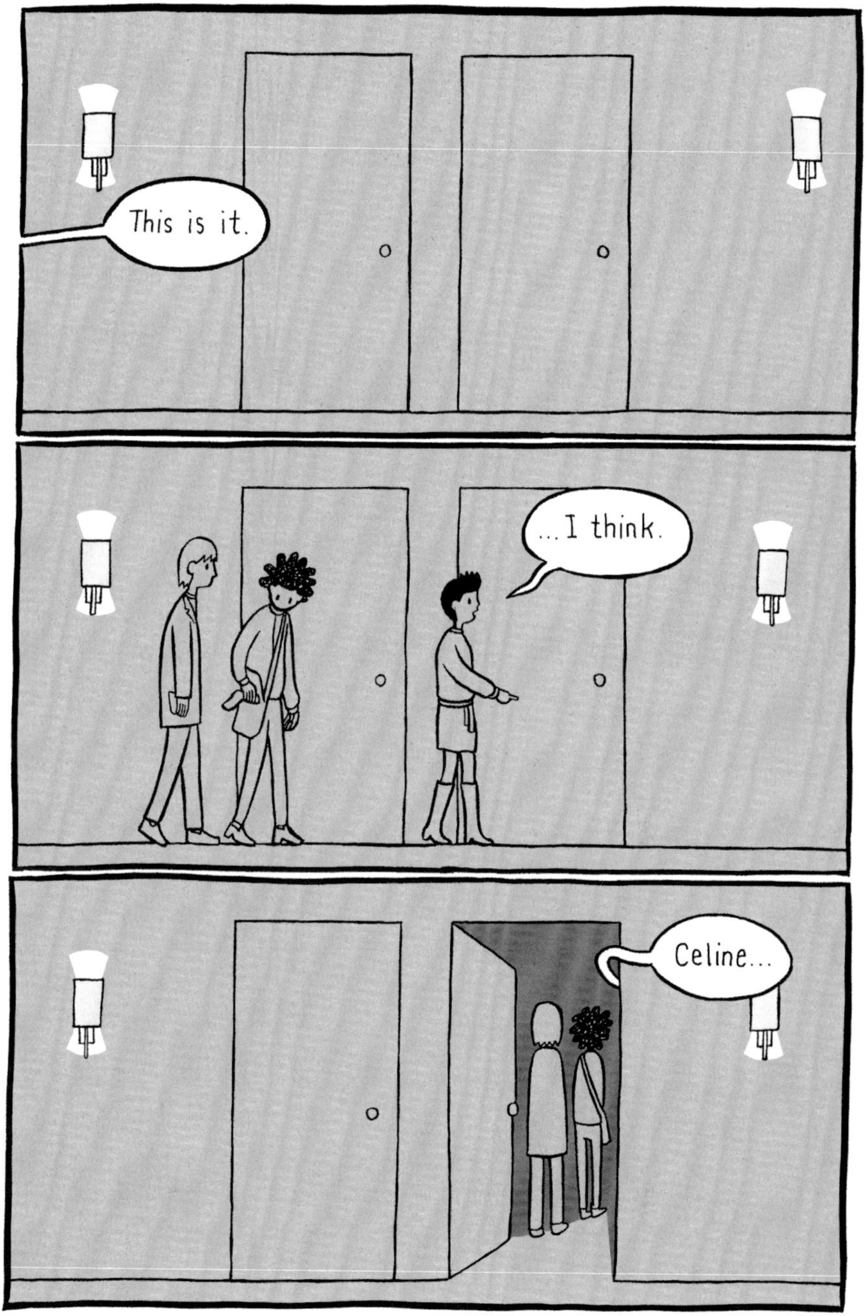
This is it.
...I think.
Celine...

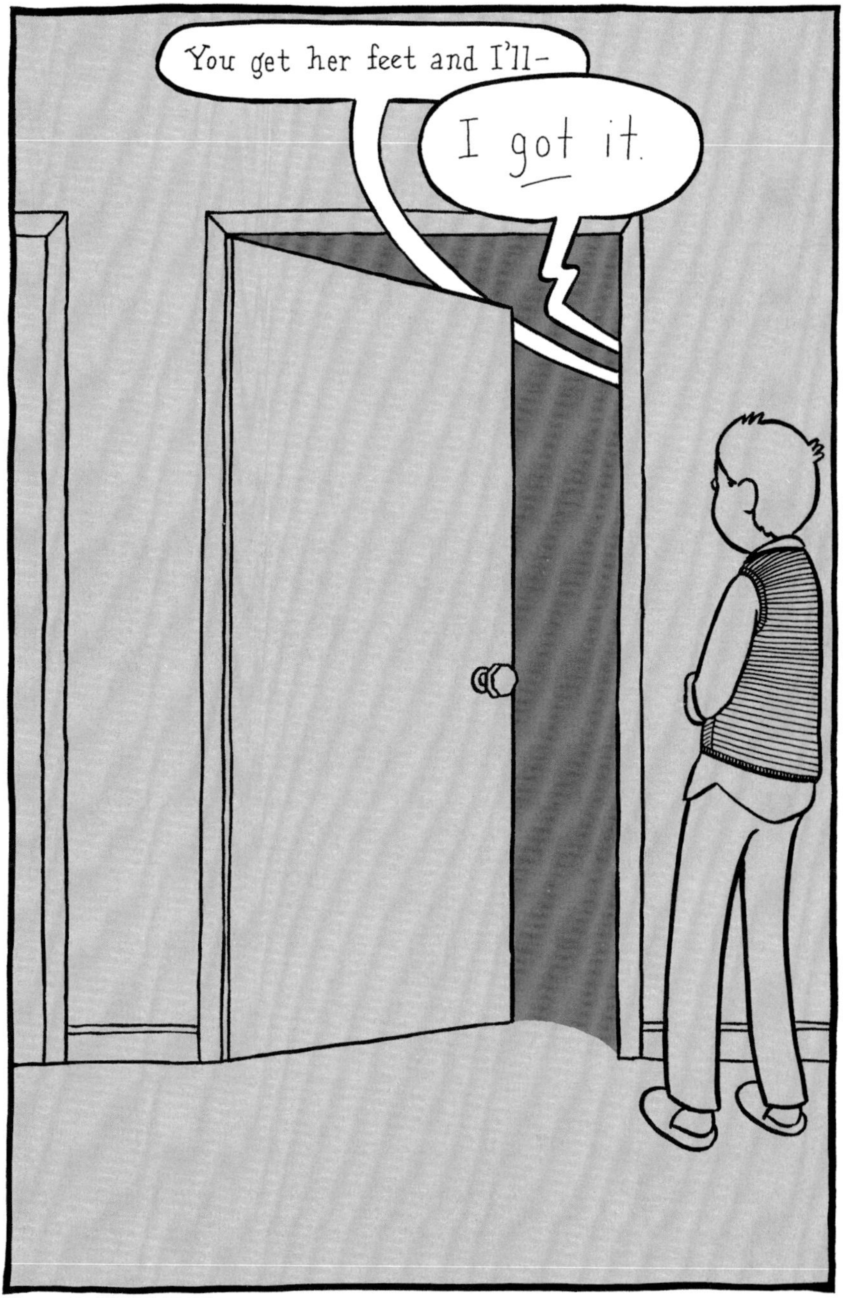
You get her feet and I'll-
I got it.

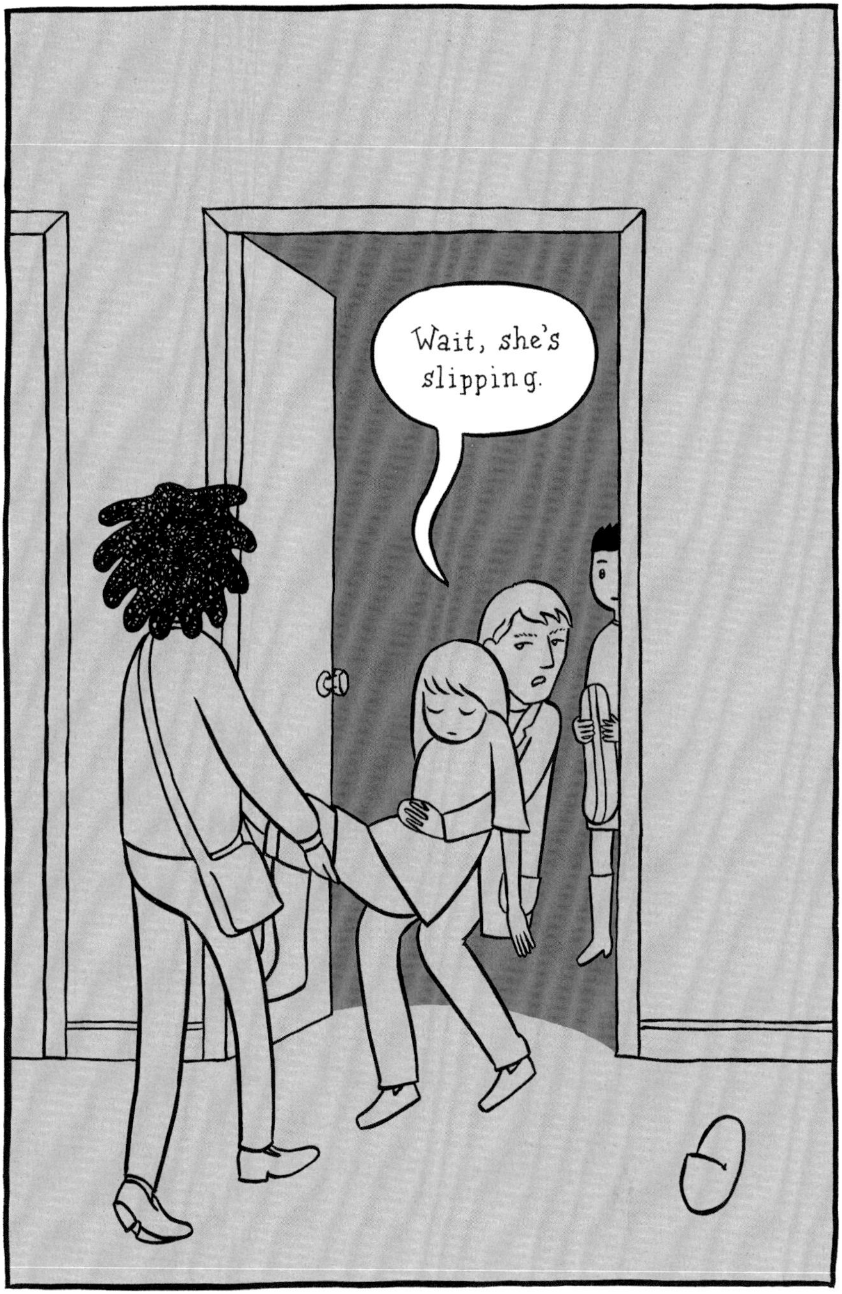
Wait, she's slipping.

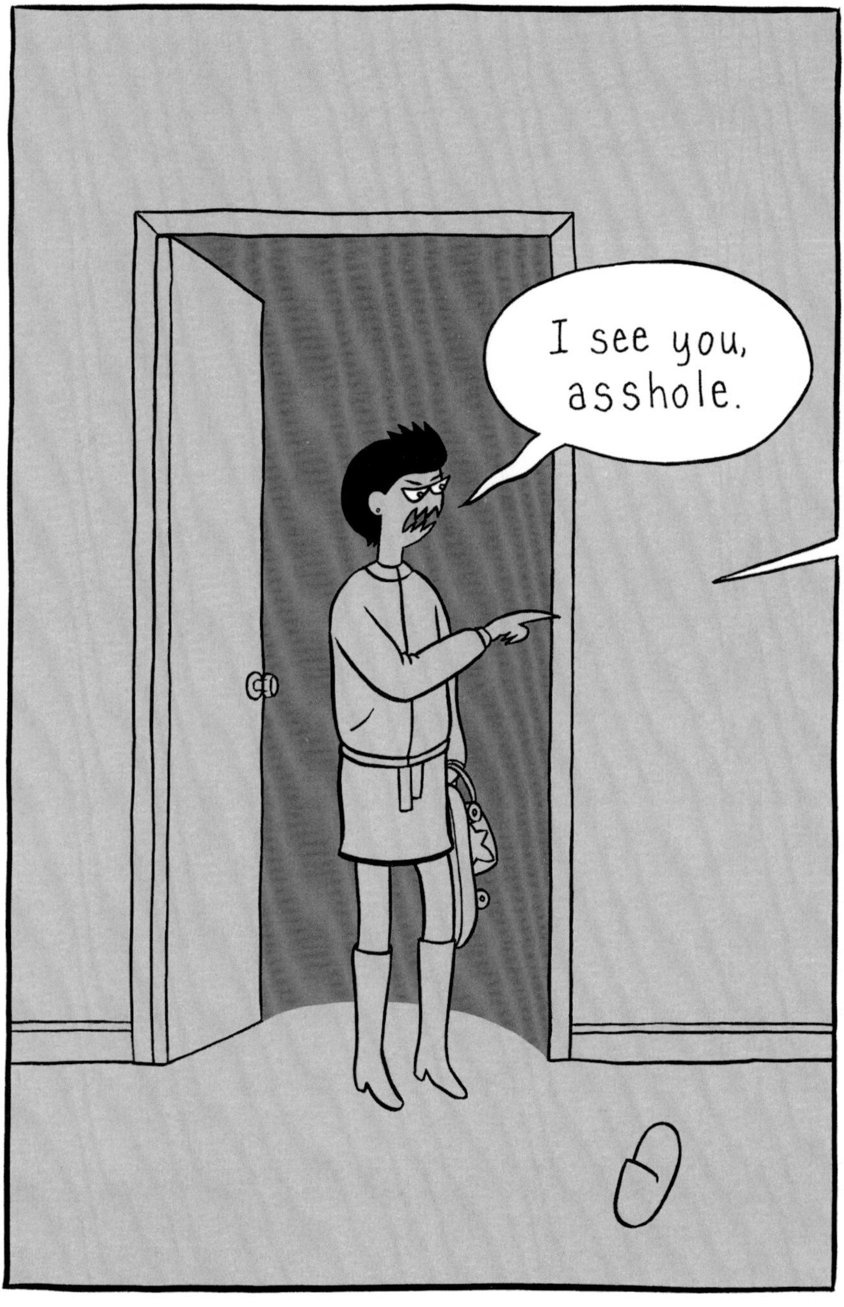
I see you, asshole.

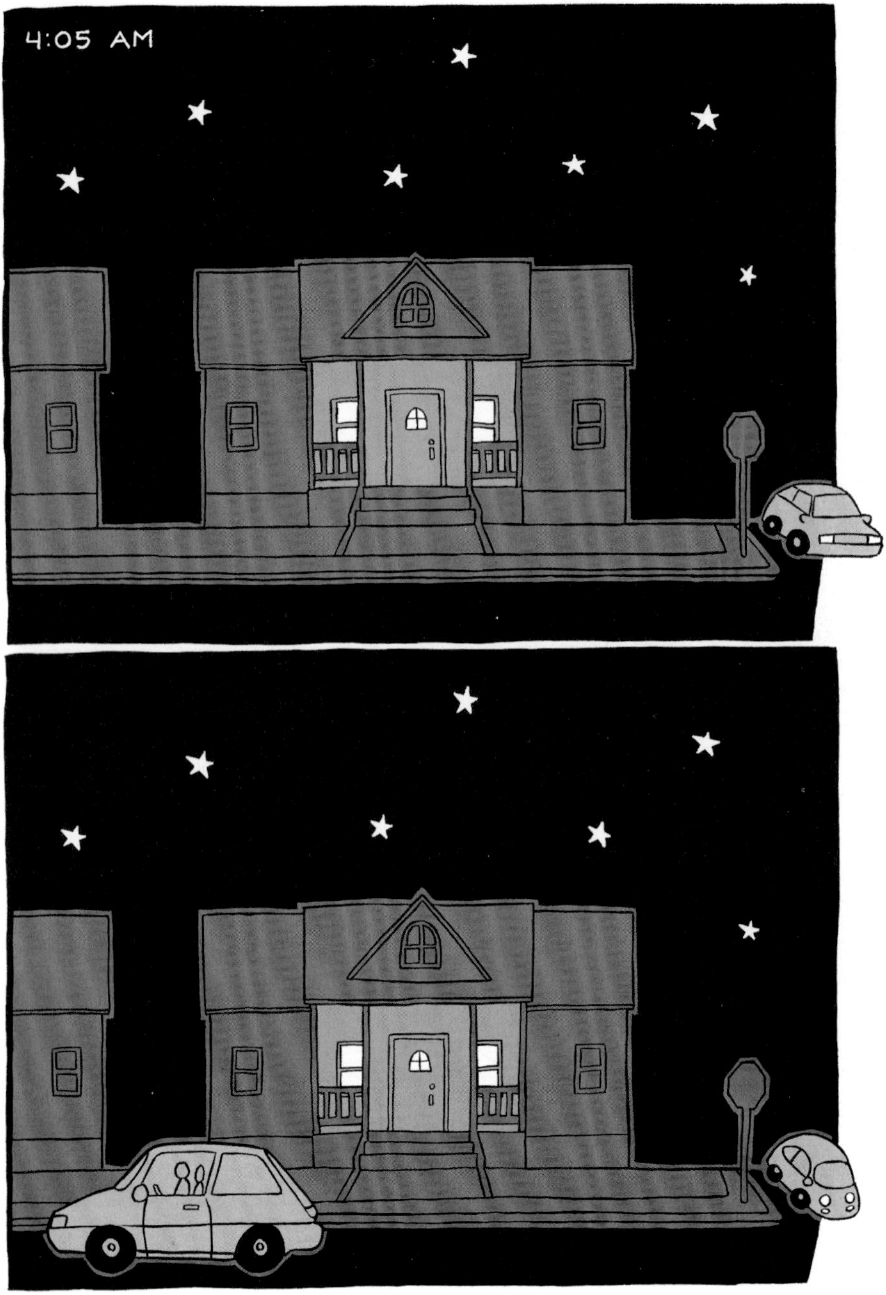
4:05 AM

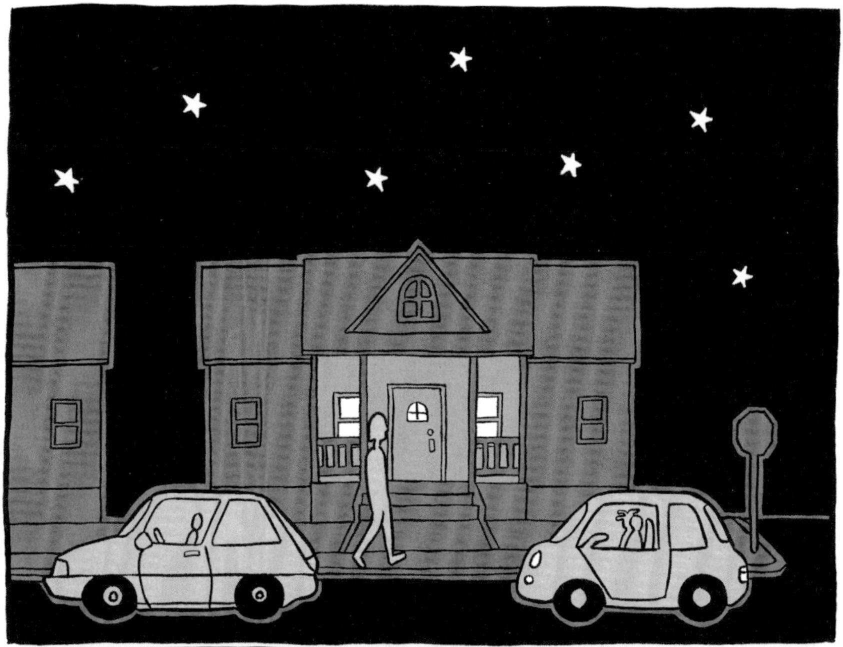

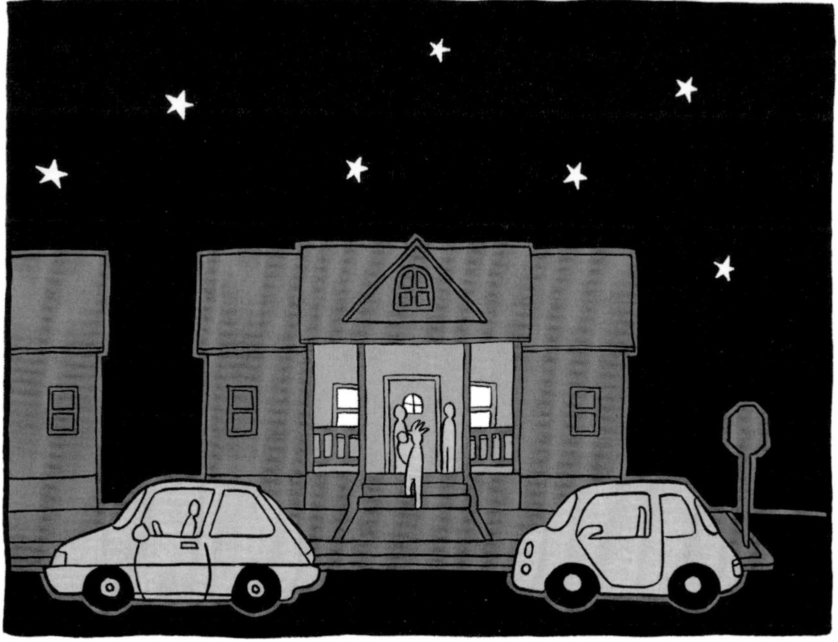

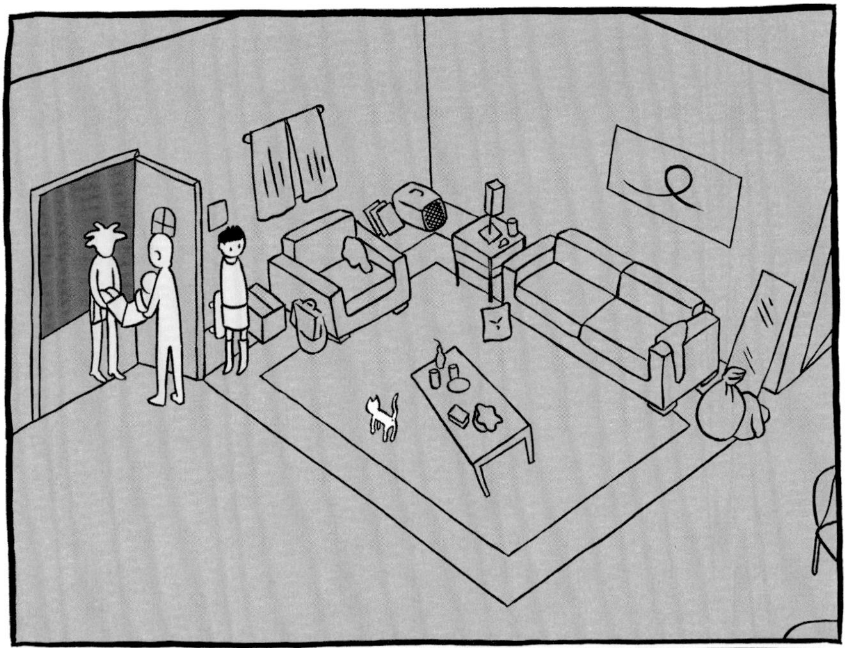

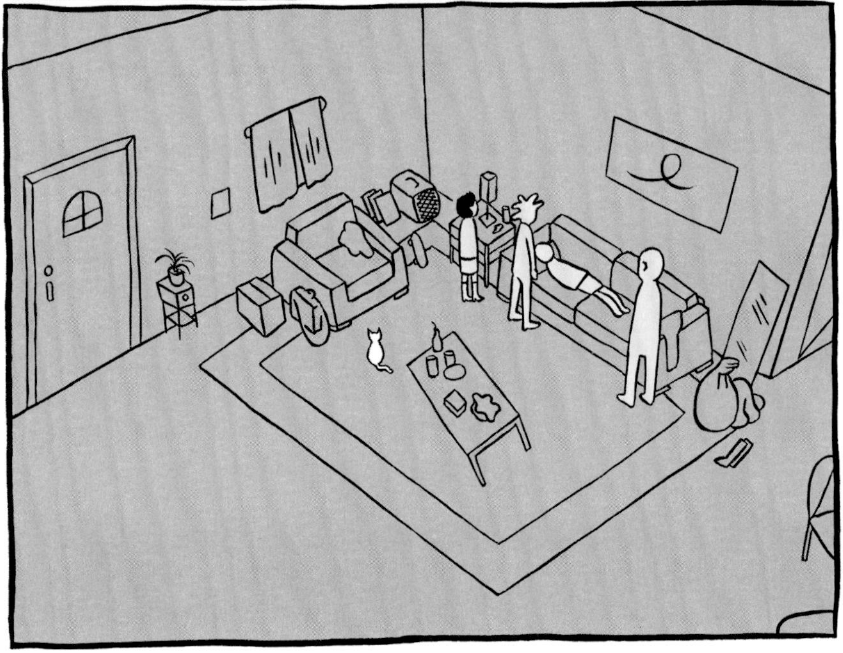

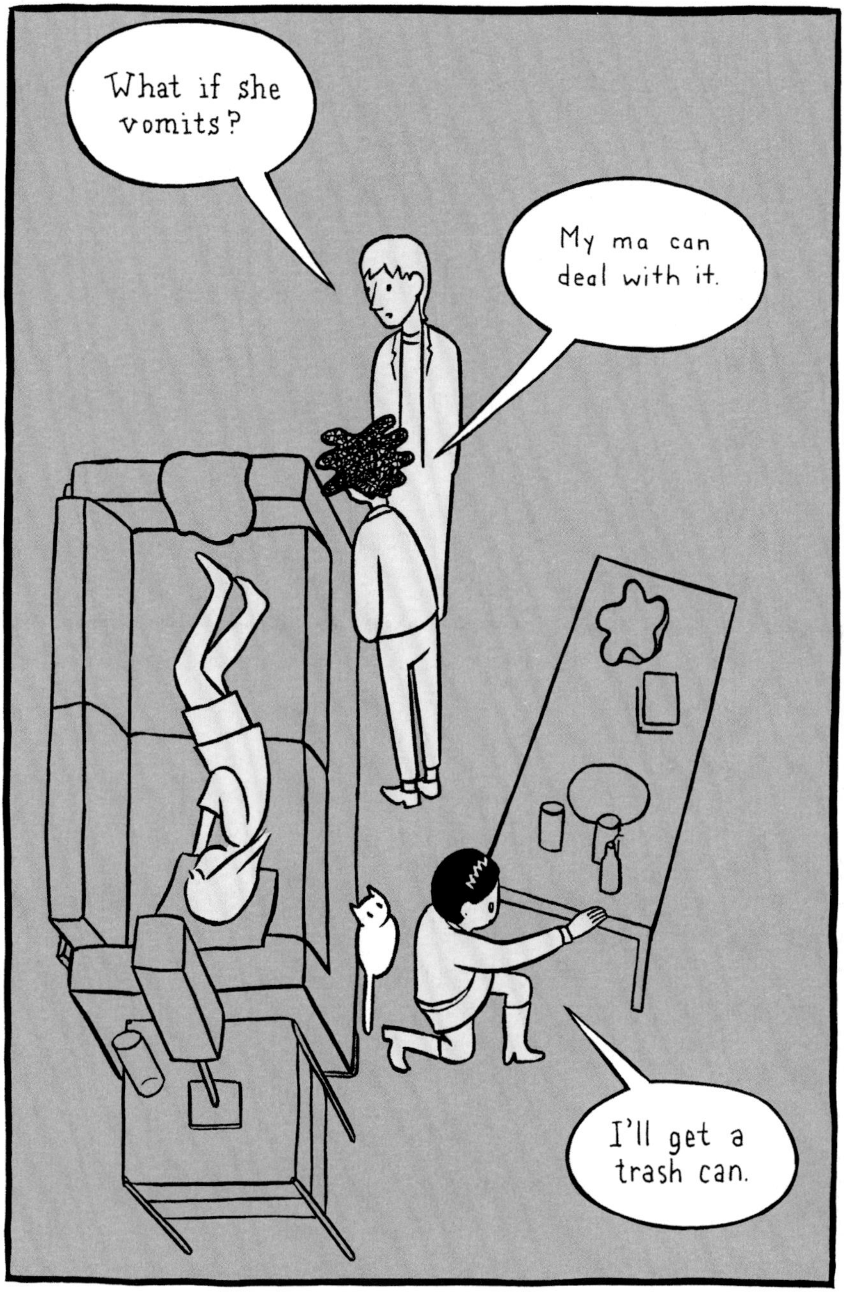
What if she vomits?
My ma can deal with it.
I'll get a trash can.

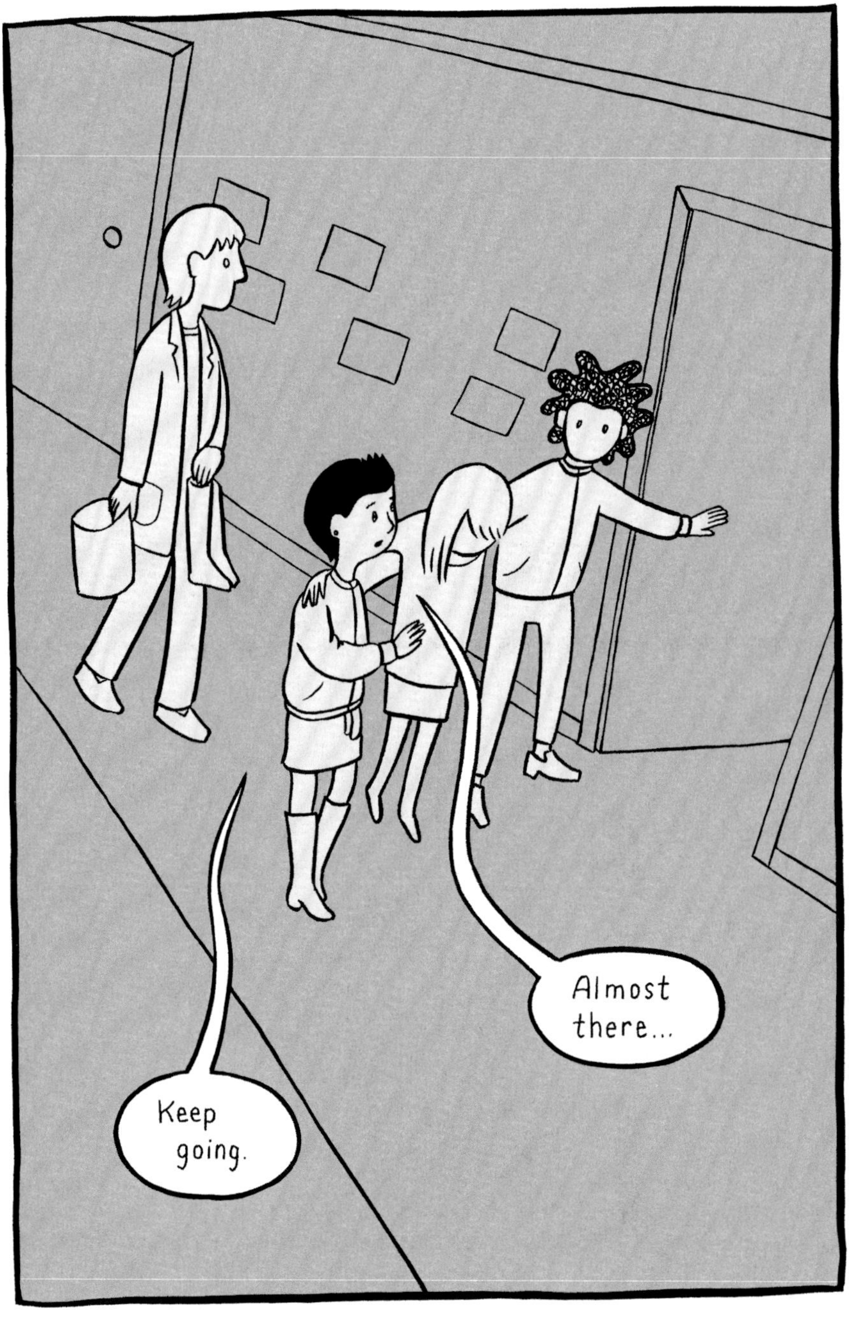
Almost there...
Keep going.

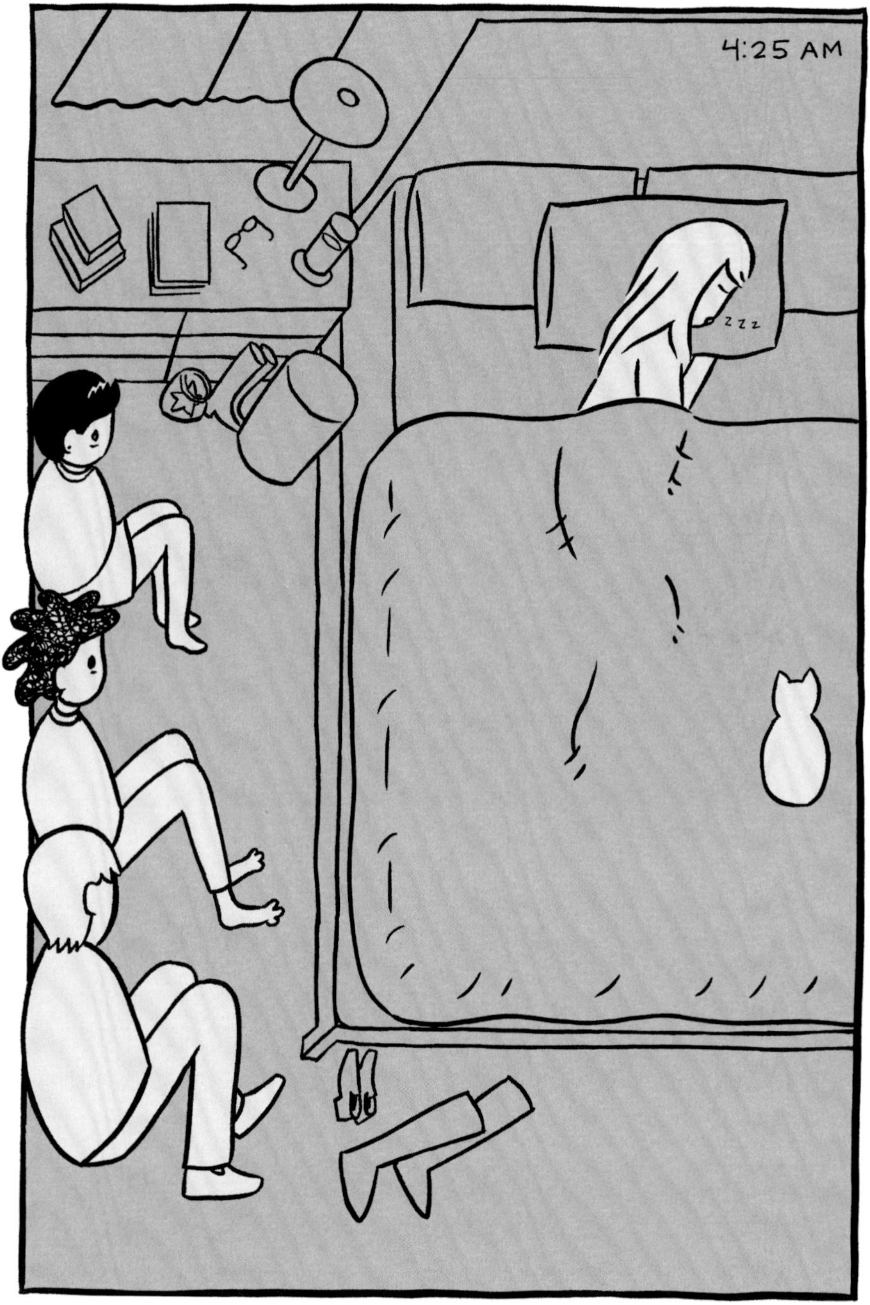
4:25 AM
zzz

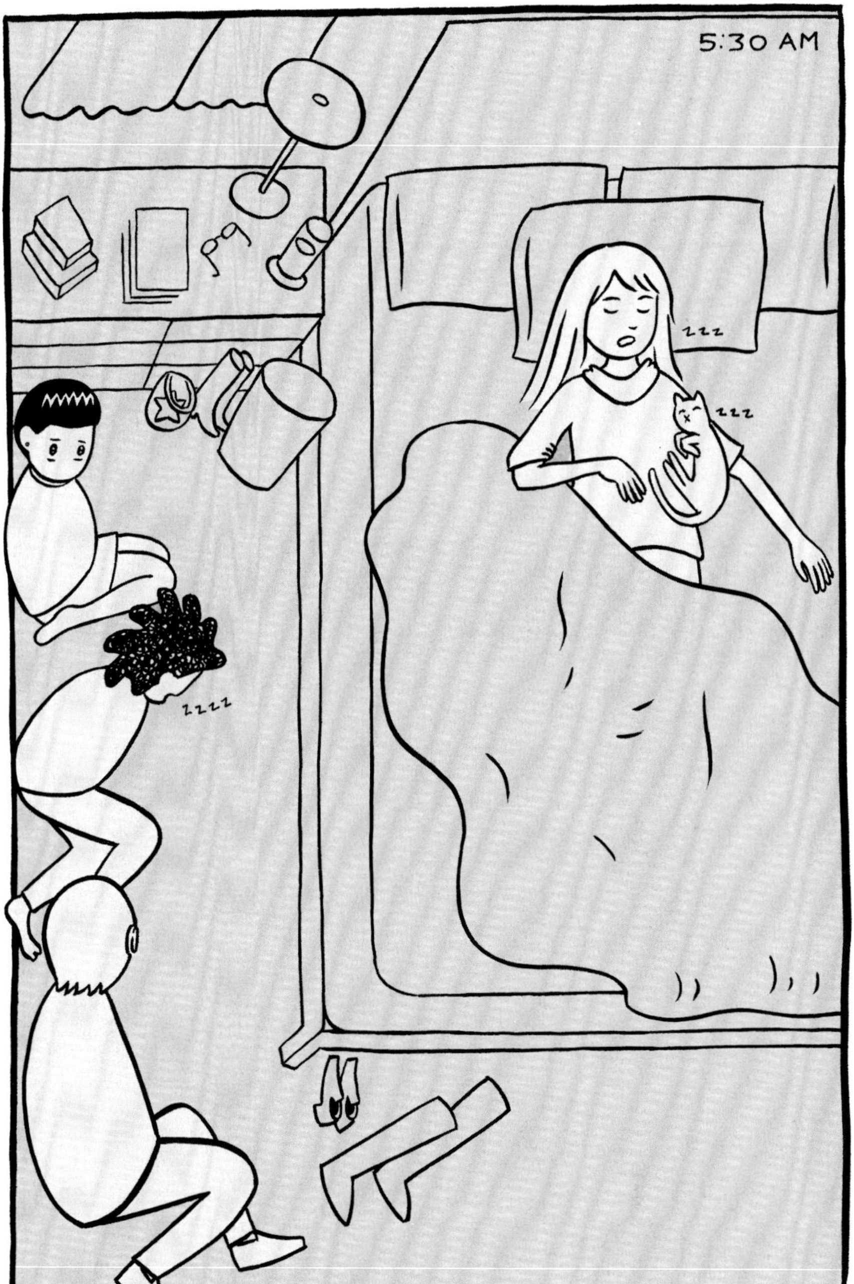
5:30 AM
zzz
zzz
zzzz

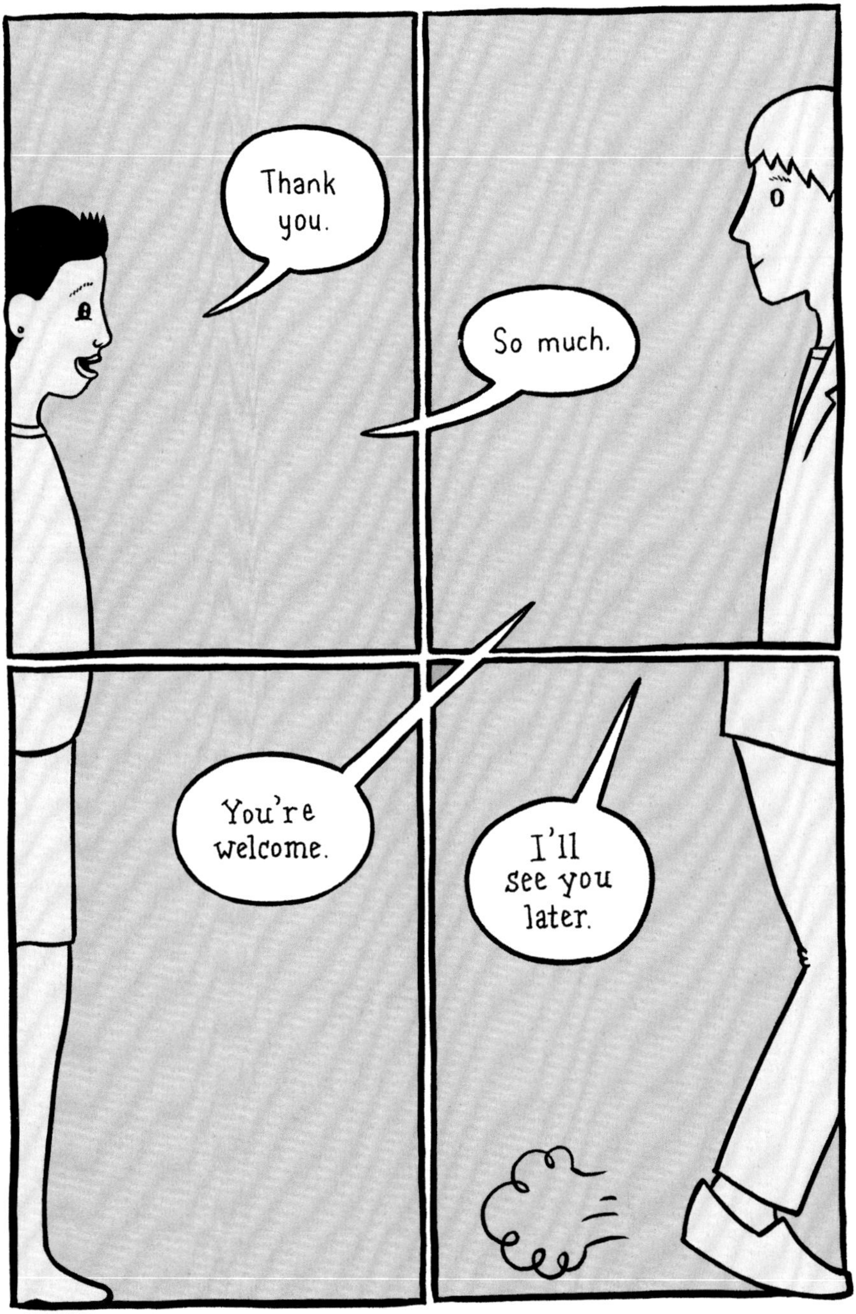
Thank you.
So much.
You're welcome.
I'll see you later.

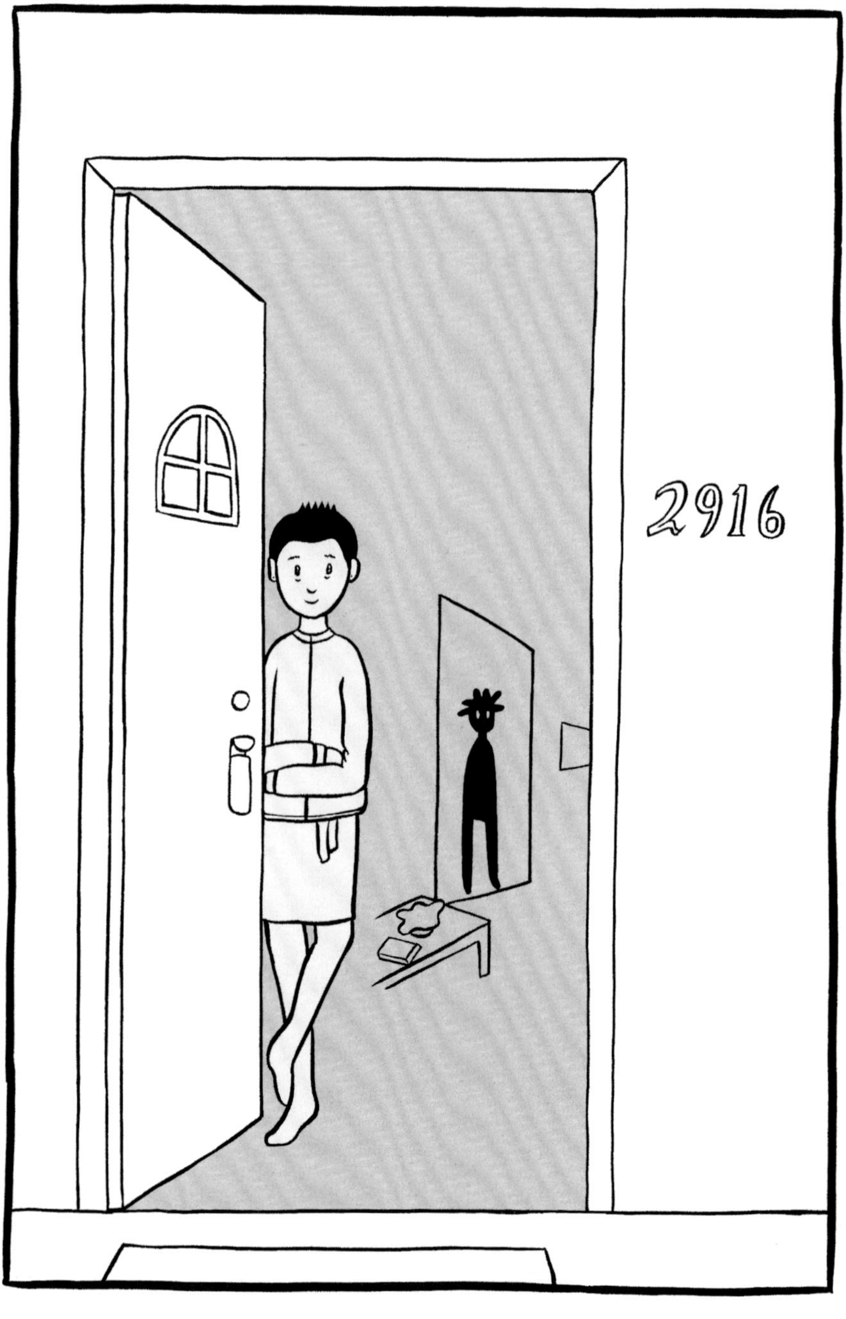
2916

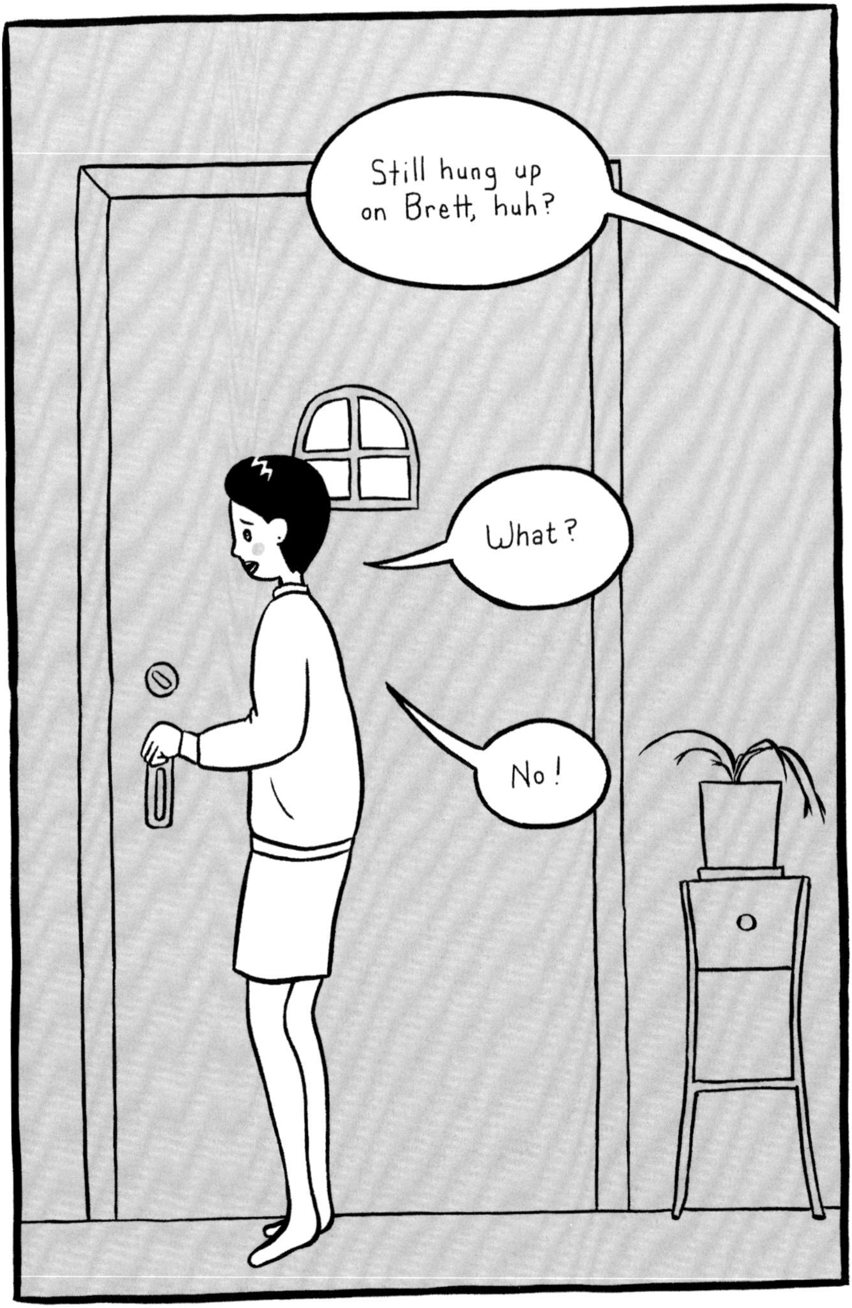
Still hung up on Brett, huh?
What?
No!

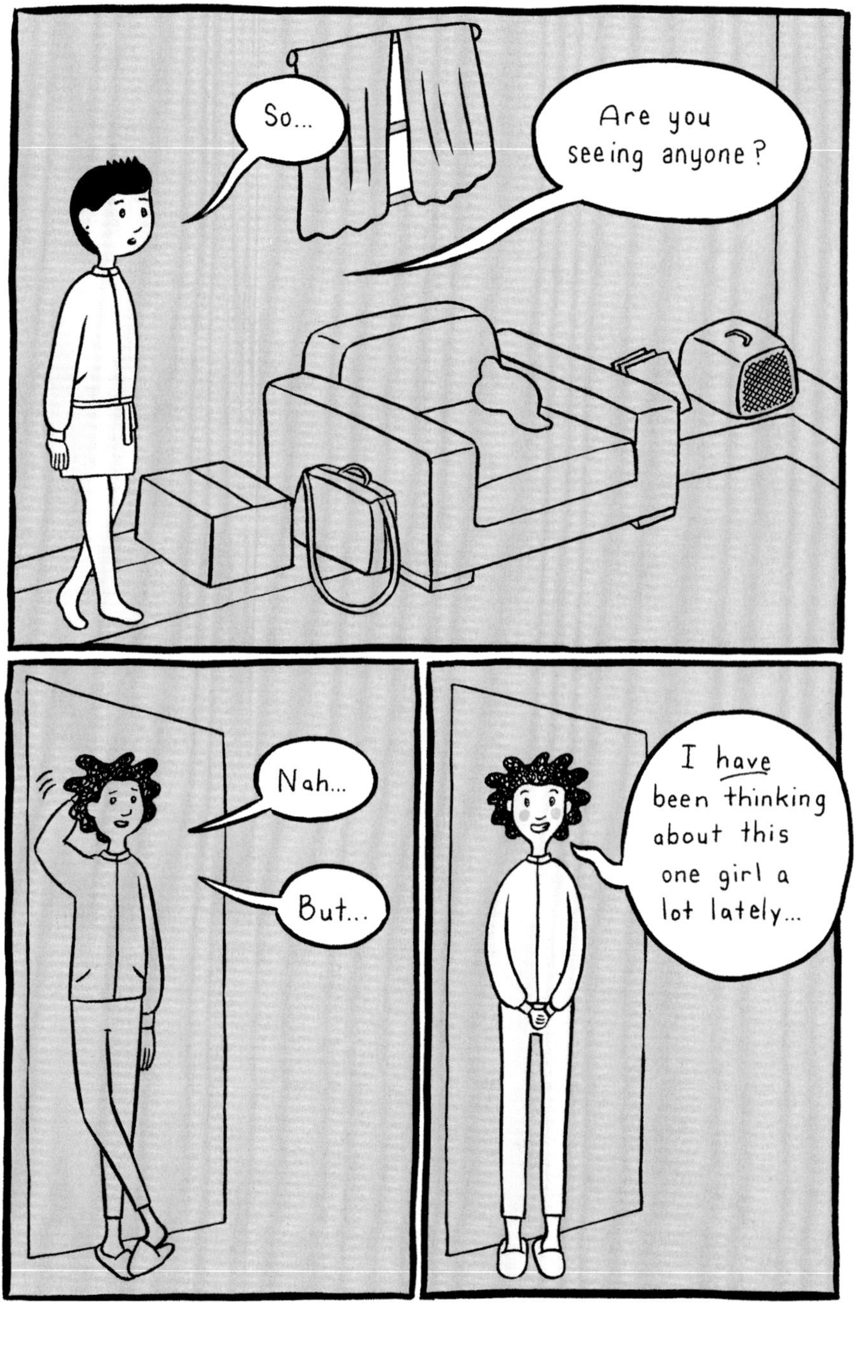
So...
Are you seeing anyone?
Nah...
But...
I have been thinking about this one girl a lot lately...

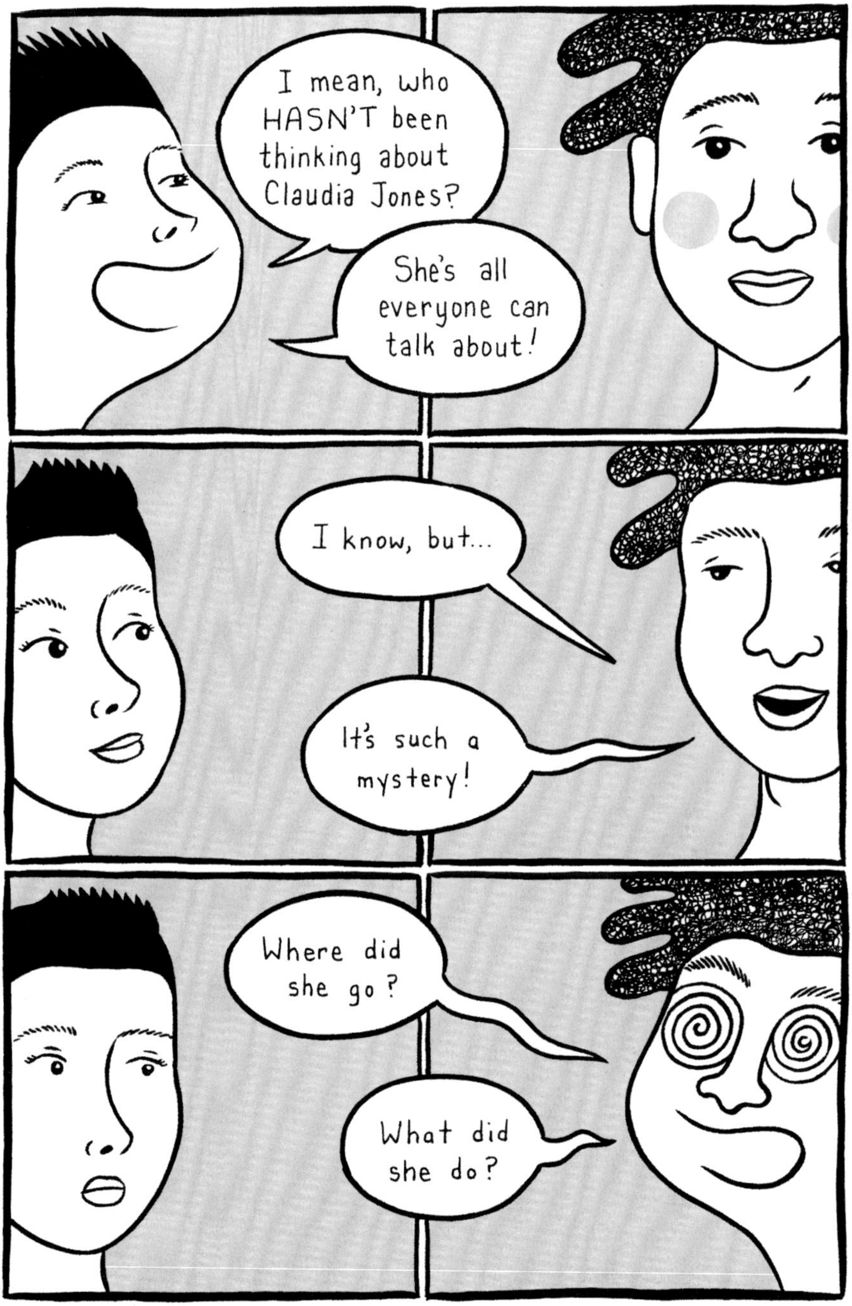
I mean, who HASN'T been thinking about Claudia Jones?
She's all everyone can talk about!
I know, but...
It's such a mystery!
Where did she go?
What did she do?

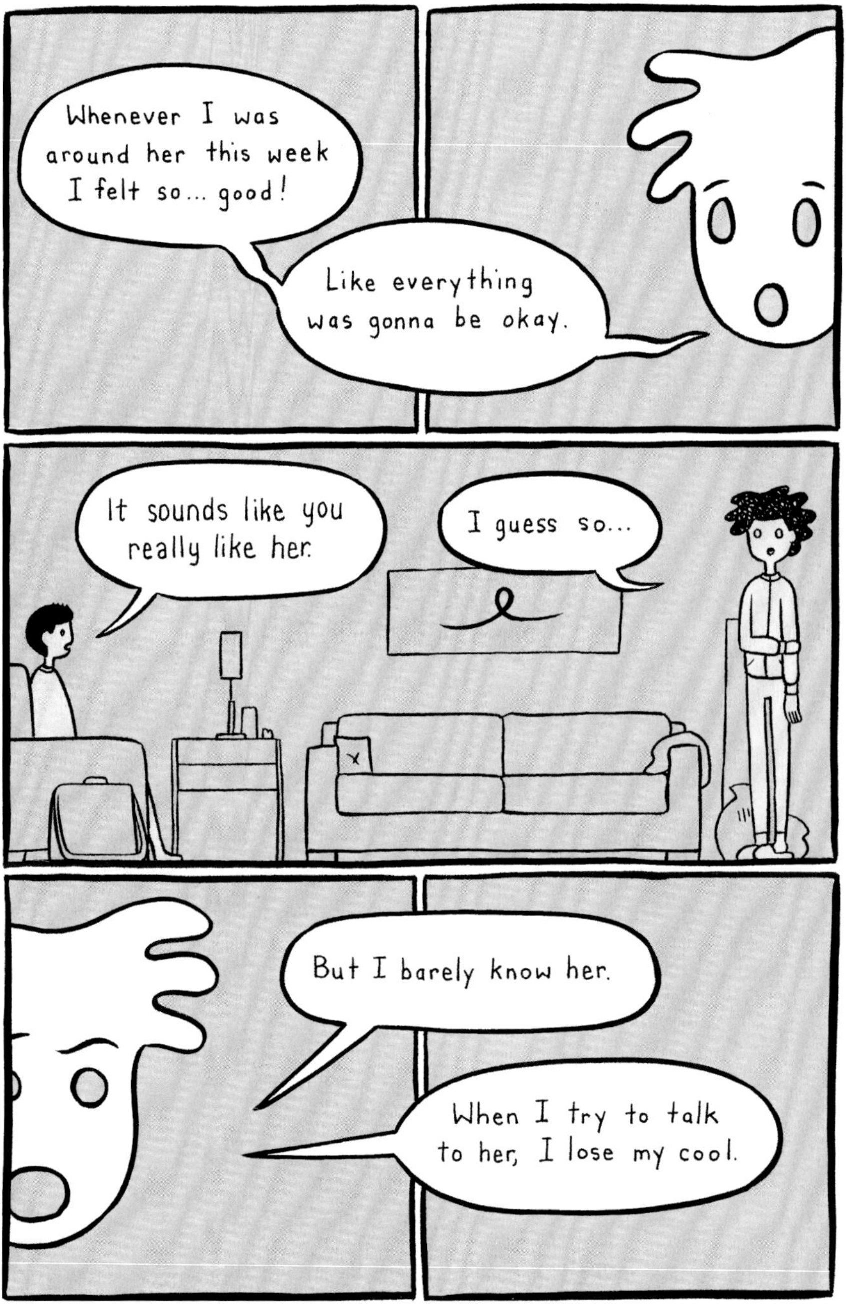
Whenever I was around her this week I felt so... good!
Like everything was gonna be okay.
It sounds like you really like her.
I guess so...
But I barely know her.
When I try to talk to her, I lose my cool.

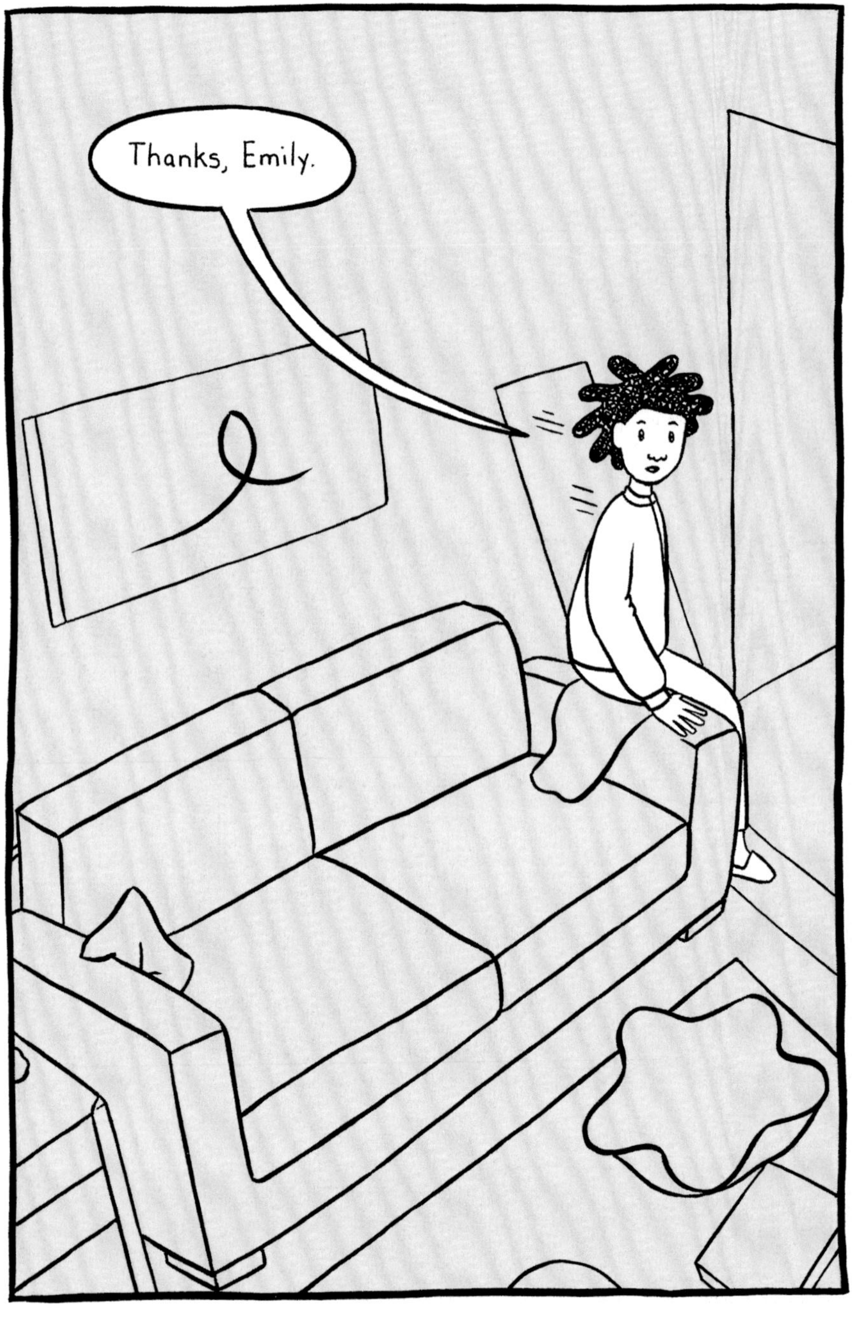
Thanks, Emily.

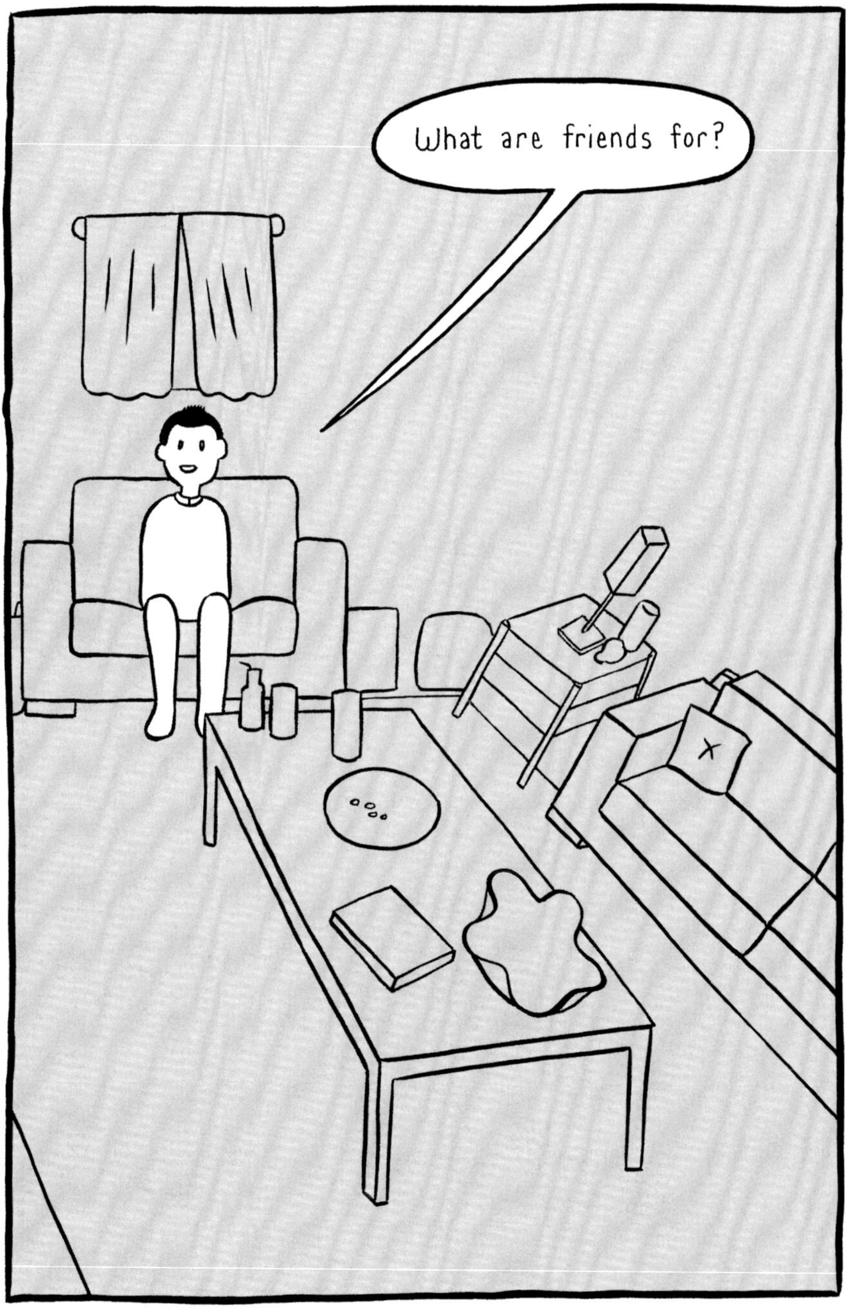
What are friends for?

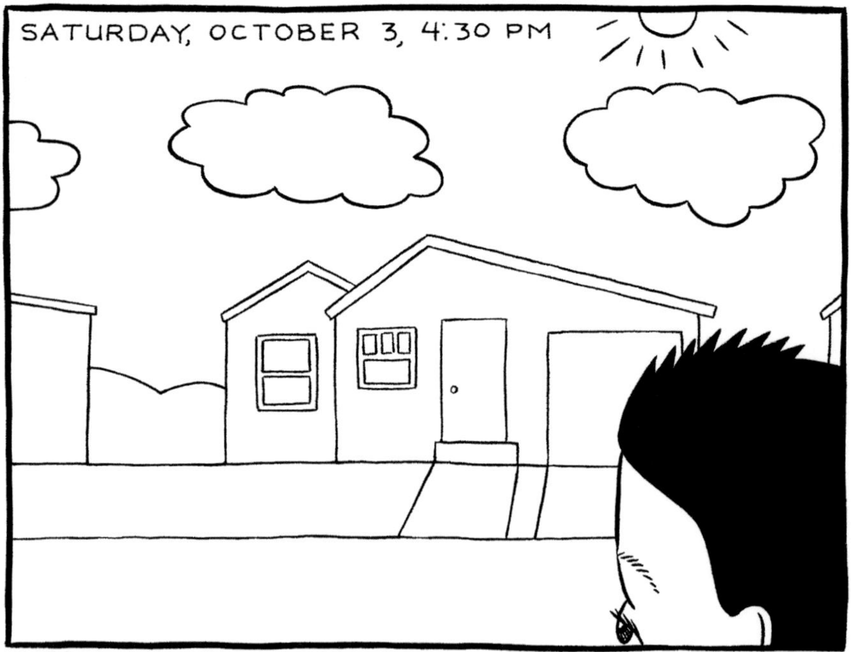
SATURDAY, OCTOBER 3, 4:30 PM

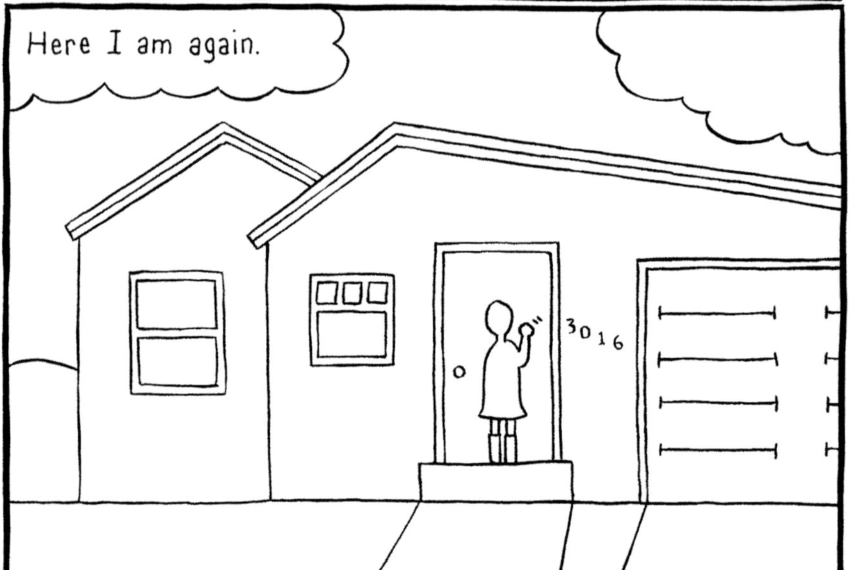
Here I am again.
3016

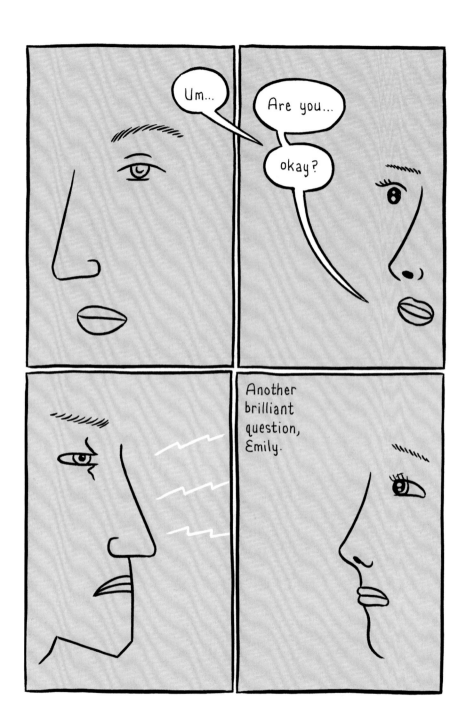

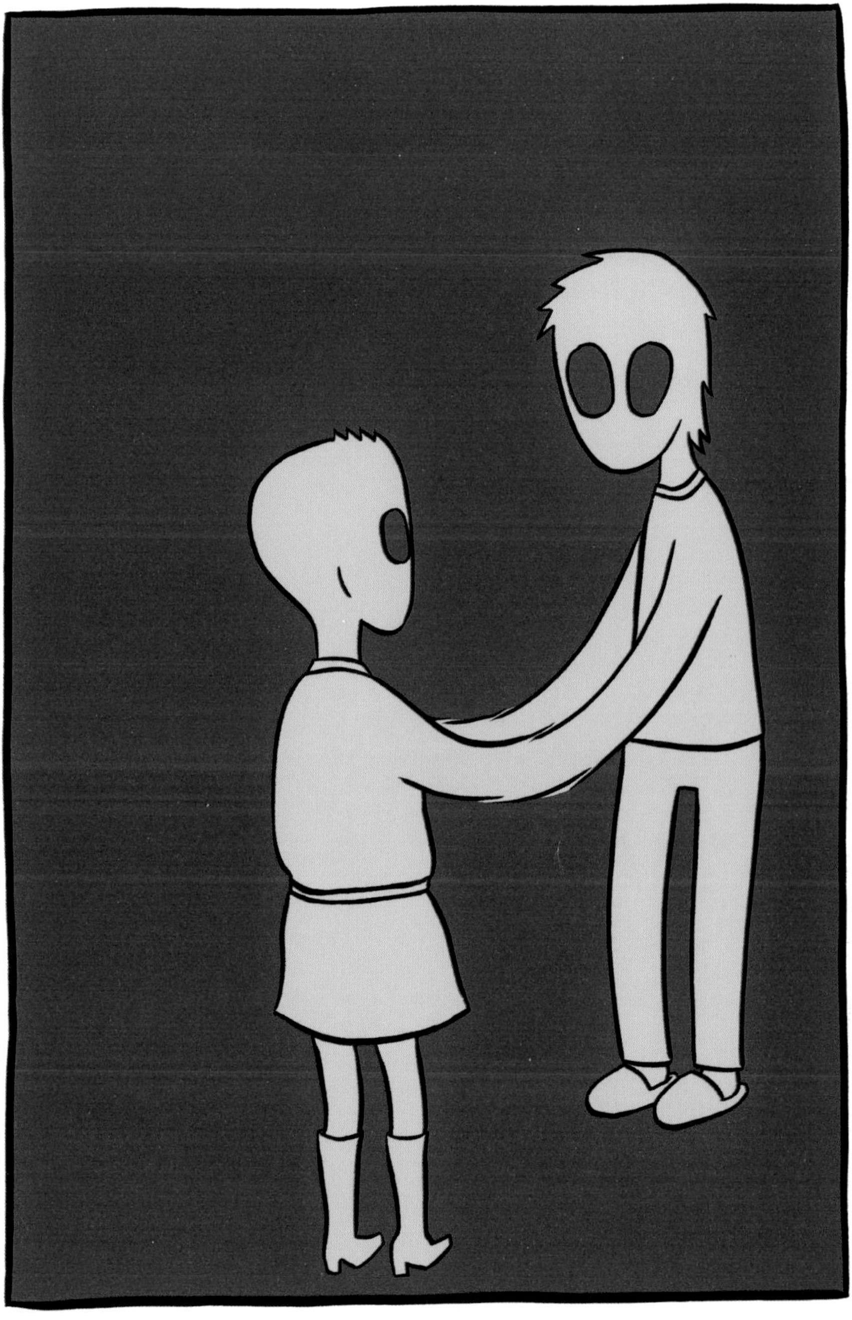

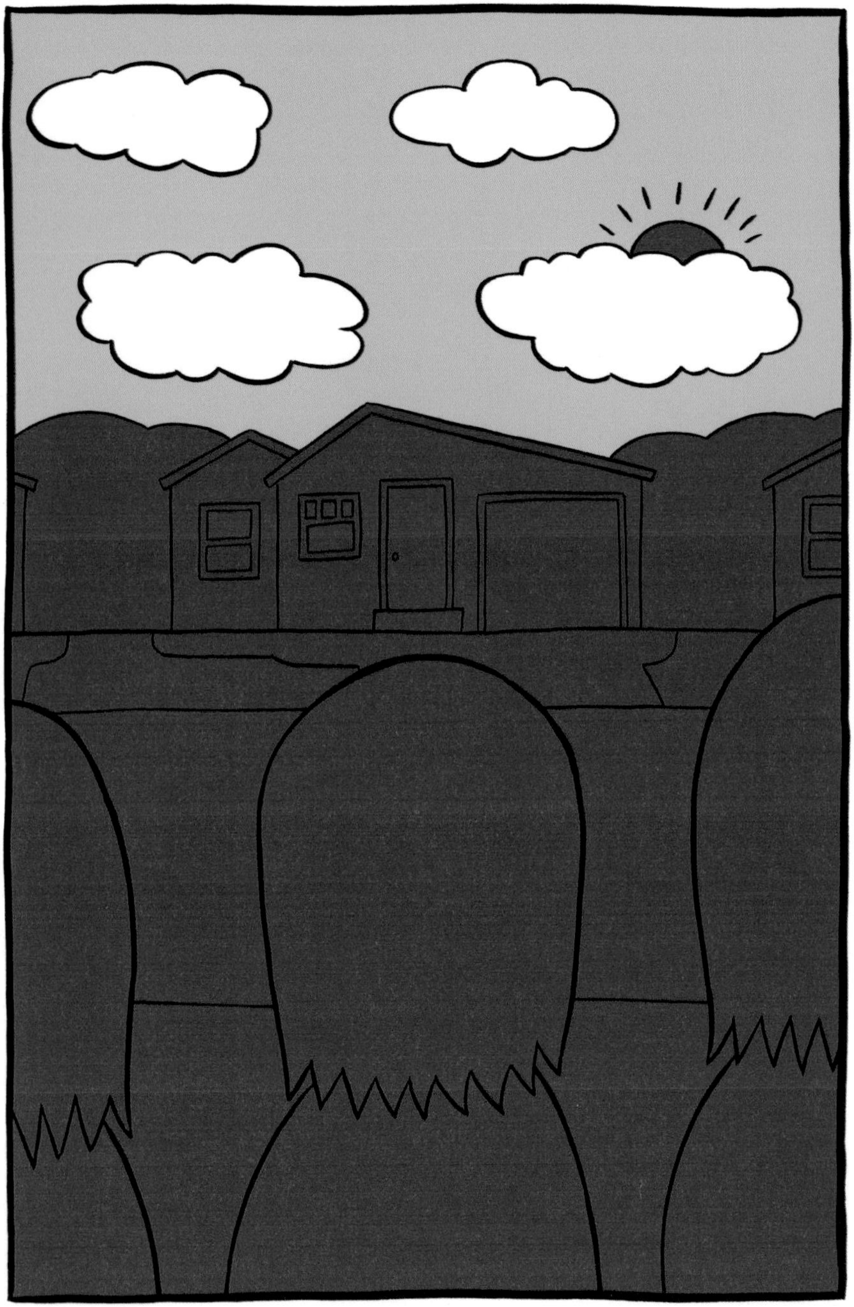

PART FIVE

Claudia Q. Jones

MONDAY, OCTOBER 5, 11:30 AM

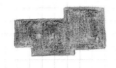

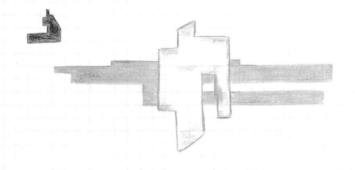

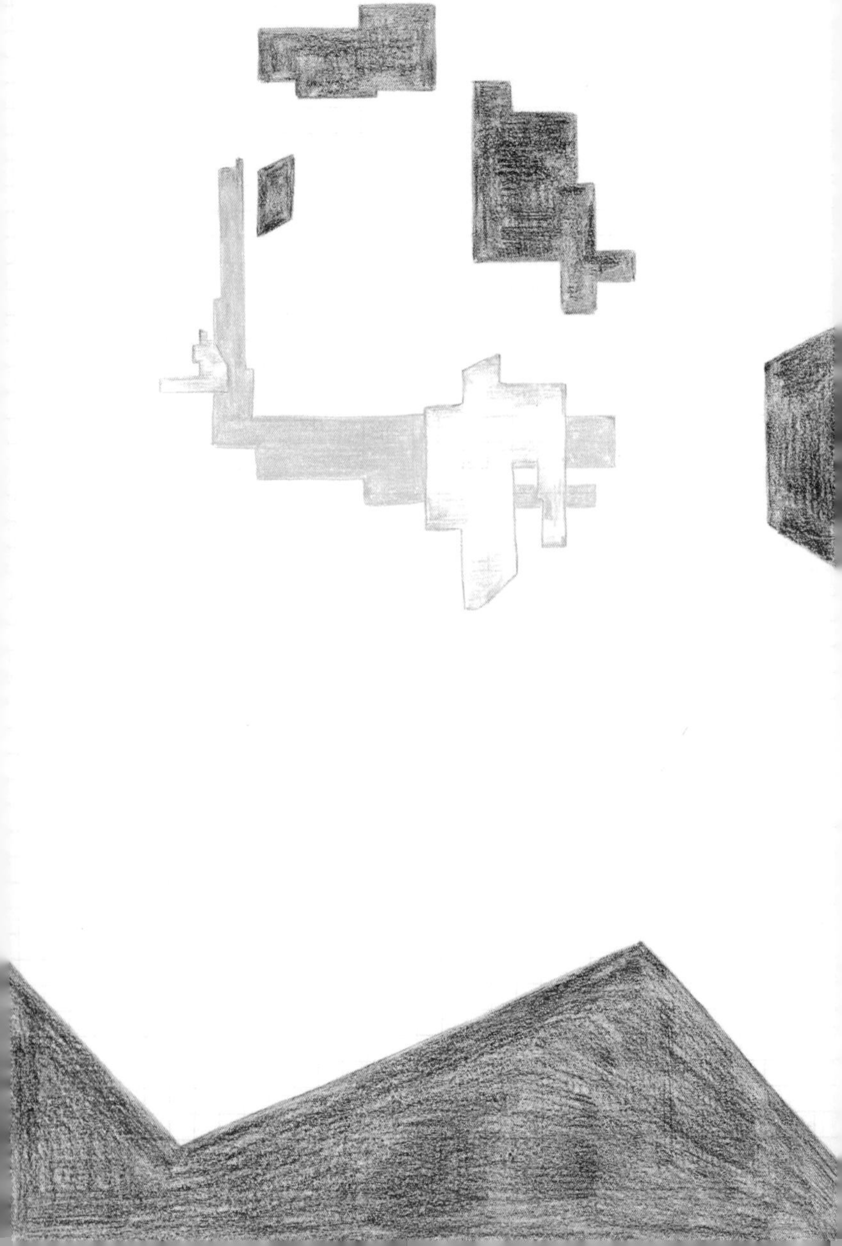

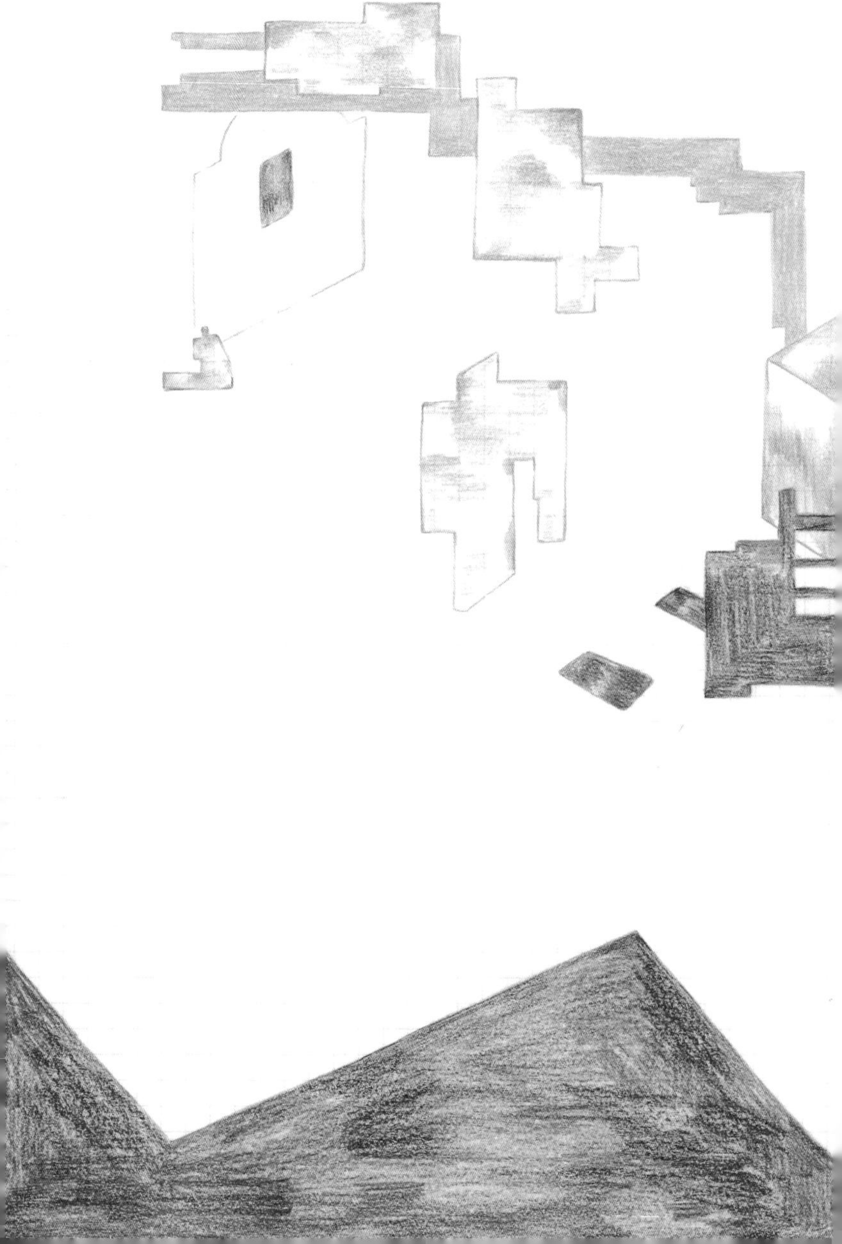

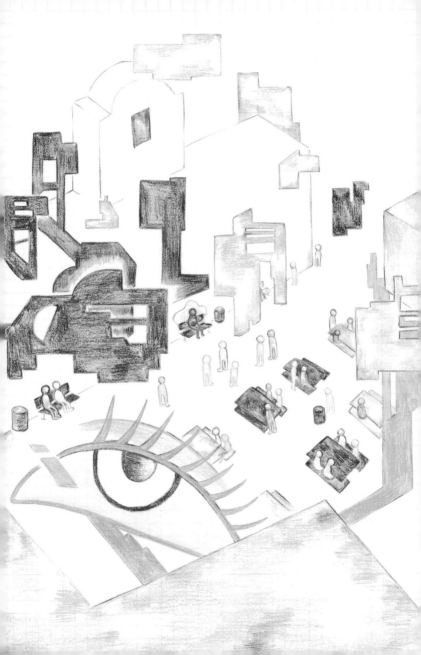

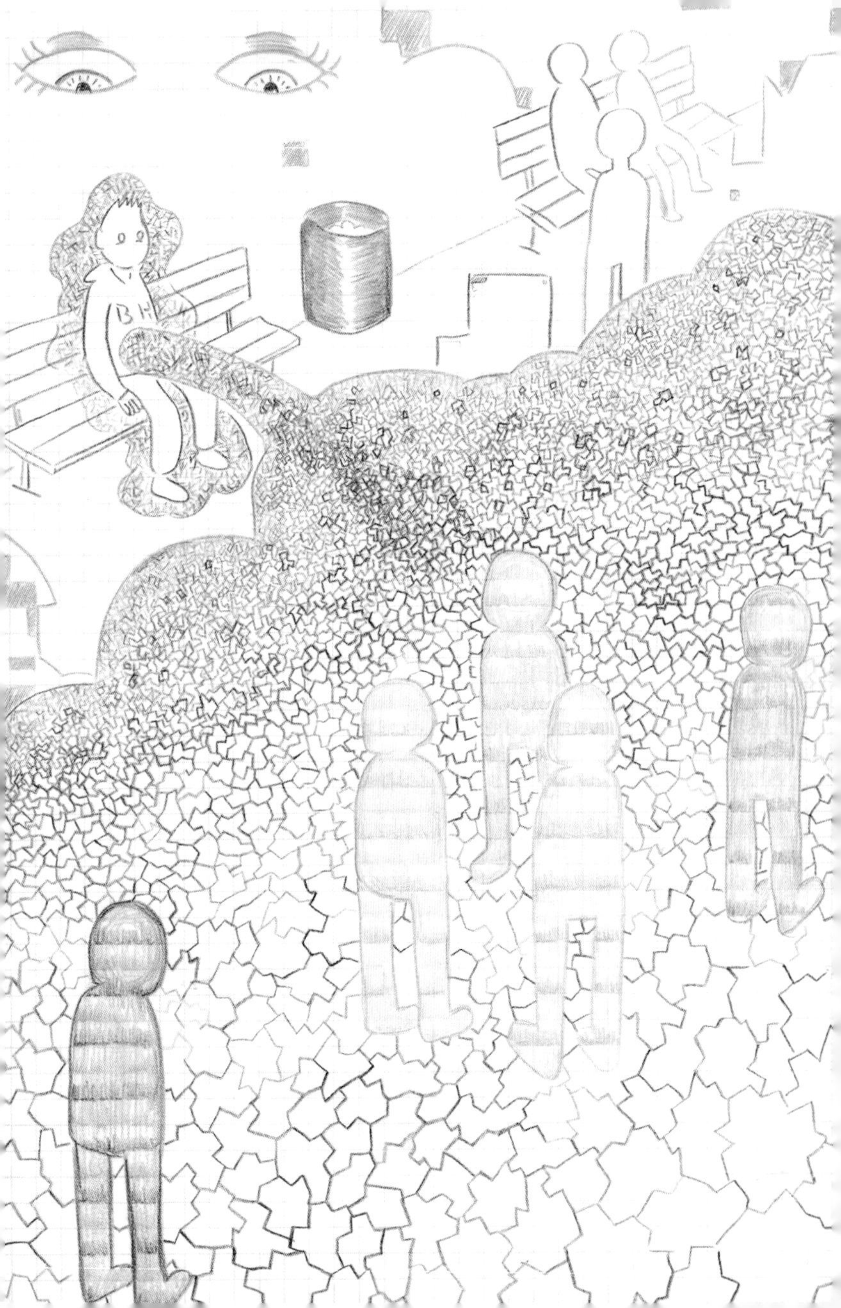

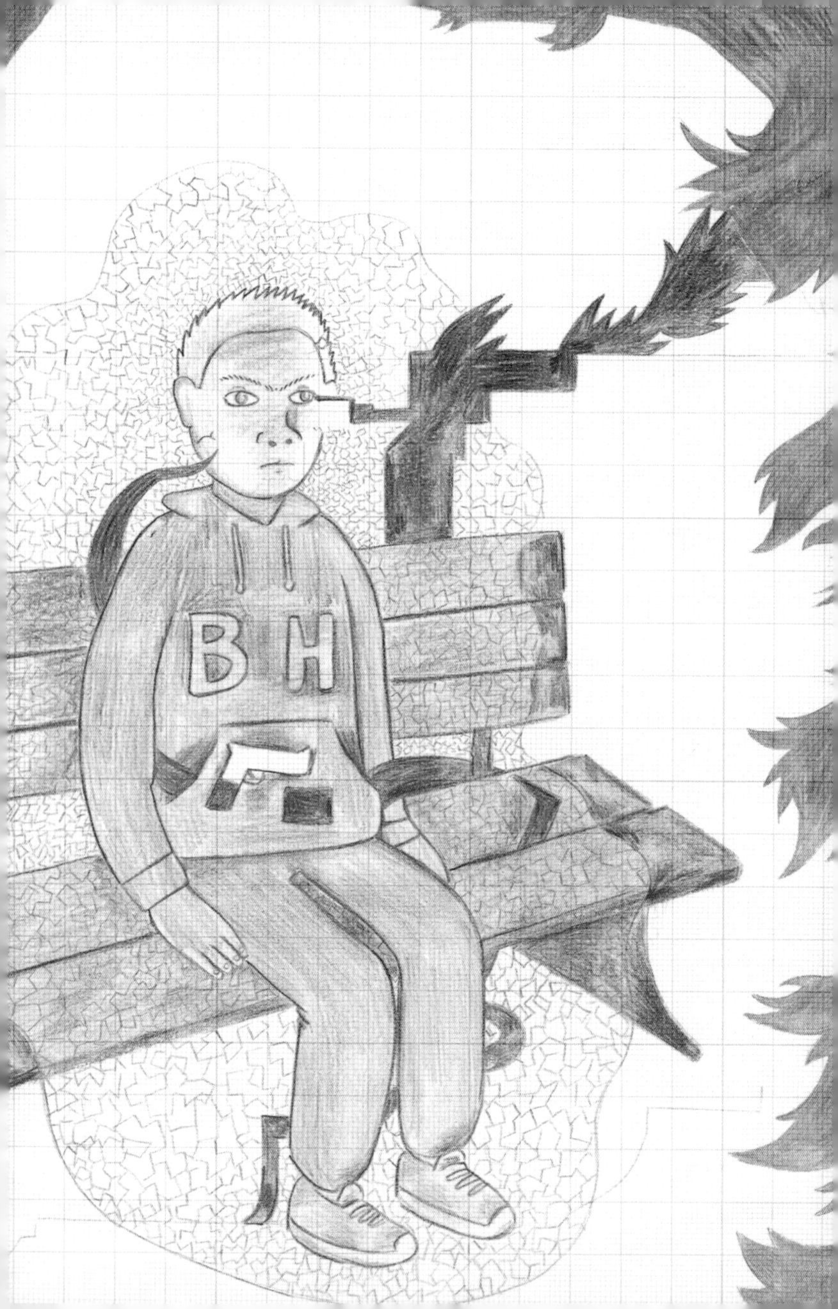
B H

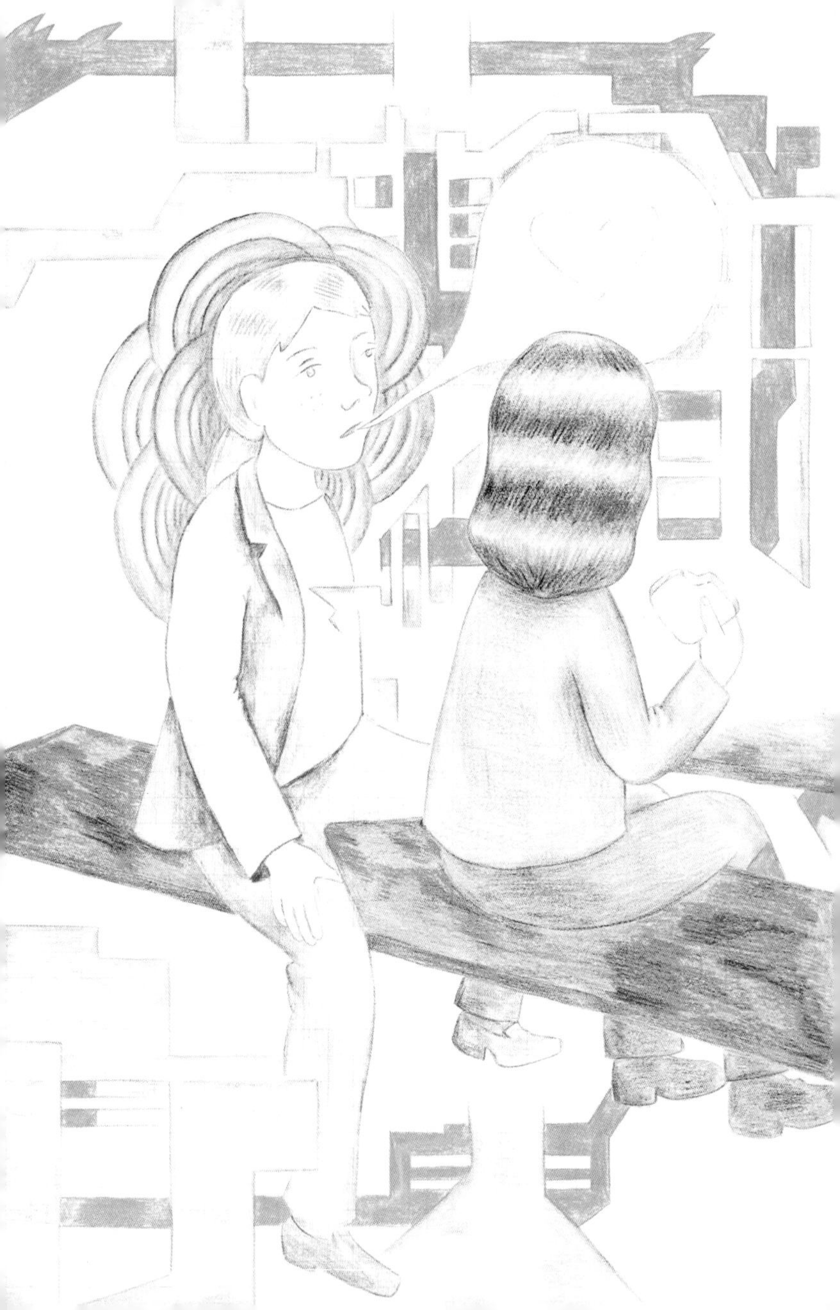

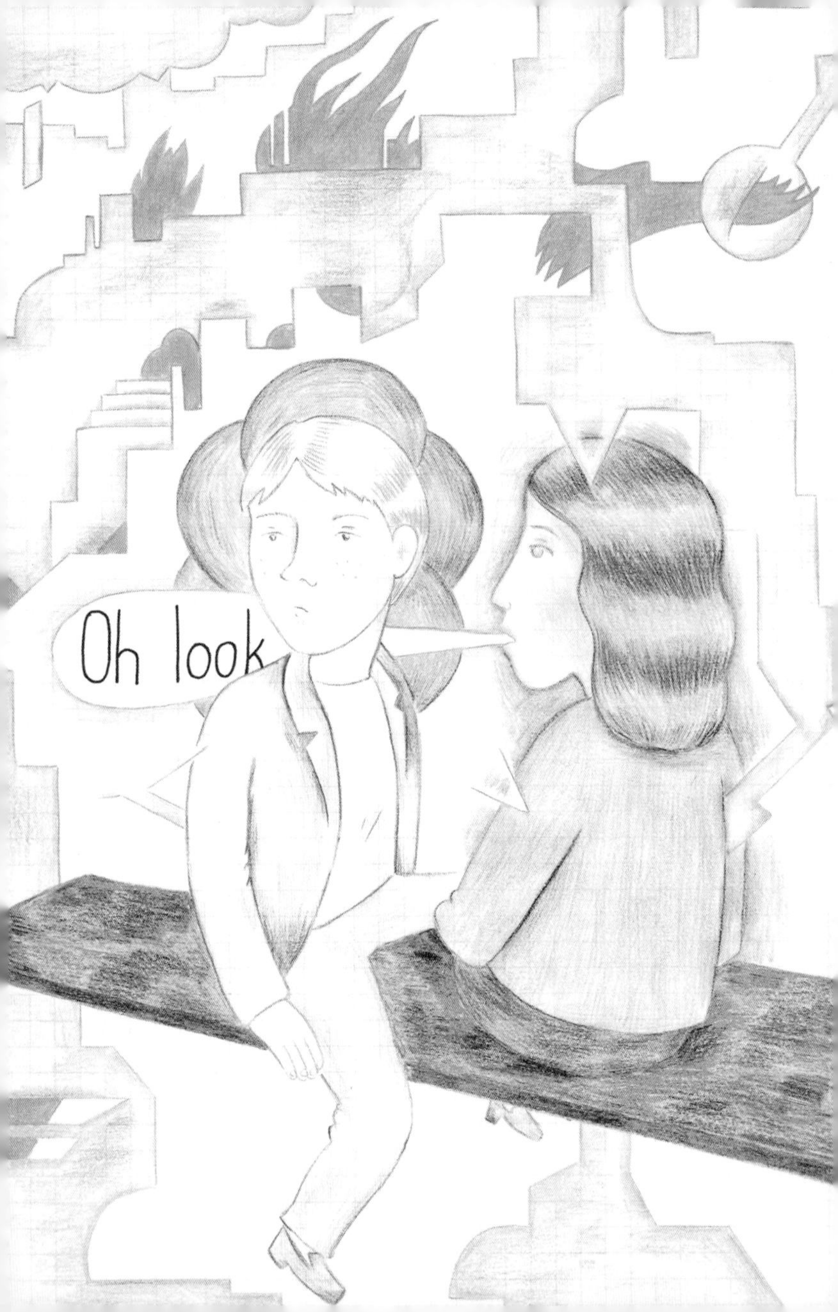
Oh look

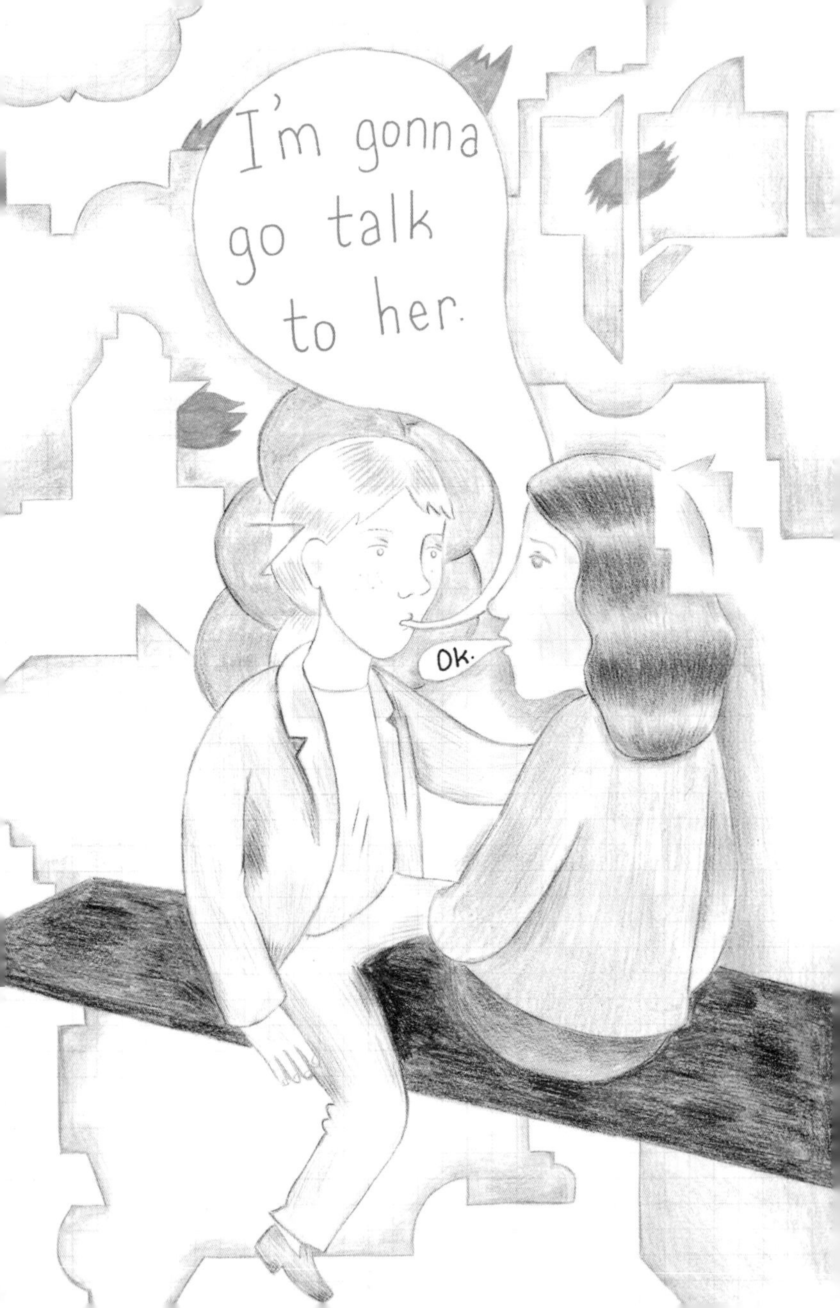
I'm gonna go talk to her.
OK.

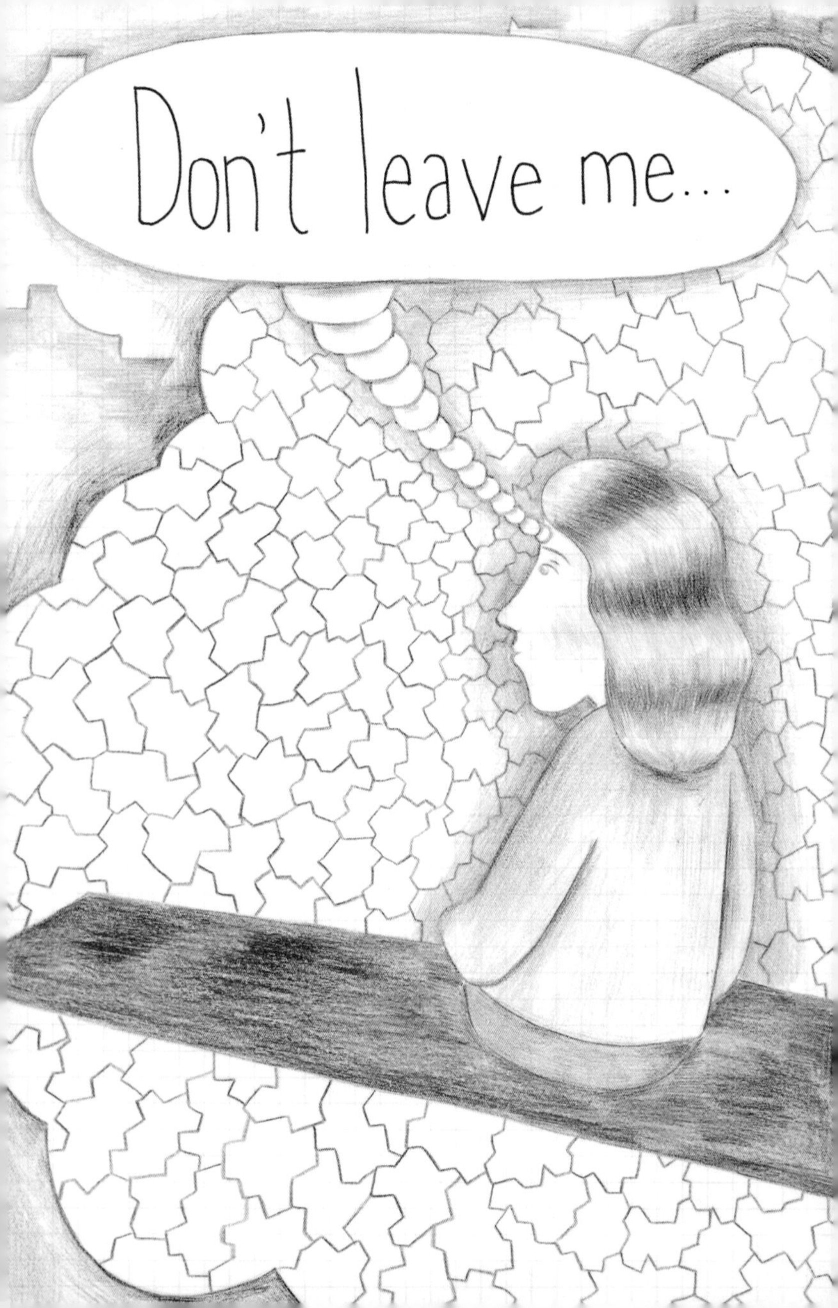
Don't leave me...

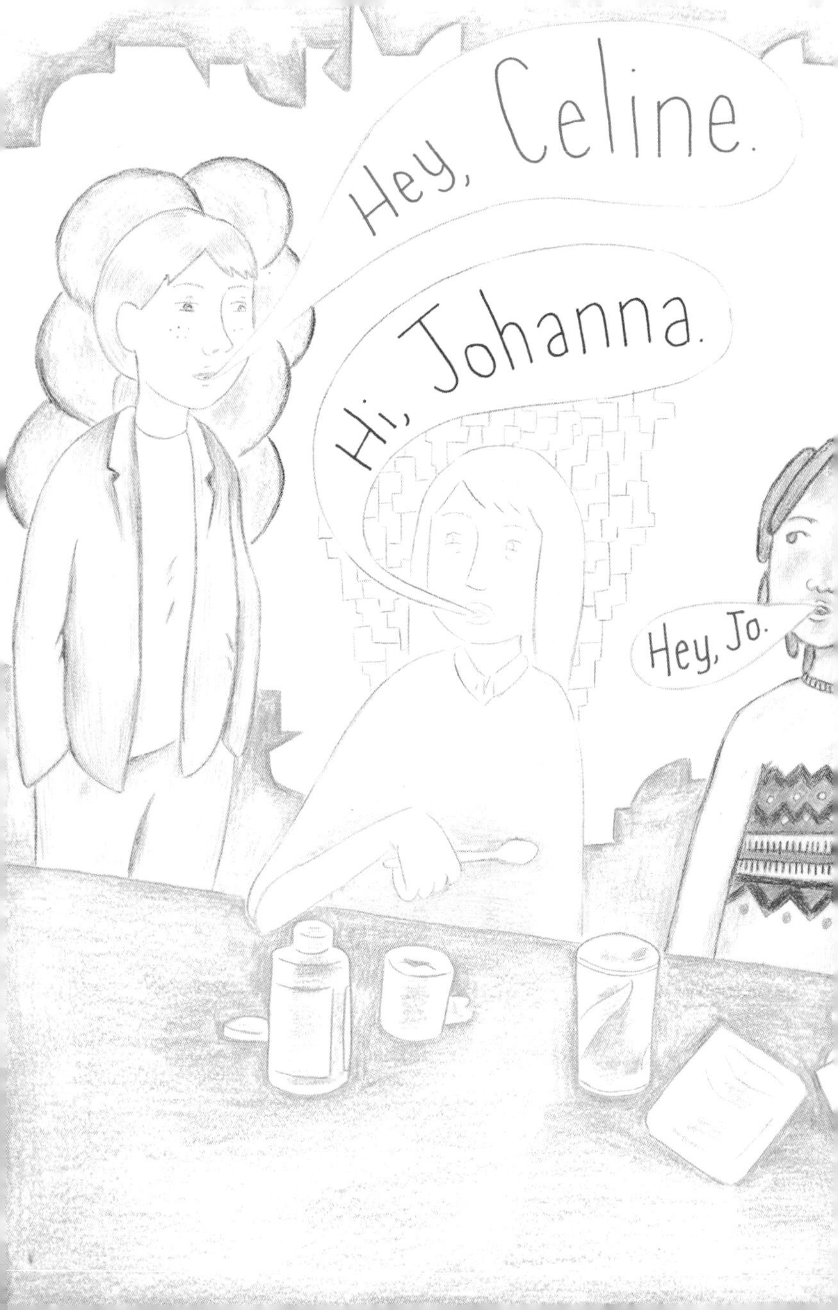
Hey, Celine.
Hi, Johanna.
Hey, Jo.

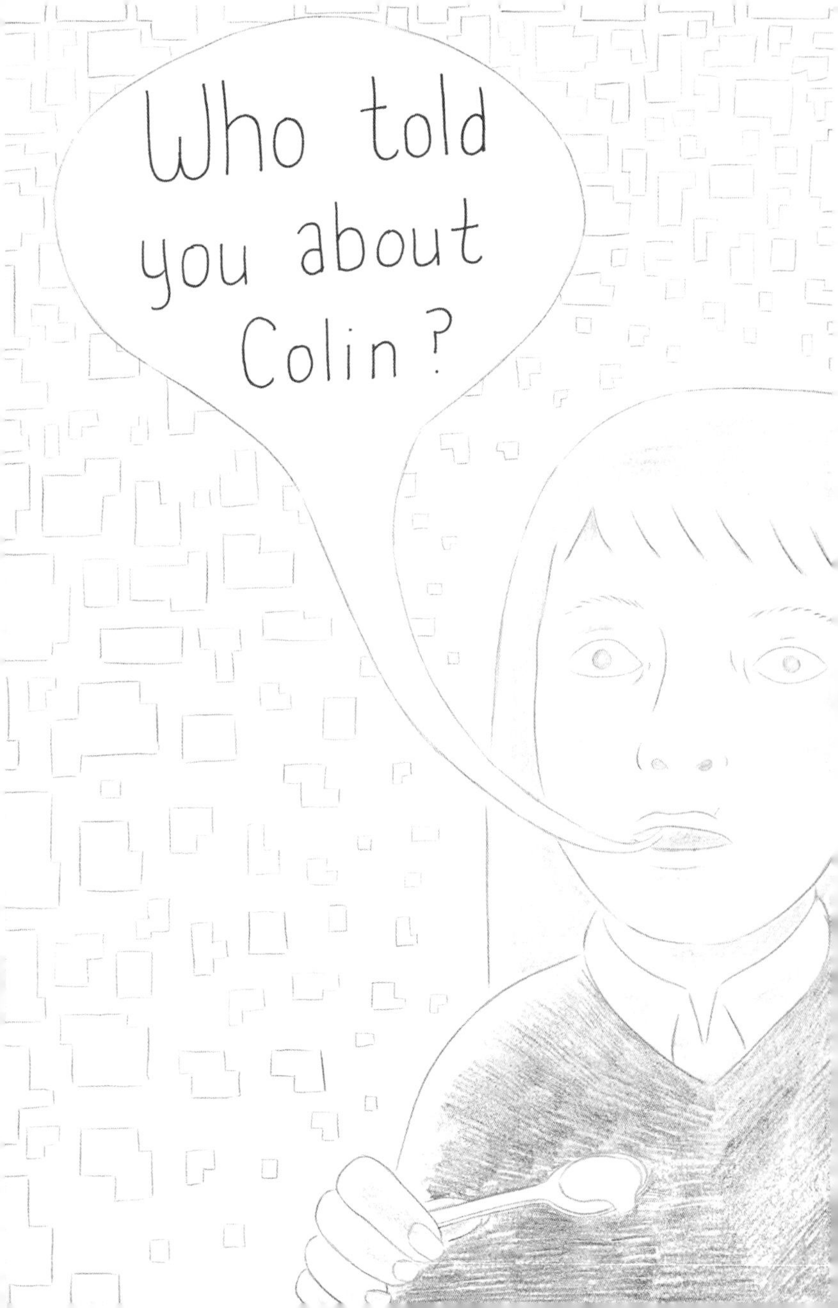
Who told you about Colin?

What's a guy supposed to do?
isn't the first time he
first
scared to get
why didn't any
so betr
He seemed like
a horrible human being.
I'm so embarrassed
think it runs in the fa
about
n't have to
Just ca

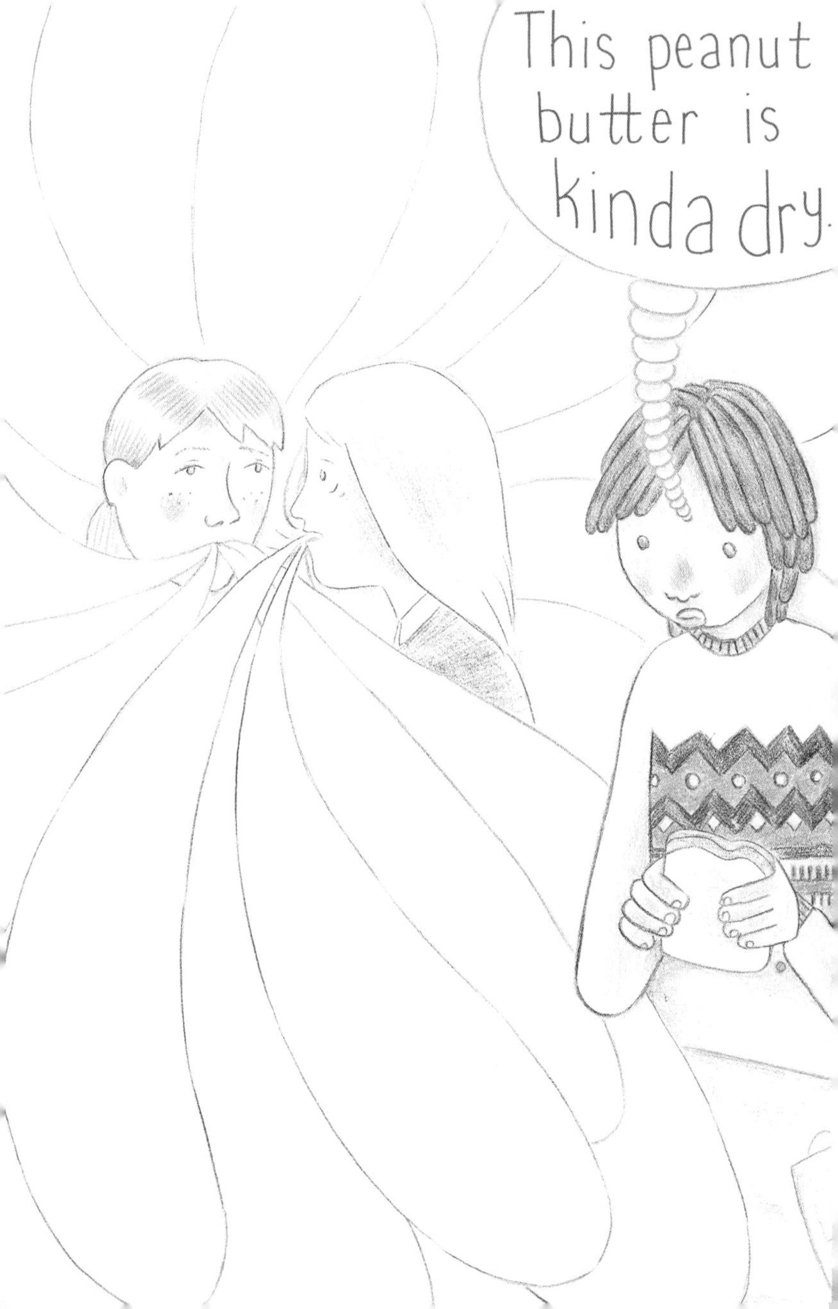
This peanut butter is kinda dry.

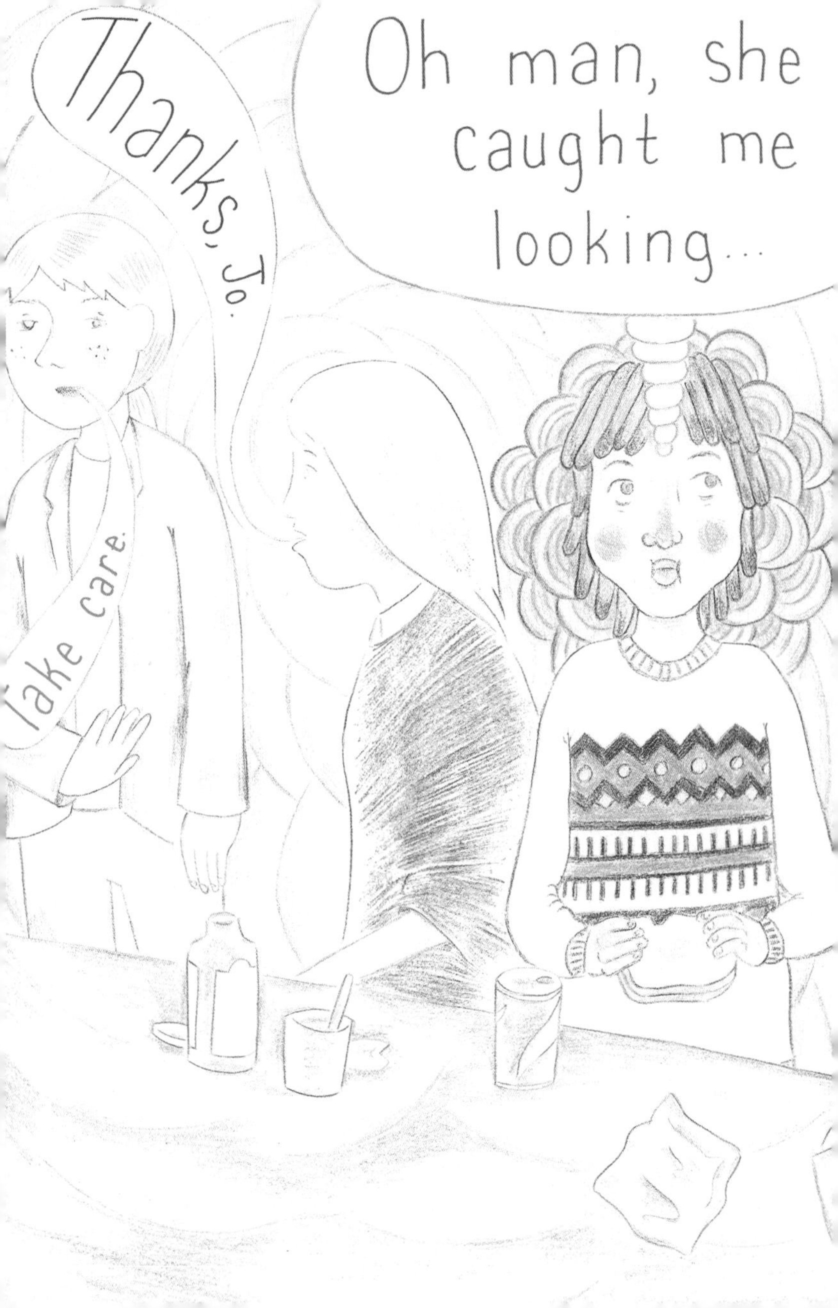
Thanks, Jo.
Take care.
Oh man, she caught me looking...

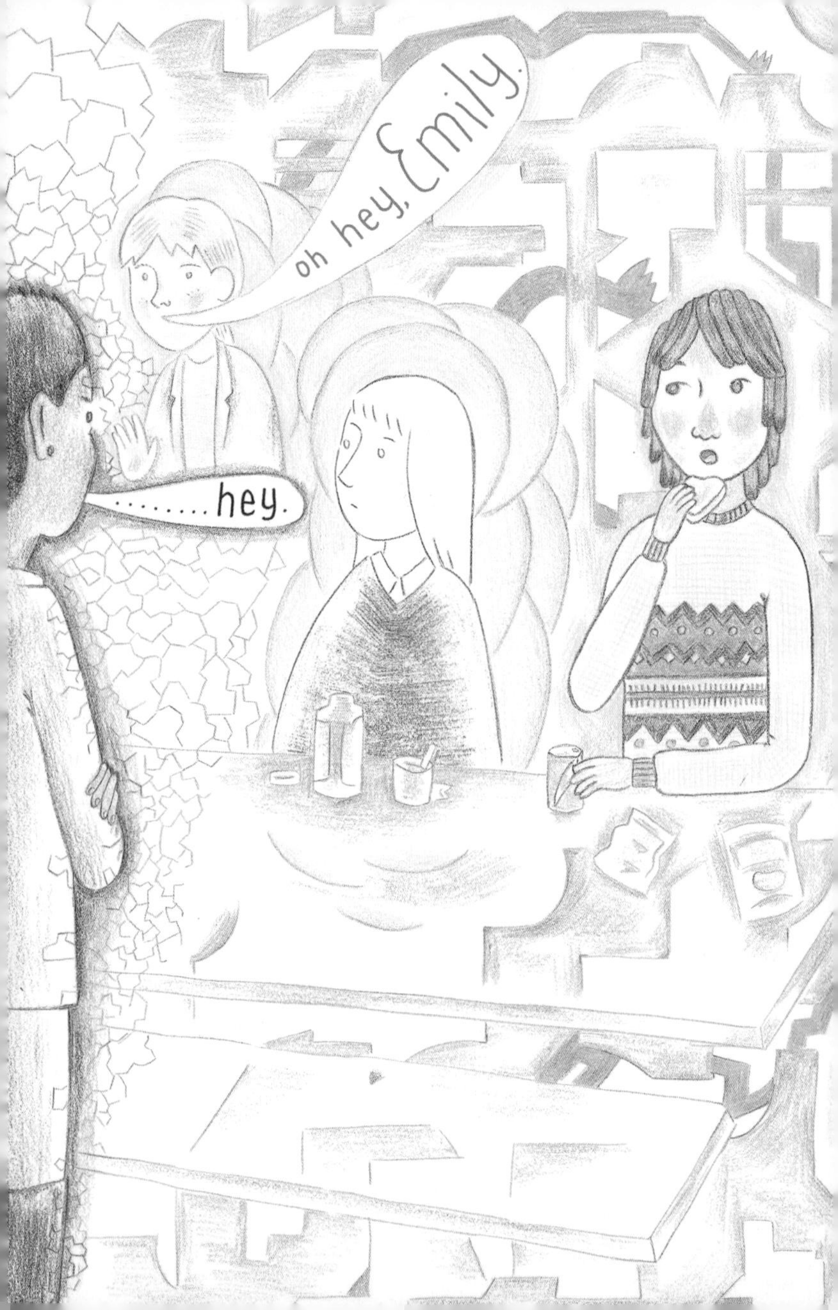
oh hey, Emily.
.........hey.

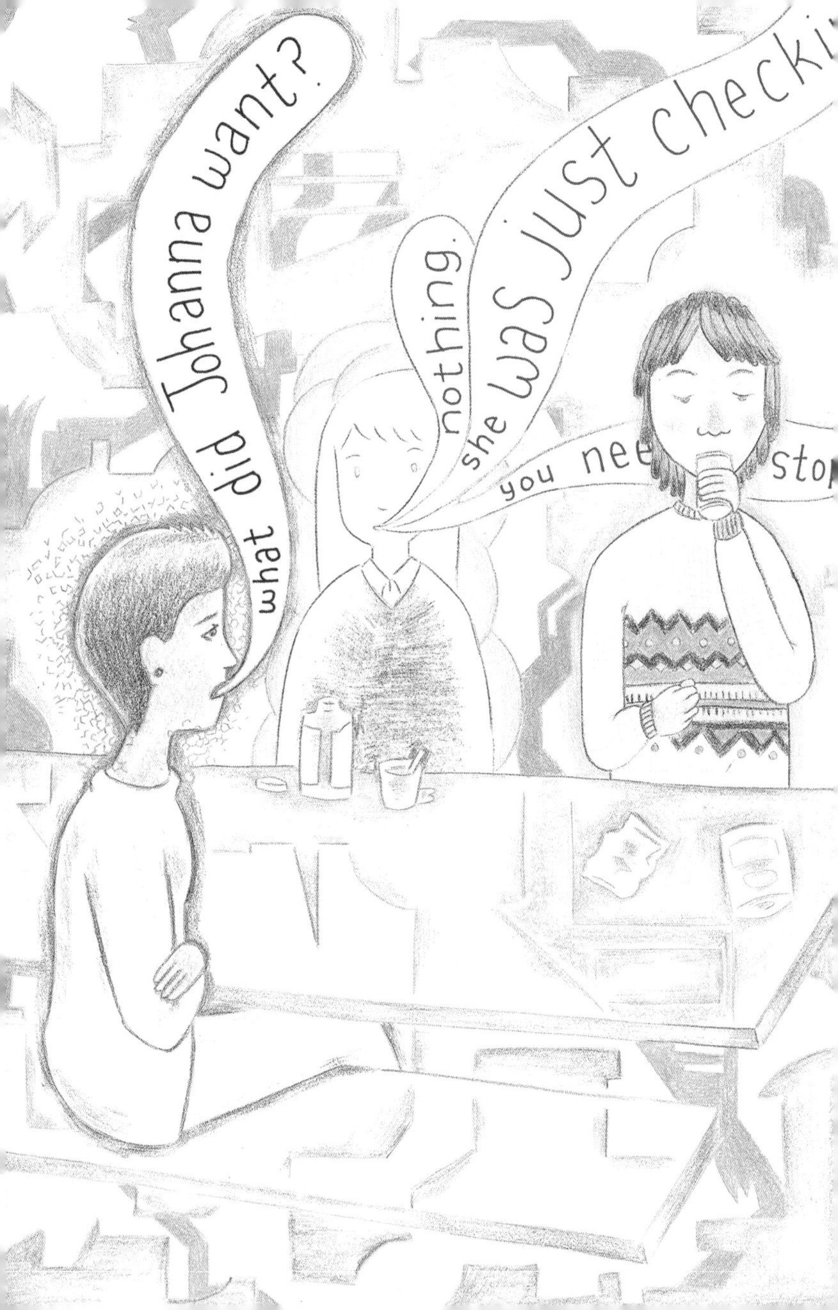
what did Johanna want?
nothing.
she was just checkin
you nee
stop

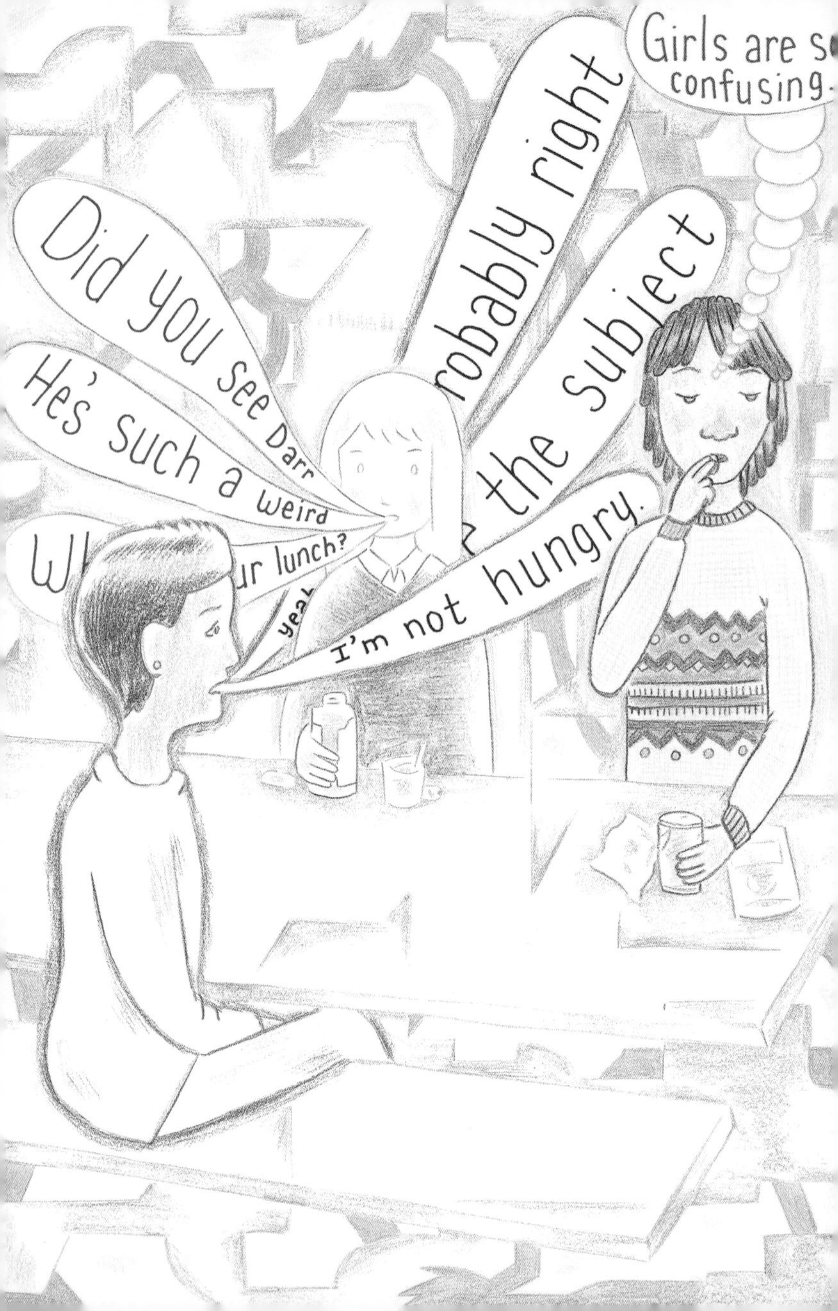

Did you see Darr
He's such a weird
Wh ur lunch?
robably right
the subject
yea
I'm not hungry.
Girls are so confusing.

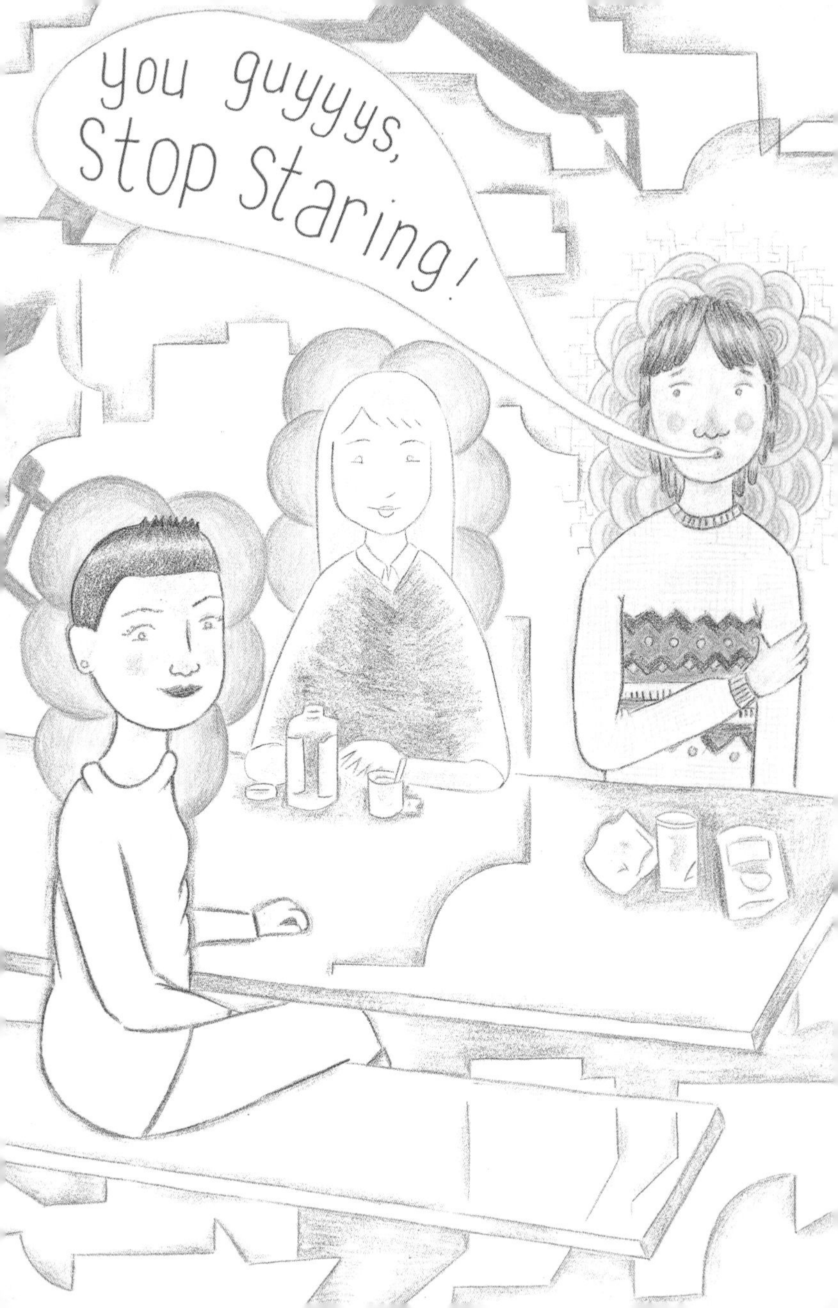
you guyyyys, Stop Staring!

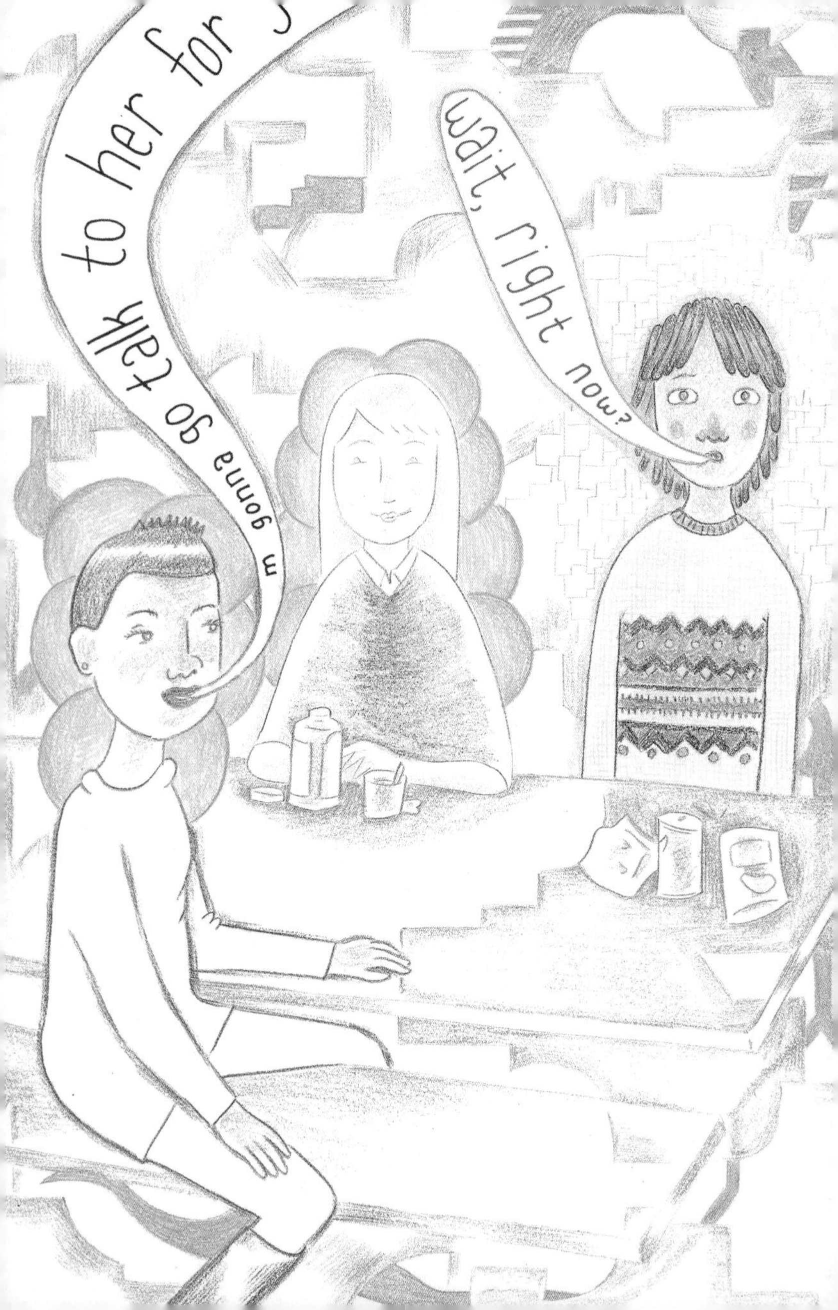
m gonna go talk to her for
wait, right now?

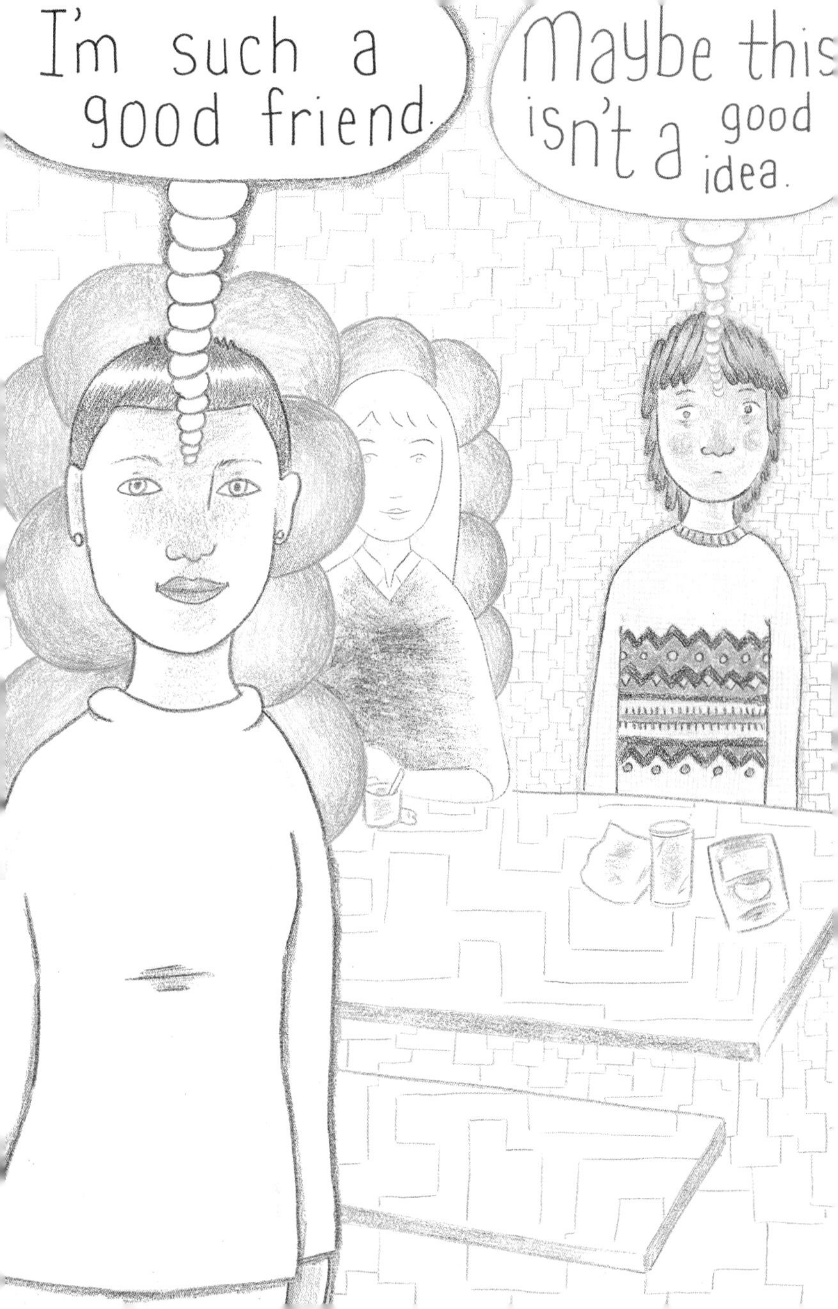
I'm such a good friend.
Maybe this isn't a good idea.

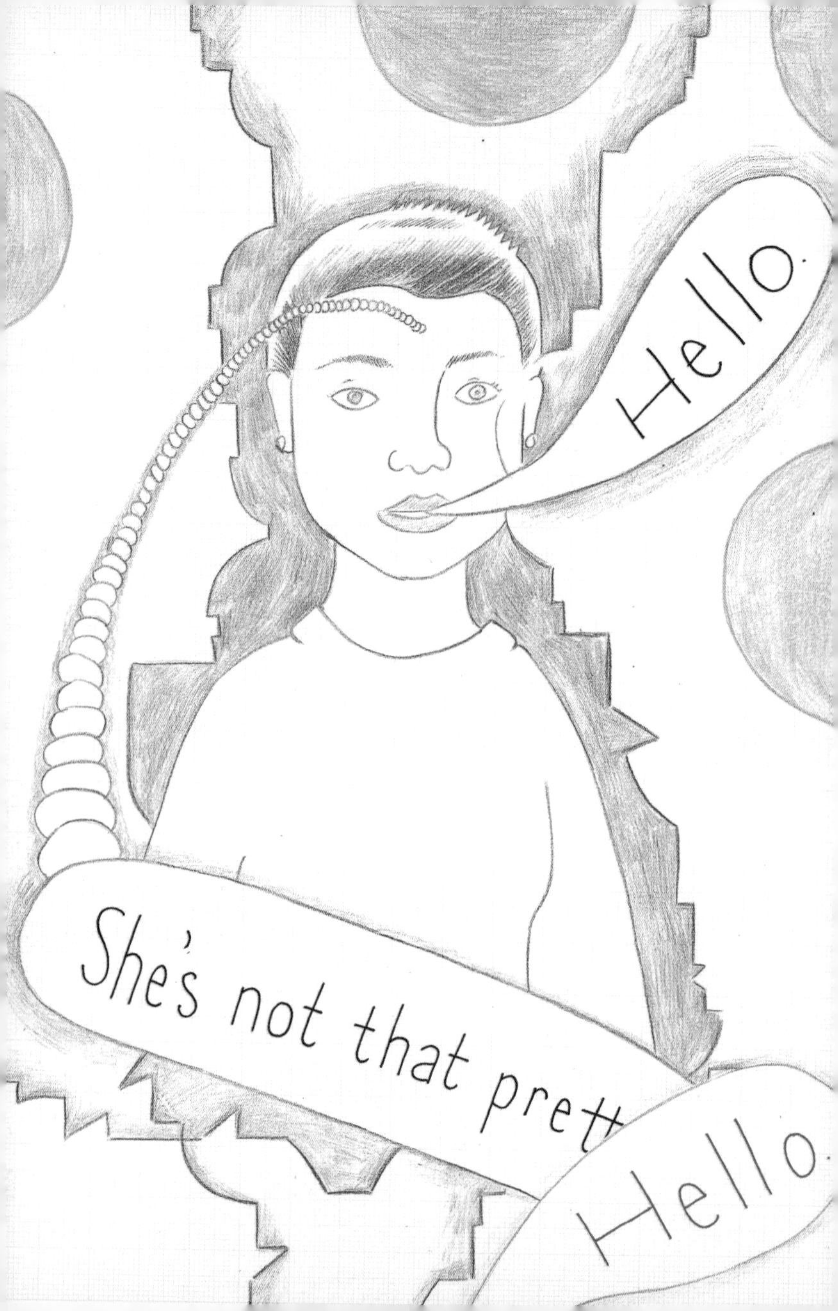
Hello.
She's not that prett
Hello.

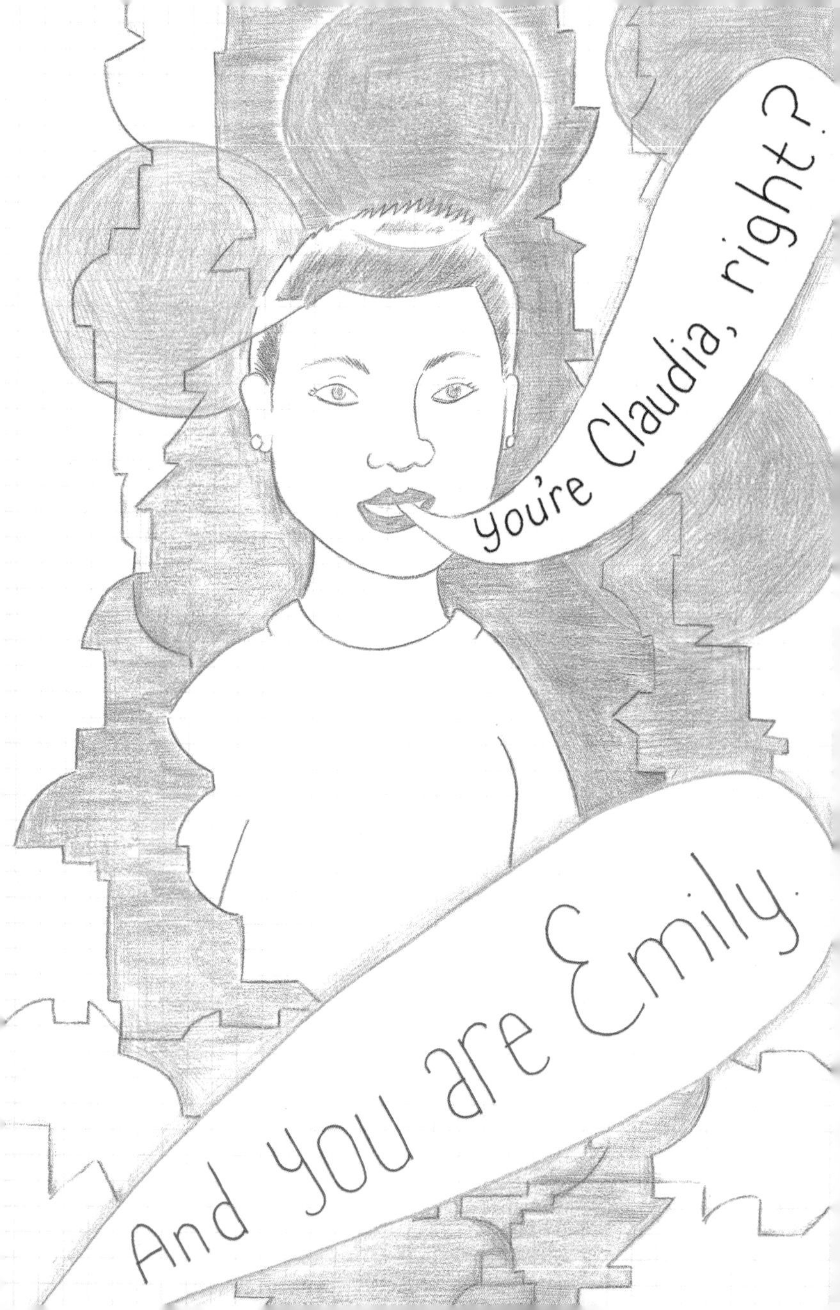
You're Claudia, right?
And YOU are Emily.

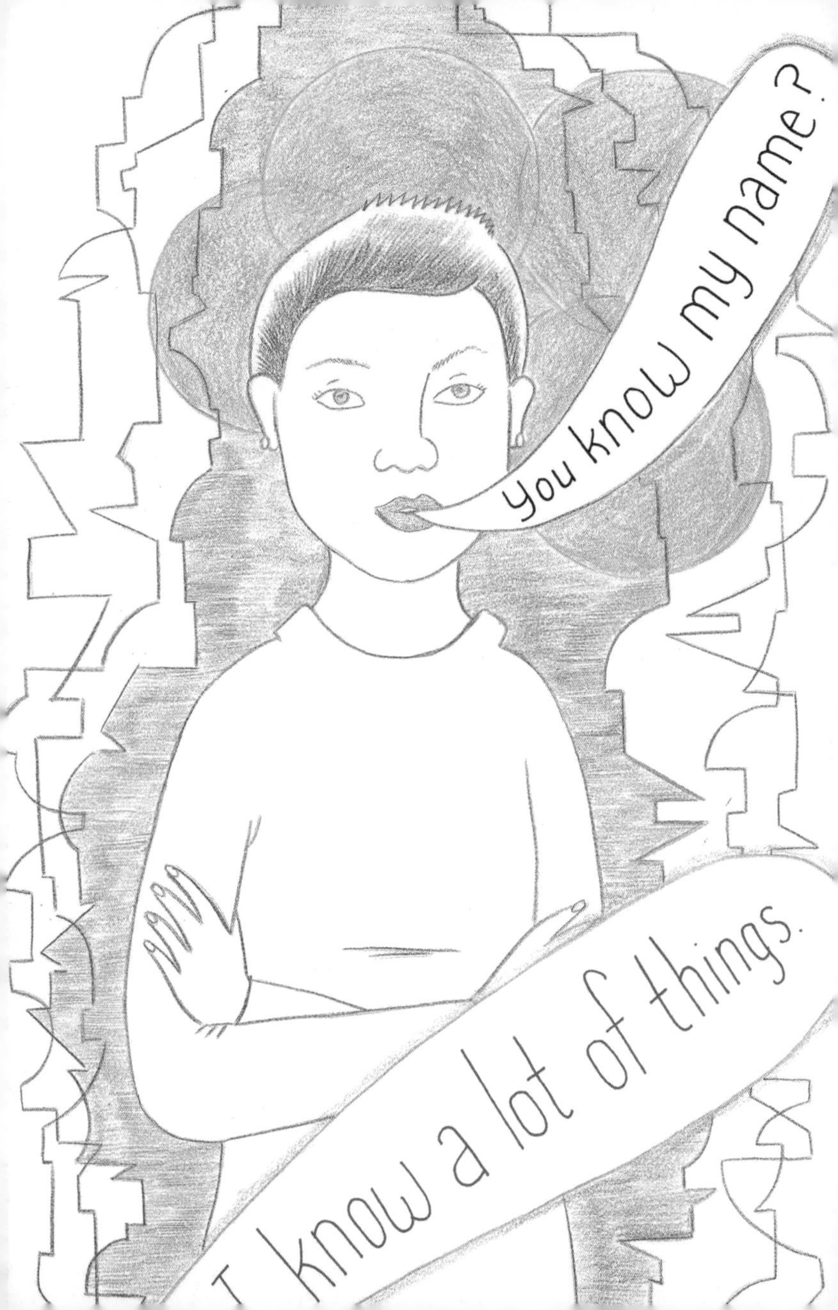
You know my name?
I know a lot of things.

such as........
you
avoid
your good
friends, the lovers,
despite your forgiving
nature.
Wait, what?
who
?

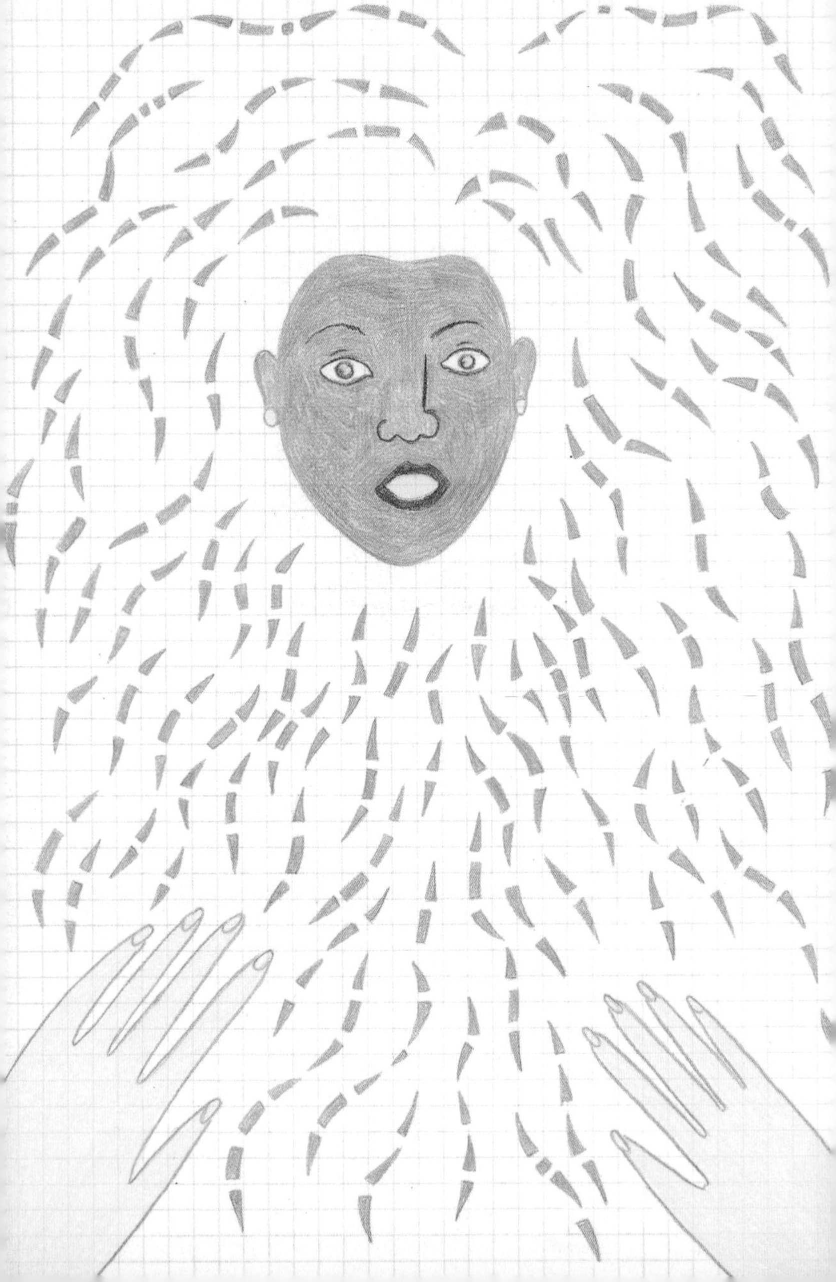

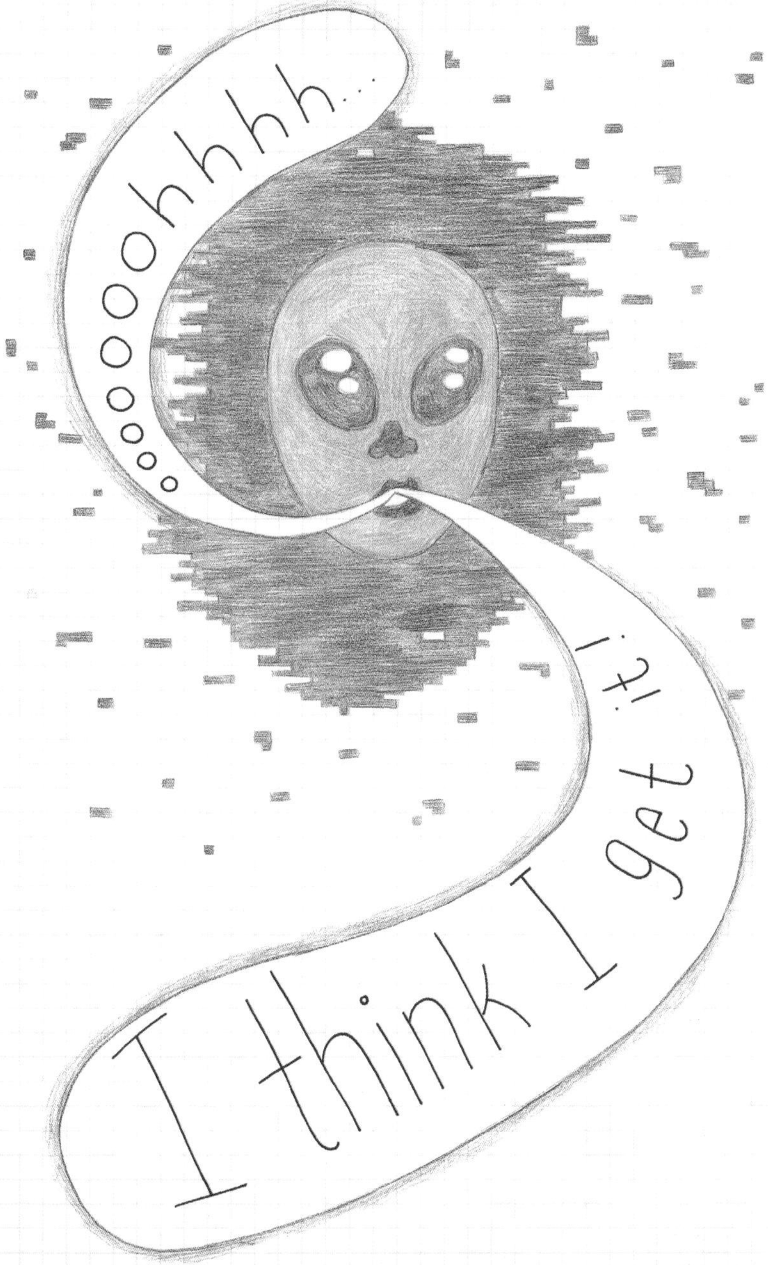
ooooooohhhh...
I think I get it!

I didn't realize...
you choose not to see many inconvenient truths.

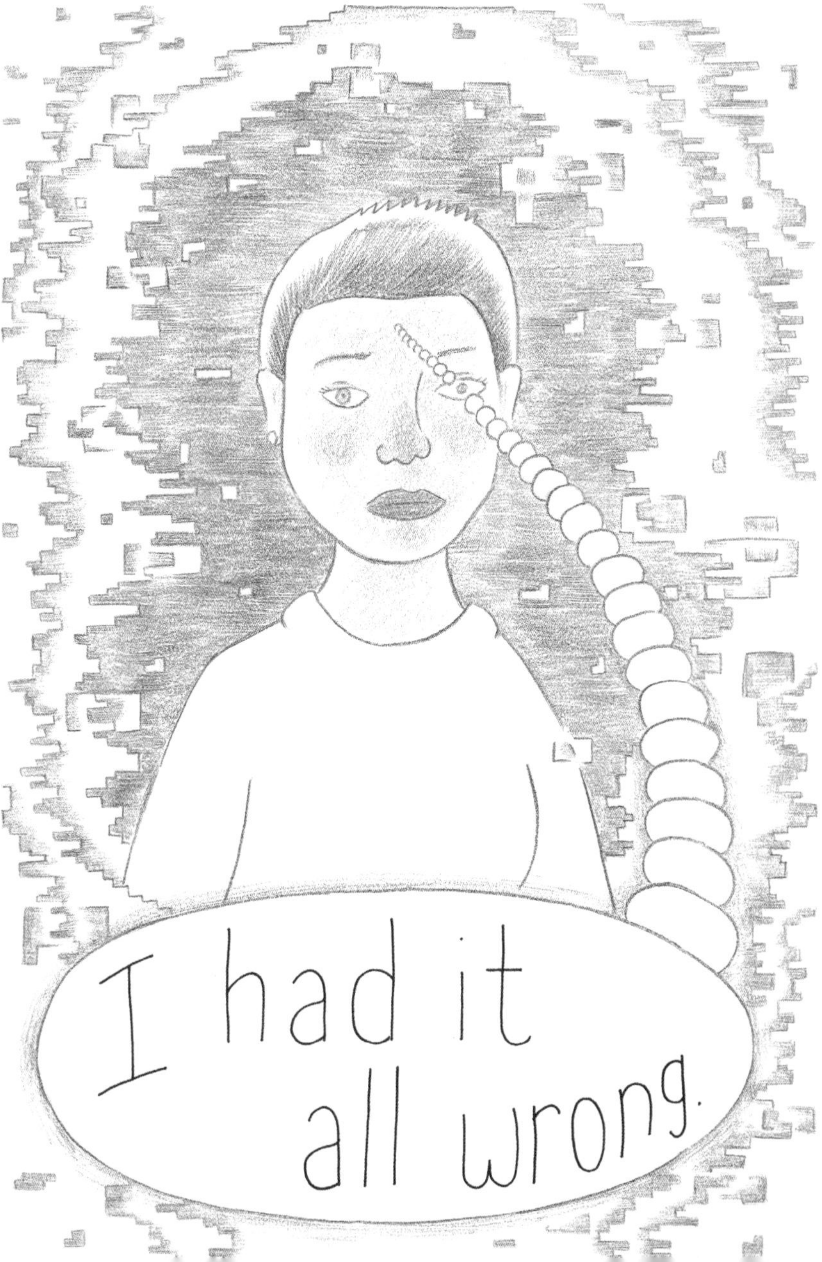
I had it all wrong.

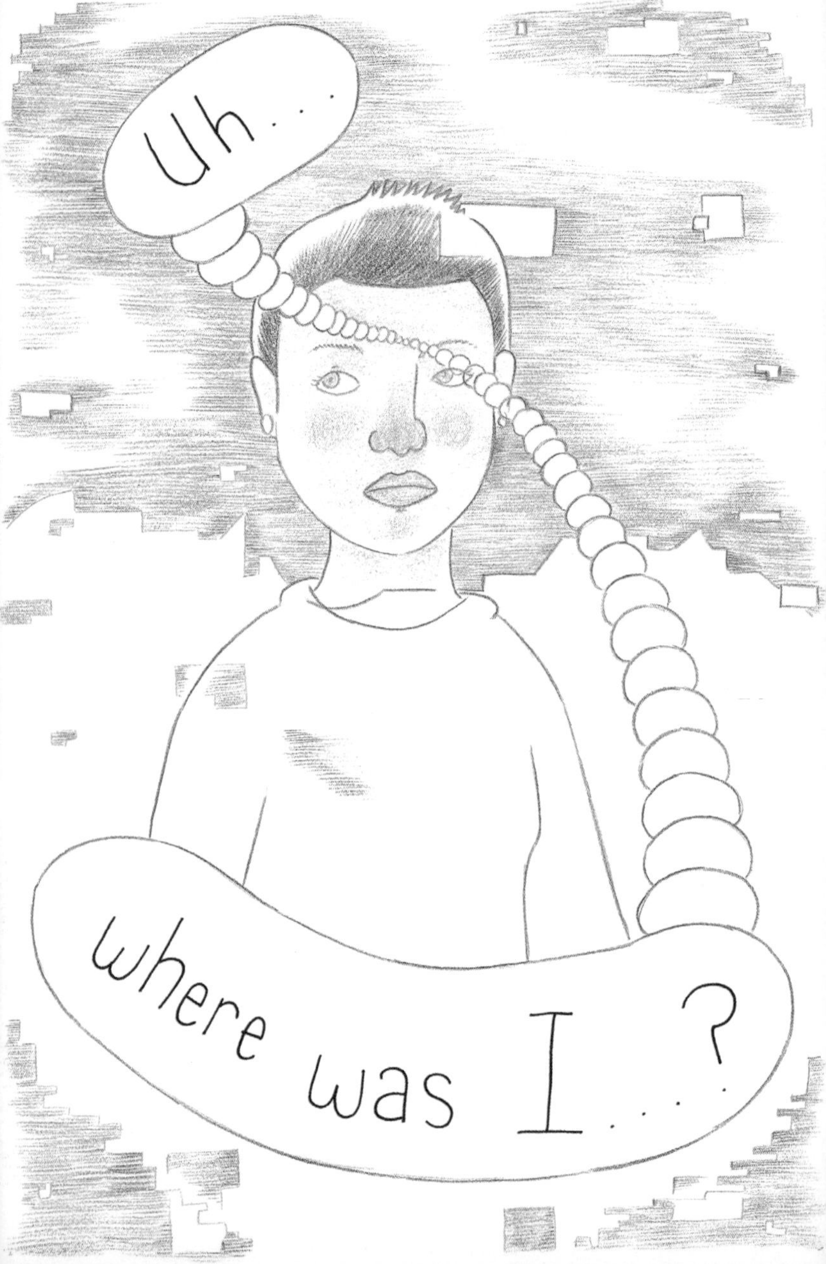
Uh...
where was I...?

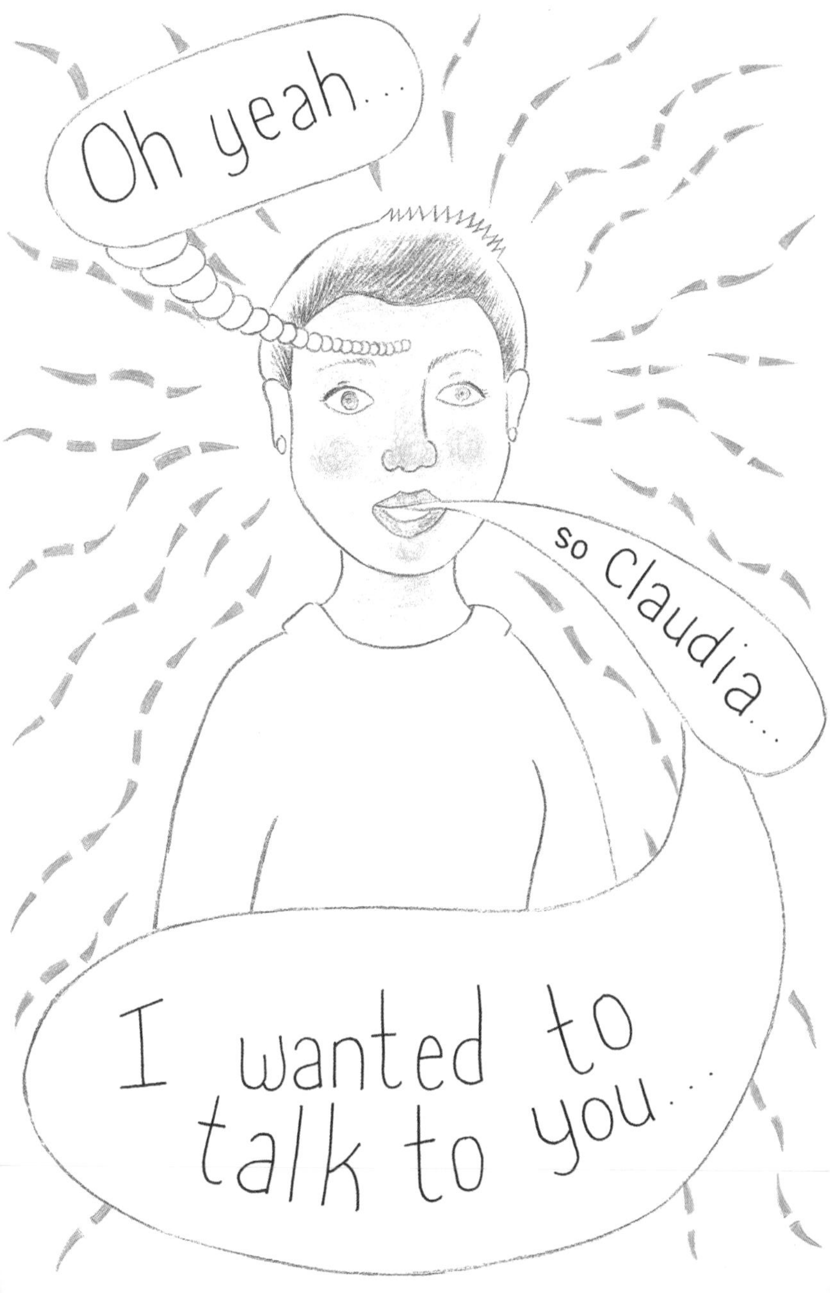
Oh yeah...
so Claudia...
I wanted to talk to you...

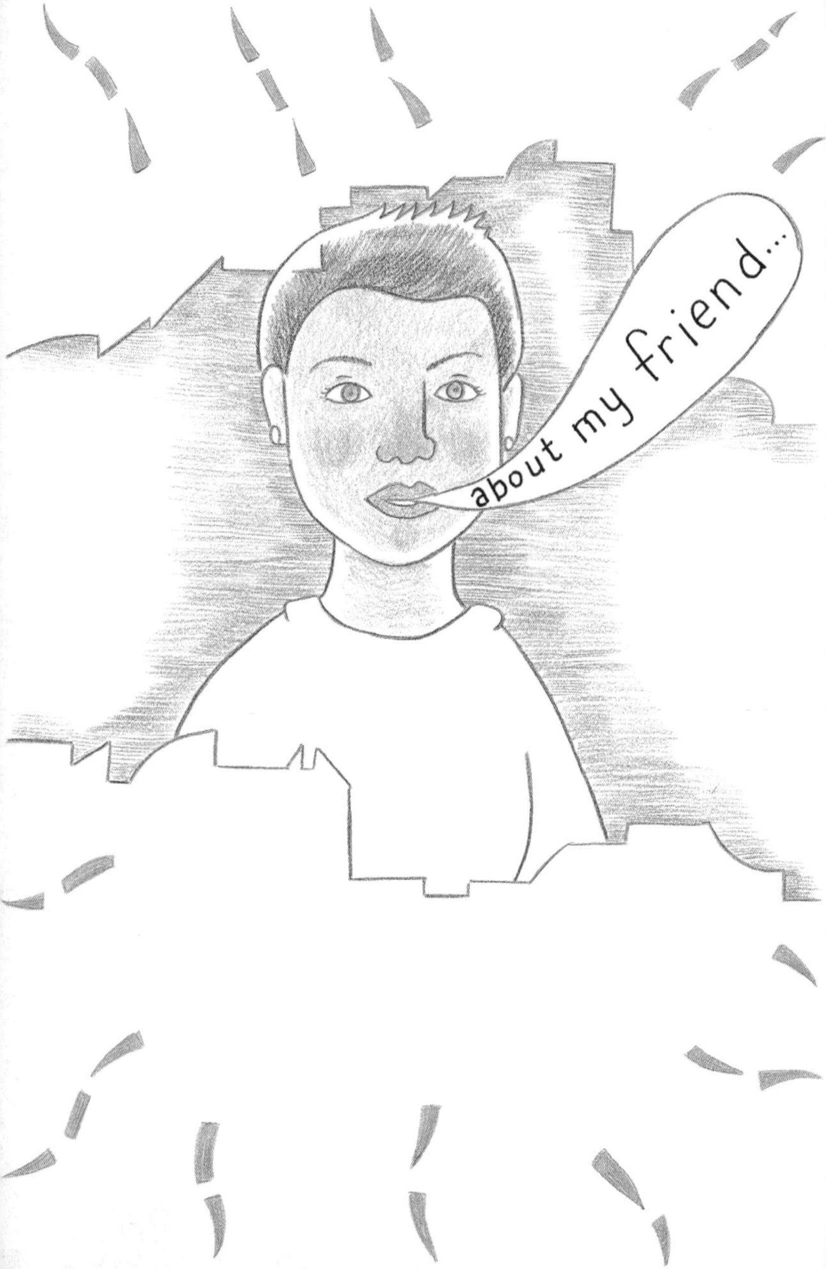
about my friend...

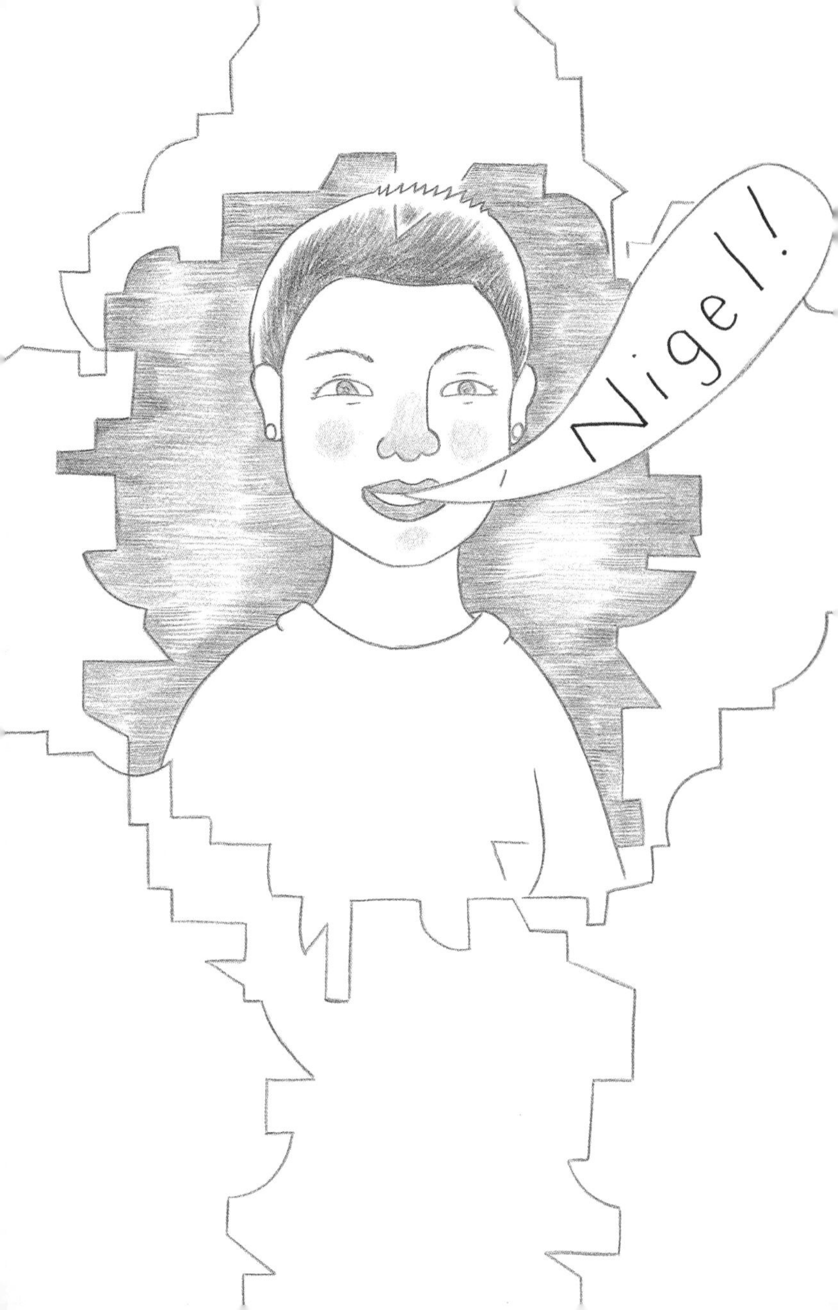
Nigel!

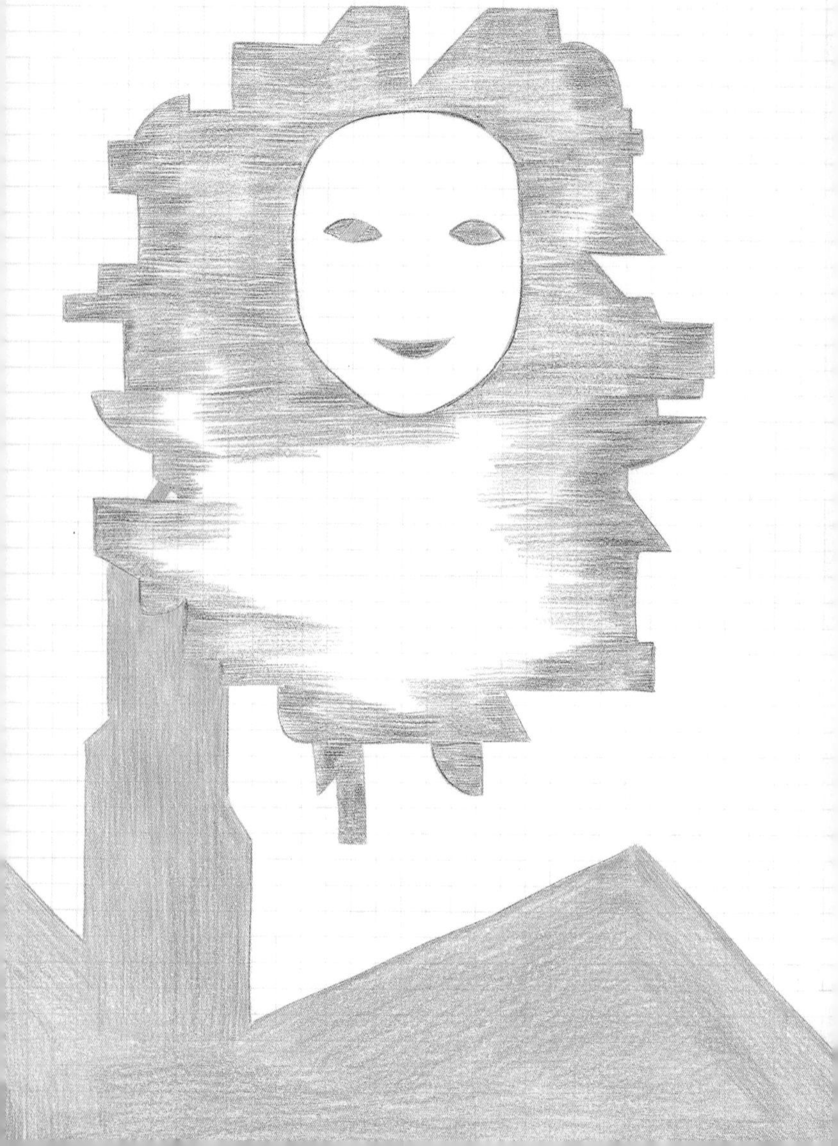

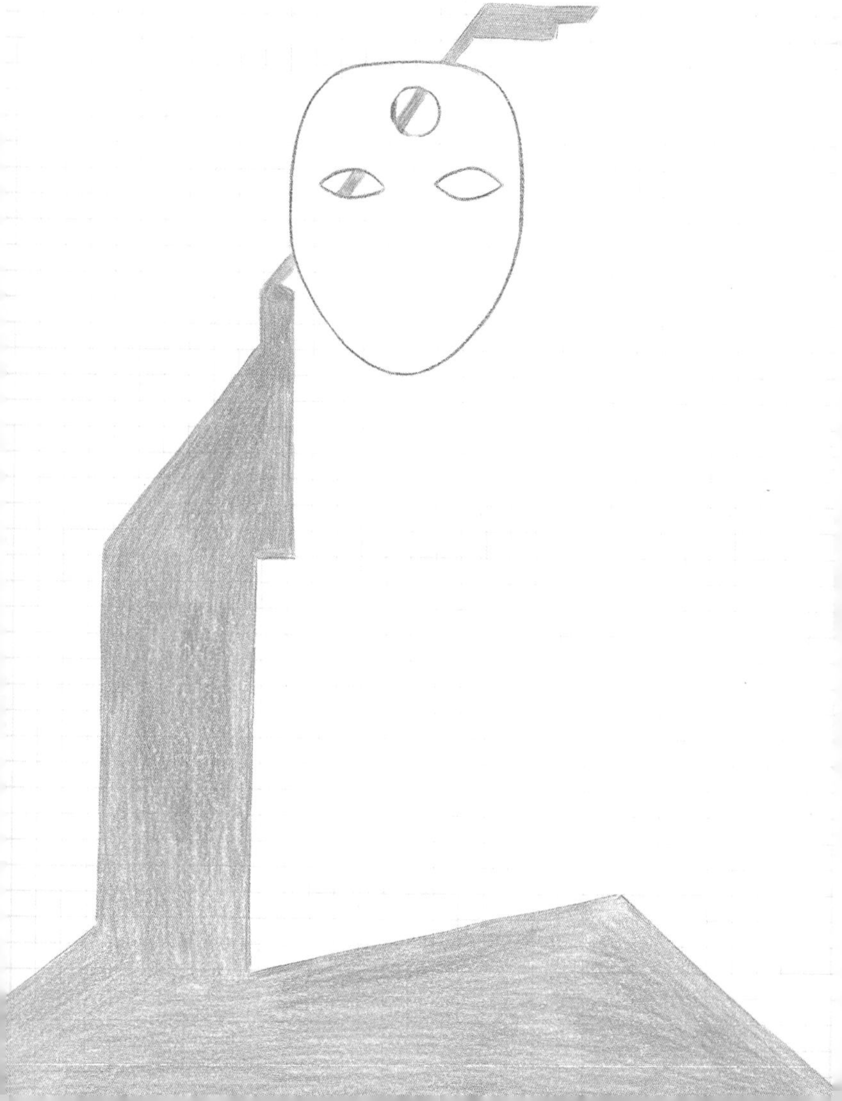

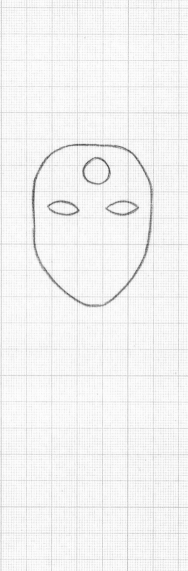

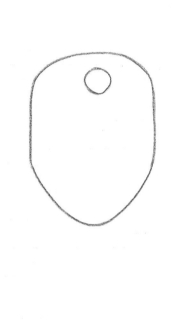

PART SIX

Nigel Q. Jones

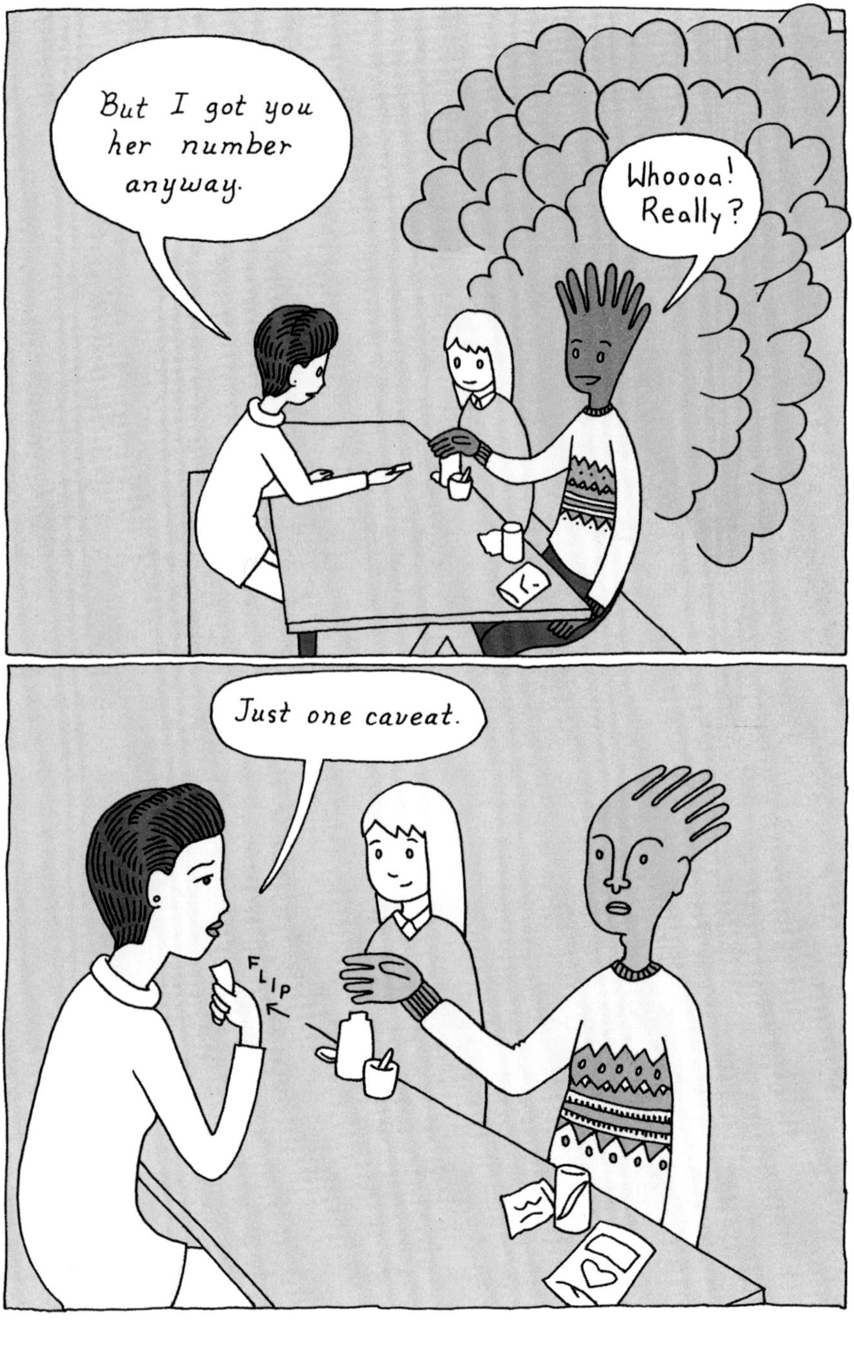
But I got you her number anyway.
Whoooa! Really?
Just one caveat.
FLIP

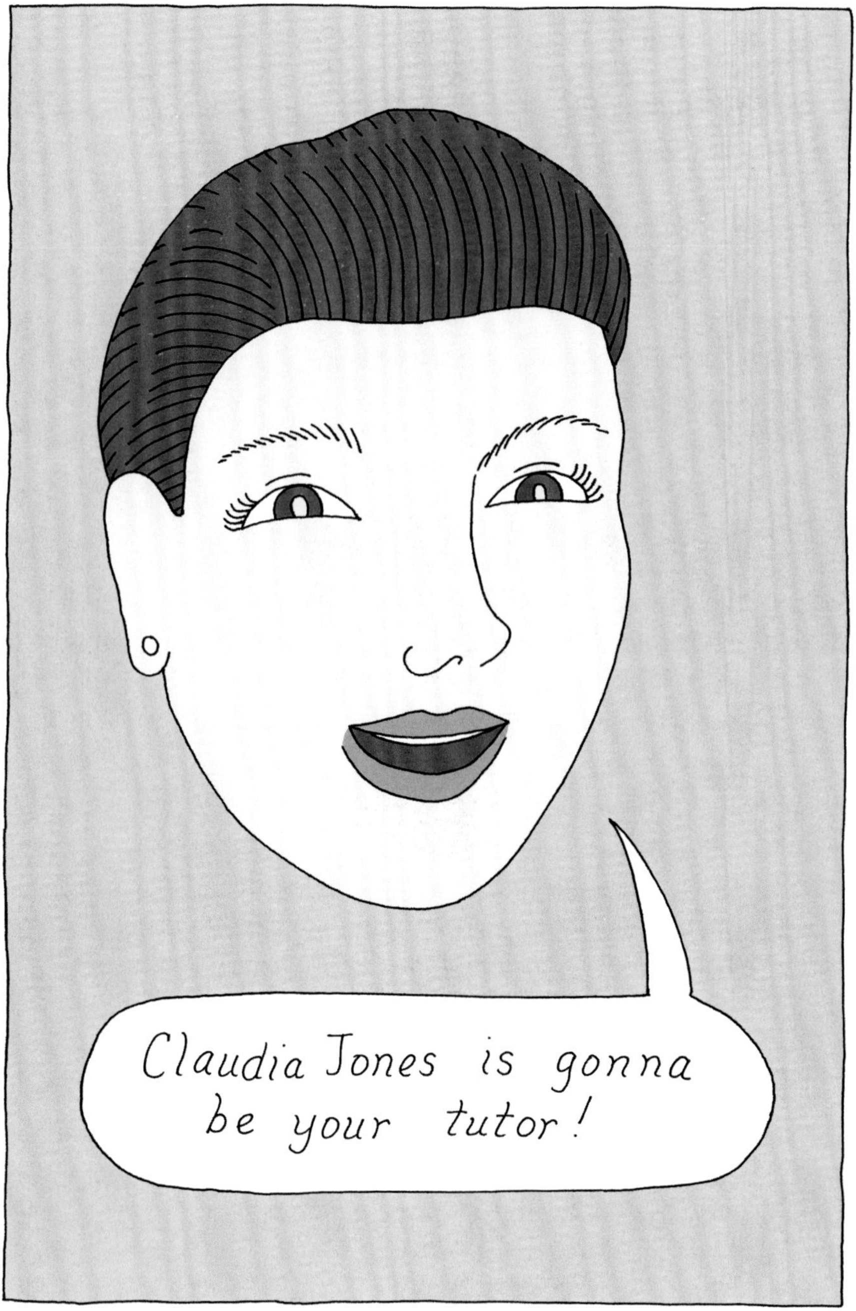
Claudia Jones is gonna be your tutor!

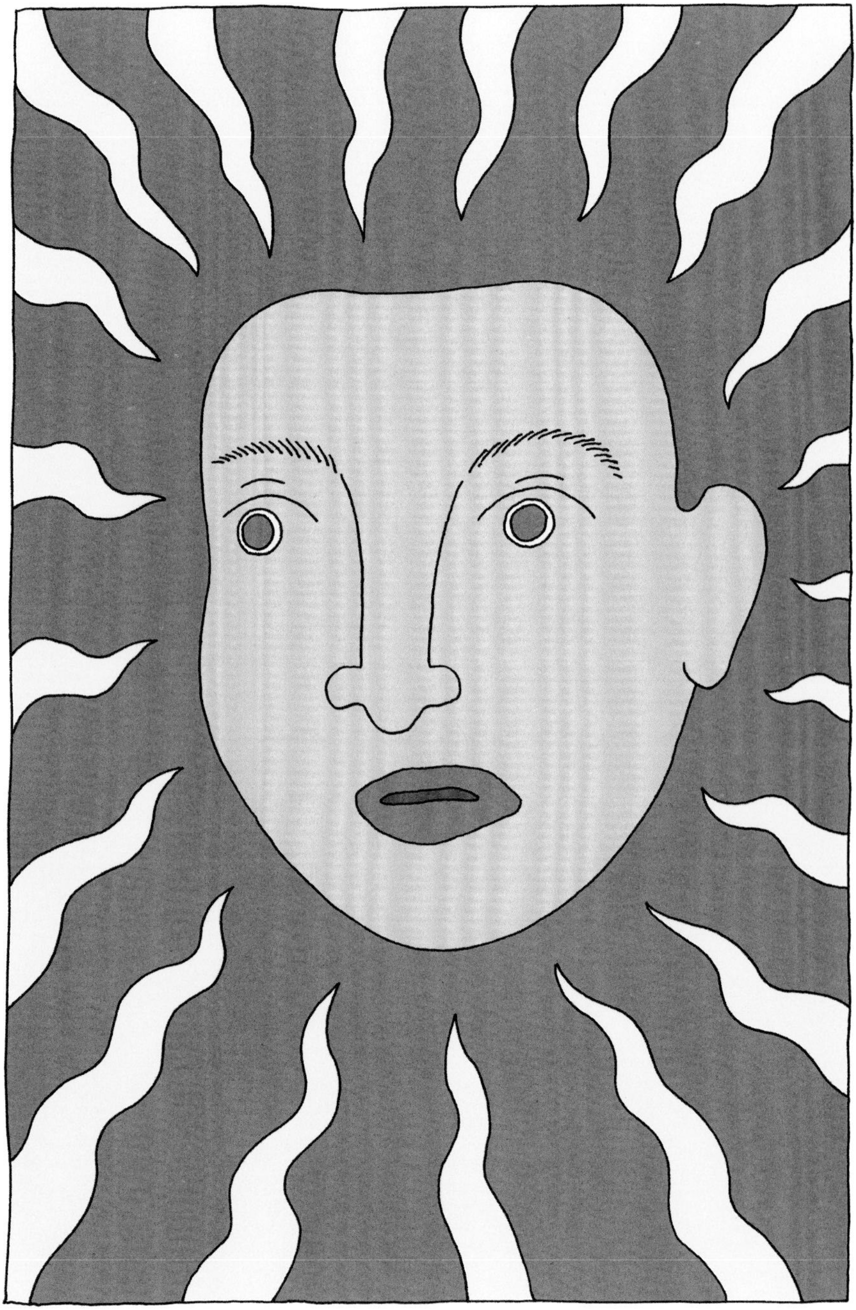